THE MAN WHO GOT AWAY WITH IT

Twenty years ago, young Inez Bailey was strangled to death, and the killer was never found. On a trip to California to visit his sister, Chicago police inspector Roy Malley finds this old crime intriguing. He's sure he could have discovered the murderer if it had been his crime to solve. Busman's holiday or not, he starts to dig. And uncovers more than he intended when he sets the wheels in motion in this small community. Because the killer is still among them, a respected member of society, a family man and business owner. He is in tight control of himself, has been for years. But with just a little push, he could let himself go. But letting go is the one thing he can't let himself do.

THE THREE WIDOWS

The Bladeswells are on vacation, traveling by car from Omaha to California. While in Santa Cruz, they hear about a man found dead on the beach, which brings to mind a similar event which occurred while the couple were vacationing in Yellowstone—a man found dead with no identification on him. When Mr. Bladewell hears about another similar case in Yosemite, he begins to wonder if there isn't someone on a select killing spree. The next night finds them at a cabin resort in Escondido, where they join their hometown friend Chet. The unmarried Chet is enjoying the attention of three older women vacationers, all recently widowed. This sets Mr. Bladeswell to thinking—three dead men and three widowed women—that perhaps there is more than coincidence at work here … that maybe one of them is a murderer.

Bernice Carey Bibliography
(1910-1990)

Novels:

The Reluctant Murderer (1949)

The Man Who Got Away With It (1950)

The Body in the Sidewalk (1950)

The Beautiful Stranger (1951)

The Three Widows (1952)

The Missing Heiress (1952)

Their Nearest and Dearest (1953;
abridged as The Frightened Widow, 1954)

The Fatal Picnic (1955)

Stories:

He Got What He Deserved (*The Lethal Sex*, 1959)

The Man Who Got Away With It

The Three Widows

TWO NOVELS BY

Bernice Carey

Introduction by Curtis Evans

STARK
HOUSE

Stark House Press • Eureka California

THE MAN WHO GOT AWAY WITH IT / THE THREE WIDOWS

Published by Stark House Press
1315 H Street
Eureka, CA 95501, USA
griffinskye3@sbcglobal.net
www.starkhousepress.com

THE MAN WHO GOT AWAY WITH IT
Originally published and copyright © 1950 by Doubleday & Company, Inc.,
New York. Copyright © renewed October 7, 1977 by Bernice Carey Martin.

THE THREE WIDOWS
Originally published and copyright © 1952 by Doubleday & Company, Inc.,
New York. Copyright © renewed January 10, 1980 by Bernice Carey Martin.

Reprinted by permission of the Bernice Carey estate. All rights reserved under
International and Pan-American Copyright Conventions.

"Bernice Carey: An Introduction" copyright © 2019 by Curtis Evans.

ISBN-13: 978-1-944520-80-9

Book design by Mark Shepard, SHEPGRAPHICS.COM
Proofreading by Bill Kelly

First Stark House Press Edition: May 2019

FIRST EDITION

Bernice Carey: An Introduction

By Curtis Evans

American mystery writing of the 1940s saw a fundamental shift away from the brainteasing between-the-wars clue-puzzle detective novels ingeniously devised by such crafty crime concoctors as Ellery Queen, John Dickson Carr, Freeman Wills Crofts and the "Queen of Crime" herself, Agatha Christie, toward other, more visceral forms, namely hard-boiled, noir, espionage, naturalism and psychological suspense, the latter pair of which were concerned not with tangled railway timetables and ingeniously locked rooms but the vexing conundrums presented by the vagaries of human character. While the hard-boiled and noir subgenres were dominated by men such as Raymond Chandler, Cornell Woolrich, David Goodis and James M. Cain, women authors quickly carried the field of naturalistic mystery and psychological suspense, producing such outstanding Forties crime tales as Margaret Millar's *The Iron Gates* (1945), Charlotte Armstrong's *The Unsuspected* (1946), Helen Eustis' *The Horizontal Man* (1946), Dorothy B. Hughes' *In a Lonely Place* (1947), Elisabeth Sanxay Holding's *The Blank Wall* (1947), Hannah Lees' *The Dark Device* (1947), Sara Elizabeth Mason's *The Whip* (1948), Ursula Curtiss' *Voice Out of Darkness* (1948), Mildred B. Davis' *The Room Upstairs* (1948), Evelyn Piper's *The Innocent* (1949) and Dorothy Salisbury Davis' *The Judas Cat* (1949), most of which happily have been brought back in print over the last few years.

Following fast on the footsteps of these pioneering mid-century women crime writers was transplanted California author Bernice Carey (1910-1990). Carey published her first of eight crime novels, *The Reluctant Murderer*, in late 1949, and her last, *The Fatal Picnic*, in 1955. Thereafter, despite high praise for her work from *New York Times* mystery reviewer Anthony Boucher and others, she unaccountably fell by the wayside in the United States for the next 64 years, until the reprinting by Stark House in 2019 of the book you are reading now, a twofer volume of her novels *The Man Who Got Away With It* and *The Three Widows*.

Arguably the most significant contribution of Bernice Carey to mid-century crime fiction was her commitment to exploring realistic social conditions in her novels. A few years before Carey published her first book, Raymond Chandler in his essay "The Simple Art of Murder," (originally published in 1944) had praised—in a sideways jab at the cozy country house school of genteel crime fiction—hard-boiled trailblazer Dashiell Hammett for having given "murder back to the kind of people that commit it for reasons, and not just to provide a corpse; and with the means at hand, not with hand-wrought dueling pistols, curare, and tropical fish." Hammett "put these people down on paper as they are," continued Chandler, "and he made them talk and think in the language they customarily used for these purposes." Although, in contrast with Hammett and Chandler, Bernice Carey in her crime fiction largely eschewed dealing with professional criminals, she nevertheless set her mystery plots spinning in everyday California communities, anatomizing the well-off, to be sure, but focusing her greatest attention on the men and women of the more modest white and blue collar classes. These people may not have been any more likely in reality to have encountered murder than Lord and Lady Caraway-Crumpet at Hot Toddy Hall, yet their fictional lives in fact mirrored those of the vast majority of Americans who actually read mysteries.

In a 1951 review of Carey's fourth crime novel, *The Beautiful Stranger*, Anthony Boucher, though a devoted fan of classic mystery from the so-called Golden Age of detective fiction (the period between the two world wars), welcomed what he deemed the long overdue shift, which Carey represented, toward more commonplace settings rather than the Georgian country manors and posh urban penthouses that were still frequently found in detective fiction in the classic mode. Traditional mystery writing, as Boucher saw it, left a landscape which utterly failed to mirror the real world:

> There's a belief among publishers and editors that American readers prefer, in their escape entertainment, a "nicer" sort of life than that which they themselves lead. I'm not sure how justified this belief is; but it results in the fact that the lower middle class and the working man are almost completely absent from the detective story....The man from Mars, reading a year's crop of whodunits, would wind up with some strange ideas as to the prevalence of penthouses and country estates, and would never even learn of the existence of trade unions.

The man from Mars would have gotten a much different—and more accurate—picture of the modern world from the crime fiction of Bernice Carey, however. In the first work collected in this volume—Carey's third crime novel, *The Man Who Got Away With It* (1950)—the action is set in the small town of Los Alegres, among "nice" middle class shop owners and the like, some of whom, like the titular anti-hero Ben Sterling—

have risen from working class origins and are painfully anxious to leave their humble beginnings far behind them. There are other things, as well, that the people in lovely little Los Alegres want to leave behind them—like the shocking murder, two decades earlier, of wayward working class beauty Inez Bailey. "Why, we don't even have murders in Los Alegres," laughingly declares Beth Sterling early in the novel to inquisitive visiting Chicago cop Roy Malley, conveniently forgetting the brutal unsolved Inez Bailey strangling, in which her husband had been a suspect, like many another man in the town. But when a man gets away with murder can he ever stop with just one? Readers may well witness history repeat itself in *The Man Who Got Away With It*, a novel which, uncharacteristically for Bernice Carey, hews closely to the patterns of male-oriented noir fiction, though Ben's wife Beth reveals unsuspected depths behind her prattling surface personality.

In contrast with the noirish *The Man Who Got Away With It*, Bernice Carey's fifth detective novel, *The Three Widows* (1952), which she dedicated to her mystery reading father Charles, a Wisconsin farmer, has a more satirical, mordantly humorous tone. It details the amateur (and sometimes amateurish) investigations of well-meaning Mel Bladeswell, a plain spun retired businessman from Omaha, Nebraska, who is vacationing in California with his wife Elsie. While staying at "Escondido," a resort (half dude ranch, half motel) near San Luis Obispo, Mr. Bladeswell, drawing on previously unsuspected reserves of imagination (he has recently read a mystery novel), comes to believe that one of three widows who clearly harbor designs on his and Elsie's well-off bachelor friend Chet Hoffman, also a paying guest at Escondido, has not merely matrimony in mind but murder! He thinks that one of these ladies might be, in short, a black widow killer. But which one, that is the question....

"How often did ordinary, decent people run into murderers?" Mr. Bladeswell fretfully wonders. "And these women were all just plain, everyday people like him and Elsie." Although it is a man, Mr. Bladeswell, who functions as the amateur sleuth in *The Three Widows*, what should most intrigue readers of the novel are the enigmatic personalities of the three widows themselves, along with the sardonic observations of the author, who herself married very young at the age of eighteen and divorced at the age of thirty-two. Over the course of *The Three Widows*, Mr. Bladeswell comes to believe that women truly may be, as the saying has it, deadlier than the male and that feminine crime writing may have something to offer, after all:

> There were always lots of mysteries mixed in with the other books [at the Escondido store], and [Mr. Bladeswell's] eye lingered on one

showing a frightened young woman in a filmy negligee staring up into the darkness of an open stairway. When he did read detective stories he liked them with mostly men characters and lots of action and guns; but he picked up the frightened young lady and thoughtfully turned the pages. The author was a woman, a name he was unfamiliar with. Ordinarily he would never have given the book a second glance, but there was something about the combination of women and mystery and murder that drew him now.

Women and mystery and murder: an enticingly deadly combination, as Bernice Carey and other female mid-century crime writers proved to the delight of their devoted readership, male and female alike, over and over again. Happily Bernice Carey can now demonstrate this once more to a modern-day mystery reading audience.

—December 2018
Germantown, TN

Curtis Evans received a PhD in American history in 1998. He is the author of *Masters of the "Humdrum" Mystery: Cecil John Charles Street, Freeman Wills Crofts, Alfred Walter Stewart and British Detective Fiction, 1920-1961* (2012) and most recently the editor of the Edgar nominated *Murder in the Closet: Essays on Queer Clues in Crime Fiction Before Stonewall* (2017) and, with Douglas G. Greene, the forthcoming Richard Webb and Hugh Wheeler short crime fiction collection, *The Cases of Lieutenant Timothy Trant* (2019). He blogs on vintage crime fiction at The Passing Tramp.

The Man Who Got Away With It

- - - - - -

Bernice Carey

CHAPTER ONE

He stood on the flagstone path by the house smoking his second after-dinner cigarette and watching the languidly turning arms of spray thrown out by the sprinkler. Drops spattered on the hydrangeas along the back fence and left a half moon of darker colored stones at the edge of the patio floor.

The regular swishing against the hydrangea leaves alternating with the recurrent patter on the stones had a narcotic effect, and the man stood almost somnolent in the quiet twilight. Finally he walked over to the white-painted table beside the settee and crushed out his cigarette in an ash tray before bending to turn the key set in the corner between the walk and the patio. The streams from the sprinkler slowed and became briefly visible as slender columns which dwindled away into dying little fountains close to the metal circlet buried in the grass.

Ben moved his shoulders slightly under the short-sleeved rayon sport shirt covered in a design of horseshoes and lariats. It had felt good to get out of a hot collar and tie when he got home at six-thirty, but now at eight o'-clock the coastal California night had already laid chill fingers upon the air; so, with rather deliberate steps in his brown loafers and hand-knitted Argyle socks, Ben crossed the patio and went into the living room through the screened double doors.

Beth was coming into the room from the kitchen, alternately turning on lights and rubbing her hands to spread the lotion on them.

"I've been laying out the things," she announced, "so they'll be ready to serve. Do you suppose they'll think it's funny, serving beer instead of high-balls? I don't want to seem cheap; and goodness knows, it isn't, really. I've got pretzels and assorted nuts—I mixed in a few salted peanuts. The assorted are so high; and people just gobble them. And the Ritz crackers with bleu cheese look lovely, and with potato chips and all— Of course, the Merritts always serve those fancy cocktails. But it was so warm today, and I thought I'd just mention how beer always seems to go with hot weather. Better close the windows, Ben; we'll just leave the doors open."

She paused before the Carmel-stone mantel, and regarded the clean fire space thoughtfully. "I wonder if we ought to have a little fire. Maybe a few eucalyptus logs—to make it smell nice."

Ben, turning the catches on the windows, didn't bother to reply. He knew Beth didn't expect answers.

She glanced about the room inspectingly, and picked a folded newspaper off the coffee table and laid it on the magazines neatly stacked on the lower shelf of an end table. Then she sat down in the tapestry-covered wing chair facing the sofa.

She touched the long string of crystal beads hanging over the V-neck of her rayon dress with its floral print, and smoothed the material at her waist. Beth's hair had once been the color of ripe oats, but now the short, lightly curled locks were ashy with imperceptible gray. She was five feet two, and had had a "cute" figure when she married Ben twenty years before. It was still not bad, she told herself. At least she wasn't fat. And, after all, only Ben knew how she looked undressed, without the supporting brassieres and the girdles with the clever corsetlike waists.

She did not suspect—she was not the suspicious type—that sometimes Ben, seeing—or feeling—her in her knitted nightgowns, bonelessly soft and all of a piece, would think unintentionally of Dolores who ran the record department, or of girls his eyes followed in the store or on the street; girls who pinched in at the waist and came out solidly in front and behind.

Ben never thought of Beth critically though as he made these unconscious comparisons, even though his own figure had changed little with the years, merely becoming more solid and compact. He accepted her appearance as unthinkingly as he accepted the gray blending into and dulling his own light-brown hair, the increasing permanence of the lines on his forehead.

"You do think beer is all right?" Beth was asking anxiously once more.

"For the fiftieth time—yes."

"Well, it *is* cheaper," she reiterated. "A fifth of whisky just lasts no time, and when you count in the mixer— And they don't drink beer so fast. It ought to save two or three dollars anyway."

Ben had arranged the logs in the fireplace, and now he lowered himself to the davenport and leaned his shoulders back in the corner.

"What do you keep harping on the cost for?" he said in a mildly irritated tone. "Anybody'd think we were up against it."

"Well, Ben," she said with patient reproachfulness, "you know how business has been lately. I should think you'd be glad I take an interest."

"So all right, things have slacked off. I'm having to cut corners at the store. But we aren't on relief yet."

Beth looked worried again. "Then you don't think I should have planned to serve beer!"

Ben was taking a deep breath, closing his eyes as he did so, when the subject was changed by the noise of their daughter Shirley's descent of the staircase, her hand sliding along the wrought-iron railing.

"Where are you going, dear?" Beth inquired, looking up at the girl, who wore a full, figured skirt and flat gold sandals beneath a loose pink flannel coat which hung to her hips. Her honey-colored hair seemed to consist principally of heavy bangs reaching nearly to her eyebrows.

"Over to Ginger's," she replied offhandedly. "Pop, can I have a dollar? I had to spend the rest of my allowance for a manicure for the Teen Time dance at the club night before last."

"What do you need money for if you're just going to Ginger's?"

"Oh—Po-up," she said wearily. "You know. We may just angle on down to the Sweet Shoppe for a malt or something. And you need nickels for the juke box or something. And suppose Ginger wants to go to the show."

Ben looked accusingly at his wife. "I don't like it, her running the streets at night. Why can't they just stay at Ginger's or here? It's not safe, kids seventeen traipsing around the streets at night. It don't look right either. What kind of girls will people think they are?"

"Oh, Ben." Beth chuckled tolerantly. "In Los Alegres what can happen to them? It isn't as if this was a big city. My goodness, Shirley knows everybody." She smiled archly at the girl. "And we know why they do it, don't we, sweetie? The boys get thirsty, too, don't they? And then they just happen to walk home with you."

"Oh, Mother, you make it sound so corny."

"Well, I don't like it," Ben insisted. "I like to know where she is and who she's with."

"Oh, Pop," Shirley sighed. "Come on. Give me a dollar. Ginger's waiting."

"Well, go get my wallet. It's on the dresser in our room."

As the girl went toward the door to the front hall leading to the street, her mother called after her, "Now be in early, darling. Eleven o'clock."

Beth glanced at her wrist watch. "It's almost eight-thirty. I suppose they'll be here pretty soon. I wonder if I ought to pick up my knitting; but then I'd just have to put it away again when they came. If it was just Lucille and Clarence I'd work on it and get that sleeve finished; but with Roy and his wife along, not knowing them, you might say, it looks as if you weren't giving your guests your undivided attention. Don't you think so?"

"What happened to the paper? I wasn't quite finished with it."

"I put it away. We don't want the place all cluttered-looking, people from out of town and all. Of course Roy is Lucille's brother and just as common as an old shoe and all; but he is a pretty big man—in his line," she appended thoughtfully. "And from Chicago. My goodness, you'd never think to look at him, would you, that he's mixed with all those gangsters and things? Head of the Homicide Department," she repeated reflectively, and then glanced at her husband defensively as she declared, "Though, actually, I suppose that's nothing more than a policeman, like Barney Granger, and nobody's much impressed with him."

"Running the prowl car in Los Alegres isn't quite the same thing as being chief of the Homicide Squad in Chicago," Ben put in dryly.

"Well, it's nice he can get away for a vacation," Beth observed approvingly. "I suppose things are kind of slow in his line in the summer too."

The chimes in the hallway between the kitchen and dining room rang softly, and Beth got to her feet. Ben followed her to the arched opening into the hall as she went to the front door and ushered in the guests. It was a little crowded and flurried in the narrow corridor, with Lucille talking in a high voice and Beth greeting everyone at once and Ben adding his welcome from behind.

Beth steered the ladies to the downstairs bedroom beyond the staircase, first collecting Roy Malley's straw hat—which in itself showed he was an easterner. Imagine a man wearing a hat in the summertime, and in the evening! Both Ben and Beth had already taken in his light suit, the coat and pants matching, and the white shirt with a pale-blue tie, and they had both felt a little undressed, even though Clarence Merritt was clothed as usual in his regular business attire, plain brown slacks and a sport jacket of subdued plaid.

When the women emerged from the bedroom, satisfactorily similar in their summery prints with short sleeves and their hair short and fluffed out, the men were still standing out from the fireplace, and there was another little flurry then of getting seated in the deep chairs and the sofa while Ben lighted the kindling under the eucalyptus logs.

"A fire will feel wonderful," Mrs. Malley was saying. "I just can't get used to it the way it cools off when the sun goes down out here."

"It's the ocean," her brother-in-law pointed out, as if he were personally responsible for the Pacific's proximity.

"At home, you know, even on the lake shore, the evenings are so balmy."

"Sweltering, you mean," her husband corrected dryly.

Beth was again undergoing mental tortures over the propriety of beer. Mrs. Malley made it sound as if she would have welcomed a hot toddy. But perhaps they would have forgotten the weather by the time they were all settled down talking and it was time to get up casually and suggest a drink.

Clarence Merritt sank into the low-backed overstuffed chair facing the fire and stretched his feet out on the footstool. He was florid and husky and hearty, and didn't look as if he had spent years as some kind of clerk in the city hall until he reached the position of street commissioner which he now held.

Lucille Merritt had seated herself in the exact center of the davenport, and was fitting a long cigarette into a holder, managing to look vivacious, with her small, bright eyes and her hair dyed to a gleaming black, her thin, nervous hands busy with holder and lighter.

The sister-in-law, Mrs. Malley, sat at the end of the sofa closest to the fire, leaning forward to watch the blaze, pleasant and nondescript with her brown hair and round arms, and—Beth noticed—rather thick ankles above platform-soled pumps.

Roy Malley had taken the wing chair, where he sat placidly with his hands on the arms, his mild blue eyes moving from the fire to one or another of the people. His appearance had disappointed Beth the first time she saw him, and it still did. Somehow you expected a police officer who dealt in murders on the scale in which Chicago produced them to look beefy and tough and gimlet-eyed; but Roy Malley always made her think of Clint Simmons who had run the Emporium since the year One.

Even though he was tall, he was sort of skinny and frail-looking, and there was a narrow path of pale skin down the center of the thin gray hair distributed along the sides of his long head, which was broader at the temples than it was below or above. With his hair not filling out the top that way, it made his head look almost pointed.

He must, though, have had lots of exciting, dangerous experiences, and she hoped they could get him to talking about them. It should be fascinating—Al Capone and everything, although that was probably before his time.

Ben sat on the end of the davenport beside Lucille, and Beth had taken the occasional chair between Clarence and Mr. Malley. They talked about the Malleys' trip and about the vacation the Merritts intended to take; and pretty soon Beth rose casually to bring in the beer. She set the tray of bottles and glasses on the coffee table, and Ben began to open and pour, while Clarence exclaimed approvingly, "You must have been thinking about me, Beth. You know my weakness. Nothing like a nice cold bottle of beer."

"Well, it was so hot during the day, and I just kept thinking how good a glass of beer would taste—"

Amidst a flutter of commending comment—about whose sincerity Beth wondered anxiously—she went out for the tray of crackers, nuts, and pretzels.

They were busily comparing the merits of eastern and western beer when she returned.

Before long the men were discussing business conditions, and Ben was expounding his view that there was nothing to be alarmed about, things were just shaking down after the war's disruption of normalcy.

"Way I look at it," Clarence was declaring, "we're gonna have some failures, but it'll be businesses that, for normal times, there wasn't no real need for. Now, like in your line, Ben. You been established for years, and then after the war Tim Bailey expanding like he did and giving you competition ... He had no business getting out of the straight repair line. Takin' on selling radios and electrical appliances. There wasn't no need for another radio store. You been handling that end. And we already got three good electrical goods stores. If Tim gets squeezed out, it's only his own fault."

"Well Tim," Ben said judiciously, "wasn't what you'd call a businessman to start with. He was just handy with tools, repairing and like that. He's a good workman and should've stuck to that end of the game."

"Oh, those Baileys," Lucille put in. "They never did amount to much. All of them have always been poor—laborers and so on. I think it's a mistake for people to try to move out of their class."

Ben nodded politely at this feminine interruption to a discussion he considered strictly masculine in character. He agreed with Lucille's point, but he was momentarily annoyed. She wasn't taking a dig at him, of course; but he hoped no one else remembered that Ben Sterling hadn't come from such a high-class family himself. His father, too, had been what she called a laborer, a mechanic in the Ford garage on Pacific Street.

Beth chirped up just then, however. "I'm sure all this gossip about local people isn't very entertaining for Mr. and Mrs. Malley. But you know how us small-town people are—provincial." She laughed comfortably. "Get to thinking the whole world revolves around us and our little affairs."

"Well, I suspect that small-town affairs aren't very much different except in degree than big towns'," Mr. Malley reassured her.

"I don't see how you can say that, Mr. Malley, considering the exciting job you have. Why, we don't even have murders in Los Alegres."

"At least not very often." Lucille laughed.

"You can't tell me," Beth repeated tenaciously, "that your job isn't simply fascinating."

"I'm afraid if the truth were known, Mrs. Sterling," Malley said with a smile, "you'd find my life pretty humdrum."

"Oh, Roy," Lucille chided, "you're just being modest."

"Don't get him started," Mrs. Malley advised indulgently, "explaining how all he does is get eyestrain from plowing through reports."

"That's about the size of it, though. People seem to have the idea that there's something glamorous about detective work; but to tell the truth, whether you're a leg man or in the office like me, it's really pretty tedious. As Marian says, most of my time is put in wading through dull reports and trying to figure out what they mean."

"And then half the time you don't, eh, Roy?" his brother-in-law jibed.

"I wouldn't say 'half' the time," he demurred amiably.

"Do you mean," Lucille said accusingly, "you don't solve all your murders?"

Her brother set his glass on the coaster on the end table, and smiled. "I hate to disillusion you, Sis, but I have to admit we don't.'"

"Why, I thought," Beth said wide-eyed, "the police always caught murderers—especially in Chicago."

"As a matter of fact, our cases fall pretty evenly into two classes, the open and shut ones where there's witnesses or an iron-bound set of circumstantial evidence that'll bring out a confession—or a complete blank where we're up against a dead end." He paused, and his quick, small blue eyes twinkled. "No pun intended."

"Well, I'm surprised," Beth said on a disappointed breath. She looked at him archly. "You do make it sound awfully dull and cut and dried. I think you're just being modest."

"We had an unsolved murder once," Lucille said brightly over hands busy again with holder and cigarette. "Remember? That Bailey girl—Inez. That's funny. We were just talking about the Baileys. This Tim we mentioned," she said as an aside to Malley, "was her brother. Of course it was years ago."

"That's right," Beth chimed in. "My goodness, the whole town was agog. Strangled. Behind the lilacs in the high school grounds. How long ago was that? Oh, I remember. It was in the spring before we were married, Ben." She threw him a glance and went on reminiscently, "That makes it just twenty years ago."

"Yeah, I remember," Clarence put in. "It was '29, the year of the crash. We shouldn't forget that."

Ben leaned forward and passed the pretzels to Lucille and offered them to Clarence, who passed them on around the circle.

"I expect Mr. Malley isn't much interested in our old murders either. We seem to be talking nothing but shop tonight, one way or another. How about it, would you folks like to have a few new records on while we talk? I've got a honey of a new album of Burl Ives stuff."

"That would be nice," Mrs. Malley said politely, and added with a humorous glance at her husband, "You keep on, and you'll have Roy digging the whole story out of you, just to see if he can't figure it out, even at this late date. Every town we've stopped in on this trip, he gets the local papers, and if there's been a crime committed, he reads every word on it."

"Habit," Malley said laconically.

Ben had gone to the elaborate cabinet at the end of the room and was putting on a record.

"Keep it low, honey," Beth called.

"You should have been here, Roy," Lucille said banteringly, leaning back with a pretzel in one hand, her cigarette holder in the other. "You might have been able to catch poor Inez Bailey's murderer. Although a lot of people said it wasn't surprising somebody did bump her off. Lord knows, there must have been motives enough. Jealous wives, husbands scared they'd be found out, jilted lovers. You see, she wasn't—well—a nice girl."

"Just wild," Beth put in with an explanatory glance at the policeman.

"Beth means," Lucille laughed, "that she wasn't a professional."

"Mercy no, Lucille. Why, she was in our class in high school. Of course she didn't graduate. That kind don't somehow. I guess there wasn't a boy in town she hadn't dated."

Clarence laughed in his usual uninhibited way. "Now, don't look at me, Beth. I only went out with her once—when we were still in school. Those days, a fellow wasn't considered a man until he'd dated Inez Bailey." He glanced up with a knowing wink at Ben, who had come to the end of the davenport and was lighting a cigarette. "Eh, Ben?"

Ben uttered a stilted laugh. "Speak for yourself, Clarence."

Lucille raised her eyebrows. "Please. There are ladies present." She looked at Beth resignedly. "What a way for our husbands to talk—right in front of us."

"It's just talk," Beth said comfortably. "I always thought that's all a lot of it was. Poor Inez, she got a bad name. And you know how boys in a small town are—they all had to climb on the bandwagon and say they'd been out with her whether they had or not."

"You mean," Roy Malley inquired seriously, "all you people in town never had any idea who killed her? Or was it just that your police couldn't get proof?"

"Oh, there were ideas," Lucille said scornfully. "Everybody who'd ever had anything to do with her was suspected. But that was the trouble; there were too many. And we didn't tell you the juiciest part. There was an autopsy, of course, and she was pregnant."

"*An American Tragedy* sort of thing then," Mrs. Malley put in helpfully.

Beth wrinkled her forehead. "Let's see. That was so long ago. I saw the movie. Such a beautiful boy played the hero. Philip something, wasn't it? And wasn't it that he drowned the girl so he could marry somebody else?"

"We never figured it was anything like that though," Clarence said with a rejecting grimace. "Everybody figured it must have been some married man got her in trouble, and she was putting the heat on and he was scared his wife would find out."

"If that was the theory, it should have narrowed it down," Malley said.

"You didn't know Inez," Lucille quipped gaily. "There'd been talk about her and at least half a dozen married men. There was that doctor that moved away a few years later. But I figured it couldn't have been him. He'd have just performed an abortion and that would have been that. And then there was the guy that managed the chain store and one of the tellers in the bank and even one of the high school teachers. Nothing definite, you understand, about any of them; but there had been rumors that she'd been seen with all of them at one time or another, in a car on a country road or something."

Ben had taken his place in the corner of the davenport again. "Well, the poor girl's dead now," he said lightly, "and we ought to let her rest in peace."

"If the truth were known"—Malley pursued the subject—"your police may have known more than you think. But in a small place like this they'd have to keep their mouths shut. Unless they had proof they'd lay themselves open to a suit for defamation of character if they broadcast their suspicions." He murmured thoughtfully, "Five or six thousand people you have here? It wouldn't be hard to check on everybody the girl knew, alibis and so on."

"Nope, you're wrong, Roy. I was working in the city hall then," Clarence elaborated, "and Jim Billings was police chief. I knew him well. His folks were neighbors of mine all our lives; and he told me they were baffled—completely baffled. There was an American Legion dance the same night; and that accounted for a hell of a lot of the men or boys she knew, along with girl friends and wives. The sheriff's office worked on it, too, and among 'em they got nowhere."

Malley shook his head, tightening his lips impatiently. "It's not my place to run down your law enforcement bodies; but I don't think they could have known their business very well. I still say, in a place this small, the proper lines of investigation would have got them somewhere."

Mrs. Malley chuckled ruefully. "Now you've roused the bloodhound in Roy. He'll worry over the case all evening."

"Maybe he'll solve it for us—twenty years later," Lucille chirruped gaily.

"No. No, it's too late now. But at the risk of sounding immodest, I'd be willing to bet if I'd been in charge here at the time, we'd have solved it to our own satisfaction, whether we got a conviction or not. Maybe I have a suspicious nature; but the thing sort of smells to me—as if somebody important around here might have influenced the police to lay off."

Clarence uttered a shout of laughter. "I'd like to see old Jim Billings's face if he heard that. By God, Los Alegres never had a more honest police chief, before or since. Fact is, he was too straight for some people's taste, and he didn't last long as chief. You know, Ben, how when Dan Miller and old man Zangoni got their heads together and got their own city council elected, Billings was soon out and Fred Colton was in. Colton," he explained to Malley parenthetically, "married the oldest Zangoni girl."

Ben nodded. "Yes, and Jim was no dope either. It was just one of those cases like you spoke of, Mr. Malley—a dead end. Personally, I always figured it was a tramp or somebody like that that didn't even know her."

"Had she been attacked?"

"Not as I recall," Clarence said thoughtfully.

"Oh, it was probably somebody she knew," Beth put in cheerfully. "Just think, all these years we've probably all of us been associating with somebody with blood on their hands. It just gives you the creeps, doesn't it, to stop and think of it?"

"Well of course," Malley said reassuringly, "the people who commit these *crimes passionnels*, if that was what it was, aren't always dangerous afterward. Knowing what they've done in a fit of passion sometimes tends to make them more controlled in the future. They realize what their emotions can do to them, so they try harder than other people to keep them under control."

"Just the same," his wife said with a little shudder, "I could never feel comfortable around somebody I knew had committed a murder. I'd know what he *could* do when he lost control, and I'd be scared stiff that he might lose his head again sometime."

"Well, there is that, of course," Roy agreed equably. "What a man will do once he may do again. That's the theory, of course, behind putting killers away."

Lucille shivered, and pressed her cigarette out of the holder into the big crystal ash tray. "How did we get on this gruesome subject? Now I'll be afraid to walk down the street alone at night, afraid somebody I've unwittingly annoyed will lose their temper when they see me."

"I believe it was you who brought the subject up," Ben said with a quiet smile.

CHAPTER TWO

When their guests had finally been bidden the last goodbys from the front steps Beth and Ben came back into the living room and she began to stack the empty glasses and bottles on the trays.

Ben looked at the electric clock on the spinet desk under the south windows, and said irritably, "Eleven-fifteen, and that kid isn't in yet."

"Oh well, they probably decided to go to the show."

"But the last thing you said to her was 'Be in by eleven.'"

"I know, but that was more just to let her know she mustn't be late."

Ben lifted his own glass and drained off the inch of flat beer remaining in it.

"Well, I don't like it," he muttered, setting the glass on the laden tray Beth had picked up. "Here, I'll carry that out."

He took it from her, and she followed him to the kitchen with the smaller tray.

"I do believe," she said jokingly to his back, "you let that talk about Inez Bailey get under your skin. You're afraid Shirley might get strangled under the lilacs by some impetuous boy friend."

"It's no joking matter," he growled over his shoulder as he pushed the swinging door open with his arm. "How do we know what kind of people she's getting mixed up with?"

"Oh, for mercy's sakes, Ben! Shirley only goes with the nicest kids in Los Alegres. And she's a nice girl. It's only the bad ones, like Inez Bailey, that get murdered."

"I know, I know," he said testily, setting the tray on the drainboard. "But these young sprouts around town ... Sure, they're mostly our friends' kids; but I know more about boys than you do. I don't trust 'em."

"My goodness, kids like Spec Miller and Bobby Whitlock aren't going to up and murder Shirley. I don't know what's got into you."

"Who said anything about murder?" he snapped. "But Shirley's no child any more. How do we know what she's doing out late at night like this?"

"We don't," Beth retorted cheerfully. "Come on, we needn't bother washing up. I'll have Shirley help me in the morning. But I figure you just have to trust your kids; and goodness knows, I've tried to bring her up with standards."

Ben went out first, and Beth snapped off the kitchen lights.

He pursued his thoughts tenaciously as they crossed the living room, Beth detouring to turn off lights. "Shirley's a smart kid and pretty as they come, and damn it, I'd like to see her settled someday with a good man. No reason she can't marry anybody she wants to—somebody that amounts to something; and the way things are in a small town like this, the kids all know each other, no matter what kind of a family they come from. How'd you like to see your daughter fall for some no-good and run off and get married—or worse—before she's even eighteen?"

"I'm not worried about it," Beth returned calmly. "Like I said, Ben, you have to trust kids. And far as that goes, it's no catastrophe if she happens to fall in love with somebody besides Tony Zangoni, the banker's son."

As she came to his side, she slipped her hand under his arm and squeezed it, smiling up at him coquettishly. "Look at me. I married a poor man's son, and it didn't turn out so bad."

"We-ell," he said with a reluctant grin, "I'm different."

"Go on with you," she chuckled.

As they were undressing, the front door slammed and in a moment they heard Shirley's steps on the stairs.

"Now," Beth said archly, sticking her head through the neck of her nightgown, "I hope you're satisfied."

Ben grunted and climbed into bed. He paid no attention as Beth kept talking, airing her opinions about their late guests. Both the talk about Inez Bailey's death and Beth's remark about marrying a poor man had sent his thoughts back twenty years to the summer of his own marriage. He had felt lucky—lucky as hell to be marrying Beth Jensen. Her father had been among the well-to-do men in Los Alegres, owning a big dairy and the creamery on the outskirts of town, which supplied all the stores and restaurants in Los Alegres with milk products. And Beth had been the most popular girl in town, cute and pert and always on the go. Their wedding at the Methodist Church had been a real social event, even though Ben knew a lot of the old cats in town thought Beth Jensen was marrying beneath her. After all, all Ben Sterling had been was the clerk in charge of Clint Simmons's music department in the Emporium.

It was really Beth's old man who was responsible for their being where they were now. Radio was the big thing in those days. Not everybody had one yet; and old Ole Jensen had lent the young couple the money for Ben to start his own shop, selling radios, with records and sheet music and phonographs as a sideline, until now Ben was one of the most prominent merchants in Los Alegres, with an entirely glass-fronted shop on the corner of Main and Live Oak streets. No one remembered any more that his family had lived in a run-down bungalow on Railroad Avenue, with old Ben Sterling a grease monkey at the Ford garage and his brother Bill a brakeman for the Southern Pacific. His father was dead now; his brother Bill worked out of L.A. So there weren't any reminders any more that his family had been close neighbors of people like the Baileys, who lived one street over down among the rows of crowded frame bungalows. For that matter Tim Bailey had come up, too, from the Railroad Avenue neighborhood days, with a store down the street from Ben's and a membership in the Lion's Club as big as you please.

Ben pushed the pillow up under his cheek. Well, maybe his wife had married beneath her and it had worked out all right; but he didn't want his daughter to do the same thing. It didn't always work out so well.

Down the street and around the corner Roy Malley stood by the straight chair in his sister's guest room, and carefully folded his gray pants over the back of the chair. He had already hung his suit jacket on a hanger and pulled off his tie, and now he began to unbutton his shirt with an abstracted air.

His wife, coming out of the bathroom which connected with the other couple's bedroom, gave him a casual glance and then steadied her eyes on him for an instant before she smilingly shook her head.

"Roy Malley," she chided, "you're thinking."

He started guiltily and grinned sheepishly. "Guess I was."

"That case got your interest up, didn't it?"

"Some, I guess."

"Well, you just forget it. Talk about a 'postman's holiday'!"

"I don't know why," he said apologetically, "but it took hold in my mind."

"Old war horse," she teased, bringing her robe and slippers out of the closet.

He never discussed his work at home. Being what it was, it didn't belong there. So he did not explain to Marian what he knew to be the reason for this interest in a twenty-year-old homicide which was no concern of his. At any rate he might not have been able to explain it to her.

It was a part of his training and his long experience. You got so you sensed things; felt them without bothering to trace the tiny, almost imperceptible stimuli which gave you the hunch, the awareness that you were getting onto something.

That feeling arose seemingly from an intangible current in the atmosphere, as if your nerve ends caught intensified vibrations in the air. And such a condition had existed tonight.

There was nothing mystical, nothing actually mysterious about it. It was simply that a man's brain and all his senses became unusually acute after being directed for years toward observation of other men. Nuances of behavior, inflections of speech impressed themselves on the delicate perceptive apparatus of the mind, made associations which did not have to be followed precisely by conscious mental processes.

Every expert in his field knew what it was like. It happened all the time, and usually one passed it off as a "hunch," the sudden knowing that, out of several people under consideration, this man was the one to keep your eye on, that this avenue, rather than another, was the one to follow doggedly, whether you saw the end as yet or not. It did not always mean that the person who impressed himself on you like that was the man you were after; but it did mean, when it happened, that his manner or something about the place he occupied in the picture had telegraphed to your brain that there was information here to guide you toward your objective.

And tonight that "hunch" had come to him, clear and insistent. It had not been distinct enough to point to any single person as the emanating source. It was only that some gesture, some word, or perhaps the whole pattern of the conversation had informed his well-trained perceptive faculties that within the group, collectively or individually, something lay hidden—knowledge, or uneasiness, or apprehension.

Even the signs that his senses had dutifully catalogued, so that his mind knew something had happened, were too slight, too indistinct to emerge in conscious analysis. Already he had gone back over the scene several times, and all he had come up with was the vaguely exciting impulse to start work on the case. And when a man got that feeling, he knew from experience that, whether he recognized them yet or not, he had seen indications of a trail. If he followed them, whether he ever came to the end or not, he would get somewhere further along than the point at which things stood at the moment.

But it was foolish, of course. It was none of his business. And it was much too late anyway. Undoubtedly there had been blocks in the case which would have stopped him if he had been there, just as they had stopped the local police years ago. That happened all too frequently.

Just the same it was frustrating not to be able to go on after you had experienced that hunch.

He woke the next morning before Marian did, and as he lay quiet and rested after a good sleep, he knew what it was that had alerted him the evening before. He narrowed his eyes toward the light shining in below the blind on the open window.

In a few minutes he got up quietly, letting Marian go on sleeping in the other twin bed, and went to the bathroom and washed, and brushed his hair. Then he tied his bathrobe around him and went down the hallway which bisected the one-story house, out to the kitchen at the rear, overlooking flower gardens and a circular clothesline tree set in a square of grass.

Clarence was already off to work, and Lucille, in a short-sleeved pink linen housecoat, was clearing the table in the breakfast alcove whose sunny eastern windows curved out into the back yard.

"Why don't you sleep, Roy," she demanded good-humoredly, "now, while you have a chance?"

"I'm letting Marian do that." He smiled. He looked across the table to the colorful borders of ranunculuses outside. "It's too beautiful a day to waste in bed."

"It is nice, isn't it? I love our breakfast room in the morning."

Lucille stood at his side and glanced about the space whose cream walls were nearly covered—where they weren't filled by glass-faced cupboards—with framed Audubon prints. The long windows, draped only by narrow chintz valances at the top, seemed to allow the blue of the sky and the green of the leaves on the trees in the next yard to become a part of the room.

"We had bacon and eggs," she said briskly. "What will you have?"

"Just my orange juice now, and a cup of coffee. I'll wait and eat later with Marian so you won't have to keep cooking breakfasts all morning."

"Okay. I'll have my after-breakfast cup of coffee with you." She grinned and lightly struck his arm with her doubled fist. "It'll be kind of fun, sitting over the breakfast table with my distinguished brother—you old bum."

Lucille fitted a cigarette into her holder across a steaming cup of coffee, and Roy, looking at her, thought with a pang that neither of them was as young as they once had been. Between the determined black of her hair, looking rather brittle in the morning sunlight, and the fresh pink of her square-necked gown, Lucille's face, as yet unmade up for the day, looked sallow and dry and more lined than he remembered.

It occurred to him that he hadn't really known Lucille well, as a brother usually knows his sister. She was ten years his junior, and their mother had died when Lucille was eleven. He had just joined the force in Chicago, a lad of twenty-one, ambitious and believing the things they told you about the chances for advancement in law enforcement if you studied hard and took your work seriously, which he, incidentally, had done, with night school and special courses in criminology, and all the rest of it. Lucille had been taken to live with an aunt in California—Aunt Kate, who had, for reasons he could not now remember, moved to Los Alegres when Lucille was thirteen.

They had a brother, Ed, between them in age, now in the trucking business in Milwaukee. Lucille had visited both brothers at two- and three-year intervals; and during the past ten years Roy and Marian had made two vacation trips to California, on the first having time only to stop overnight with Lucille and Clarence before they raced on in their car to get back to Chicago before his two weeks' leave was up. On their second trip the Malleys had not come to Los Alegres at all. Roy had been on sick leave after a session of pneumonia, and they had gone to Palm Springs for his convalescence, with Lucille coming down to spend a week with them there. Thus, among them, they had kept the family ties from breaking.

"You don't want to eat too late," Lucille reminded him now, holding her cigarette to one side. "Remember, Clarence wants you to meet him for the Kiwanis luncheon."

"That's right. But I'm on vacation. Guess I'm entitled to overeat if I want to."

She laughed. "That's one thing we don't have to worry about. Diet. Look at us, skinny as rails, both of us. It must run in the family."

He smiled and took a sip of coffee, gazing across the cup at a hummingbird darting among the fuchsia blossoms beside the corner window.

"It's nice here," he said. "Some ways I envy you, living in a nice quiet little town."

"I still think you kids ought to settle down here in Los Alegres when you retire. All respectable people come to California to die."

"Sometimes I wonder if we oughtn't to have settled down out here years ago," he said lightly, and felt a little shamefaced, deliberately lying to his own sister. He had never had any desire to live anywhere but in the city. But he was edging up to his subject, and he went on shamelessly, "After all, I could have been just as good a cop"—he grinned jokingly—"in Los Alegres as in Chicago."

"You probably wouldn't have been as busy," she said dryly. "Our criminal element isn't what you'd call a real problem."

"The work would be easier, I suspect. Before you have a crime laid on your doorstep here most of the spadework is done. That is, you already know all about the public and private lives of everybody concerned. You don't have to start from scratch, figuring out people's relationships."

"You're not kidding about that," she agreed wryly. "Nobody has any secrets for long around here. The old hens know how much you paid and where you bought every stitch you put on. And you have an argument with your husband and by noon the next day the whole block not only knows what it was about but who won."

"That's what I mean. There's very little mystery in your lives. Although that would be one of the handicaps to holding public office, I should think. Too many personal elements to contend with. Like this—what was his name?—Jim Billings you were talking about last night. I gathered he tried simply to do his job, but a few individuals wanted to tell him how, and when he wouldn't co-operate, he was out. What happens to a man after something like that happens to him?"

Lucille shrugged. "Oh, he does something else. Jim Billings is still around, in real estate and insurance now. He's done well enough. Has an office on Main Street."

"He sounded like a nice guy."

"Oh, he is; Clarence thinks the world of him. You'll probably meet him at the luncheon today."

"Good. I'd like to." With an air of seemingly idle musing he stirred his coffee and watched the busy hummingbird. "It must complicate things, being in police work, when you're in the same social and civic clubs with the man you see you may have to arrest. Like this case you were discussing last night. If the crime were committed by someone you'd played basketball with in high school and golf with at the country club, even your mind would shy away from placing suspicion on him."

"Not Jim Billings's. He's one of those stolid, conscientious sort of guys. If he caught the President of the United States overparking for five minutes on Main Street, Mr. President would get his ticket, just like anybody else." She paused and pushed out her lips. "Maybe that was one of Jim's troubles, too uncompromising."

"Yes, a certain amount of flexibility is necessary. Although even then a man can be completely defeated at times, just as they were here in dealing with the Bailey murder. I wondered while we were talking of it about the girl's family. Usually her relatives would know a good deal about her associates and could give you a line on who to investigate."

Lucille smiled skeptically. "A young girl's family sometimes knows less about her private life than you'd think. Especially girls of her kind. They make special efforts to conceal their shenanigans from the parents. And, of course, Inez had only her mother, who lived on a pension and wasn't very well—hardly ever went out. She died a few years ago. The only other relative she had was Tim. He and Etta hadn't been married long and were living with Mrs. Bailey and Inez. And they were all home together all evening the night it happened."

"Surely the brother and sister-in-law knew who Inez's boy friends—and girl friends—were."

"Oh, we all knew that. But there were so many of them."

"Yes, I suppose so." He smiled. "When even Clarence and your friend Ben admit to having been out with her."

"Oh—Clarence!" Lucille looked up scornfully as she pressed the catch on her holder to expel the cigarette into the ash tray. "I don't think he ever took her out in his life. For one thing, Clarence was two years younger than Inez, and although you wouldn't think so now, Clarence was rather shy with girls when we were kids; always hung out with his gang of boys. But Ben did know her fairly well. That's why I could have kicked Clarence last night when he started showing off about what devils they were supposed to have been in their youth. As a matter of fact, he and Ben never ran around together. For one thing, Ben is five years older than Clarence, and when we were kids, Ben wasn't really in our set. His folks didn't have much money, and they lived down in that neighborhood where Baileys did. And as a matter of fact, Ben doesn't like to be reminded of it. You know, sensitive because his people were nobodies. It wasn't till he graduated from high school and went to work for Clint Simmons at the Emporium that he started to run around with our crowd."

Her eyes took on a reminiscent glaze. "He was cute then—not that he isn't still a nice-looking man—and he always had such a nice, pleasant way about him. When we began to get acquainted with him, all of us girls got to like Ben. He always treated you as if you were something special."

"He probably knew more about Inez than any of you, then, if he lived close to her."

"I suppose he did," she said thoughtfully. "But Ben is more of a gentleman than the rest of us, I guess. He doesn't gossip. You noticed last night how he didn't chip in with some nasty cracks—the way I did," she added with a little humorous grimace. "As far as that goes," she said with returning seriousness, "the whole thing was probably less—abstract to him, having played with Inez when they were kids, walking back and forth to school in the same bunch every day. Come to think of it, I remember he used to bring her to some of the high school dances when he was a senior and Inez and Beth and I were still sophomores, I think it was. Yes, that was the year. That was before Inez started getting herself talked about. And of course they never went steady. But when you stop to remember, Ben probably knew her better than the rest of us did, and I suppose he felt bad about it; you know, a kid you'd watched grow up on the next street—"

"Was he seeing her much at that time?"

"Good heavens, no. He'd been going with Beth for almost a year, and they were crazy about each other. Now that I've got to going back in my mind over the whole thing, I remember Inez was killed the very night we had a shower for Beth. Gladys Whitlock gave it." She lifted her eyebrows at him mockingly as she pulled another cigarette from the package. "So you see that eliminated all us girls. It happened some time between nine and eleven, they figured."

"But that left all the boy friends running around loose that night," he reminded her teasingly.

"And don't think Jim Billings overlooked that point," she retorted with acerbity. "Especially after they found out she was pregnant. Jim went around doggedly checking the alibis of every male in town, I guess, who wasn't downright impotent. When the Miller-Zangoni crowd decided to get Jim out as police chief, the way he'd handled the Bailey case didn't help matters any. He'd made more people mad! People like Clarence's folks and the Whitlocks and practically all the pillars of the community who had eligible sons that Jim insisted on investigating. They were outraged, of course, that he even knew their boys had dated Inez. And, of course, the married men like that doctor and Bob Morgan at the bank—they were furious at being questioned, even though Jim tried, I think, to be discreet about it; but you know, it leaked out that they were being investigated."

"Sounds as if he was thorough," Malley said soberly.

There was a sound in the kitchen behind them, and they turned their heads as Marian said with an apologetic laugh, "Well, here's the star boarder, late for breakfast. Aren't I the nuisance though!"

"Not a bit," Lucille returned heartily. "Roy and I've just been having a good old visit." She halted, and turned suspicious eyes on her brother. "Or was it?"

She frowned at him, ignoring her sister-in-law. "Roy Malley, are you up to something? Because if you are, you stop it. This is a nice peaceful little town, and nobody wants any trouble."

"What has that man been doing?" Marian put in despairingly.

"Why, nothing," he protested innocently. "I was just listening while Lucille gossiped."

"You made me," she accused, rising. "And just for that, I won't say another word about a living soul in this town the rest of the time you're here."

"Don't pay any attention to him," Marian said lightly. "He's a regular vacuum cleaner about getting dirt out of people."

CHAPTER THREE

Roy was to meet Clarence in the lobby of the Rio Verde Hotel at twelve o'clock, and he set out from the house at eleven to walk, explaining to the girls that he would stroll around town for a while, for a little exercise. He strode briskly along, however, straight down the seven blocks to the business district. Despite his businesslike directness, his eyes lingered pleasurably on the houses and lawns bordering the paved street lined with maple trees.

There was a pleasant mingling of the old and new architecturally: brown-shingled, two-story bungalows with inset front porches and bulky shrubbery standing between brisk, low, ranch-type residences with white walls and Venetian blinds and clipped-looking yards edged by bright-colored annuals. Here and there, between the curb and the sidewalk, beds of nasturtiums or verbena assaulted the eye with their vivid hues. Occasionally, across the street on the north sides of the houses, low masses of cineraria lay against the foundations in cool purple banks; and one little gray cottage with a pointed roof was half hidden in drooping lavender cascades of wisteria.

Children flashed past on scooters or squealed at him from playpens put out in the sun. From time to time a well-polished sedan rolled by on the street with a bareheaded woman at the wheel. Fox terriers ran down stepping-stone paths, barking playfully, and fell back after a few steps to wait for the next passer-by. A plump, middle-aged woman with her hair skewered to her head in pin curls gave him a curious glance as she plodded by carrying a large brown bag full of groceries on each arm. An old man in a shabby black suit and a panama hat nodded and said, "Howdy," in a cheerful voice as they passed one another.

Whimsically Malley thought to himself that maybe there was something to Lucille's talk about the preferability of living in a small town. It all seemed so open and clean and well aired. At least scenes like this were a refreshing change from the plate glass and concrete of the city streets he walked every day at home.

Turning onto Main Street, Roy made a pretense of idle window-shopping, as if he were killing time. A few doors from where he had turned onto the main street, he noted the sign on the long, wide window, "J. B. Billings, Real Estate and Insurance." Inside he saw a girl sitting at a desk smiling as she spoke into the telephone. Farther back in the room there was another flat-topped desk, at the moment unoccupied.

Malley walked on without pausing; but when he came to a window displaying a conglomeration of merchandise comprising everything from a television screen to electric alarm clocks, he dawdled to a stop and seemed absorbed in study of a pop-up toaster. Just above his natural-colored straw hat gold letters spelled out "Bailey Radio and Electric Shop."

His eyes roved among the objects on display and came to rest on a toy accordion that "Plays real tunes." He would have to take something home to his grandson, Ronald. That might do as well as anything.

The shop was empty when he entered, and he wandered vaguely down the center aisle. In a moment a man emerged from the door behind a counter at the rear and stood under the neon sign, "Repairs," which flowed in blue script above the door.

"Anything I can do for you?" he inquired, advancing into the shop.

"I was just looking around. Trying to pick up a present for my young grandson." Roy turned, and gestured toward the window. "Thought maybe one of those little accordions."

"Very nice. Kids get a big kick out of them. Here, let me get it out for you."

He was a heavy-set man, wearing a light khaki shirt and darker khaki trousers. His round head was bald except for a plastered-down circlet of brown hair, which dipped low at the back of his head. As Malley followed him toward the front of the shop, he could hear a tuneless whistling in the back room where repairs were presumably taking place.

The man leaned across the raised display platform filling the front window and reached for the miniature accordion.

He turned and held it in his hands, pressing the keys and working the bellows, a smile on his rugged features. "See? Plays just like a big one."

"Cute, all right," Roy agreed with an answering smile.

The man held it out. "Want to try it?"

Both watched the little instrument with fatuously gratified expressions as Roy in his turn made it squeal.

"How much?"

"Only three eighty-five. And tax, of course."

"I guess I'll take it. But I'll tell you, Mr. Bailey—" He glanced up inquiringly, and the other nodded confirmingly. "I don't want to take it with me right now. I'm on my way to a luncheon at the hotel. Had a little extra time and was just idling around, how I happened to see this. I wonder if you'd hold it and I'll pick it up later. I'll pay you now, of course," he added quickly.

"Why, sure. I'll just wrap it up and put it behind the counter. We'll put your name on it so in case I'm out for a cup of coffee or something one of the boys will know what you're after."

"Fine. Malley's the name—R. Malley."

As Mr. Bailey deposited the accordion in a box and wrapped it, Roy pulled out his wallet. "I'm just a visitor in town," he volunteered, "staying with my brother-in-law, Clarence Merritt. You probably know him."

"Oh sure, sure. I've known Clarence for years. Old friend of mine. Brother Odd Fellow, in fact."

"That so?" Then Malley chuckled, as if partly to himself. "I just happened to think, a competitor of yours had us over to his house last night, and here I am patronizing another store. Sterling was the name—Ben Sterling."

Bailey accepted Roy's five-dollar bill and laughed good-humoredly as he made change. "Oh, I guess Ben wouldn't hold it against you. Far as that goes, I don't think he carries these little gadgets."

As he finished counting the change into Roy's hand, Tim Bailey leaned an elbow on the cash register and went on: "And I wouldn't say we was competitors exactly. I carry more of a general electrical line, with radios as more of a sideline. Where we get into the radio business is more on the repairing angle, new tubes and like that; and trade-ins and secondhand. Ben, he sticks to new stuff and specializes more in straight music; carries instruments and all."

"Sounds as if there was room for both of you then."

"Sure. Matter of fact—" Bailey had lost himself momentarily in the receptive expression and the kindly, encouraging gaze of his customer's light-blue eyes; and now he caught himself sharply, surprised at how he had been on the point of confiding to this stranger an idea he hadn't as yet mentioned to anyone.

A tall young figure appeared in the doorway of the back room, with the words on his lips, "Say, Pa—"

The boy paused as he noticed Roy, and he nodded apologetically for interrupting.

Tim Bailey straightened up, and Roy noticed the pride which modified the expression on the man's face as he said with an attempt to sound offhanded, "This is my boy Norman, Mr. Malley."

Malley's eyes were friendly on the handsome youth with curly brown hair, broad-shouldered, and an inch or more taller than his father.

Norman gave the stranger a quick smile that was nonetheless impersonal.

"Mr. Malley is Clarence Merritt's brother-in-law," the older man elaborated. "Visiting in town a few days."

At that the boy's brown eyes came back to Malley's face with candid curiosity. "I read about you being here—in the *Clarion*. I never expected to meet a big-time detective." He gave a boyish laugh. "I wasn't sure they really existed except in Ellery Queen."

For a moment Roy wished the kid had kept out of the place; but he smiled with a deprecatory air. "Compared to the sleuths of fiction I'm afraid I'm a disappointment."

Bailey was regarding him wonderingly. "That's right. Seems to me I did hear Clarence's brother-in-law was a big policeman from Chicago. But it slipped my mind. 'Fraid I don't read the local paper as careful as Norman does."

Roy directed a kindly smile at the boy, who was still gazing at him expectantly, as if he thought the detective might at any moment perform some kind of a trick with magnifying glass and fingerprint powder which he didn't want to miss. "Looks as if you have a good husky helper here, Mr. Bailey."

"Oh, Norman just helps out summer vacations. He's going to engineering college at U.C. Going to be an electrical engineer," he stated proudly. "Don't reckon I'll be able to keep him here in a little old shop in Los Alegres after he graduates."

The boy grinned at his father. "I may be glad to get a lob with you fixing electric irons. They're turning out so many of us engineers I can't see how we're all going to find work."

"You'll find something. You wait. Anybody'd be glad to hire a smart boy like you. Getting the education first, that's the main thing; isn't that what you say, Mr. Malley?"

"It is indeed." Roy pulled his watch out of the pocket at his belt and consulted it. "I've got a date for twelve, so guess I'd better be running along. It's been very nice to have this little chat with you."

Tim Bailey followed him to the door. "Sure glad to have met you. Just drop in any time you're downtown. I always have time to stop and chew the fat. Things ain't so rushed right now—as you can see," he finished with a rueful grin.

Walking down the street, Malley wondered if he had learned anything from meeting Tim Bailey. The first step, however, was always to look over all the people even remotely involved in a case. With a little inner smile at his own expense, Roy realized that he was enjoying himself. It had been a long time since he had got out and rustled for himself. As Inspector Malley of the Chicago police force he was too big a figure to do leg work anymore. And it was fun, in a way, coming down from the post of general to that of private, going out after information himself rather than delegating such work to subordinates.

Although, he told himself whimsically, all it would probably amount to was exercise. Which, of course, was what vacations were for, the pointless exercising of muscles you wouldn't use again when you were back on the job.

The lobby of the Rio Verde Hotel was dusky and somber, with maroon-velure chairs having high, carved backs in an old Spanish style and standing under dreary tapestry hangings which depicted the days of the dons in faded colors.

Malley sat down to watch for Clarence on a long sofa trimmed with velvet rope and fringe. Men were arriving singly and in pairs and trios, joining others in little knots to exchange hearty salutations before entering the elevator opposite the desk which would pull them up to the banquet room on the third floor. He saw Ben Sterling come in, deep in conversation with another man.

It occurred to Malley that he would be almost conspicuous in the crowd, in his carefully buttoned double-breasted suit and starched white collar. These were presumably the town's leading businessmen, but they looked like a Saturday afternoon golf club crowd back home; pants and jackets seldom matched, open-throated shirts were the rule, and shoes ran from the moccasin type to fancy stitched, rubber-soled affairs. A few men were even in shirt sleeves.

Malley realized that from his conservative necktie to his plain black ox-fords he had city and East written all over him, and he mused ironically that this was a violation of the conventions of his trade; for a detective ought to blend into the surrounding mass of humanity like a quail in the underbrush of a California hillside.

As Clarence came through the open double doors and glanced about seekingly, Roy stood up and moved forward. Their progress across the lobby and up in the elevator was a series of introductions, during which Malley recognized only one name that was of interest to him at present.

They rode up with Mr. Zangoni, whom he had heard referred to as one of the crowd "who got Jim Billings out." In keeping with his position as president of the bank, Roy noticed that there was slightly more formality in Mr. Zangoni's attire. His tailored suit, it was true, was made of a sub-dued plaid twill, and he wore brown sport shoes; but the coat was buttoned neatly and he wore a necktie with a quiet pattern. Mr. Zangoni was small, and slender as a knife blade, and his sleek dark hair and black eyes had also the shine of polished steel; but he showed his teeth in frequent smiles and went out of his way to manifest good fellowship—the way some ministers and undertakers try too hard to be hearty and jovial in an effort to belie the traditional public conception of their professions. Underneath Zangoni's effusive manner, however, Malley could see the traits which had given validity to the prototype of the banker as a tightlipped creature with dollar signs instead of pupils in his eyes.

There was really little use in a man's trying to act a part other than that which his work assigned to him. The basic pattern was there for the discerning eye to find. For instance, you could not have as your primary concern, day in and day out, the making of two dollars grow where one had been before, with its concomitant shrewdness as to how far you could risk other people's money in a fellow man's hands, without running the risk of reducing life itself to terms of monetary percentages, with a resultant hardening and constriction of one's outgoing impulses toward others.

Roy's thoughts, in their glib generalizations about other people's professions, suddenly came up short against the Public Conception of his own line of work: the blunt-featured, flat-footed, stolidly heavy plain-clothes man chewing on a cigar and wearing a dark felt hat. He himself had never fit that description—physically, at least. As a matter of fact, as he had mused earlier, it was a detective's job not to fit noticeably into the characterization the public had built up for him. It was a part of his technique to look like whatever type of person his job called upon him to represent. But beneath the chameleonlike technique was there not something accurate in the prototype created by the omniscient Public Mind? Was he not even now, beneath the role of pleasantly nondescript brother-in-law and visitor, being true to that Type, bluntly, flat-footedly, stolidly and unfeelingly spying upon the people whose hospitality he graciously accepted?

With philosophical amusement at his own expense Roy accepted the self-judgment to which his reflections had led him.

Upstairs, in the anteroom to the dining room set with long, white-covered tables, they ran into Dan Miller, who shook hands cordially as Clarence presented his brother-in-law. This, then, was the other Power in Los Alegres affairs. He was a big man, fat and with grizzled hair above deceptively vague, washed-out gray eyes. He talked loudly, with painfully obvious good will toward all. Just a plain old western rancher, common as an old shoe. Malley, in his imagination, could hear people thus fatuously describing old Dan Miller.

But Malley had run across his kind before—in different clothes and in different settings. He sympathized fraternally with Jim Billings. These were the ones who made life difficult for men in the public employ, like heads of police departments and mayors of cities, big or small. They had power and they knew it, and if they saw fit to use it, they did; and there you were, frustratingly forced, perhaps, to sacrifice work you had painstakingly accomplished over months of application before you discovered that what you were doing wasn't going to turn out acceptable to the Dan Millers.

This one, he had learned from casual comments made by Lucille and Clarence, owned land all over the county, was the biggest stockholder in the bank, and prided himself on coming from a pioneer family.

The two men, Miller and Zangoni, were not, he suspected, important to the particular case that had ensnared his interest; but the whole of an environment always played a part in any crime, even if so remotely that it had no immediate bearing on the case. It never did any harm, Roy had found, to see the whole setting. If you were aware of the framework within which your people moved, your vision was likely to be more discriminating in its consideration of specific details.

It was Jim Billings that he particularly wanted to meet; but he waited patiently. Clarence would miss no one in town if he could help it, in showing off his city relative.

As the crowd moved to take seats at the tables among which Filipinos in white jackets were already moving with laden plates, Clarence hailed a man in front of them. "Hey, Jim, I want you to meet my brother-in-law. Mr. Billings, Mr. Malley. Roy's out here for a couple of weeks to soak up a little good old Los Alegres sunshine."

The man ahead of them turned and smiled, and Roy extended his hand.

"Well, you couldn't come to a better place for climate," Billings said.

"That's your real-estate man talking," Clarence chortled.

Roy moved up abreast of Billings, leaving Clarence to the rear in a group which closed around him. It was easy to keep chatting with Billings about the residential advantages inherent in the city of Los Alegres, and Roy kept at his side until they found themselves sitting down next to one another at a table, with Clarence crowding up to take the next chair.

Malley was pleased to find that his mental picture of the former police chief had proved correct in general. He was a thickset, slow-moving man, with meager iron-gray hair, deliberate eyes under bushy brows, and a stolid chin beneath straight-set lips.

It was easy to see why a man with a face like that, if he held a key position in local affairs, would cause some uneasiness to a man like Dan Miller. Those smoky-blue eyes would wink at nothing. If it was the law, it was the law, and that was that. And if he were hired to enforce the law, he would enforce it with a stubborn single-mindedness of purpose that would ignore any subtleties of interests or shadings of expediency which might be involved.

As they attacked the beef stew on their plates, Jim Billings gave Roy a speculative glance. "Understand you're in police work."

"Yes, I'm an old flatfoot," he returned humorously. "Been on the force for thirty years."

"Well, it's interesting work."

"It's a job," Roy said dispassionately. He paused with his fork over his plate. "Seems to me Clarence mentioned that you used to be in the game."

"Yeah, took a whirl at it when I was younger. Worked for the sheriff's office a few years over at the county seat."

"I understood Clarence to say you were chief here for a while."

"Yeah. For a while." Billings was silent for a moment over a mouthful of french roll, and then he added laconically, "Guess I wasn't cut out for it."

"I know what you mean," Roy said dryly, and met the other's impassive eyes with a slightly sardonic gleam in his own. "Politics," he added quietly.

Billings nodded. "Yeah. Politics." He grinned. "Me, I never learned diplomacy."

At this point the man across the table broke in with the inevitable query, "Well, how do you like California, Mr. Malley?"

"This isn't my first trip out here, of course," he smiled. "My wife and I made a couple of flying trips out several years ago."

"I been telling him," Clarence declared, "they oughta come out and stay. Settle down right here in Los Alegres."

"Well, you can look anywhere you want to, but you'll never find a better climate," the citizen over the way informed him solemnly. "And variety. Drive ten miles one way and you've got the beach, five miles the other and you got mountains—foothills, that is."

"Billings is the man can tell you about that," Clarence said heartily, leaning forward to look at the latter. "Eh, Jim?"

"That's right. Can't sell you a couple of acres, can I?" he said jokingly.

Roy replied with just the proper show of reluctance. "We-ell, to tell you the truth, I wouldn't mind sort of looking the ground over while I'm here— in case I did see a spot that appealed to me."

"Glad to show you what I've got," Billings said equably.

"Oh, I wouldn't want to take up your time," Roy demurred, "when I'm not sure I'm really a prospect."

"Don't worry about that. Right now I've got more time than money. Things aren't moving the way they did for a while there after the war. Be a pleasure, far as that goes, to show you around the country a little. Like Ed here says, this is about as nice a locality as you'll find anywhere in California."

"Well, if you put it that way, I do have time on my hands. The girls are going to some kind of hen party this afternoon, and I was just going to drift around till dinnertime."

"If you want to then, I could drive you around after the luncheon."

"Fine, if you're sure it won't put you out."
"No. Not a bit of it."

CHAPTER FOUR

As they drove in Billings's gray sedan up into the light-brown hills dotted with live oaks overlooking the curve of the valley, where the river's course among the cultivated fields was marked by a curving green line of willows that led up to the uneven cluster of buildings and foliage which was the town, they talked casually of Los Alegres's natural advantages and its residential desirability.

Long, low homes with terraces and swimming pools and, occasionally, stables, lay back from the road here and there, appearing to sun themselves as they viewed the scene below, where, far in the distance, in a gap between the low hills where the river met the sea, a brighter blue ran out to merge with the skyline beyond the Pacific.

With seeming loquacity Roy talked of himself, his plans and his life, coming down at last to his work, with its fatigues and its problems until he was, in a gossipy way, recounting the details of a difficult case they had turned over to the district attorney just before he went on his vacation.

They parked on the black-top road and walked out on a level site about an acre square. The dry grass was matted underfoot, and live oaks drooped gracefully at intervals above it. The lot was bounded on the south by a dry gully overhung with old sycamores. In winter a stream tumbled down the ravine, Billings said, to meet a larger creek flowing into the river. They sat down in the shade of one of the oaks, hands clasped about their knees as they gazed absently off across the sweeping vista toward the sea.

Real estate was forgotten as they chatted idly, Malley rambling on about his last case, Billings asking occasional questions and listening with obvious enjoyment, neglecting the ostensible purpose of their trip in the chance to talk thus casually of matters which still interested him abstractedly, though he had long since abandoned the profession to which they pertained.

He shook his head musingly. "Lot goes on in a big city, don't it, that the average man never realizes?"

"As far as that goes, a lot goes on anywhere, where there's people, that never comes to the surface."

"You're not just talkin' when you say that." Billings pulled out his pipe, and filled it, carefully pinching out the match flame afterward and digging down through the grass to bury the head in the soil.

"Even here, I guess," Roy said with an appreciative glance at the peaceful landscape in which the scolding of a jay among the sycamores was the only harsh sound above the murmur of insects and the occasional trills of other birds from the hillside behind.

"Yep, even here."

"My folks got to talking last night, for instance," Roy went on casually. "Gossiping about old times, and it brought up a murder you had here some time back, never caught up with the fellow that did it."

"What one was that?" Billings said cautiously.

"They called it the Bailey case—young girl strangled. It's terrible the number of sex fiends you run across." Roy clucked deprecatingly.

"I never figured it was anything like that, that killing."

"No?"

"No." He grinned wryly. "Guess they didn't mention. I was chief of police here then. Did most of the work on that case."

"That right?"

"Of course the sheriff's office lent us a hand. Put a good man on it too. Plain-clothes man. Between us, we dug up a lot of dirt; but that's all we had when we got through—dirt. Poor girl."

"You knew her personally, I suppose."

"Sure. I guess I know everybody for twenty miles around. Did in those days, anyway. People been comin' in so fast the last twenty years, though, that I can't keep up with 'em all like I used to."

"I gathered from the way the folks talked, this girl wasn't much good."

"Oh, I wouldn't say that. Full of life, pretty much of a flirt. One of those kids that need a restrainin' hand an' never had it. Her dad, old Tim Bailey, died when young Tim was about fifteen and Inez ten or so; and the mother was always sickly, just let the kids run wild. An' you know how it is, a pretty young girl, full of ginger, thought it was smart to have all the men after her. Which they was, of course. I always figured—and it turned out I was right when we got to goin' into things after she died—there was more smoke than fire in the talk about her. Not, you understand, that she was above lettin' a man lay her once in a while if it happened to suit her; but it wasn't nothing like the wholesale way the women in town liked to let on. Mostly she just strung the guys along."

"What happened the night she was killed?"

From the way Billings had loosened up and started to talk, Roy could see that the affair had lain rankling in the depths of his mind for all these years. He knew how it was. A defeat made a man sore. He never really got over it.

"Well, you know how the town's laid out, the Civic Center right in the middle with all the public buildings together. The back of the American Legion hall's right across the street from the high school grounds. Well, that night there was a big benefit dance in the hall. According to her family's story, Inez went out alone a little after nine, intending to wind up at the dance eventually. There wasn't anything unusual about that. She often left home alone to meet her dates somewhere else, and didn't tell her folks where she'd be.

"The fellow running the service station at Live Oak and Hydrangea saw her pass there, headed downtown, but he wasn't sure what time; and that's the only trace we had of her from the time she left home till some kids playing found her body the next morning. Her folks went to bed around ten-thirty, they said, and never even missed her till I called 'em up the next day to tell 'em we'd found the body. She slept in a room by herself and they just figured she was sleeping late that morning."

Billings's pipe had gone out, and he paused to strike another match, his face furrowed with recollection. Roy was not surprised at the freedom with which details flowed out from the man's memory. Every phase of the case was by now worn smooth from handling by speculation and reflection, both at the time and afterward.

"The whole thing was complicated by that dance. Half the town was there. And a lot of the young blades out on their own. The girls in the upper crust were having a party for Beth Jensen—Mrs. Sterling she is now; and that left a bunch of fellows, one or another of whom had all been out with Inez, running loose without dates that night; and they all showed up at the dance. You remember we still had prohibition then; and most of this young crowd had bottles cached in their cars in the parking lot behind the hall across the street from the school and up and down the street in front of the lilac hedge where they found her."

He halted and squinted off across the valley. "Funny thing, I never've liked the smell of lilacs since then. They was in full bloom."

He drew on his pipe and went on. "Well, the men and a lot of the women, too, was in and out all evenin', havin' drinks and carrying on in their cars, and most of 'em pretty high even before eleven o'clock. Me and a couple of the boys was there at the dance, keepin' an eye on things."

He cast a defensive glance at Roy. "Don't think I winked at the bootleg racket. God knows we done our best to keep this town shut up. I closed down more'n one place for sellin' it. And in Los Alegres, by God, it wasn't easy to buy a bottle. But you know how it was, them days; you padlocked one joint and another sprung up down the road; an' I only had jurisdiction in the city limits. I remember that night we packed two or three of 'em off to jail for the night, guys flashin' flasks inside the building and gettin' too noisy and unsteady on their feet."

He grunted an ironical laugh. "I remember me an' the boys congratulatin' ourselves after the dance, the way we kept it nice and peaceful and respectable, no fights and nobody actually acting stewed on the floor. And all the time that poor kid layin' there with her tongue out and her face purple, choked to death with somebody's bare hands."

He scowled down at his cold pipe and poked his thumb into the bowl.

"Do you think it was premeditated?" Roy said quietly, removing his hat and running his hand over his faintly perspiring head. "Or do you think it was the liquor and the excitement and a sudden fit of rage?"

Billings lifted his heavy shoulders and let them fall. "Hard to say."

"No one saw her at the dance?"

"No, don't think she ever got there. She might've met her killer on the way, or getting out of a car on the street there. He might have planned it for the time and place, on account of it being hard to trace anybody's movements. And that was hard, by God. You know how it is at a dance. People are on the floor; they're in the rest rooms; they're buying cokes in the anteroom off the kitchen; they're stepping outside 'for a smoke.' They're circulatin' up and down the sidelines. And there's four outside entrances. Double doors on each side of the hall, with sidewalks running back to the parking lot, and a back door by the orchestra pit, and the front entrance. Us boys kept all the entrances covered, but, hell, with all them people milling around you couldn't remember afterwards who went in and out by themselves; and it would've been easy anyway, with the dim lights in the parking space and them young squirts whoopin' and hollerin' around, full of bathtub gin, for somebody to have drifted out in one bunch and slipped away and come back in with another bunch, and none of 'em noticing the difference."

"Could it have been done somewhere else and the body put there? Were there any signs of a struggle around where she was found?"

Billings shook his head. "It was grassy there, been mowed the day before; and you know short grass, springs back up after it's been stood on. There were a few marks of the girl's high heels though, and the ground was chewed up some around her feet, from her kicking to get loose, we figured, while she was being attacked. Looked as if she'd been held down flat on the ground while it was done."

"Were her fingernails examined for traces of skin or cloth? In a strangling case usually the victim claws at the assailant's hands till unconsciousness sets in."

"No. That was another funny thing. Her arms were bruised on the inside of the elbows. The way we reconstructed it, the guy threw her backward with his hands on her throat and got astride of her and managed to pin her arms down with his knees just so she couldn't leave marks on him. Sounds like a tough proposition for a man to handle, but if he was strong, he could pin her down that way, and of course it wouldn't take long till she couldn't resist any more."

Malley's eyes rested preoccupied on the distant skyline. "Sounds calculated. His thinking of preventing scratches."

"Not necessarily," Billings returned slowly. "An intelligent person's mind seems to operate on two levels. Even while they're out of their heads with rage, the old instinct for self-preservation goes ticking right along, and they think almost automatically of the steps they have to take to protect themselves."

Malley nodded approvingly. "That's true." They were silent for a moment, and then he went on, "Anybody hear anything suspicious along there, any sounds of a struggle or quarreling voices?"

Billings shook his head. "But that didn't mean anything. It was all parked solid along there by nine o'clock. Things start early here in Los Alegres. The dance was goin' good before Inez even left home. And pedestrian traffic to the hall was all on the other side of the street. People coming either direction crossed at one of the corners above or below the block where the lilacs grew. And anybody that might've been hangin' around the cars parked on that side, what with havin' their minds on a woman or on gettin' a drink, and the music comin' out the open windows along the roof above the orchestra pit, and cars goin' in and out of the parking lot, a herd of buffaloes could've been chargin' around the high school grounds and nobody've noticed."

He paused, and dug at the dried grass with his heel until he had uncovered the soil, and then leaned forward and emptied his pipe on the bare spot, after which he slowly pounded on the dottle with the back of his heel.

"Did any of the young crowd have their cars parked across the street by the high school?"

Billings slewed his eyes quickly under their fringed brows toward Malley, and then stared down at his foot again. There was an instant's hesitancy before he uttered a dry laugh and said, "To tell you the truth, your brother-in-law, Clarence Merritt, had his car—or his dad's—parked down near the corner by the walk into the grounds."

"He had a crowd with him, I suppose?" Roy said equably.

"Oh yes. Far as that goes," Billings assured him, "I never connected Clarence up with the girl. His name was never linked with hers. There was five other boys drove down to the dance with Clarence. They had a bottle, of course, in the glove compartment; and later on, in the evening, Clarence and two others took off to the country—for a little fresh air," he explained wryly, "and came back and found the place still open and reparked the car."

"Who was in Clarence's bunch of passengers?"

The names came flatly off Billings's tongue. They had obviously been ineradicably engraved on his mind at the time. "Bob Jensen—that's Beth Sterling's older brother—he's in business over in the San Joaquin now; and Ben Sterling, and Pete Zangoni—he was a few years older than the rest of the crowd, but the girl he was going with and married later, Dotty Miller, old Dan's daughter, was a friend of Beth's and was at the party for her; so Pete was along with the rest of the boys; and Jim Foley, and Tracy Whitlock. They're still around. Jim owns a restaurant on Main Street, and Tracy's one of our leadin' lawyers. Nice bunch of fellows, but they all knew Inez. All—except Clarence—been seen one time or another taking her for a ride in their cars or having a drink with her at that roadhouse down the river near the beach. I had to question them," he concluded sourly, as if the memory was unpleasant.

Malley silently sympathized, allowing only a slightly quizzical gleam to show in his eyes. Himself, he preferred straight routine cases among the criminal classes for whom homicide was simply a by-product of their means of livelihood. When you had to invade the private lives of the upper crust they always seemed more outraged at the impudence of your investigating them than they were at the murder itself, running squawking to the political bosses with requests to know what kind of a police department their taxes were supporting. They rapidly got to the point where they were more concerned with stopping the police from looking under their beds and poking about in their dirty linen and dragging skeletons out of their closets than they were in finding the murderer.

Roy could see that that was what had happened here, and that Jim was further handicapped by not being able to keep any of the witnesses on ice until they made up their minds to remember, or to sweat anything out of a suspect. Not, Malley reminded himself virtuously, that he was in favor of third-degree methods; but the police had a job to do, and sometimes you had to be a little less than polite if you wanted to get results.

"Most of these young fellows, I've gathered from what local gossip I've heard," Roy said conversationally, "had money to spend buying drinks on the sly for the town's 'bad' girl, feeling like regular hellers as they did it; but I gathered from remarks made by my sister that Ben Sterling didn't come from the set that had money for cars and bootleg liquor. How did he fit in?"

"That's right. But Ben—well, Ben knew her really better than the rest of 'em. He had been practically a—boy friend. Earlier, that is. So naturally he had to be looked into. But his relationship with her—what there had been of it—was open and aboveboard, which didn't throw him in such a bad light."

"You didn't get a line on any of Clarence's crowd having gone out to the car and come back alone early in the evening?"

"That's where we were up against it. They all swore they never saw her that night, and nobody admitted making any solo trips out to the car; and you couldn't sort out their movements enough to show who might have. They were all high as kites all evening. I noticed them myself, at the dance. Kept an eye on 'em for fear some of 'em might get too gay and cause some commotion. You see, the girls they were all mixed up with were all up at the Whitlocks' to the Jensen girl's shower; and the boys was sort of cele-bratin' bein' on their own, stag, for one night. They was kind of incoher-ent in general about where they'd been an' who with, and it bein' dark out, half the time they didn't know who was in the gangs that went out for a snort—not that any of 'em ever owned up that's what they did go out for."

"Who would you say stayed the soberest of the lot?"

Billings shot his companion a shrewd glance, and his lips curved slightly in a dry smile as he began absent-mindedly to refill his pipe.

"That's easy. Ben Sterling. But he was always," he added immediately, "a quiet, unobtrusive kind of a lad. Don't know as I ever saw him tanked up."

Roy kept his eyes on the ground and picked up a twig and poked at the dry earth through the flattened, yellow wild grass.

"The kind of fellow," he said tonelessly, "that kind of melts into a crowd, and afterward people couldn't really swear to it whether he was there or not."

"That's right."

They met one another's eyes expressionlessly, and then they both looked out across the shimmering valley and the low brown dunes beyond to the glitter of blue which edged them; Billings sucked at his pipe, and Malley's fingers still pushed the stick up and down absently.

"You see what I was up against," Billings said flatly.

"Yes, I see."

The gossamer hints Roy's mind had registered almost unconsciously in the Sterling living room had hardened now into solid opinion. He re-membered how, on waking in his bedroom at Lucille's, he had been able to pick out the cobweb-thin pattern of incongruity.

People, he had learned from experience, were avid to talk about murder cases. It could be that such talk satisfied vicariously a streak of cruelty in every human being, or it could be that dwelling on the wickedness of an-other was a way of reassuring oneself that "Of course I would never do such a thing," or perhaps it was an assuagement of unrecognized fear: "It was someone else who fell before an enemy—not me, not me."

But Ben Sterling had moved almost at once to shut the discussion off with a change of subject, and, that failing, with music. He had even removed himself physically to the other end of the room. His reply to Clarence,

"Speak for yourself," had rested beneath its jocularity on a note of denial, of rejection. And when Ben reminded Lucille with a smile, "It was you who brought the subject up," there had been disapproval behind the quiet words.

Some people, of course, were more sensitive than others, found no pleasure in the contemplation of violence. But Ben Sterling seemed a prosaic, not particularly imaginative man. He led the conventional, unexciting life that usually predisposed people to enjoying the spectacle of other people's unsocial exploits.

CHAPTER FIVE

When they drove back to town Billings parked his car in the alley behind his office, and the two men came in the back way. Malley made a few vague remarks about the property they had viewed and about seeing what Mrs. Malley thought, and, feeling something like an impostor, made a leisurely exit to the street, on his way to pick up the toy accordion.

It was warm on the east side of the street, and he tried to keep in the shade of the awnings. He had unbuttoned his coat, and was tempted to take off his necktie and unfasten the top buttons of his shirt; but he couldn't quite bring himself to thus practically undress in public.

As he passed the door of the Sweet Shoppe, the insistent strains of a juke box beat upon his ears. There were booths built along the sidewalk windows so that the occupants could see and be seen as they took refreshment. The present patrons, Roy noticed with amusement, were all under twenty, and of mixed sexes; and he appreciated the business acumen behind this table arrangement. Sometimes it seemed to their elders that the younger generation had but one object in life—to be heard and seen over as wide a range as possible.

A girl with deeply tanned skin and honey-blond hair that fell across her forehead in bangs and lifted over her ears in the suggestion of a curl was leaning forward across the table with a cigarette in her rounded lips, accepting a light from the youth facing her, her blue eyes looking up coquettishly into the boy's brown ones. A white T-shirt enclosed her square young shoulders and round breasts, and, under the table, shapely tanned legs extended beneath crisply pleated white shorts to end in ribbed white socks and thick-soled tennis oxfords.

Malley walked slowly, taking note of the fact that the girl was Shirley Sterling—Lucille had pointed her out to him on the street—the young man Norman Bailey, the latter wearing the slightly fatuous, tolerant expression of the "older man" being agreeable to a mere kid. The girl, Malley could tell even in this passing glance, while acting the gay, unconcerned part, was putting everything she had into making time with what she would describe as a "college man." There were two other girls in the booth, one acting bored with it all by means of a masklike face under sleek black hair, one being "a lot of fun" in a bouncy, round-faced, ejaculatory way. Shirley and Norman were oblivious both to the sophistication and to the vivacity.

Malley walked slowly. The picture of the two young people framed behind the glass brought him back to the old tragedy behind the lilacs. It was strange how, since it first came up in the Sterling living room, Inez Bailey's murder had infused his thoughts. The girl had died; but for him at least the crime still lived, as it must live with her murderer, his inescapable companion. Would the twenty-year-old crime emerge even yet to affect the living?

Malley was certain now that Billings knew, just as he knew after his talk with the former police chief. They had nothing to go on, nothing but their intuitive opinions. But when you'd been in the business as long as he had, you got so you could tell. You could read it in the face and manner and actions of the guilty. Billings had had enough experience, enough natural talent along those lines so that he could do the same thing. But it was often like this. You were left helpless, with nothing but your own conviction; no evidence—nothing.

Without feeling smug about it Malley knew also that if he had been in charge here twenty years ago he would have won out. He was simply better at that sort of thing than the forthright Billings. He could have handled it even without the rough stuff which was proscribed by the setup here in Los Alegres. The persistent wearing away of defenses, the psychologically calculated questions, the choice of the exact moment for remaining in ominously knowing silence, for lashing out with accusing declarations ...

He turned his back to the street and stood in the shade of an awning, staring unseeing at a display of women's shoes, flat-heeled things made of cloth, elaborately cut-out and strapped and buckled sandals, sleek little colored slippers utterly plain except for a narrow strap.

Even yet, if he really exerted himself on the problem, he might possibly be able to extract a confession. It was all in knowing how, once you had your suspect nailed.

It was foolish, of course, giving so much thought to the affair. He had no intention of doing anything about it. But there seemed to be in almost all human beings—if they weren't demoralized in one way or another—an instinct for workmanship. The human mind liked order, recoiled from sloppiness. Especially in one's own line of work, whether it was carpentry or cooking, or, as in his case, detection, you liked to see things finished, complete and neat to the last detail. The sight of a job done with inferior workmanship was subtly irritating.

But even if he could do it, just for his own satisfaction, it would be cruel. More than one life would be darkened, if not ruined.

But Inez Bailey's life had been more than ruined; it had been ended. Whatever depths or heights that life might have attained in after years, whatever she might have given or taken away from society, no one now would ever know.

Malley had no illusions about the purposes behind man's laws. In the crime of murder he knew that, where the punishment was concerned, revenge played a part. And was vengeance always worthwhile for society?

But a part of the reason for punishment was self-protective. Men felt it was dangerous to allow other men, who had resorted to killing, to move freely among them.

In a case like this, though, was there any danger?

Malley frowned, his eyes fixed on a flat-heeled green slipper.

The murder could have been premeditated; and a man who deliberately plotted and carried out murder was, no matter how you looked at it, a decided menace to anyone who might get in his way again.

But he doubted if this had been a planned crime. The murderer had probably not realized as he did it that he was killing the girl. It was a common expression—"I could have choked him." In a moment of rage the hands went out to the neck of a weaker creature and did not let go until the passion was spent in action.

And the boy's mind had been unsettled with alcohol, his emotions strained beyond endurance by the girl's threat to his future. With everything he wanted in life practically in his hands, she threatened to dash it all away.

Malley thought perhaps that the girl's "wildness" was an indirect result of her love—or, at least, her desire—for her murderer. Besides the natural youthful desire for a good time, excitement, constant movement, admiration, she had probably been "showing him," ever since he sloughed her off to enter a "better" circle, one that rejected her.

And the boy had undoubtedly been torn by another conflict. Malley suspected that he had been more physically attracted to the girl than he wanted to be, since she did not fit in with his hopes for the future; that he had been seeing her surreptitiously off and on, even after he had decided he was through with her.

And the girl had probably submitted, though unwillingly, to this secret alliance, influenced by a love which irked her but which she could not overcome. The emotional attachments aroused in late childhood and early adolescence often sank deep and tenacious roots, remaining stubbornly alive beneath later outgrowths.

Malley shook his head slightly at the green slippers, and turned away. Well—that was that. He must put the whole thing out of his head and settle down to enjoy his vacation.

Bailey's shop was empty as it had been that morning, except that now its proprietor was sitting on a stool behind the counter at the rear, a pencil in his hand, an account book open in front of him. He delivered the package to Malley, called a friendly farewell after him, and returned to the columns of figures, the customer forgotten. After a few minutes of frowning concentration on the book, he turned the pencil over slowly in his hand until the eraser struck the page at a slant. He tapped the eraser slowly on the paper, his eyes focused on the edge of the counter beyond the book.

Then he stepped down off the stool, closing the ledger with one hand and sticking the pencil behind his ear. With his hands in his pockets, he walked to the front of the shop and out through the open doors down the broadening aisle between the display windows.

His eyes turned speculatively toward the corner to the northwest a few doors down across the street. He could see the gold Spenserian writing over the glassed-in front, "Sterling for Sterling Quality." A woman with a shopping bag came out of the doors which extended diagonally across the corner of the building, and no one else went in or out while Tim Bailey stood there gazing with unreadable eyes.

He pushed his lips out and twisted them a little, and turned slowly to go back into the store.

It wasn't that his business was in danger. He could make expenses, meet his bills, get by. But he wasn't, you could say, making money. And neither, he figured, was Sterling. Ben had gone in debt—he was sure of it—when he moved to the new location, had all that remodeling done, took on a television line. Sterling, in fact, was probably having a hard time meeting his commitments. Business had been slower for everybody, starting even before Ben expanded.

Tim put his hand around his jaw and rubbed his thumb up and down his cheek. He was foolish, maybe, not to sit tight, content just to keep his head above water.

But the whole thing offended his conception of economical procedure. It was wasteful. Ben didn't have enough stock actually to make a showing in that big corner place, especially with the record department on the mezzanine. Here they both were, paying rent, doing advertising, paying utility bills. His own repair business brought people into the shop, helped make sales that by right should be Ben's. He kept Mike Whitehead on steady in the workshop out back, hardly touched repair work himself anymore; and, when Norman wasn't home, kept a full-time salesman in the shop. You had to have a man there while you took care of business errands, lunch time, conferences with salesmen and the rest of it.

Besides Dolores in the record department Ben also had to keep a salesman out front while he was busy off and on with other things. If they combined forces, they could eliminate two men's wages right there, and both of them have more free time. As partners, neither would have to stick in the place almost every minute. They could spell each other off.

Ben might figure, if he came to him with a proposition, that Tim was only trying to get in on the better location and swankier setup. But, on the other hand, Ben was probably carrying quite a loan at the bank, while Tim would come in with no liabilities, his stock clear, and a pretty good clientele with him. If Ben was the businessman Tim thought he was, he ought to see the advantages.

But Ben was a funny fellow some ways; Tim didn't feel he was very well acquainted with Ben, even though he'd known him all his life. Quiet, and not particularly friendly. That is, he was always a little standoffish except with his own crowd. In a way Sterling seemed to pride himself on an exclusive trade.

But in Los Alegres you couldn't live on a "fashionable" trade, and Tim knew his own shop had cut into Ben's business. That was probably one reason Sterling didn't act particularly chummy with his old neighbor from Railroad Avenue. Not that he'd ever been unfriendly, just—reserved, Tim supposed was the word.

He walked around the counter and picked up the ledger and shoved it into the drawer under the cash register, and made up his mind. No harm in trying. He'd talk to Ben and see what kind of a reception his proposition got.

As he looked up, and down the aisle to the sidewalk, he saw Norman at the entrance with his hands in his pockets grinning down at Shirley Sterling's slightly tilted blond head, her eyes grinning up at him coquettishly.

Tim smiled to himself, as at an omen. He was glad Norman was able to do the things he had never quite been able to, go to high school in good clothes with enough spending money to run with the kids that set the styles, go to college and be asked to join a fraternity, be invited to the big-bugs' homes here in Los Alegres because their kids liked him.

And he and Etta would do the same things for Sharon, who was just starting high school. In the long run he figured they'd make more by going in with Sterling. But if Ben said nothing doing, why, to hell with it! The shop would see the kids through school, even if he had to mortgage himself into bankruptcy making it do so.

Over on his corner Ben sat at his desk in the glassed-in corner of the mezzanine floor and gazed stonily at a bill for records. He frowned a little, hearing the voices of a trio of bobby-soxers descending the stairs.

The next moment Dolores appeared in the open door to his office and ran a hand through the soft curls which sprang out around her face.

"I'm going to run out for a coke now, Mr. Sterling. Can I tell Harvey if anybody comes in for records while I'm gone you'll look after 'em?"

He turned in his swivel chair to face her. "Sure." With a glance at his wrist watch, he added, "You usually go earlier than this, don't you? I didn't realize it was so late."

She leaned a shoulder that was half bare in a low-necked peasant blouse against the doorframe.

"I would-a gone half an hour ago. My tongue's fairly hangin' out. But those kids! Patty Hagen and that bunch. Played every Sinatra and Como record in the racks, and bought one measly little number—a Vaughn Monroe." She straightened and shook her short mop of hair. "Use this for a place to kill time; that's what they do. Well, I'll be dashing off. I'll be back in a few minutes."

"Don't hurry," he said with a smile. "Things are slow today."

His eyes followed the slim white ankles above plain, childish kid slippers with a strap across the instep as the full printed cotton skirt above them swished jauntily toward the stairs. She was supposed to take fifteen minutes for her relief in the afternoon, but he knew she'd be gone almost half an hour.

His brows drew together slightly in impatience with himself. She took advantage of him. He knew it. He oughtn't to put up with it. There was no reason why he couldn't save money, summers, by putting Shirley in charge of records. It would save giving her an allowance and also enable him to keep an eye on her daytimes. But, even disregarding his weakness about discharging Dolores, he didn't want his daughter to work. It would make it look as if she had to.

But he should get rid of Dolores. The situation made him uncomfortable. He didn't like the way his eyes followed her smooth bare legs as they had just now, the way they would rest involuntarily on the curved line of her throat and shoulder out to the edge of the thin blouses she wore in hot weather.

But most of all he didn't like her receptiveness toward those glances, toward the occasional contact of their hands or arms in the course of work. A girl like that—who so obviously liked men—was dangerous to have around.

Doubly dangerous in this case. It wasn't until she had been working in the shop for several weeks that Ben had become aware of the way she felt about him. He began to notice that every time he happened to glance her way she was looking at him; that she made opportunities to touch him, to stand close, looking over a sales slip or an invoice; that she asked unnecessary questions, leaning over his desk at his side so that her perfumed hair almost brushed his cheek.

At first he had been amused and flattered, understanding what had happened; that it was a simple case of a young girl with a "case" on an older man. She was twenty-two, and something of a nobody. That is, her mother lived on a pension and did sewing to help out, and had brought up her two daughters to be respectable—among the "nice" girls in Los Alegres but still just "the Baldwin girls," neither a part of nor yet apart from the leaders of Los Alegres society.

Ben could see how he appeared to Dolores. He wasn't a rich or powerful man, but he and his family were prominent, of the "better" class. They moved with the people who were somebody; and that impressed Dolores.

And, after all, without conceit he realized that he was good-looking in a quiet way, his eyes a soft blue, his features regular, his skin still firm and practically unlined, his hairline still almost in the right place despite its increasing scantiness at the crown; and he dressed well, was careful to wear becoming colors and styles.

Yes, it had been rather pleasing to know he had made a hit with his pretty young salesgirl.

But he was becoming increasingly uneasy about it, partly from distrust of the physical sensations her proximity aroused in him, and partly because he knew she had become aware that he was not unmoved by her attractions. She had grown almost self-assured about the whole nebulous situation.

The last thing in the world he wanted was any messy entanglement with a young woman—or any woman, for that matter. He loved Beth, and except for a few business worries, his life was ideal. He didn't want any disruptions of it.

And there were times when he didn't trust himself, that was the hell of it.

Like that incident at the Firemen's Benefit Ball at the American Legion hall last spring. Everybody went, whether they danced or not, to be seen and to show public spirit. It was a sort of civic duty. He and Beth had gone with the Merritts, and he had danced once with Beth and once with Lucille, and with Dotty Zangoni. He had become separated from Beth in the crush and found himself beside Dolores, who clasped her hands on his arm and demanded kittenishly, "Aren't you going to ask me for even one dance, Mr. Sterling?"

So of course he had led her out on the floor; and it had been worse than he bargained for, having her in his arms, her body unfortified by the controlling girdles and wired brassieres that his wife's friends went in for. She seemed to have very little on underneath the heavy crepe dress falling in folds to the floor—which was nothing unusual. He often fussed at Shirley for the sparseness of her costumes. But every inch of his body from knees to chest where Dolores rested lightly against him was hotly aware of hers under the clinging dress. The feel of a woman hadn't affected him like that since—well, for years.

When the music stopped they were close to the side doors, and Dolores linked her arm in his and suggested boldly, "Let's step outside for a minute. It's so stuffy in here."

Against his better judgment he had let her pull him along through the doors.

"Got a cigarette?" she had demanded, and kept moving along the sidewalk.

By the time he got her cigarette lighted they were down along the wall away from the couples who had overflowed about the side entrance of the building. He did not take a cigarette for himself, but pushed the package back into his pocket slowly, his eyes on the girl's impishly upturned face, a dim white oval in the semidarkness. He could still feel the blood beating heavily throughout his body. Deliberately he took the cigarette from her fingers and gave it a sideways fling into the grass, his other hand on her arm pulling her toward him. She came into his embrace willingly, with a muted little mew of pleasure, and he kissed her greedily and forgetfully, pressing her close.

He relaxed his arms and took a step back. She could not see his face well enough to decipher its expression, but it was stiff then, and blank. He drew in his breath, and let it out.

"Let's go inside," he said evenly.

She released a little giggle, and reached for the handkerchief in his breast pocket. He stood still, and she dabbed lightly at his mouth.

"The evidence." She laughed softly.

He took the handkerchief out of her hand and wiped his lips thoroughly. He looked at it for an instant when he had finished. It was plain white linen, like a million other handkerchiefs.

He held it out to her with a whimsical smile. "Here, you'd better keep the—evidence. I can hardly take it home with me."

She made a chuckling sound in her throat and tucked the crumpled linen down the top of her bodice.

He had dreaded seeing her at work on Monday morning, for it was going to take the utmost care to establish what had happened in its proper perspective. There must be not the slightest deviation from his normal manner.

When she arrived for work on Monday he had quickly noticed her air of veiled expectancy, indicating her private conjectures as to how much more this would lead to. Ben had realized with horror that as far as the girl was concerned she wouldn't care where it led. When he was his courteous, pleasant, and slightly reserved self, Dolores had taken her cue and gone on as usual. But Ben knew that, even yet, she had not fully made up her mind as to what it meant. Had his sudden unrestrained kiss been "just one of those things," meaning nothing? Would he have done the same to any girl in like circumstances, or was Mr. Sterling really terribly attracted to her alone? Was he the victim of an overwhelming passion which he was manfully repressing for the sake of both her and his family?

Ben was certain that the girl's romantic mind was dwelling on all these possibilities. And he wished to God she would settle on the first. But he didn't know how to convince her of it without telling her in bald-faced words that the embrace had been merely an impulse. And he couldn't do that. All he could do was ignore the episode and hope she had sense enough to see what he meant.

He knew what he ought to do; he ought to discharge her on some pretext or other. Then it wouldn't matter what significance she imputed to the whole affair. She would be out of his hair anyway.

He stood at the window and looked down at the floor of the shop below, and said, "Hell," under his breath.

The real reason he ought to get rid of Dolores was that he was reluctant to do so. He liked having her around. Actually he wanted to hold her in his arms again, and for a long enough time next time.

And it wouldn't do. It simply wouldn't do. He ought to know by this time that it didn't pay to be dilatory about these things.

CHAPTER SIX

When Ben got home a little before six-thirty he paused at the kitchen door in the front hall, and Beth, with an oiled silk apron over the flowered chiffon she had worn to the tea for Lucille's house guest, made a detour from the icebox with a head of lettuce in her hand, and kissed him quickly before going on to the sink.

"Dinner's just about ready. We're eating in the alcove. I hope you don't mind. But it was almost six before I got home, so I've been a little rushed. Get washed up, dear. Shirley's setting the table."

"Hi, Pop," the latter called from beside the table set in the square made by the front windows whose Venetian blinds were closed against the sun. She still wore the T-shirt and shorts.

"Won't it be a little warm there in the alcove?" Ben ventured mildly.

"We'll pull the table down this way. And the fan's on. It just seemed like so much work—"

Ben could hear his wife's voice still going on as he went into the cool living room with the doors and windows open at the end.

"—setting the table across the hall in the dining room. We had a lovely time. Phyllis's tea table was beautiful. Red and white carnations—"

Ben had been carrying his jacket over his arm, and he threw it over the back of a straight chair and went on to the doors and across the patio floor to turn on the sprinkler, which slowly came to life on the shady lawn.

He watched it for a moment, and came back, and went through the bedroom to the bathroom, where he washed his face in cool water after rolling up the long sleeves of his rayon sport shirt. So far as he knew they were staying home tonight; so he did not bother to shower and change clothes. He changed his oxfords for the moccasin loafers, and came out into the living room. He picked up the Los Alegres *Clarion* from where it lay folded on the coffee table, and settled with a small sigh on the davenport. It was good to be home.

When they were seated around the red-topped table with hand-woven place mats under each service Beth asked if the Kiwanis luncheon had been interesting, and as soon as Ben had answered her question sketchily went back to tidbits she had picked up at the tea.

"Lucille said they're trying to talk Roy and Marian into buying a place here and settling down permanently when Roy retires."

"Don't look to me as if Malley's old enough to be thinking of retiring."

"Well, he's well past fifty. There was a brother between him and Lucille, you know. And policemen get pensions, don't they, after so many years' service? And I should think he'd want to get out of that work as soon as he was financially able to. Nobody could possibly enjoy murders. Although they say he has a wonderful record. Like the Canadian Mounties in the old silent movies. Always got their man. Remember James Oliver Curwood, Ben, when we were kids? I forget who the actors were, but I remember the pictures. The girls wore fur parkas, and long curls."

She paused and looked at Shirley. "You aren't eating anything, honey. Aren't you hungry?"

"Not very."

"I suppose she was eating banana splits all afternoon in the Sweet Shoppe," Ben said with a note of disapproval.

"I was not. Two cokes, that was all."

"Well, don't start worrying about keeping your weight down," Beth interposed. "Not at your age. You're almost too thin now. It'll be time enough when you're my age. Goodness, to think I was that skinny once! Remember, Ben?"

"You weren't skinny," he reassured her.

"I'll get enough to eat before the evening's over," Shirley said lightly. "Where do you keep those marshmallows, Mom, that you said I could take?"

"I'll put them out for you."

"What is it tonight?" Ben inquired.

"Beach party. A bunch of us are going down to Horseshoe Cove and build a fire and roast wienies and marshmallows. Some of 'em are planning to go swimming if it isn't too cold—which it will be, I expect."

"What is it, a church affair, or your sorority?" Ben asked idly.

"No, just three or four couples of us; we thought it'd be fun."

Beth raised her eyebrows archly at Ben. "And she has a new beau tonight."

"That so?" he said with more attention.

Shirley tried to look and sound offhanded. "Oh, Mom, you make it sound so corny. Just Norman Bailey, Pop, picking me up in his car—his dad's, that is. Ginny and Spec Miller and Bunny Simmons and Freddie are going in the same car. It's not even like a regular date," she added, a trace regretfully. "We're just all riding down together."

Ben opened his mouth and closed it again. Then he said with an attempt at jocularity, "Isn't Norman a little—old for you?"

"My gosh, Pop, he won't be twenty till next fall. And I was seventeen in February. Do you want me to go out with children?"

"I just didn't think he ran around with your crowd," he said noncommittally.

"Well, he didn't used to. He was at Berkeley last winter, of course. And he's three years ahead of me in school. But naturally, as a person gets older, well—they don't just go around with the people in their own class in school." She laid down her dessert fork and regarded him sternly. "Pop, you're not going to object to Norman?"

"Can't I even be allowed to know who you're associating with anymore?"

"Of course he's not objecting, silly," Beth broke in. She reached over and patted Ben's wrist. "Your father's just concerned about your welfare. That's what comes of having only one child. We hover over you like two old hens with one chick between them."

"Well, I hope sometime you'll quit treating me like a child."

"If it's not too inquisitive of me," Ben asked sarcastically, "may I ask who else is going on this expedition besides the ones you mentioned?"

"Oh, Bobby Whitlock maybe, and Georgia Foley, and Tony Zangoni if Betty decided to ask him. She didn't know whether to invite him or that new guy that's moved in next door to her."

"Um," Ben grunted in response, and devoted his attention to his iced tea, only slightly reassured by the thought that there was safety in numbers. Beth gave him a quick glance. It bothered her a little, the way Ben worried so about Shirley. It impressed her as being not quite normal somehow. You worried some, of course, about a young girl being out on her own socially; but it seemed to her that sometimes Ben overdid it. And he was so calm, so placid really, about most things. She couldn't see why he had become so overprotective about Shirley since she started to run around with boys. All girls went through that boy-crazy age.

Even if the child had seemed a little more keyed up than usual about Norman Bailey when she told her mother about her date tonight, and even if Shirley got serious about him, Beth couldn't see anything wrong with it. She had never heard anything against him. He seemed like a very nice boy.

But she could tell Ben hadn't liked the idea when he heard Shirley was going out with Norman. Of course, Tim and Etta Bailey were rather common, and then Tim being a competitor and all ... That was probably why Ben had reacted unfavorably to the name.

When Shirley went upstairs to dress she, too, mused rebelliously about her father's attitude. He hadn't used to be that way. It was only in the last year or so that he'd become so fussy about where she went. And it was getting under her skin. She would never have believed that Pop was going to turn out like this, putting on the heavy father act. He had always been so good to her when she was a kid, and she had been crazy about him, thought he was a lot better as a father than most of the other girls' dads were.

Her fair face hardened as she turned on the shower and pulled a cap over her hair. She wasn't going to put up with it much longer; that was all. If it kept up, they'd have a showdown; and she bet Mom would be on her side. Which was a reversal of the way things used to be in their family. When she was a kid, quite often she and Pop had been conspirators plotting to wring privileges out of Mom for Shirley's benefit.

She dressed as carefully in her rolled-up jeans and flannel shirt as if she were preparing for a formal ball, rubbing herself lavishly with toilet water and being painstaking with lipstick and the fluffing out of her hair, and forgetting Pop as her thoughts ran forward into the evening.

It was the first time a man of twenty—well, practically twenty—had ever paid any attention to her; and Norman was really smooth, knew how to act—not like Spec and those callow kids in her own class at school, with their loud laughs and strings of pet phrases that you got so you knew what they were going to say before they even said it. Poise, that was it. Norman had poise. And the other girls, Ginny and Betty and Bunny, they had been impressed all right when she said she thought she'd ask Norman Bailey to go on this beach party they were getting up.

She had been scared herself at the thought of casually suggesting it to him, and terribly relieved when he didn't make up excuses to get out of it.

She had all her stuff together on the hall table before the doorbell rang: the boxes of marshmallows and the long barbecue forks and the Navaho blanket for spreading on the sand. So when she opened the door she simply piled the stuff in Norman's arms, ran back to the living room archway to call good-by to the folks, and skipped out quickly.

She didn't want to have to bring Norman in to say hello to the folks, with Pop probably looking him over gloomily as if he were a criminal, and Mom making kittenish remarks that would give the impression she thought Norman was calf-eyed about her daughter. Lately Shirley had wondered sometimes if life wouldn't be simpler if you just didn't have parents.

Some of the boys were willing, when they got to the beach and had a fire going, to show they were he-men by taking a dip in the surf; but they were easily talked out of it. It was clear for once, with no fog rolling in from the west; but it wasn't what you would call warm, and they all knew from experience that even in the daytime the ocean this far north had an icy sting.

So they played noisy games for a while on the hard-packed sand left by the receding tide, last couple out, and drop the handkerchief.

And then they gathered around the fire and ate charred wieners imbedded in cold buns smeared with mustard, and sticky, scorched marshmallows, washing them down with bottled cokes.

Thus gorged, they sat on the blankets encircling the fire upon which they had thrown more wood, and smoked cigarettes and talked in incoherent shrieks until Tony Zangoni began to start songs in his pleasant tenor voice. Desultorily they rendered a few popular numbers until Tony led off with "Clementine," which all the voices took up enthusiastically. Tony, who was in the Glee Club at school, and had played the lead in the senior operetta, knew all the verses, and they mumbled along with him on the middle ones which they didn't know so well, and came in strong on the chorus, "Oh, my da-ar-ling, oh, my da-ar-ling, oh, my da-arr-ling Clem-en-tine—"

Then Tony tried to lead them in some songs from *Pinafore*, but nobody knew the words very well and the music gradually died out as the real purpose of the party asserted itself. In the light from the dying fire the group resolved itself into pairs lying close together on the blankets, and the beach was quiet beyond the white, irregular lines of breakers falling with a dull roar upon the wet sand.

Shirley and Norman had been sitting facing the fire and the sea, their shoulders against a log at whose base dry seaweed had collected and which they had covered with the blanket. During the singing the boy had put his arm around her shoulders. For a time they sat thus, looking out past the fire to the great star-studded canopy that faded into the darker expanse of the Pacific far out toward the horizon.

It was all so beautiful and so right that Shirley thought she just couldn't breathe.

Norman put his other arm around her, and with a little nestling movement they drew closer together, and he brought his face down to hers and kissed her. Then Shirley was sure that she couldn't breathe.

The next morning about eleven o'clock Ben had just finished rearranging a display of sheet music in the window when he glanced up in surprise to see Norman Bailey's father turning into the shop, bareheaded and in shirt sleeves.

With the professional smile he used on customers, Ben came forward to meet his fellow tradesman.

"Come over to take a look at some *good* radios?" he challenged Tim jokingly.

"Looking is about all anybody does nowadays, ain't it?" Tim countered with a grin.

"That's just about it. Summer, you know. Nobody stays inside to listen to music."

"I got a line of portables that's moving pretty good," Tim volunteered. "You busy this morning? I got something I've been wantin' to talk over with you."

"Sure. Like to come up to the office where we won't be interrupted?"

Ben remained suave and self-possessed as they mounted the stairs; but he was as alert as a cat who has caught sight of a seemingly well-intentioned dog.

Tim took the room's other chair, and Ben sat in his swivel chair at the desk and offered Tim a cigarette which the latter refused.

"Never got the habit." He leaned forward slightly in his chair. "I won't beat around the bush. I been doin' some thinkin', Ben. Ain't no gettin' around it; we're in a recession. Temporary, maybe; but the way I see it boom times is over for some time. And it's like this. Los Alegres ain't big enough for two businesses as near alike as ourn are. I'll tell you frankly, I'm gettin' by. I make a living. And my business is out of the red. I don't owe a dime. But my income—peanuts! Now I don't know nothin' about your financial status; but it's pretty well understood around town you got a loan when you took over this corner last fall and fixed it up. I know what business has been like, with television in the undecided state it's been, and all that. And I figure you're a long ways from out from under. So I figure like this—why don't we throw in together, cut the overhead for both of us. You got enough room in your storage space back there"—he jerked his head toward the rear of the building—"for my repair shop. That brings in a lot of trade for new stuff. And you got plenty of room for a small electrical line, clocks and gadgets and so on, in your showroom downstairs—"

He went on to outline the savings in rent, help, and general overhead, which a combination of forces would bring about, concluding, "So, the way I look at it, the savings would enable both of us to make decent wages, even with no more volume of business than we got between us now."

Ben had managed to keep on his face an expression of calm and intelligent interest; but behind it he was completely flabbergasted. To go into partnership with Tim Bailey!

"We'd have a monopoly on the radio business in town," Tim was saying smugly.

"What's to prevent somebody else going into business in competition to us?"

Tim spread his hands with a slight shrug. "Not a thing. But look what he'd be up against. An established concern on one of the best corners in town. And, between us, we got the good will of practically everybody in the whole community. Ones that aren't personal friends of yourn are of mine. And what's going to stop somebody setting up shop in competition even if we don't merge? Take any more trade away from either of us, the way we stand now, and we're both done for. Together, we could stand it better."

Ben crushed out his cigarette in the ash tray, following the movement carefully with his eyes. This was a proposition he ought to jump at. But he didn't think he could stomach being thrown into this intimate contact with Tim Bailey.

It would look funny, though, if he turned the thing down flat right off the bat.

"I'd have to think it over," he said slowly, his eyes still on the crumpled cigarette butt in the ash tray.

"Sure. Sure. A man can't decide anything like this offhand. And I realize there's a lot of angles'd have to be worked out. Terms and legal arrangements and all."

He stood up. "Tell you what you do. You think it over; talk it over with your wife, and see what you think about it, and we'll talk about it again in a few days."

As Tim began to move toward the door Ben rose, and with a gesture at the papers on his desk, said, "Mind if I don't see you out? I've got some things to look after here."

"Sure." Tim chuckled. "You got a pretty big place, but I guess I can find my way out without getting lost. Well, see you in a day or so."

Ben sat down again slowly, and stared frowning at the blotter.

He knew Tim hadn't done it deliberately, but the remark about referring the matter to Beth smarted a little. Everybody knew he had started in business on her father's money.

Now there was nothing further to look forward to from the Jensen estate. After the old man retired he had used up a good deal of his money; and there had been six children in the family, so that when Ole died a few years back, that made six of them to share the inheritance; Beth's share had gone into the new house. They had stinted nothing in the building of it; and it had cost plenty, what with a two-car garage and a single apartment over it for servants—if they should ever have any.

Ben moved restlessly in his chair. He shouldn't have had to go in debt for this expansion of the business. Enough money had gone through their hands in the past twenty years, heaven knew; but that was the trouble. They spent so much—furniture, new cars every three or four years, fur coats for both Beth and Shirley, expensive vacation trips in the summer, all three of them going to Hawaii first-class one trip, and to Mexico by car another, and to Canada, and flying to New York.

They lived too high; that was the size of it. But they had to, if they were going to get any fun out of life.

He wished Tim hadn't reminded him of Beth. He would like to have just let the matter drop without mentioning it to her. But he knew he couldn't. Even if she never heard of Tim's having approached him, Ben knew he wouldn't dare not to tell her about it. There was something about the business having been started with old man Jensen's money that put her in a different position than most wives. He'd say this for Beth, she didn't butt in, didn't try to run the business from the back seat. But he felt a moral obligation to keep her fully informed of what went on regarding the business. And she herself felt her right to be on the inside on everything, as if she were a silent partner.

And he was afraid to have her learn of Tim's proposition. Beth talked a lot aimlessly, and was seemingly silly about little things; but sometimes Ben had an uneasy feeling that her flightiness was in part a pose, one she had found so useful that it had become a part of her personality, and that if or when she ever needed to, she could be as decisive and as stubborn as she thought the occasion demanded.

She was stupid about some things. But not all the way down the line. And he foresaw that, garbed in inanities and irrelevancies as it would be, her opinion on this would amount to approval of Tim's proposition.

And what reasons could he present for its rejection? The whole thing might precipitate an unpleasant crisis at home.

Beth didn't mind economizing if it was necessary; but she also liked to spend; and if she saw a way to have more money, she would want to adopt it. He didn't see how he could successfully oppose her if she made up her mind that he ought to enter a partnership with Tim Bailey.

He slapped his fingers down on the blotter, the heel of his hand against the edge of the desk, and for the second time in twenty-four hours said "Hell!" under his breath.

CHAPTER SEVEN

Dinner was served in the dining room as usual that night; and during the meal Shirley did not find it necessary to mention her date for the evening, and Ben had a good excuse not to talk business before Shirley. Beth had been busy all day with a committee of ladies from the church on preparations for the annual summer garden party and supper to be held out of doors in the grounds between the parsonage and the church. While they ate, she entertained her family with an exposition of the difficulties involved in working with a committee made up of so many differing minds.

"If I didn't feel it was my duty," she declared, "I would simply never take on any responsibility in the Guild. In anything to do with the church you have to work with just anybody. It isn't like your own circle of friends, where you choose the people that are congenial. And with the ladies in the church—honestly, absolutely the only thing you have in common with some of them is that you're all Christians." She veered off suddenly. "Why they made Etta Bailey chairman of the Arrangements Committee I'll never know. Not that she isn't a nice woman. I have nothing against Etta; but you have to push her every step of the way. Just keep prodding at her, or not a thing would get done. A chairman, it seems to me, should give some leadership."

Ben sighed slightly. Another Bailey. They seemed to be buzzing around his head like gnats the last day or so.

"I don't see why," Shirley put in reasonably, "you bother with the Guild. All you do is gripe every time you have to do anything in it."

"Well, you have to support it. I try not to get mixed up in too many community things; but you do have to take an interest once in a while in improving the place you live in."

"I don't think I'll live in a small town when I grow up—when I'm out of school," Shirley corrected herself hastily. "I think I'll live in a city, like San Francisco—or Los Angeles. You don't have to pay any attention to 'the community' in a city."

Her eyes rested dreamily on the Venetian blinds facing the street. She wondered just what an electrical engineer did. Did they go out to godforsaken places and build dams like the engineers you read about in stories, or were they connected with big factories or dynamos and things in dreary industrial places like Detroit?

After dinner Ben settled on the davenport with a magazine, and when the dishes were done Shirley ran up the stairs to her room. The doorbell rang at seven-thirty, and Beth came out of the kitchen to answer it.

As she ushered Norman into the living room Ben glanced up over the back of the davenport, then slowly brought his feet to the floor until he was sitting up with the magazine still clenched in one hand. He nodded, and smiled stiffly at the boy.

"Sit down, Norman," Beth invited cordially. "Shirley's upstairs. She'll be down in a minute."

She sat down on the occasional chair and gazed at him blandly. "Been another warm day, hasn't it?"

"Yes. And it's still nice out this evening."

He had seated himself uncomfortably on the large matching footstool standing against the armchair facing the fireplace; and to the accompaniment of his awkward smile, the conversation then died.

But Beth brightly administered first aid. "Shirley says you're going to the show. Bob Hope, isn't it?"

"Yeah, that's right. They say it's pretty funny."

"Oh, I love Bob Hope. We always listen to him on the radio. That is, I do, while I'm getting dinner. In the wintertime he comes on just while I'm busy in the kitchen. Ben hardly ever gets to hear him though, because that's right when he's closing up the shop and coming home. He likes his pictures though."

"We haven't seen this one, Beth. Why don't you put on your coat and we'll all go?" Ben said, as if on a sudden inspiration.

Beth gave a high little laugh. "Oh mercy, not tonight. I was down at the church all afternoon, checking over the silver and dishes for the garden party. And I'm just worn out. I expect your mother's done up tonight, too, Norman—all the responsibility as chairman."

"I suppose so," he said uncertainly, obviously unaware of his mother's heavy social obligations.

"Here's Shirley now," Beth exclaimed brightly as the girl in her pink coat and a thin dress and sandals came running down the stairs with a blithe "Hi!"

Ben rose as the young couple moved toward the front door. He tried to make his tone light as he said, "You were out pretty late last night, Shirley; so try to make it early tonight."

"We won't be late," she returned carelessly; and Ben was frustratingly certain that she wouldn't come home until she was good and ready.

When the door had closed behind them he turned to Beth accusingly. "That's two nights in a row with the same boy."

"Relax, darling. There's absolutely nothing you can do about it."

Beth dropped into the wing chair, switched on the table lamp, and pulled her knitting bag into her lap. "You might as well resign yourself. She's developed a full-sized crush on Norman Bailey, and we just have to let it wear itself out."

He flung himself onto the sofa again. "Suppose it doesn't wear out."

"Well, it's bound to happen sometime that she settles down to going steady with some boy." She glanced up over her now steadily moving needles. "I know, I know—the Baileys are rather common, and there was that awful scandal about Inez years ago; but Norman seems just as bright and well behaved as the other boys she runs with." She lifted her hand, pulling at the yarn to loosen it from the ball. "Anyhow, I don't believe in holding a person's background against them. It's un-American," she said smugly. "You should judge people on what they are themselves."

Ben frowned at the neatly swept hearth and said nothing. There was nothing to say. For Beth was completely in the right.

"To tell you the truth," she was going on placidly, "it's a problem, this whole question of boy friends. You're always so pleased when she dates Tony Zangoni; but suppose she decided to marry him when she grows up. Did you ever stop to think, the Zangonis are all Catholic. And you know what that means where marriage is concerned. They'd have to raise the children in the church; and there'd just be nothing but friction over it. And Spec Miller. Sure, the Millers own everything in sight. But—" She raised her eyes and looked at Ben meaningly. "Shirley talks to me quite a lot. And if you knew what I know, you wouldn't want her going out with Spec. Shirley says he's a terror. Hardly any of the girls will go out with him anymore unless it's in a crowd. And Bobby Whitlock—nice enough, of course; but dumb, my goodness! He flunks practically everything in school, and they just keep passing him along to get rid of him—"

Resignedly Ben let her words lap over him. He knew he was going to have to keep his mouth shut and accept the situation. He didn't have a leg to stand on. Probably, if he were made of sterner stuff, it wouldn't faze him. At any rate, he couldn't let on either to Beth or to Shirley that it was purely psychological on his part.

He closed his eyes wearily. He was beginning to feel trapped somehow; and it was the more uncomfortable because there was nothing tangible to put his finger on as the reason for the sensation. It was simply this distaste for entanglement with the Bailey family. And it was irrational, because he had nothing to fear from them.

"Etta Bailey made a peculiar remark to me today," Beth was observing inquiringly. "We were alone for a few minutes in the kitchen at the church, and she said with a sort of a smirk, 'I hear our men had a little talk this morning.' Mrs. Jackson came in then and I didn't get to ask her what she meant. What did she?"

Ben drew in his breath and let it out audibly. Well, that decision had been taken out of his hands. Now he had to tell Beth.

So he did, quietly and dispassionately.

She let her knitting lie idle in her lap while she listened. When he had finished, slowly she lifted the oblong of soft coral wool depending from her needles and began to knit, keeping her eyes on the work.

Ben waited, like a little boy before his teacher. When she did stop talking—in her desultory, witless way—and withdrew like this into herself, Ben knew that side of her that he always suspected was there, and which she kept in abeyance behind her fluffy, unconsidering manner, had assumed supremacy for the moment.

Finally she asked quietly. "What do you think of it?"

"From a practical standpoint it sounds O.K. On the personal side, I don't like it. I'd rather be independent. I don't like entanglements with other people."

Her needles moved swiftly. For a while there was no sound except the rhythmical clicking of the steel.

Then, with no cessation of the movement of her fingers, without raising her eyes, Beth said tonelessly, "Business is practical. You can't make a go of it any other way. And as far as being independent goes, we owe money to the bank. That's not independence. We're entangled with people right there."

"It's not the same thing."

"No." She lifted her eyes and let her hands and the work drop in her lap.

Ben, glancing at her sidelong, could see his wife "coming back." She had retreated to the bedrock of her personality to draw her conclusions, and now she was going to become "natural" again.

"It's more efficient," she said glibly. "The trends today are all toward consolidation. Look at the chain stores." She lifted her work and started the needles briskly. "Tim keeps a man in the front of the shop all the time, except now when Norman's helping out. There's one salary that could be cut out right there. And you could let Dolores go and just keep Harvey on. You and Tim could spell each other off on the main floor when Harvey had to work on the mezzanine. It'd be better to keep Harvey instead of Dolores," she elaborated casually, "him having a family to support and all, and you need an extra man to help, moving heavy stuff around and unpacking and all."

Ben felt a slight prickling under his skin when she mentioned Dolores.

Beth had been very quick to see the possibility of eliminating the girl.

He let his eyes fall casually on his wife. She had never let on; but did an attractive young woman in the shop give her some uneasiness? Of course she had kidded him occasionally about having picked out such a cute girl to work for him; but that's all it had amounted to—kidding. He had always felt that Beth was complacently sure of him.

The speed with which she had seen an opening for getting rid of Dolores jarred him a little. It indicated that more than he gave her credit for might have been going on in those recesses of her personality whose existence he only suspected.

It was obscurely frightening, the thought that Beth might be secretly unsure of his faithfulness, that she might be suspicious of him. He needed to feel that she was placidly, solidly confident of her hold on him, just as he was of her. It shook the foundations of his own sense of security, like the hardly perceptible jar of an earthquake tremor, to think that she might have doubts of him.

She was prattling on in her usual skipping way so that he did not have to pay attention, and he lay still with his hands behind his head, his face inexpressive.

He had hardly considered this aspect of it before, the fact that in actuality Beth had reason to be jealous. He knew that Beth need have no fear of losing his affection, let alone of his ever breaking off with her. But had she known of the things that had gone on in his mind regarding Dolores, and of the kiss outside the dance hall, Beth would have felt betrayed.

Against his will he remembered the seductive warmth of Dolores's body in his arms, the vibrant responsiveness of her lips; and the springs of heat glowed involuntarily in his own body.

He was angry suddenly, feeling cheated, and—again—trapped.

A lot of other men in his place, with a hot-blooded young girl throwing herself at them, would simply take her, get their satisfaction and forget the whole thing, and their wives never any the wiser; or, if they were, the two of them would battle it out in a few tearful scenes, and that would be that.

But he—he didn't have the guts. He stood here cringing, on the one hand afraid to enjoy a surreptitious affair with the girl, on the other too much dominated by the desires she aroused to put her conclusively out of reach.

There was nothing to stop him from taking Dolores up on the promise her manner toward him offered, with Beth never finding out a thing about it. Nothing except this fear. If things had been different in his life, he knew he would have done it, taking what risks there were as part of the gamble involved in living.

Heavily it dawned upon him, staring into the empty grate, that he hardly ever took action boldly, with a sense of freedom and independence.

It was probably not in his nature to do so; but it seemed as if he had been like that once—when he was young.

But he had hewn out his life on the lines he wanted it to follow, had achieved what he wanted; so why then did he have this feeling now of not having moved freely, in command of himself, a feeling that his actions had been guarded, cautious, held always within bounds somehow?

He thought of the worn jocular expression: Are you a man or a mouse? And he realized with a shock that he felt like a mouse.

And it was absurd, because he had always done exactly what he wanted to do.

Except, of course, now in this instance of Dolores. It occurred to him, surprisingly, that she was the first woman he had wanted since he married Beth.

"What are you frowning about, dear?" the latter inquired lightly.

He adjusted his thoughts quickly, and smoothed out his face, looking at her with his usual self-contained smile. "Worrying about this proposition of Bailey's, I guess."

"Well, there's no need to rush into anything. You can take your time and think it over."

He pulled himself up off the sofa and came over to her. She lifted her face with a faint smile, and he bent and kissed her cheek. His hand pressed her shoulder for a moment, and then he turned away.

"Guess I better turn off the sprinkler."

Ben woke the next morning without feeling rested. He had lain awake until long after he heard Shirley come in at eleven-fifty by the illuminated face of the alarm clock.

This partnership with Tim Bailey, it would draw the two families closer together, strengthen the developing bonds between the two young people. Norman Bailey might in time become his son-in-law, might someday, despite his fancy education, take over the business here in Los Alegres after the older men retired.

Ben couldn't see how he would dare to turn Tim down on the partnership. It would leak out that the deal had been proposed. If it had been the other way around, that Ben had approached Tim to buy him out or go in with him, no one would think anything of it if Tim refused. But people would see that most of the advantages in a merger lay on Ben's side; and they would think he was crazy if he turned Tim down.

He tried to argue himself into resignation to the situation, into being sensible about it. There was no reason for this panicky feeling, this revulsion.

Dressing carefully in the morning, shaving himself close and clean, brushing his light brown hair till it lay smoothly back along his head, the slight wave showing with apparent carelessness where it rose a little over his forehead, he tried to accept an attitude of resignation to the way things had developed, tried to be unemotional about it.

Walking downtown, however, in the cool, still-moist morning air, with the sunlight clear and golden on the quiet lawns and flower gardens, he still felt rebellious, frustrated, trapped. Deep inside him he was angry—at the Baileys, at life, at himself. He didn't know why he felt this undirected resentment, this sense of constriction, of pervading annoyance.

The interior of the store was bright in the eastern sunlight; and he went about the routine tasks methodically, unlocking, counting out change into the cash register, rolling down the awnings, exchanging greetings with Harvey.

He was out back in the storeroom when Dolores came in. She hadn't entered his mind until he went upstairs with the morning mail to sit down at his desk and go over it and saw her moving around among the racks at the other end of the mezzanine floor.

He sorted out a heavier envelope from the bunch in his hands, and moved toward her.

"Here's a new brochure from Columbia. Like to look it over?"

"Sure." She took the folder and spread it out on the glass case before which she stood, her elbows on the glass, her head bent as she scanned the advertising.

He stood beside her, looking over her shoulder, reading the heavier print. From her glossy hair a penetrating, spicy scent rose to his nostrils. His eyes ran down the nape of her neck onto the soft flesh of her shoulders revealed in a deep half circle above the ruffle of her blouse. His gaze was held fascinated by the smooth, curving depression between the softly padded flesh over her shoulder blades.

He felt a sudden reckless surge of rebellion, as if in the girl's warm young flesh his inchoate disturbance found an available means of release. He bent and pressed his lips against the warm skin between her shoulder blades.

She straightened, startled at first, and then with a slow, slyly mischievous grin said softly, "Why, Mr. Sterling!"

He looked down into her knowing young eyes with a slight, cryptic smile, feeling inexplicably, all at once, poised and sure of himself. He put out his hand and closed it for a moment with a caressing pressure on her bare arm above the elbow, and turned and walked composedly toward his office, his hands shuffling through the packet of letters, his eyes blandly occupied with the mail.

He refused to go back and consider his previous feelings, his fears and misgivings regarding the girl. This feeling of having asserted himself, of having defied something—he was not just sure what—had done too much for him—giving him a sensation of release, of satisfaction, of power—temporarily anyhow—to allow him to be worried about its dangers. He had followed an impulse, by God—the way any man would, in the casual, carefree way that a man had a right to act once in a while.

The church garden supper was on Saturday evening; and, in company with Harvey, Ben walked over to the pleasantly bustling churchyard lawns after closing the shop.

There was a big turnout, and Ben saw both his wife and daughter flitting among the tables in organdy aprons. Card tables and chairs had been set up in corners; and lawn furniture, borrowed wholesale from the congregation, reposed in sociably inviting groupings under the trees of the parsonage grounds.

Ben knew everyone who was there, and he dawdled along on his way to the homemade awninged counter where food was being dispensed, buffet style.

The Malleys were still in town, and Ben nodded and smiled toward Lucille and Marian where they sat on a wicker settee with Clarence standing beside them, a cup of coffee in his hand. Ben glanced about, seeking Roy Malley, and saw him stretched out in a canvas chair, talking in a serious manner to Jim Billings, who was settled uncomfortably in a similarly rickety folding chair. The two men were isolated at the moment, set apart in a pool of shade thrown by a graceful Japanese willow tree. They had an appearance somehow of settled intimacy, like old cronies who had peacefully removed themselves from the chattering crowd.

Ben's eyes tarried upon the two, and his face was blank. It happened that the men looked idly in his direction at the moment; and for an instant both pairs of eyes rested dispassionately upon him, their expressions identical.

Ben smiled and raised his hand in a gesture of greeting. As he turned away, he saw each face stir in a smile of response, with Billings casually lifting his own hand slightly in recognition of Ben's salute.

As he sauntered down the walk toward the food counter, Ben felt tense. He imagined their eyes following him meditatively. He remembered Clarence's idle remark one day that they were trying to get the Malleys to come out for good. Ben's brows drew together slightly in uneasiness as he realized for the first time that he wouldn't care about having Roy Malley around all the time.

The two men did for a moment follow Ben's progress down the walk with impenetrable expressions. Then Billings caught sight of his wife down near the counter, and he turned his head toward Malley with a resigned smile.

"My old woman's motioning at me. Guess I better see what she wants."

He heaved himself up out of the belt of canvas which made the body of the chair, and plodded away.

Roy continued to lie back, glad of a moment's solitude. His eyes followed Ben's movements idly. He saw the minister come up and the two men shake hands. Then Tim Bailey approached them eating a piece of pie off a small paper plate. He made some laughing remark, and the two other men responded in an evidently joking manner. Shirley came by carrying a tray full of dirty cups and halted beside her father, tipping her head at him pertly. Ben put his arm around the girl's shoulders with a paternal gesture, and all three of the men looked at her smilingly, the whole group indulging in a moment's bantering exchange before the girl tripped lightly away.

Roy put his head back and gazed up into the slender, pendent clusters of leaves above him, satisfied that no good could come of his meddling in things that didn't concern him.

That old eye for an eye, tooth for a tooth philosophy, did it not sometimes do more harm than good? Perhaps the damage to human happiness that it effected was greater than that resulting from the loss of the original eye or tooth.

CHAPTER EIGHT

A tinge of resignation crept deadeningly over Ben's thinking in the course of the week end; and he began to bolster his spirits with assurances that it might not be so bad. It would get on his nerves terribly, being associated with Tim Bailey; it would worry him, the way it would further the intimacy between Norman and Shirley. But you couldn't ignore the stabilizing effect the merger would have on his financial condition; and he would just have to steel himself not to let being thrown with the Baileys get too much on his nerves. He had weathered things that called for greater emotional control than this did. A man got caught in a position he didn't like, and he simply held on to himself and toughed it out. That's what he'd have to do now.

And, as far as Shirley went, she was frivolous and fickle; perhaps if he just bided his time she would get over Norman.

He stood beside the cash register, one arm draped across it, his body half turned, to stare broodingly into the sunny street, empty of pedestrians, but with a few of the merchants' cars nosed into the curb, a light delivery truck or a station wagon or a convertible passing now and then, with the sunlight splintering off the chromium trimmings.

Ever since Saturday evening, now and then his mind had brought up the image of Billings and Malley regarding him silently from the shade of the willow tree. He saw them now, superimposed on the leisurely Monday morning scene outside the broad plate glass.

In some ways it was probably a good thing, this partnership with Tim Bailey. If there were, or if there had been, conjectures; if there was still anyone who silently wondered—although he was sure there hadn't been, even at the time; he had always been a cautious, careful man—still, now his and Tim Bailey's going into business together would kill the last vestiges of suspicion or doubt that might linger in some unknown mind, even after twenty years.

Ben's pleasantly curved lips moved in a slight, sardonic smile; and for a moment his revulsion at the current turn of events was wiped out in a cynical sense of triumph. Now that he had made up his mind to accept this latest development he had for the first time a vaguely complacent feeling. It was as if now, with Tim Bailey coming to him, simply as one businessman to another, in friendliness and co-operation, a final key had been turned, and Ben could at last indulge in the luxury of relaxation, even of a small, sly feeling of self-congratulation.

It was something new, this first faint stirring of a new attitude toward the whole thing, something he hardly evaluated and recognized for what it was.

Standing there, having made his decision, he did realize, however, that heretofore there had been a buried, unconscious fear associated with the Baileys in his thoughts, and that now in the course of deciding to take Tim Bailey up on this offer, his hitherto unrecognized fear had changed into something else: a sense of power over, of superiority to, his future partner. At first he hadn't seen it in that light; but there was, after you thought of it, something immensely reassuring in Tim Bailey's innocently trusting impulse to become his partner.

Ben's eyes and face were blank as he stood there slowly trying to appreciate the fact that, astonishingly, he was going to get a sort of guilty pleasure out of association with Tim.

His mouth hardened, however, as he thought of Shirley. Somehow—some way—he would squash this budding love affair. That far he could not go, to give his daughter to Inez Bailey's kinsman. Shirley was young; there would be time. He would wait. Ben felt strong, self-confident all at once; and he lifted his chin a little. He was through with that querulous, nagging watchfulness of his daughter. In the course of this little crisis over the partnership a change had taken place in his attitude. He had a strange new heady sense of being able to cope with things. He would handle Shirley, assert himself if he had to, when the time came.

From the back of the shop he heard Dolores's treble laughter and Harvey's baritone chuckle blending for a moment. Ben turned and glanced back to where he could see their heads and shoulders above a Philco console displayed along the aisle.

His eyes rested thoughtfully on the girl's oblivious head. This new feeling had begun to emerge, he realized uncomprehendingly, at that moment of rebellion, of self-assertion, when he had said to himself, "To hell with it!" and bent to kiss the gentle hollow of her spine.

His senses, thoughts, emotions quickened at sight of her, as if she were a talisman, the touch of which brought him strength.

He was a man. He would not cringe, restrain himself, hesitate any longer under the bonds of self-distrust, fear of the world and of people. He was not a mouse. He was a man. He was through watching himself, guarding himself, putting restraints on his every action and thought. He had a right to live, to move freely, to let his impulses function like other men's. He was not going to be a prisoner of himself any longer.

He saw himself clearly for a moment, a quiet, respectable, conscientious, small-town—his mind groped for a descriptive term, and it came to him contemptuously—bourgeois. That's what he had always been, a dull, uninteresting bourgeois.

And he was through, he told himself defiantly. He was going to live from now on.

He looked down at the hands he had clasped on the rounding top of the low cash register. It was strange the way in the last few days things had got so stirred up in him. He had gone along for years and never felt that he wasn't living, never thought of that silly phrase, "Are you man or mouse?" which had suddenly begun to run through his mind like Mark Twain's, "Punch in the presence of the passenjare."

And now all of a sudden some kind of strange revolution was going on within him.

Dolores came swaying across the floor in a pink cotton bolero dress fitting smoothly across her hips and flaring around her legs.

"Think I'll run out for a cup of coffee," she informed him carelessly.

"Good idea. I'll go with you."

Ben moved easily out from behind the counter, noting with amusement the brightened expression on the girl's face. Since the incident at the dance he had been careful to refrain from these little companionable gestures.

"I'm going out for a while, Harvey," he called. "Carry on."

They sat on stools at the drugstore counter, and Ben lighted Dolores's cigarette and one of his own. He made a frivolous remark to Billie White behind the counter in her crisp white uniform, and talked lightly to Dolores, who responded with unconcealed eagerness.

When he had finished his coffee Ben dropped two dimes on the counter and stood up. He touched Dolores's shoulder lightly with the tips of his fingers and said, "I'm going down the street for a while."

He walked down the sidewalk to the pedestrian crossing in the middle of the block, and crossed to the shaded east side of the street. Norman was waiting on a woman who was considering a small radio for her son's birthday; the boy nodded and smiled at Ben. As the woman went out Norman approached Ben questioningly.

"Your father around?" Ben inquired affably.

"He just stepped out to the bank. He ought to be back any minute. Oh—here he is now."

Tim came in with a genial wave of the leather change bag and the soiled deposit book, talking as he moved along back to put them in the drawer beneath the cash register.

Norman inquired, "Is it all right if I go back and give Mike a hand now, Pa? He's got a couple of jobs to get out before noon."

"Sure. Run along. Well, Ben, been thinkin' over what we were talking about?" Tim demanded amiably, resting his elbow on the register.

Ben pulled out his cigarettes and took one, smiling containedly. "Doesn't look like there's much I can do, if you really want to go into this." He flipped out his match soberly. "I'll be frank with you. I like being independent. I'm a little dubious about having to consult a partner on every move."

"Sure. I see your point. Feel something the same way myself," Tim agreed seriously. "But we've got plenty of time to talk it over, settle on the division of responsibilities and then make up our minds to stick to them. My lease here runs till the first of September; so we got all next month for getting moved and working out the details."

"When I've had any legal matters to be taken care of," Ben observed, "Tracy Whitlock has always handled them. Is it all right with you if we talk it over with him and have him draw up the papers?"

"Sure. Sure. Tracy's O.K. with me. You and me can get together first and get it straightened out where we both stand, and make an appointment to see Tracy. I can show you my books right now if you want."

"Well, perhaps some evening, when we won't be interrupted. We can get together in my office and go over mine at the same time."

"That's O.K. by me. How about tomorrow night?"

"Well, tomorrow night is my lodge meeting. How about—say, Thursday? Far as I know I'll be free then."

"I'll check with my wife and see if we've got anything on that night."

When Ben emerged onto the sidewalk again the stimulation which had stiffened his emotional fibers earlier had worn off. He felt now rather numb. His eyes fell on the maroon glass bricks of Joe's Cocktail Bar across the street, and followed the neon column of color which flowed around the outlines of a manhattan glass framed in the center of the brick front, the cherry in the bowl lighting into ruby brilliance as the neon current completed its course and then set out once more on its tracing of the goblet.

The whole garish façade looked incongruous in the brilliant morning light; and Ben rejected the urge which had suddenly manifested itself, to go in and have a straight shot.

Ben always walked to and from work, believing that it helped to keep his figure trim. It was still warm under an unmarred blue sky as he walked home that evening, and he carried his jacket over his arm.

He was very tired, much more so than usual for some reason, as he came up the steps and walked down the hall. The Venetian blinds were closed all over the house, and it was dim inside, but the air was still and warm and vaguely stuffy despite the doors and windows standing open at the shady east end of the living room.

He saw Beth sitting in one of the white iron chairs in the patio, dressed in a low-necked blue silk dress. She was knitting as usual, and she waved to him cheerily.

"We're out here, dear."

Shirley glanced up from the magazine *Seventeen* over which she was poring, to say, "Hi, Pop."

She was sitting with her back against the arm of the settee, her feet in the seat; and Ben noticed that she wore a light dress instead of the usual sunsuit.

He dropped his coat on a chair and sighed wearily before going to the open doors.

"You'd better shower and change clothes, dear," Beth advised. "We're due at the Merritts' for dinner at seven."

He pulled the back of his hand across his forehead. "Damn, I forgot."

He threw himself into a pretty, uncomfortable chair with short arms, and unbuttoned his shirt. "Well, I'll have a cigarette first."

"Tired, dear?" Beth murmured sympathetically.

"Dead," he grunted.

"Busy day at the store?"

"No, I'm just tired, that's all."

"Well, you needn't snap my head off about it," Beth countered placidly.

They all walked down the street together after a while and around the corner and down the next block to the Merritts' green-shuttered white house. As they approached they could see across the side lawn to the terrace which opened off the dining room and was sheltered from full view of the street by the jutting rear wall of the living room.

The Merritts and Malleys were seated out there in the shade; so the Sterlings took the path around the side of the house to join them. They settled into the upholstered terrace furniture grouped around a rattan coffee table while Clarence came out with a tray holding a cocktail shaker and glasses. The drinks were martinis, and Ben didn't care so much for gin; but he sipped the cocktail gratefully. Even the shower had not lessened his nervous fatigue, but with the second drink he felt himself relaxing.

Idly he watched Shirley, who was playing with the yellow mother cat and her two kittens on the grass at a little distance from the brick terrace.

He turned his head with a slight start as Clarence's voice pierced the haze which had fallen on his thoughts.

"What's this I hear about you and Tim Bailey going to consolidate?"

Ben uttered a wry chuckle. "Don't tell me that's got out already?"

"You should know by now, Ben, that nothing stays a secret in this town," Lucille reminded him with a laugh. "But I hadn't heard about this yet. How did you get it, Clarence?"

"Just heard a rumor," he said knowingly. "Anything to it, Ben?"

"Well, we've been discussing it," he acknowledged cautiously.

As he leaned forward to pick up a canapé he caught a glimpse of Roy Malley's face, which was turned toward him. Inexplicably the man's expression made Ben uneasy. Why should a stranger to the community be surprised at hearing of a simple business deal like this? But Malley had definitely had the look of a man caught off guard in a moment of astonishment.

As the talk trickled on, however, over their reactions to this news of the partnership, Malley was only politely and disinterestedly attentive; and Ben forgot the flicker of discomfiture which had stirred in him as his eyes crossed Roy's face.

As they sat around the table later Lucille announced triumphantly, "I've persuaded the folks to stay a week longer than they planned to, instead of going on to L.A."

"We only have a month," Marian explained. "We'd been planning to drive south the end of this week; but Lucille has talked us into going back straight from here, the northern route."

"We've decided," Roy added, "to take a few side trips, using this as our base, the Monterey Peninsula, and maybe a day or two in Yosemite."

"That's nice," Beth put in approvingly. "We'll all be able to see more of you."

Ben murmured politely; but he experienced a vague irritation. Since Lucille and Clarence were practically their best friends, this meant that he and Beth would be further thrown into plans for entertaining the house guests. He told himself that he was only annoyed because the Malleys bored him; he and Beth had so little in common with them.

The evening was like a hundred others when Lucille had them over for dinner. Shirley helped Lucille with the dishes before she skipped off to one of her girl friends' homes, and at ten-thirty Beth and Ben walked quietly back around the corner to their own house.

Tonight, however, Ben did not feel the usual lethargic contentment with which they usually concluded a social evening, looking forward comfortably to their bed. He felt moody, vaguely depressed, a little restless.

From the way Beth acted, he could tell she would be willing to have him make love to her; but he felt no inclinations of that sort tonight.

She soon fell asleep; but he lay awake and uncomfortable. The mood of that morning was gone; and as he lay there he was plunged even more feverishly into his formless revulsions against the deal with Tim Bailey; the distaste for Shirley's affair with Norman returned with accentuated pressure. Again he felt desperately that against all logic, all reason, he didn't like it. He wanted no part of the Baileys.

Now he felt no sense of power, of triumph, of self-confidence. He felt only harried and angry and disgruntled.

In the morning the face of life wore a more cheerful expression, as it will sometimes after a man has slept. While he brushed his hair before the bathroom mirror Ben resolutely rejected the misgivings and the shadows which had hung over his thoughts the night before.

His sense of well-being increased as he strode jauntily toward the business district under the warm summer sun, aware that he made a good appearance in the gray sharkskin suit he had chosen to wear with a paler gray silk shirt open at the throat. He felt like what he told himself he was, a prosperous businessman in the prime of life. Why, actually, he was a young man, with the best years ahead of him. Forty-two wasn't even middle-aged, really. The business was bound to do better in the future. There was a lot Tim would contribute; and having two bosses at the shop would mean he wouldn't be so tied down. He could get out more—for golf, for an occasional trip.

His nerves had just been getting the best of him lately; that was the only reason he'd felt so down in the mouth last night. Been working too hard, worrying too much about the bank loan and the poor sales. Actually, he had nothing in the world to fear.

What was it Roosevelt had said?—"... nothing to fear but fear itself."

Walking along briskly, he thought of Dolores, and allowed lustful thoughts to rise unabashed in his mind. Once he quit being nervous about it, it made a man feel good to know he'd made a hit with a cute little number like that; made a man realize he wasn't a back number yet, not by a long ways.

His lips curved in a faintly self-satisfied smile; and for the first time in a long, long time he consciously enjoyed the awareness of his own sexual attractiveness; was glad that his posture was good, his waistline still within bounds. He wasn't as slim as he had once been; but he was just heavy enough to have a dignified, mature appearance.

He had no intention of going out of his way to make passes at the girl; but neither was he going to continue as he had been, avoiding openings for getting involved with her. He would just take things as they came. He was through, that was all, with retreating from life. Through with this infernal carefulness at every step. He had been, in the secret places of his own self, a mouse too long, as if he were afraid of the man he had a right to be.

The bright morning euphoria clouded for a moment. Ben felt somehow less cheerful, less optimistic, as if even this oblique contemplation of himself as a man and not a mouse was alarming.

But when Dolores breezed into the shop a little later his stability returned. His now fully admitted desires toward her acted as a stimulant, rescuing him from that depressing seesawing between conflicting emotional states.

By the time he had really got down to business for the day he had, as he expressed it to himself, got hold of himself.

There was little time at home that evening before he had to leave for the lodge meeting. But it was time enough to see Norman arrive in the Baileys' car to pick up Shirley "for a ride."

Ben found himself wanting to protest; but he restrained the impulse. The intimacy was developing entirely too fast; and he felt a definite vexation with Beth for allowing the girl to run around so much at nights—in cars at that. But he grimly reminded himself that in September the boy would be going away to school and the affair would taper off. Shirley would start looking for someone more available.

He took out his own car to go to the meeting. Usually Clarence and he drove down together, but Ben didn't even give him a ring tonight, assuming that Clarence wouldn't be coming, since he had guests.

The attendance was not large, but Ben enjoyed the meeting. The ritual was soothing, took his mind off himself; there was a reassuring sense of solidarity in being there quietly with his brother members.

After the meeting a group of them dropped into Joe's for a drink, lining up on stools at the bar. The dusky lighting, the red leather *décor*, the black and white images on the television screen, the bursts of laughter, and the occasional raising of a voice—it was all cozy and comradely and pleasant.

Two men played shuffleboard at the table against the wall, and in the alcove at the rear the juke box played.

Ben and his friends turned on their stools to watch the game of shuffle-board. Several people had sauntered up from the alcove to watch, and Ben noticed Dolores among them. She smiled at him, narrowing her eyes and wrinkling her nose impishly. After a moment he eased off the stool and casually moved over to stand beside her.

They exchanged a few sallies of rather labored repartee before Ben inquired offhandedly, "You here alone?"

"No, my sister and her boy friend are in the back." She jerked her head to indicate the low settees beyond the arch. "I just came along for something to do."

"Like a ride home?"

"Love it. I'll tell them I'm going."

Ben stepped over and set down his glass, then unobtrusively made his way toward the entrance. As he stepped out of the open doors he saw Dolores swinging down the room and knew she had noticed him at the exit. He halted just out of sight around the door, and in a moment she was beside him.

As they walked down the street to his car, he said lightly, "Did you tell them I was taking you home?"

She gave him a quick upward glance before she chuckled, "No, I figure what people don't know won't hurt 'em."

Ben was at the same time relieved at this indication of the girl's discretion, and inexplicably disturbed by it. She had almost too adeptly established their relationship on the clandestine basis which he, of course, wanted, making its illicit nature an accepted fact between them.

Ben found himself feeling as inept and inexperienced as a boy on his first date. He made conversation, and not too skillfully, as they rode through the quiet streets. In her block he parked at the curb two doors down from where she lived, as if unsure of the exact house; but they both recognized the impulse toward deception involved in the choice of parking place. At least no busybody could say that she had seen Ben Sterling's car parked in front of his salesgirl's house.

As he lifted his arm to lay it along the seat back, Dolores moved naturally into the curve of his shoulder, smiling up at him with what he recognized as a rather childlike confidence.

It was irresistibly appealing. Ben forgot all his qualms, all the inhibitions that had bothered him, as he drew her close and kissed her the way he had been wanting to.

He did not stay there very long, parked at the curb. It was too risky. One never knew whose headlights might pick them out, turning the corner, whose eyes might recognize the car from the sidewalk.

Driving home, he pondered over how to manage things. It wasn't easy,

in a town this size, carrying on an affair. For a married man it was next
to impossible to do it without discovery.

But when the driving forces are strong enough a person can usually find
ways. Within the week he had contrived the first rendezvous. It turned out
to be simpler than he had expected. Beth was invited to a baby shower in
the evening, and he was ensconced on the sofa with a new magazine when
she left. He told her he intended to go to bed early. Shirley, of course, was
at a movie—for once without Norman.

As soon as Beth had gone Ben walked out the back way and down the
alley and across town to Dolores's home six blocks away. If anyone tele-
phoned or called at the house while he was gone and mentioned it afterward, he had a story ready; it had been such a nice night that he had gone
for a walk.

Dolores had managed to dispose of her mother and sister, also at the
movies; and she admitted Ben through the back door. He spent two hours
with her in her bedroom at the rear of the house, safe from interruption
behind the locked doors, their only light that from the crescent moon shining in through the west windows.

He was in bed, feigning sleep, when Beth came home a little before midnight.

He had wondered a little, ahead of time, how he would feel afterward
around Beth and Shirley; and he found, slightly to his surprise, that it hardly
bothered him.

And in all other ways he felt wonderful. Better than he had in years. There
was a new zest to life. He felt alive, alert as he had not since—well, since
he couldn't remember when.

His thoughts were so full of the hours he managed to snatch with Dolores, and which were so completely satisfying, that he hardly remembered,
as he went ahead with the partnership deal, that at first he had feared and
hated it. For days on end he forgot to wonder how often Shirley was seeing Norman.

He felt young, dashing; even, he admitted a little sheepishly to himself,
rather glamorous. It was as if wanting and taking Dolores had released him
from some spell he had been living under.

She had worked out perfectly. She did not talk, upsettingly, about the future, about the meaning of their feelings for one another. She seemed content merely to accept things as they were. Which was how Ben wanted it.
He knew that eventually it must stop, knew even that in time she would
become merely a habit, and after that stage eventually a boring habit at
that. But she was just what he needed now.

Sometimes he reflected uneasily on whether she would be troublesome
when the time finally came to break it up. There was no question about

it, she had gone completely overboard for him. When they were together she fairly consumed him with her ardor; and he was disturbingly aware that it was not entirely from pure physical passion.

Well, she knew what the score was. They had never talked about it in so many words; but the very secrecy he maintained in regard to seeing her, the circumspection of his manner in public—these things ought to show her that she would never be openly a part of his life. She knew that he had neither the desire nor intention to break up his marriage. At least he assumed she knew.

Once in a while he felt a certain anxiety, a trace of fear in connection with these reflections; but he didn't let it distress him. He was too happy.

It was funny; he had thought he was happy all along; but now he realized he had been so only in the sense that a cat is happy lying sluggishly in the sun.

CHAPTER NINE

The Sterlings saw less of the Merritts and the Malleys than Ben had expected in the two weeks the visitors remained in Los Alegres; but on the Saturday evening preceding their departure Lucille and Clarence gave an informal *bon voyage* party for the guests.

While Ben and Beth dressed for the occasion in their room they heard the volcanoes of shrieks and guffaws in the living room which indicated that some of Shirley's friends had invaded the premises.

Ben was wearing his good dark-blue suit and a white shirt for the party, and as he stood before the mirror over his chest of drawers drawing the broad end of his necktie through the four-in-hand knot, he raised his eyebrows questioningly at Beth's reflection in the glass.

"Is Shirley throwing a party tonight?"

"Oh no. She said some of the kids might drop over this evening, is all. I left some stuff for sandwiches and a few bottles of coke in the icebox."

Ben turned, arranging a hemstitched handkerchief in his breast pocket, and regarded Beth affectionately. She looked sweet tonight, he thought, in her flowered chiffon, her hair fluffy and soft above her round, rather girlish face. He was proud of his pretty little wife. Everybody liked Beth, with her artless, inconsequential chatter, her impulsive friendliness. A sense of well-being possessed him as he stood there in their stylish Swedish-modern bedroom. They could have been models for an advertisement in a woman's magazine, two well-dressed, good-looking people of the solid American middle class, typical examples of the most fortunate breed of people in the whole world.

He went over and put his arms around Beth and sniffed at the flower fragrance she had sprayed on her hair, then laid his cheek lightly against hers. She put her hands on the lapels of his coat, and kissed him, lightly, so as not to smear her lipstick.

Then she pressed her forehead against his chin and murmured, "Maybe it's just my imagination, but it's seemed to me lately you've been sweeter to me than ever, Ben."

He tightened his arms around her protectively. Yes, he had noticed it himself. Except in regard to physical passion he had been more attentive to Beth than usual since his happiness with Dolores. Trying to salve his guilty conscience, he supposed ironically. Paradoxically enough, as her words indicated, Beth had actually gained from his affair with Dolores; she had been given more tenderness, more of the little attentions she liked, as he unconsciously sought to make up to her for his emotional defection.

Well, it would not go on forever, his infidelity. Before too long he would have got his fill of whatever it was he had needed that Dolores was giving him. He would not go on forever risking what he had here with Beth. But somehow Dolores had been necessary to him at this stage in his life. He hid a slight frown in the softness of Beth's hair. A hazardous necessity perhaps. But a man simply couldn't spend his entire life in the consolidation of safety. There seemed to be a psychological need to indulge in the stimulant of danger once in a while.

He went out into the living room while Beth was putting on her coat, repressing an impatient reaction at the sight of Norman Bailey already there, leaning on one end of the radio console. Shirley was on her knees on the floor, dragging records out of the cabinet. The loud-speaker was giving out the vocal strains of "Pretty Baby," and Ginny was showing Bobby Whitlock a new dance step in the middle of the floor. Bunny Simmons was leaning over the back of the sofa to watch, her knees on the cushions.

On the whole, Ben was reassured by the scene. He felt safer about Shirley when she was within the walls of his own house and surrounded by a crowd. Then he knew that some ineligible boy was not initiating her into the mysteries of sex, getting her started on paths that did not lead to the goals her father had marked out for her, goals remarkably similar to the one he had attained with Beth.

It was a mellow moonlight night, warm for the Coast; and a rather large crowd had gathered at the Merritts', over-flowing onto the terrace and circulating through the living and dining room with highball glasses and cigarettes. Besides her own intimate circle of the Sterlings, the Whites, and the Foleys, Lucille had invited the elite of Los Alegres society, the Whitlocks, Pete and Dotty Zangoni, Fred Colton, the police chief, and his wife, who had been a Zangoni girl. Ben was a little surprised to see Jim Billings and his wife there, not that—despite Jim's unreliability as a Guardian of the Law in the interests of his own class—the Billingses were not among the town's solid citizens; but, being older, they did not mingle frequently with the "younger" set. Clarence had probably invited Jim because Roy seemed to have taken a liking to him, to prefer his company indeed to that of his fellow policeman, the current chief, Fred Colton, who was also a substantial property owner in the community.

Dimly the idea of that sudden friendship was disquieting to Ben; but he brushed away the sense of uneasiness. He had steered clear too long of those betraying apprehensions to start entertaining them now.

Tim and Etta Bailey were not invited, of course. They were neither close personal friends of the Merritts nor among the social big bugs who accepted the Merritts and Sterlings and the Foleys as part of their "set" but who invited them only to their "big" parties.

As the evening went on people began to feel good; nothing boisterous, but they talked rapidly and loudly, and there was much laughter and moving from group to group and self-serving of drinks at the tiled drainboard in the kitchen.

Ben was always careful about liquor. He never seemed to turn down a drink; but he kept his eye on the clock on the buffet in the dining room, and pursued his usual quota of no more than one drink every hour.

His program of calculated spacing enabled him to keep in a sociable mood, however; and tonight he felt especially warm and agreeable. Before they left home he and Beth had sat in the patio watching the moon slide upward into the deepening blue of the sky over the roof of the Smiths' house on the next street, drinking a cocktail of their own making, "to put us in a festive mood," as Beth had said gaily.

Ben was particularly attentive to Beth at the party, more so than usual, inquiring as to whether she wanted another drink, bringing the tray of canapés to her, gravitating again and again to the group she was in, sometimes as they stood talking to people, slipping his arm casually about her waist, meeting her eyes across the room with an intimate smile. He could see she was gratified by his quiet gallantry. Husbands in Los Alegres were inclined to take their wives for granted, and Ben had always been more punctilious toward his wife than most of his friends were to theirs. He could see that she comfortably interpreted his manner tonight as simply a continuation of the impulse that had moved him to the gentle embrace there in the bedroom before they left the house, a result of one of those inexplicable moods of heightened tenderness and closeness which sometimes arise for no apparent reason in a happy marriage.

There was nothing deliberate in his tendency to move closer to Beth tonight. Ben didn't even attempt to analyze it; he simply followed an instinctive prompting.

He did not talk very much to Roy Malley, but paused beside him once or twice to ask the expected polite questions about how he had enjoyed his vacation, to express conventional regret that the visitors couldn't stay longer in Los Alegres.

Ben told himself that he felt no emotion at all toward the Chicago policeman. The man simply left him cold, did not have the sort of personality with which he would ever feel chummy.

Ben was in the kitchen a little after midnight, having his fourth drink and his last before the coffee and hot dish which Lucille was preparing to serve at the table in the dining room. The others in the room, standing about with highball glasses in their hands, dropping cigarette ashes on the inlaid linoleum when their first cursory glance did not spot an ash tray, had consumed considerably more than four drinks apiece; and they were flushed and convivial. Clarence was telling a dirty story—which Lucille interrupted as she came out to pick up the Silex coffeepot from the stove: "Clarence Merritt, don't you finish that story while I'm in the room!" She winked laughingly at the men cluttering up her kitchen. "You see, I know how it ends."

As she sailed through the dining-room door with a swirl of her ankle-length skirt Clarence went on boisterously. Jim Billings's heavy shoulders shook with laughter, and Tracy Whitlock let out a bray of appreciation. Roy Malley, half sitting with his hips against the chromium-trimmed worktable, chuckled, and Ben smiled and took a sip of his drink.

Roy's eyes slid good-humoredly over Ben's pleasant, composed features, the soberest ones in the house at the moment. Roy had been drinking fairly steadily all evening, sticking to straight shots and plain water, aware of his ability to hold his liquor. He had made up his mind not to think about Ben Sterling any more, but his treacherous brain would not relinquish interest in the man.

It was probably because it was an affront to his pride that a simple little strangling should baffle the practitioners of his profession.

He had suspected it before; but tonight he had become certain that Ben didn't like him. Roy didn't know whether Ben himself was aware of his own antipathy, but Roy could read it in the man's scrupulously pleasant manner toward him, the unobtrusive way in which Ben avoided being near him.

Roy was used to not being liked. The men he hunted down were of course his enemies, and he had political and professional enemies; but social acquaintances almost never reacted unfavorably to him.

There was wry amusement in the thought of this confirmation of his suspicions.

Something else though had bothered him tonight. Again it was one of those seemingly psychic phenomena. He seemed to sense a wrong note in Ben's deportment. His sensitive perceptions telegraphed a message of warning, of something off key. And in the realm of crime anything off key could mean potential danger. The criminal nature was an unsafe entity when subjected to vibrations which jarred it from its habitual adjustments.

Roy walked over to the drainboard and poured himself a shot, oblivious to the voices and laughter around him. He'd been drinking too much, that was all; getting maudlin, feeling things that weren't there. What in the hell had been any different about Ben Sterling this night, different in a way anyhow that made him a character to keep your eye on? It was a purely subjective thing on his part, born of annoyance at having to contemplate a man who had got away with it under the noses of the police. All he was doing was unconsciously looking for reasons to consider the man a menace so he'd have an excuse for going after him. It was no wonder the poor guy didn't warm up to him. People sensed things about other people's attitudes toward themselves, and Sterling had sensed the policeman's intrusive, distrustful thoughts.

Some of the men were moving out of the kitchen, and Roy followed. Lucille was urging people in the other rooms to help themselves from the steaming chafing dish on the lace-covered table.

Roy stood back as the guests began to crowd around with plates and napkins. He saw Ben go to Beth, who had wandered into the dining room with Marian. Ben inclined his head and addressed his wife with a smile, and she looked up at him, her face dimpling. They linked arms, and Ben continued to smile down at her, speaking in a low voice. They moved toward the table, still arm in arm, and as they reached the pile of plates at the end, Ben withdrew his arm with a lingering contact of his fingers on Beth's arm. His eyes lifted as if by accident and caught Roy's, and Ben smiled perfunctorily.

Just then Roy heard Marian's voice raised across them. "Better get a plate, Roy." He knew that she had been feeling her drinks for at least an hour; so he was not surprised when she added crassly, "Maybe some of Lucille's tamale pie will help put a little flesh on your bones."

Those standing near her laughed, and Lucille added shrilly, "Maybe I ought to take that plate away from my old man. He doesn't need any extra weight."

Dotty Zangoni giggled and pointed a finger at her husband, while with her other hand she patted the pale-green lace over her ample hips. "Pete, don't you dare get into this conversation about people's figures. This is my night to howl, and to heck with the diet."

Amidst further connubial banter and the laughter it elicited Roy circled the table inconspicuously and wandered out of the open doors to the now abandoned terrace.

He pulled out his cigarettes, and walked over to the breast-high brick wall which shut out the back yard, leaning against it and gazing across the lawn dappled by the designs the moon had spread upon the grass with the shadows of the trees.

So a man publicly showed his devotion to his wife, did so consistently all evening. Was there anything wrong with that? Any reason for this conduct to set up those little warning connections in his brain? Wasn't that the way any married couple ought to act?

The trouble was, as had just been demonstrated, married people in Los Alegres didn't act like that. Out in a crowd for a good time they seemed to forget about each other except for good-natured raillery such as had just taken place in regard to the tamale pie. Any gallantries that were bandied about were usually exchanged heavy-handedly with other people's mates.

But there were differences in temperament. Everybody didn't act the same.

Roy frowningly pulled on his cigarette. But that was the trouble. Differences in temperament ... A change took place—if the abnormality was not already there—in the psychological make-up of a human being who had gone beyond the proscribed bounds of aggressive behavior to the extent of taking another life. And those differences which came about in the temperament were significant. They bore watching.

What had given him this warning to be watchful tonight was that he had not, in their previous social contacts, seen Ben demonstrate the same attitude that he had revealed tonight—as if he were deliberately showing everybody or somebody how wrapped up he was in his wife.

Previously he had been—although a shade more deferential—as casually acceptive of his wife's presence and status as any of the other men in his set were of their wives'. But tonight Ben Sterling had seemed constantly aware of his wife, almost propitiatory in his manner toward her.

And when people popped up with a new line of behavior it indicated that something had occurred to make it necessary.

Roy threw his cigarette down and stepped on it, and, standing sideways with his arm outstretched on the brick wall, drummed his finger tips on the rough surface.

One day when he had lunched with Clarence they had dropped in to see Ben's shop. Ben and the salesman had both been out to lunch, and only the girl who worked there had greeted them, exchanging a few flippant remarks with Clarence, smiling cordially at Roy when he was introduced. He had noted idly that she was a very attractive girl, vivacious brown eyes, full red lips, enticingly a shade plumper than the average fashionably emaciated young woman.

He remembered now how, after they had left the store, Clarence had delivered a few coarse remarks about her charms, and added bumblingly, "Wouldn't mind having a piece like that in our office. Seems like all we get's the skinny old maids that can't find a man."

"I'm surprised she isn't married. She looks like the type that could be if she wanted to be."

"I'll say. But as far as I know Dolores isn't even going steady with anybody right now. Hasn't since she broke up with the Mathews kid a year or so ago." Clarence chuckled lewdly. "Damn shame, her wasted there on old Ben. He's so damn proper it probably never even occurs to him to snitch a little feel now and then."

Roy had smiled dutifully and forgotten his brother-in-law's crude humor. He knew it was just Clarence's way of trying to appear manly.

Now in the moonlight he remembered the girl and the remarks. The whole thing made a disturbing grouping in his mind. Beth, Ben, and a sexy-looking young girl. There was a situation that Roy didn't like.

Suppose Ben was carrying on, as Los Alegres would call it, with his employee. Naturally the whole thing would be utterly secret, unsuspected— with Ben handling it. Why should he, Roy, feel this alarm over the possibility of the triangle's existence? It was nothing unusual. Such things happened frequently, and often as not ended without undue commotion for all concerned.

It was part of his training and experience, Roy decided. He distrusted killers. Perhaps he even feared them a little. It was almost instinctual with him by this time to watch their movements warily, prepared to see a menace in their most innocent behavior.

He felt a moment's irritation with Jim Billings. Twenty years ago was the time to have stopped the whole thing, before the happiness of wives and children was involved. He knew what Billings had been up against, of course: nothing but an intuition, without a damn fact to back it up. And a charge of false arrest was something a small-town officer had to watch even more carefully than the city police did.

But he knew that if he had been handling the case he would have kept hammering away until one or the other was worn down to defeat in the contest. And no criminal had ever worn Roy Malley down yet.

He clenched his fist and struck the knuckles on the wall, permitting himself a sheepish grin. Well, maybe none of them had ever worn him down; but he had run up against characters as tough as he was, whom he had never been able to wear down either.

He decided to go in and get a cup of coffee and some food, and this time he would put the whole thing out of his mind.

The night had become cooler, and no one had brought plates out to the terrace to eat; so he went back into the buzz of talk and laughter which was quieter now that they were all busy eating.

It was almost one-thirty when the Sterlings came wearily up their own front steps. The Whitlocks had given them a ride home. The house was dark, and at the front door Ben discovered that he had forgotten the keys both to the front and to the side door into the kitchen in his other pants; so they trudged down the driveway and around to the patio doors in the rear, which were usually left unlatched.

"It's no use to ring the bell," Beth said ruefully. "If Shirley's asleep, she'd never hear it. She can sleep through noise that would wake the dead."

But as they opened the gate between the driveway and the back lawn they found that Shirley was not asleep. The moon was now high overhead, its light falling benignly on the long white settee where two figures lay at full length, their heads close together on a cushion brought from the house and propped against one of the hard arms of the seat.

The settee's occupants had obviously not heard the quiet footsteps on the driveway, but as the little wooden gate creaked open Shirley raised her head, her tousled blond hair shining silver in the moonlight, and Norman turned his shoulders and came to a half sitting position against the cushion. As he recognized the two standing at the gate in the bright moonlight he swung his legs awkwardly off the settee and sat up.

Shirley squirmed into a sitting position, her legs drawn up on the seat. "Oh—hello," she said with a futile simulation of aplomb. "We—we didn't hear you."

"Apparently not," Ben snapped. "Do you know what time it is?"

"Why—no," Shirley said, too casually. "About twelve, I guess."

"It's one-thirty," Ben pronounced ominously.

Norman had risen to his feet. "I didn't realize it was so late."

"I should think you children would be cold," Beth interposed flutteringly before Ben could speak again. "Outdoors so late."

Norman uttered a low, embarrassed laugh. "We've only been out here a few minutes."

"Yes," Shirley chimed in quickly, "the other kids just left. It was such a lovely night we thought we'd just sit out here a few minutes and watch the moonlight."

"Well," Norman said awkwardly, "I guess I'd better be going."

Shirley scrambled off the settee. "I'll walk to the front with you."

"You'll go in the house," Ben commanded grimly, "right now."

Both the young people turned startled eyes upon him; then, before Shirley could speak, Norman announced with an attempt at nonchalance,

"I was just going to leave anyhow. Good night, everybody."

Glancing uncertainly at the girl, he made his way around her parents to the gate. Ben stepped back stiffly to allow him to pass.

"Good night, Norman," Beth said in a rather high voice.

Without a word Shirley turned and stamped across the flagstone floor, letting the screen door slam behind her. By the time her parents had reached the door she had turned on one of the lamps and was facing them with furious eyes which fastened hard on her father.

"What do you mean," she demanded, "taking that kind of an attitude, embarrassing my friends?"

For the space of a second Ben was taken aback at the girl's attacking him instead of waiting for him to take the offensive; but he retorted angrily, "What do *I* mean! I'd like to know what you mean, laying around in the dark with a man in the middle of the night."

He advanced toward her a step or two with a contorted scowl on his face. "Has it got to the point where we can't trust you alone in the house for fear of your going to bed with any young squirt that wanders in?"

"Ben!" Beth ejaculated with horror. Then she quickly whirled and closed the glass doors so the sound would not carry outside.

For a moment the girl's expression was bewildered, and she stood silent, her eyes aghast upon her father's angry countenance.

"I'll have no more of it, you understand!" he shouted.

Beth's voice rose behind them, cold and decisive. "And I will have no more of this. Shirley, go up to your room."

The girl's lips trembled, and then she wheeled and ran to the stairs. On the steps she turned, and with both hands clenched on the banister, cried, "I don't have to take this, being humiliated, insulted." She glared tremulously at her father. "I won't be treated like this, as if—as if I was a—a prostitute or something. You needn't think you can get away with it."

Sobbing and stumbling, she ran on up the stairs.

Ben shouted after her futilely, "And don't think you're going to get away with talking to me like this either."

Breathing heavily, he turned his head toward Beth.

"Have you gone crazy?" she said levelly. Her eyes were hard and her face set.

As Ben's eyes rested on her truculently, slowly his passion subsided under the sobering recognition that the Beth whose concealed presence he suspected had emerged and taken over.

Now she was eying him not so much angrily as speculatively, as if probing for the sources of his conduct.

"I suppose," he said bitterly, "you think it's just fine to come home and find your seventeen-year-old daughter in a man's arms in the middle of the night?"

"I don't think it's just fine," she replied coolly, "but I'm not particularly surprised by it; and it certainly doesn't make me fly into a rage. Why," she whipped out sharply, "does it upset you so much to find your daughter necking with her boy friend? They all do it."

"That doesn't make it right. Nor any the less dangerous. Do you want her to come up pregnant one of these days? Do you want a shotgun wedding in the family?"

"Poppycock," Beth said rudely.

Uncertainly Ben looked back into her scornful eyes. He was suddenly stopped cold. His anger had drained away, leaving him feeling hollow and brittle.

He turned away brusquely, muttering as he stamped toward the bedroom door, "All right, have it your own way. She's your daughter, bring her up any way you want; make a floozy out of her if you want to."

Beth turned out the light and followed him, retorting vehemently, "If necking on a moonlight night with a perfectly nice boy like Norman Bailey is going to make a floozy out of my daughter, then I guess she's just going to have to be one."

He had pressed the switch on the bedroom wall, and now Beth met his eyes accusingly and said with the air of one making an unpleasant discovery, "You're evil-minded. That's what's the matter with you."

Ben yanked at his tie, and uttered an obscene epithet under his breath.

Occasionally as they undressed Beth erupted into angry phrases of reprimand for the man, defense for her daughter.

Ben was sulkily silent. He pulled the covers up around his ear. It took Beth longer to get ready for bed, and he lay there, closing his eyes against the light, more upset than he cared to recognize. He and Beth had had quarrels during their married life, arguments when they couldn't agree on some practical decision, hurt feelings on her part when she blamed him because something hadn't turned out the way she wanted it to.

But they had been superficial, a temporary blowing off of steam, with each of them unadmittedly recognizing that character in the fuss. Tonight, though, he saw that he had aroused hatred and contempt in Beth, not a diffused, undirected hostility for which she merely used him as an outlet. This time she had withdrawn from him emotionally in contemptuous distaste. For the time at least she loved him not at all.

The knowledge of this was, for some reason, terrifying. It was no longer important to him whether he was right or wrong about the subject of the quarrel. At the moment he was no longer even concerned about Shirley. His anger at the girl and Norman had been wiped out by the fear Beth's attack had generated. He could not—dare not—leave himself open to rejection by Beth.

Beth flounced into bed and jerked the chain on the light. The movements with which she settled herself on the mattress were eloquent of the displeasure which still pulsed through her.

Once settled, she lay rigidly, without speaking or moving. Ben held himself tense, waiting for a few minutes; but he knew he couldn't stand this state of affairs. It was too unsettling. So he rolled over and tentatively clasped her arm in his hand.

"Maybe I was hasty," he said hesitantly.

"Hasty!" she snorted. And added mutinously, "It's your attitude I don't like."

He went on with soothing, explanatory words. He wanted all the best for Shirley. He was overprotective maybe. He'd been tired tonight. Saturday, and a busy day at the store. Anybody could fly off the handle sometimes.

He moved closer to her, so that their bodies were touching, and passed his arm around her waist. She was a little more relaxed than she had been, but she only muttered unintelligibly in response to his voice.

"Don't be mad at me," he whispered, half facetiously; and put his face down and lightly moved his lips against her neck under the hair at the back.

He pulled at her gently with his arm, urging her to turn to face him. Grudgingly she rolled over and let her arm lie limply over his at her waist.

Ben began to breathe easier. He felt relieved, safer somehow; and with real sincerity he fondled and caressed her until she was again his in the physical unity of marriage.

CHAPTER TEN

Sunday morning at the Sterlings began late, and was not a happy time. By tacit consent Ben and Beth did not call Shirley to eat with them; and when she did come down Ben was puttering in the yard, loosening the earth at the roots of the shrubs, pretending to do a little gardening. As he dug around under the kitchen windows he could hear Beth's voice, and by the tone he could tell she was trying to "smooth things over."

He went around to the back and talked for a while over the hedge to Fred Morrison, who was washing his car. Ben had come out in old slacks and no shirt, and he found the sun was getting too hot on his shoulders; so he went into his own garage and "straightened up" for a while in desultory fashion. He didn't want to go into the house where he would have to encounter his womenfolk; but finally he wandered in through the patio doors and went to the bathroom to wash his hands. When he came out he listlessly sank into his usual place on the sofa and unfolded the Sunday paper.

All he admitted to himself was that he was "restless" this morning. He read with the wrinkles between his eyebrows showing deeply.

The relief and relaxation he had felt at re-establishing contact with Beth before they went to sleep last night had left him while they slept. Now he felt only a deep disgruntlement. It did not occur to him that the dissatisfaction was with himself—for having seen himself so dependent on Beth's good will, for having given in on every point in order to regain it, for having in the first place lost control of himself in attacking Shirley. He had only a confused sense that everything was a mess.

His approach to the girl had been a tactical error. It would only throw her more closely into young Bailey's arms. He should have kept his mouth shut, played it smart. But damn it, a man got tired of concealing his feelings. He wanted to express himself sometimes, be able safely to think, "To hell with everybody! This is the way I feel, and you can take it or leave it."

He felt stirred up inside every time he thought of how he had quit fighting with Beth and turned quickly to currying her favor.

A man had a right to rip and roar once in a while, whether he was in the wrong or not. But not him. Not Ben Sterling, the model citizen, model husband, model father.

He lowered the brightly colored comic page and glared at the smooth grain of the Carmel stone in the mantel.

He was damn sick of being a model man. He would like to be able to be just a plain man for a change, a man who could fight with his wife and let her be the one to get over it, who could lay down ultimatums to his child and dare to disapprove of a boy friend on a mere whim if he chose, who could stand up and say, "I just don't want that man for a partner," and let people figure out any kind of reasons they liked for his behavior.

But not Ben Sterling. He set his teeth as the answer came unbidden to the unspoken question: Why not Ben Sterling?

He had forfeited the right to act as he chose. He had to be, like Caesar's wife, above suspicion; the pleasant, perpetually well-behaved, respectable member of the community.

The thought of Dolores cut across the stormy surfaces of his mind like a ray of sunlight striking the sea on a cloudy day. The muscles of his face relaxed; the lines between his eyebrows were not so deep.

There was one way in which he had stepped out of character. He was not so perfect after all, if they just knew. He was a man with a mistress. He had asserted himself in defiance not only of his own self-imposed restrictions but against those of the world in which he functioned.

After these reflections he had the inner steadiness to approach Shirley with a quiet smile when she came downstairs, to say to her placatingly, "I'm sorry I was sharp with you last night, Shirley. I probably sounded more severe than I meant to."

She surveyed him with inimical but guarded eyes under the smooth bangs, "Let's forget it, shall we?" he said coaxingly, lightly.

Her lips trembled a little, and then she tossed her head. "O.K. I guess I was pretty—sassy, maybe."

"We were all tired, I guess." He smiled. "You know that at bottom I'm just concerned with your welfare. Don't want to see you do anything foolish."

"I know," she said reluctantly, and added stiffly, "but I have to start taking responsibility for my own actions sometime. After all, I'll be eighteen next winter."

He should have felt better after this exchange with Shirley; but he was soon restless again, unable to settle down. Shirley vanished from the premises about one o'clock; a little later he and Beth drove out to the country club and Ben played eighteen holes of golf while Beth played bridge with friends in the lounge of the clubhouse.

Shirley, Beth informed him, was to eat supper with Ginny's family; so he and Beth stopped at the Hacienda outside town for a light dinner, and went to the movies afterward.

The next morning as they breakfasted in the alcove Beth said cheerfully and irrelevantly over her coffee cup, "Well, the Malleys are gone now."

"That's good," Ben returned absently.

Beth set down her cup and laughed. "What a thing to say. Sounds as if you were glad to see them go."

His eyes lifted quickly to her face, and then he chuckled carelessly. "I just meant I'm glad they got away all right."

He gave a little sigh, and folded his napkin, pushing it into a ring of polished redwood. "Well, we sign the papers today." He smiled at her ruefully. "There goes our independence."

"Nonsense," Beth said stoutly. "It's a godsend, Tim wanting to go in with you. A lot better than floundering around and going into bankruptcy before we're through. Have you two decided on how you're going to run things after September first, about help and all?"

"Well, Tim told me he's already notified George West he won't be needing him again this fall after Norman leaves. It was probably quite a blow to George. He's been working in one of the packing sheds north of town, to fill in this summer while he's laid off at Bailey's. Don't know what he'll do this winter now."

"Have you talked it over yet whether you're going to let Harvey or Dolores go?"

"Not—specifically. We've agreed we can let one of them go." Ben frowned over the lighting of a cigarette. "But we may decide to try keeping them both for a while. It might be pretty confining for me if we cut down too much on help. You see, Tim gives Mike a hand occasionally on the repair work; and of course he'll oversee all that; and I'll have more bookkeeping now, expanding like this."

Beth gazed thoughtfully at the back of a chair across the table. "Maybe the thing to do is get a girl with business training and have her do office work part time and selling part time."

"That might be a good idea," Ben said equably.

He could see right now that Dolores was going. Even if he wanted to he couldn't safely get around Beth's veiled insistence on her dismissal. He wondered with a panicky flutter in his stomach if Beth actually suspected anything. Had he slipped anywhere in his scrupulous precautions for concealment?

But he kissed her good-by casually and went off to work as if he had nothing to worry about except the phrasing of the partnership agreement.

In the afternoon Ben strolled from his office over to the counter where Dolores leaned with her elbows on a glass case looking at a magazine. She lifted her head and smiled at him with slow, lazy pleasure.

He put his arm along the case, and flipped the bundle of envelopes in his hand with his thumb.

"Well, looks like we're going to have to order new stationery. From now on it'll be Sterling and Bailey."

She folded her arms on the glass. "It's going to seem funny, having two bosses."

"I haven't said anything before," he said soberly, "but I probably ought to give you some warning. You see, one of the reasons for this merger is to cut down on the help. Bailey and I haven't gone into that angle very thoroughly yet, but he may figure that with both of us on the floor all the time we won't need someone just for this department."

She was staring at him incredulously, and Ben dropped his eyes.

"You mean—you'd let me go?"

Again Ben's eyes shied away from the suddenly lost look in hers. He attempted a light tone.

"Well, only in a business way," he murmured meaningly.

But she did not look comforted. Her voice was low, but it held a wailing note. "But, Ben, what would I do? I have to work. We need the money. Mamma doesn't make enough anymore with her sewing to keep us."

He reached over and squeezed her arm playfully. "I don't think you'd have any trouble getting another job. There isn't a businessman in town that wouldn't be tickled to death to have something as pretty as you under his eyes all day."

There was no response in her startled brown eyes, and Ben was aghast to see them suddenly fill with tears.

"But I want to be with you," she said plaintively.

Ben moistened his lips, and then patted her arm reassuringly. "Don't make such a tragedy of it, darling. After all," he added brightly, "it isn't settled yet. I just wanted you to know there was that possibility."

She blinked, trying to drive back the tears which had risen, and managed a twisted grin. Her tone was playfully coaxing as she said, "You talk Bailey around if he wants to fire me." She caught his hand in both of hers and challenged him archly, "You wouldn't want to not see me every day, would you?"

"Of course not." He pulled his hand away gently, and with an encouraging smile went out to mail the letters.

It was no more than was to be expected, that she would be distressed at being torn away from daily contact with him. Deliberately Ben pulled down the opening of the mailbox and pushed his letters through. It was plain now, however, that she must be laid off. With things as they were it would be disastrous to keep Dolores on. It wouldn't take Tim long to sense something in the air. Little actions, little mannerisms that he and Dolores wouldn't notice might betray them to the eyes of another man who worked with them every day. Ben recoiled with horror from the thought of Tim Bailey's suspecting an intimacy between his new partner and the clerk.

He walked back into the shop with his eyes on the sidewalk. Had Harvey already caught and interpreted significant exchanged glances between them? The girl's expression was sometimes unguarded. She had a way of looking at him doe-eyed and fatuous.

Ben raised his head and drew a deeper breath as he passed through the entrance. Women could be a hell of a nuisance. They could be a downright menace to a man. Fleetingly he wished he'd never given in to the impulse to take Dolores.

The week went by, and he found no opportunity to be with her. He did not care particularly, was only vaguely irritated over the difficulties involved in arranging their rendezvous.

But on the following week Beth decided it was time to do something about Shirley's clothes for school; and Shirley began to tease for a shopping trip to San Francisco.

"What can you get here?" she demanded. "Everybody's seen ahead of time whatever you buy at Simmonses' or at the Betty Ann Shop. They've all handled everything and tried it on themselves."

"Well, we could run over to Coastville," Beth suggested.

"Why can't we go to the city? Everybody else does."

"It's such a trip," Beth protested. "And you can't get anything done in one day. You have to leave so early and get back so late, if you drive; and you're just dead before you get there."

The discussion had taken place at the dinner table; and Ben proposed mildly, "Why don't you make a holiday of it? Go up on the train one day in the morning, and come back the next evening; stay in a hotel and take in a show while you're there."

"But, Ben, it's so expensive," Beth objected.

Shirley, however, was all eagerness. "Oh, Mom, don't always be worrying about expenses. A person has to have some fun."

Ben let Dolores know ahead of time of his family's expected absence, but on the day of their departure Dolores informed him resignedly that she wasn't going to be able to get her own family out of the house. Once or twice Ben had gone there when Mrs. Baldwin was safely asleep in the front bedroom; but the absence of the younger sister Barbara was a necessity, even though she had her own bedroom. Sister-like, she had a way of walking into Dolores's room without knocking, bent on borrowing nail polish or costume jewelry; and a locked door would only have elicited poundings and demands to know what Dolores was doing in there in the dark.

"Mamma has one of her sick headaches," Dolores confided ruefully, "and Barbara's staying home to give herself a Toni; and she always stays awake reading till all hours."

"I was thinking," she continued tentatively, "why couldn't I come over to your house? I'll just tell the folks I'm going out; they never bother about where I'm going or when I'll be in." She smiled up at him with a fetching combination of shyness and audacity. "We could have almost a whole night together. I wouldn't have to leave till just before it begins to get light."

Ben's first reaction was one of recoil. He didn't like the idea of bringing the girl into Beth's house. But there seemed to be no alternative; so he agreed.

When she tapped gently on the patio doors after dark he admitted her, however, with an exciting upsurge of anticipation sharpened by the subtle wickedness of the situation. It had been, after all, quite a while since he had been alone with her; and he was feverishly eager as he pulled her into his arms and buried his lips on hers.

He had locked the house carefully and permitted only one light, the small lamp on the bedside table. The Venetian blinds were closed tightly; but Ben drew a sigh of relief as he turned out the bedside light when he slipped under the covers beside Dolores. Now the house looked vacant, deserted, shut tight against invasion.

He had hardly settled down, however, to a rapt and purposeful kiss enthusiastically participated in by the girl when, muffled by distance and closed doors, the telephone's ring penetrated to their seclusion. Ben withdrew his face and muttered, "Hell!"

She moved against him voluptuously, murmuring languorously, her bare arm pressing against his, which had made a motion of withdrawal. "Let it ring."

As she fastened her lips on his with clinging sweetness, he pulled his head away and muttered uneasily, "I probably ought to answer it. I forgot; Beth often calls in the evening if she's away for the night."

"If she says anything," the girl said huskily, "tell her you were out for a walk." Lingeringly she drew her parted lips against the skin of his shoulder, and slid her leg over his.

Reluctantly Ben stayed where he was, but as long as the phone continued to ring he was a passive recipient of her caresses.

Later Ben turned on the light and set the alarm clock for 3 A.M. Dolores lay back on the pillow with a sensuous, amused expression on her face, watching him.

"We might fall asleep," he explained defensively, "and find it broad daylight when we woke up."

She stirred under the covers with a lazy, writhing movement, and said in a throaty chuckle, "I'm warning you, darling; I have absolutely no intention of falling asleep tonight."

He smiled down at her over his shoulder, and twisted around to kiss the tip of her nose playfully before he switched out the light.

After he had walked to the alley above her house with her before dawn he came back and fell wearily into a heavy sleep that was shattered by the alarm clock at seven-thirty. As he lay in bed trying to fight off further sleep, his nostrils expanded at the alarming presence of a scent unfamiliar to the room; and he turned his head and pressed his nose against the pillow where Dolores had lain. It reeked of her perfume.

He sat up abruptly, running his hand distractedly through his hair. As he got out of bed he pulled his robe around him and went to the windows, jerking up the blinds and flinging the casement windows wide. He threw back the covers on the bed and inspected the sheets narrowly. Avidly his eyes swept the room for possibly forgotten signs of the girl's presence; but there seemed to be nothing.

When he had dressed and shaved he bent to sniff at the pillows now thoroughly aired by the slight breeze from the windows; but the flowery, biting scent still lingered on the linen.

He cursed under his breath, and looked about the room anxiously, moistening his lips. He didn't dare change the pillowcases and sheets. Beth would handle them anyhow when she did the laundry; and he knew that perfumes were deliberately manufactured to cling to what they touched.

His eyes strayed to the bathroom door, and abruptly he headed toward it briskly. The citronella. Sometimes they dabbed it on their skin to keep off mosquitoes when they sat in the patio in the evenings. He would tell Beth if she made any comment that a mosquito had kept him awake the night before. He sprinkled the pungent liquid around the head of the bed, and sniffed with satisfaction. The smell of that damn stuff would kill anything.

He felt listless and heavy all day at work. Not enough sleep, he told himself. And he kept remembering that telephone ring. Not that he couldn't explain it if Beth asked about it. He would say he'd been out in the garage looking for a back number of a magazine, and hadn't heard it.

Nevertheless, the awareness of nervous strain, of tension, that he carried with him all day almost wiped out the gratification left by those uninterrupted hours with Dolores.

He met the city train at eight o'clock with the car, and brought his wife and daughter home.

"What were you up to last night, Pop?" Shirley demanded gaily. "We called you about nine, and the phone rang and rang. Not stepping out on us, were you?"

"You did?" He surveyed them with surprise. "That's funny. I was home all evening. Went to bed early."

"You couldn't have been asleep at nine already, could you?" Beth said, puzzled.

"No. No, I don't think it was that early." He let his face fall into lines of sudden illumination. "I know. It must have been while I was out in the garage. Somebody mentioned an article in *The American Magazine* the other day, and I decided last night to read it. I guess it had been put out already; so I went to look for it."

"What was the article about?" Beth asked casually.

"Oh, something about Russia—how they run the government. I never did find the number it was in," he added offhandedly. "Well, how about you girls? Put a big dent in the bank roll?"

"I got the darlingest suit—" Shirley exclaimed, and chattered ebulliently the rest of the way home.

As Ben followed Beth into the bedroom carrying her overnight bag, she glanced at the unmade bed, and then stepped closer to it, sniffing.

"What in the world?"

"Oh, that smell." He sniffed innocently. "You can still smell it, can't you?

A couple of mosquitoes got in last night, and I couldn't sleep for 'em. So I thought I'd dab a little citronella around to discourage 'em. Guess I spilled a little," he finished sheepishly.

Beth chuckled indulgently. "Well, I guess you did. I'll have to change the sheets and pillowcases both. Maybe you can sleep with that stink, but I can't."

In the living room Beth stretched out in the long chair and kicked off her shoes.

"I'm dead," she announced, "just dead. I say it every time, but this time I mean it; I'll never go to the city shopping again. My poor feet."

Shirley was talking on the telephone in the hall, her voice kept low, little gurgles of laughter punctuating her share of the conversation. She had wasted no time in calling up Norman, Ben thought wryly.

He counted on Beth's fatigue to save him the effort of whipping up a semblance of passion after they went to bed; but he made the expected advances and was forbearingly resigned as Beth murmured sleepily, snuggling down on her pillow, "I'm so tired tonight, honey."

CHAPTER ELEVEN

Ben conferred with Tim the next day in his office at the shop; and it was he who brought up the question of personnel. "I figure," Ben said, "that we'd better let the girl go."

He could see Dolores talking to a customer across the building, her eyes straying anxiously at intervals to the glassed-in space where the two men sat.

Ben made a helpless gesture with one hand. "Of course I don't pay her as much as Harvey. It would be more of a saving to drop him. But he has a family and all."

"The way I look at it," Tim said, "it's handy having a man around for heavy work, loading and like that."

"I think," Ben said, "I ought to give her two weeks' extra pay."

"O.K. If you think you ought to."

Ben shrank from telling Dolores the decision had been made; but that evening before closing time he caught her alone upstairs and rather apologetically informed her that they couldn't keep her on.

She regarded him with stricken eyes.

"I can't help it," he said unhappily. "Mr. Bailey feels it's better to keep Harvey."

She swallowed once, and then burst out in a low voice, "You could have opposed him!"

He shot her a startled glance, dismayed at this show of resistance.

"There wasn't anything I could do, honey."

Her lips quivered, and suddenly her eyes gleamed angrily. "You want to get rid of me!"

While she gazed at him defiantly her face began to crumple and tears gathered in her eyes. She whirled without another word and hurried toward the door to the women's lavatory at the end of the room.

Ben was standing by the cash register later when the girl passed on her way home. He raised his eyes from the pad on which he was figuring the discount on an order. He could see that she had been crying.

"Good night," he said kindly.

She smiled feebly. "Night."

He tightened his lips impatiently as he bent his head over the pencil again.

So it was going to be troublesome. Just as he had been afraid it would be when he first became aware of his inclinations toward her. His original wariness had been right. He ought never to have succumbed to his cravings. He wasn't exactly sorry. It had been worth it in many ways. Not only the pleasure, the downright happiness he had had, but the lift to his ego, the sense of personal gratification, of satisfaction with himself. Dimly he sensed that all of it had given him strength while undergoing some kind of crisis of whose exact nature he was not clearly aware.

But the inconveniences, the risks where Beth was concerned, the tension involved in concealment. He had had enough of all that.

It would be easier after Dolores went to work somewhere else. He could let the affair dwindle off, using as an excuse the difficulties contingent upon arrangements for meeting.

He dismissed the whole thing from his mind; and a week passed without his seeing the girl except at the store. As the days went by and he made no proposals for another rendezvous he noticed a certain sulkiness growing in her manner, and at times a deliberately wistful look in her eyes, as if she were reminding him of his remissness as a lover.

In spite of himself Ben began to feel a little sorry for her. She was hurt, and he didn't like to make her feel any worse than he had to. Besides that, he did still want her. He hated to have to give her up finally. There was no use in rushing it.

On the night that Beth's lodge was to meet he proposed seeing Dolores. Her manner became instantly its usual bright, eager self at this evidence of his interest; but she approached him on the day of the lodge meeting with rueful discouragement. One of her aunts from out of town was coming to visit for a few days, arriving that afternoon. The house would be too occupied to allow Ben's stealthy approach through the rear.

"Couldn't you pick me up on a corner somewhere in your car?" she suggested hopefully.

Ben's teeth caught his lower lip thoughtfully. It was risky, but there was a renewed physical eagerness in him; so he agreed and they made the appointment.

A small shop in Coastville had written him about selling its stock as they were going out of business. He could tell Beth he was driving over to consult with the owner.

The evening had turned foggy. The puffy gray banks which had lain languidly against the skyline of the Pacific all day began to move about four o'clock and advanced with silent purposefulness until the whole coast lay cooled and subdued under their impalpable weight.

They drove toward the sea and branched off from the highway on a side road which skirted the cliffs surrounding Horseshoe Cove. Ben turned off the road onto the hard-packed earth and nosed the car toward the sea.

He felt uneasy at having his car parked in this area, well known as lovers' territory. But the night was not one to lure pleasure drivers to cruise along the ocean, and any other cars on this road would be seeking the same kind of privacy he and Dolores were. The nature of their quest would insure their putting as much distance as possible between his car and theirs.

Dolores herself added to his uneasiness though. Heretofore her manner when they were together had been always enthusiastically gay, as if she bubbled over with the excitement and pleasure of finding herself with him.

But tonight there was an intensity about her that he didn't like. She was dramatizing herself, he thought disdainfully. Her caresses were made not in the usual spirit of "What fun this is!" but in the mood of one imbued by a Grand Passion in the Hollywood tradition. If she had been old enough to have been influenced by that artist Ben would have suspected her of imitating Greta Garbo—say, in *Anna Karenina* or *Flesh and the Devil.*

He was convinced now, if he hadn't been already, that he was through. But he took her and enjoyed her.

Afterward, half reclining across him, her legs curled up on the seat, the steering wheel at her back, with her hand against his cheek she demanded huskily, "Do you love me?"

"Of course," he said with a light smile; but he was wondering how soon he could announce that it was time to start back. It was obvious that she intended to talk about Love; and he stiffened mentally. They had never mentioned it before except in the meaningless whispers accompanying the physical acts which presumably symbolized the emotion.

"I don't know how," she sighed, "I'm going to live through it, not seeing you every day after I leave the shop."

"Oh, we'll still see each other," he said easily.

"I don't think you care," she said with intentional sadness, "as much as I do. I don't mean as much to you as you do to me."

"Silly," he said indulgently, and moved his chin against her forehead, "you know I do."

She clutched at him and pulled his head down and kissed him long and desperately.

"I'll never let you go," she panted in a whisper. "I simply couldn't live again without you."

Although Ben was irritatedly conscious that she was acting the part as cheap literature and the movies had taught her it should be played, he was icily aware that the emotion which actuated her was inescapably real. She was deeply, tempestuously infatuated with him; and she was trying to force the issue.

Now, however, he was not flattered by the knowledge of his conquest. He was frightened.

In an effort to quiet her temporarily he floundered even deeper into the morass which he felt rising under his feet. If he didn't play along with her, pretend to share her sentiments, she would become even more dramatic and emotional. With horror he realized that she might even cry.

So he tried to make her feel better by murmuring with hypocritical solemnity, "Life isn't always just the way we want it to be."

"You would rather always be with me then, wouldn't you?" she demanded eagerly.

"We have to think of others. You can't go around—hurting people."

"But what about us? Why should we be hurt?"

Ben's mind squirmed under her persistence and groped futilely for another suitable, equivocal platitude.

Gradually he pacified her, combining words and caresses to steer her away from this dangerous preoccupation with the future.

Safely back in his own house, he regained some inner poise. Time was his ally, and soon greater distance and the petty obstacles to the alliance would have their weakening effect on her tenacity.

He sank into his place on the sofa with a deep breath, like a hunted thing which has escaped to its haven. His eyes followed the clean, sweeping lines of the mantel's buff-colored stone rising flush with the wall to the beamed ceiling; roved over the conservative, tasteful furniture; the soft, unmarred nap of the rug; the sand-colored plastered walls. His fingers moved on the rough surface of the dark-blue sofa, as if to reassure themselves of its substantiality.

He avoided making another date with Dolores before her last day at work, excusing himself regretfully with reminders of how busy they were preparing for the Bailey influx.

She was again becoming covertly resentful; and he attempted to neutralize her rebellion by presenting a painstaking scheme for their making contact when they no longer saw one another every day. It involved setting a time twice a week in the afternoon when he would take coffee at the drugstore and when she could wander in casually and they could make arrangements for meeting. Privately Ben intended to keep only the first two or three of these loose appointments, giving regretful reasons at each why he could not see her before the next, and finally being detained even from these meetings.

She would get mad; but she'd get over it, he thought callously. It wouldn't be long until she'd give the whole thing up as a bad job.

On the first occasion when he dropped in at the set time for a cup of coffee, he saw her sitting in one of the booths with a Coca-Cola and a cigarette, and he slid into the opposite seat with the manner of one having a casual encounter with a former employee.

She fairly glowed at sight of him, irradiated by the expectancy of the specific date they would make. But as he ruefully recounted his commitments, revealing that there was no possibility of their getting together that week, her lips fell into a mutinous pout, the glow in her eyes faded out. For the ten minutes that they sat there afterward, she was sullenly quiet.

Going back to work, Ben felt uneasily that there had been something ominous in her abrupt taciturnity.

He wished again that he had been smart and never started this thing.

But life was settling down into its new routines. He kept a certain aloofness where Tim was concerned, and with a surprising tact the latter kept out of Ben's way. Tim was often in the back room with Mike, where the worktables and shelves had been set up for the repair shop, and they were seldom together on the floor of the salesroom. They spelled one another off, Ben working up in the office or in the record department while Tim waited on customers. Tim usually had business elsewhere when Ben was on the floor. And Norman went back to Berkeley early, to arrange for his room and the part-time job he carried during the school term. So Ben no longer had to stumble over the boy every time he turned around at home.

Life was taking on a steady, monotonous pace that Ben found restful after what, in retrospect, seemed a rather feverish, unsettling summer. Sometimes, lying across from Beth where she sat with her inevitable knitting in the wing chair while he read *Time* or the *American*, he thought with a little deprecatory inward grimace, "I must be getting old. No longer care whether I have any excitement or not."

The next time he kept the drugstore appointment with Dolores he no-

ticed immediately a difference in her manner, a certain competent com-
posure that was new. She listened dispassionately to his suave, apologetic
reasons for not being able to see her in the next few days.

"I've got to see you to talk to," she asserted calmly. "Right away. I'll be
on one of the benches at the south end of the Eastside Plaza at eight tonight.
You'll just have to figure out some way to get away for half an hour or so."

The Eastside Plaza was a city block not far from Ben's home, with tennis courts at one end and lawns, trees, and graveled walks at the other. Children played there in the daytimes, and old men sat on the benches talking
together through the pleasant afternoons.

Chill warning signals flickered along Ben's nerves. He took a moment to
register the conviction that women were a deceiving entity. You went along,
accepting them as one thing, the way they showed themselves to you day
after day; and then, like with Beth, every so often you stubbed your toe on
some hard, unyielding substance in their natures, like an outcropping of
granite through the soft surface covering.

He suspected that, for his own good, he had better not resist this coldly
calculating mood. Whatever the girl was up to, he had better meet her and
have it out, once and for all.

After dinner he said vaguely, "I think I'll straighten up some of that mess
in the back of the garage after a while. Get some of those magazines ready
for the Goodwill."

Shirley had gone to Ginny's on some vague purpose having to do with
the clothes they were going to wear to school the first day, and at ten minutes to eight the telephone rang.

"Oh, Lucille," Beth cried effusively into the mouthpiece. Through the
archway into the hall Ben saw her sink onto the small chair beside the
phone table and lean on her elbow. "I was just thinking about you. I haven't
seen you for ages. What's new?"

Ben drew a relieved breath. It was going to be one of those things. They
should be good for at least half an hour. He gathered up an armful of *Life*
magazines from the shelf under the end table, picked up his jacket from
the chair back where he had thrown it, and slipped quietly out the patio
doors. When Beth stopped talking she would remember his remark about
straightening up in the garage and would go about her business, thinking
he was there. He went in through the side door of the garage, switched on
the single globe in the rear so that she would see a light in the back side
window of the building if she looked out, and, dumping the magazines on
a box, he hurried through the alley door, slipping into his coat as he went.

If Beth did wander out to see what he was doing, he would explain his
absence by saying he had run over to the Morrisons' or Smiths' to see if
they wanted some back numbers of the magazines before he tied them up

for the Goodwill people.

It should take him less than five minutes each way from the Plaza. The only risk lay in being seen en route. But it was another cool, foggy evening, the fog this time lower and damper than it had been the night he took Dolores for the drive. No one would be out for a pleasure stroll, and it was fairly dark between the corner street lights.

Dolores rose from a bench facing the entrance path, a long, loose coat buttoned under her chin, a kerchief tied over her hair.

Ben took her arm, and with a furtive glance around, said, "Let's get back off the path." They stepped onto the grass and found a bench secluded in a corner made by the privet hedge and an oleander bush. Before they sat down Dolores flung her arms around his neck and kissed him passionately, straining against him. He returned her embrace dutifully, and with his hand on her arm guided her to the seat.

She unbuttoned her coat at the neck and flung it back a little, nestling in the curve of his arm.

"It's been such *ages*," she murmured with a little pleasurable moan.

He brushed her cheek with his lips and said, "I haven't much time, darling. What is it that's so urgent?"

She drew away a little, her eyes shining out of the white oval blur of her face in the darkness.

"Ben, this can't go on. We've got to do something, decide what we're going to do. We can't just keep drifting like this." Her voice was soft, persuasive, wheedling, with seductive undertones.

"But what is there to do?" he murmured, trying to keep the impatience out of his tone.

"I know," she said, "it's going to be difficult, but you do love me, more than anything, don't you?"

In the covering darkness Ben set his teeth. "Well, of course I'm very fond of you."

He could not see her expression well enough to read it accurately, but her face seemed stiff, disturbingly still.

Suddenly she bowed her head and put her hands over her face. In a moment, muffled through her fingers, her words came pitifully, "I'm going to have a baby."

It was almost funny, Ben mused with a strange detachment. He wanted to utter a dry, harsh laugh. There was something so familiar about everything: the girl, the way she sounded, the grass underfoot, the dark mounds of shrubbery, the way he felt. Not, the way people said, as if you had experienced the same thing before. But its familiarity, as if you had known all along what was going to happen.

He found himself speaking practically, flatly. "You're sure?"

"Of course I am,"

His tone was clear-cut with anger. "I thought you took precautions."

"I did," she said on a sobbing breath. "But, you know—it isn't always sure. Accidents can happen."

Ben looked down at her with cool, silent clarity. She had done it deliberately, probably that last night in the car, thinking to trap him. He felt a cutting contempt. She had it all figured out; and her next breathless rush of words confirmed his suspicions.

"I can go away—to Los Angeles or somewhere—until it's over and you have your divorce, and then you can come to where I am and we'll get married quietly before we come back here. People will talk; but they forget those things in time."

She reached out and clasped his hands feverishly. "And afterwards—oh, darling, we'll be so happy—for always."

Ben gazed down at her incredulously, unmoving. She had really thought all that, thought he was that far out of his mind about her.

"It's impossible," he said shortly. "You'll just have to get rid of it. I'll pay for it, of course," he added bitterly. "You can go to San Francisco. There're doctors there will handle it."

Slowly she pulled her hands away. "I won't," she muttered, a hysterical note coming into her voice. "It's your child, and I want it. I thought you loved me," she finished with an accusing break in her voice.

"That has nothing to do with it. I can't break up my whole life over a thing like this."

"What about me?" she gasped. "What about my life? I won't give you up," she cried on a rising, hysterical inflection.

He grasped her arm roughly. "For God's sake, keep your voice down."

She was getting out of control, and she continued wildly, "You're just afraid—afraid to face your wife. You want me; I know you do. You'd rather have me than her. I'll go to her, I'll go to her myself—"

"Will you shut up?" he demanded hoarsely.

"I'll tell her. You'll see; she'll give you up of her own accord, when she knows. It'll be simple, really. You'll see. You have to have courage," She was babbling now, desperately, incoherently. "It can all be handled in a civilized way. She won't want to keep you when she knows you love somebody else—"

In a detached way Ben realized that for several minutes he hadn't been what you could call thinking; he was just moving along in an inexorable series of developments both objective and subjective. Dispassionately it occurred to him that if she knew what was good for her she would quit talking. But she kept on, and he reacted almost automatically, somehow suspended—apart from himself. It was not like a repetition. It was an odd sense of following a path so familiar that habit carried him along, habit so strong that only a tremendous effort of will could have made him change his responses.

Impersonally and with seeming irrelevance he recalled his original disinclination to get mixed up with the girl at all, taking note, in passing as it were, that his original misgivings were being confirmed. The mouse had known it was not to be trusted when it allowed itself to be the man that its meek gray vestures concealed.

Distantly, almost wistfully, he was conscious of wishing she would stop talking.

But she went on, pleading, accusing, even goading him a little, as if by argument she could bring him to her way of thinking. And her voice kept going up dangerously.

He had to keep her quiet.

He put out his hands and they closed on her throat.

CHAPTER TWELVE

When he was back in the garage Ben looked at his watch. Eight twenty-five. He had been away no more than half an hour. He switched out the garage light, and walked swiftly into the house. As he opened the patio doors he could hear the murmur of Beth's voice in the hall.

His lips twisted in a cynical smile. He went into the bedroom and took off his jacket and hung it over the back of a chair. He looked at his hands, and, remembering the scent on the pillows, raised them and smelled of the palms. He couldn't smell anything, but it wouldn't hurt to wash them.

When he came out of the bedroom Beth was entering the living room at the other door.

"That Lucille," she chuckled. "Just can't get away from her on the phone. I'll bet we talked for twenty minutes."

"Only about fifteen, I should say," Ben reassured her with a smile. He glanced at the fireplace. "How about a little fire? It's sort of cool tonight."

As he arranged the kindling and laid on a pair of small logs he thought rather abstractedly that he wasn't jittery this time. The same sort of deep, numb feeling though.

Jim Billings was dictating a letter to his stenographer the next morning when Walt Gordon, who ran the barbershop next door, came hustling past the window and opened the front door which had been closed against the morning air that at ten o'clock was still sunless and damp from the night's fog.

"Hey, Jim," Walt called as he strode past Edith's desk. "Heard the news? They found Dolores Baldwin murdered out in Eastside Plaza."

Jim had been leaning back in his swivel chair, his ankles crossed and his feet resting on a half-open desk drawer. Slowly he let his weight forward until the chair came upright, and lowered his feet to the floor. Edith's eyes were fixed on Walt, her lips slightly parted.

The barber lifted the side of his white coat and put one hand in his pants pocket, dropping to the desk top on one leg.

"Found her about an hour ago," he elaborated. "Bill McGovern just dropped into the shop an' told me. They took her to the undertakin' parlors. Choked to death, they say."

"Why," Edith breathed, "I just talked to her in Simmonses' yesterday noon." She looked from one to another of the men, as if defying the veracity of Walt's information. "Why, I've known her all my life."

"Guess we all have," Walt agreed. "Terrible thing. Happenin' right here in Los Alegres. Makes you wonder." He met their eyes accusingly. "Gives you a feeling the town ain't safe."

"What else did Bill say?" Jim asked heavily.

"Nothin'. That's all he knew. Fred Colton's busy investigatin' a-course, and they got the coroner over from Coastville. Got 'em jumpin' around like cats on a hot stove down to the city hall."

"I wonder who did it," Edith said fearfully.

Walt reached for his cigarettes in the breast pocket of his coat. "That's somepin else again. Remember that Bailey case, Jim, back when you was chief? Kinda resembles it, some ways. Bill says the girl's folks never even missed her; she ain't workin' now and they just thought she was sleepin' late. Same thing with the Bailey girl, remember? Only difference is, it wasn't kids found Dolores. Clem Burroughs found her. He was out there to start cuttin' the lawn this morning."

Jim was looking at Walt silently; and the latter stood up, his cigarette in his fingers. "Well, gotta get back. Left Joe alone in the shop. Wa'n't no customers, but you can't tell. Seems's if every time a man steps out for five minutes half the town makes up its mind to get shaved. Thought you folks'd like to know though."

Jim nodded slowly. "Sure. Thanks, Walt." As the barber made his way out Jim made a dismissing motion with his hand. "We'll finish that letter later, Edith."

She closed her notebook and, murmuring shocked phrases, retired to her desk in front.

Jim pulled out his pipe and filled it. He remembered Dolores Baldwin in braids and barefoot sandals, running up Main Street in a sunsuit over a skinny little chest, two front teeth out and knobby knees. They grew up so fast—made a man feel old.

But what could he have done? He hadn't had a scrap of evidence. All his questions—even bullying—had elicited only blank, innocent, and finally aggrieved stares. And, in the position of officer of the law, you couldn't go around blabbing about something that was only your hunch, especially when no one shared your suspicions, not even the men from the sheriff's office. They had even insisted there was less against Ben than there was against half a dozen others.

No one, that is, but that fellow from Chicago. A smart customer that. To get onto it twenty years later. But Malley hadn't blamed him. He knew how it was.

But now it was different. Too late. But different. The pattern repeated. And again a tie-up with Ben Sterling, the girl having worked for him for a year.

Jim's craggy brows drew closer over his eyes. He wasn't what you would call chummy with Fred Colton. Colton probably wouldn't appreciate hearing the inside dope on what Billings had really thought twenty years ago. And if the case ran true to form, again there would probably be no evidence.

But he had no choice but to go and talk to Colton.

As Jim paused in the doorway to his office, his eyes turned toward the corner up the street, resting on the sign extending out over the sidewalk, "Sterling and Bailey, Radio and Music."

The news which was licking up and down the street like a prairie fire had just penetrated the shop behind that sign.

Harvey stood talking excitedly to a knot of people just inside the door. Ben had retreated to the cash register with an appropriately saddened face. As he stood there Tim came out of the back room and plodded forward, wiping his hands on a soiled white rag, his face set and lowering.

"Heard the news?" he asked Ben grimly.

Ben nodded. "I can't believe it."

Tim dropped the rag on the counter, and Ben's eyes rested on the fist clenched on the cloth.

"It brings it all back," Tim said thickly. "Inez."

Ben raised his eyes as if surprised. "It is," he said, as if appalled, "something the same."

Tim turned his eyes on Ben, and they were cold and deadly. "That's past," he said. "I couldn't never do anything about it. But if I knew who the bastard was that did this, I'd tear him apart with my bare hands."

He turned his head and glowered toward the front windows, breathing heavily. After a moment he said in a more controlled tone, "She was a good kid."

Ben's hands were gripping the sides of the cash register. "Yes," he said with difficulty. "Yes, she was. I've felt—sick"—the words came out in a low-toned rush—"ever since I heard."

Tim turned his eyes toward his partner, and his expression softened slightly. "Yeah. You look it," he said dispassionately. He glanced toward the front of the store. "I guess it's worse for you an' Harvey, workin' right along with her all this time."

Ben lowered his head and rested his forehead on the top of the register. He hadn't been lying when he said he felt sick. The feeling of weakness, of vertigo had hit him as he listened to Tim. He must not seem to be hit too hard by the news; but still it was safe enough to show this much feeling. It was natural for a man to be horrified and almost nauseated at the news of a former employee's violent death.

He raised his head after a moment and said with an attempt at briskness, "Well, I suppose I'd better get to work. But I don't mind telling you this knocked me all in a heap." He fumbled for his cigarettes. "Having a daughter of your own, it kind of scares you."

"Yeah," Tim muttered glumly, "I know how you feel."

As Jim Billings walked south toward the Civic Center he argued with himself gloomily. What did he have to say to Fred Colton, after all? That a girl had been murdered in a similar way twenty years ago; that Ben Sterling had known her, lived in the same neighborhood, gone out with her occasionally when they were both in high school. That Ben had also known Dolores well; that she had worked for him up till two or three weeks ago. And Fred Colton would say, "So what? Everybody in town knew both girls." And you couldn't tell your successor as police chief that you knew because you had a feeling, and because a big man from a city police force had got the same feeling just from being around the man when the case came up in conversation.

Jim plunged his fists into his pants pockets, and walked on doggedly. He'd just have to try to explain why he felt so sure, whether it went over or not. He'd never feel right if he didn't try.

As he mounted the broad cement steps with the big, round white globes on pedestals at either side of the flight—the steps that had once been so familiar to him—he thought impatiently, too, that Fred was undoubtedly not in this morning. He would be busy on the case. He ought to have phoned before he came down.

But Jim tramped down the hall with its brown linoleum, its darkened mustard-colored walls, and opened one of the heavy brown double doors which had "Los Alegres Police Department" painted across them at eye level.

He spoke to the young man in a tailored, dark-blue serge shirt and black tie who stood back of the railing which shut off straight wooden benches set against the corridor wall.

"The chief in?"

"Not right now. Can I help you, Jim?"

"No, I wanted to speak to Colton."

"Better make an appointment. He's very busy today," the young man concluded importantly.

At that moment an outside door across the room opened, and Colton came in alone, wearing his jacket with the badge, and his official, visored cap.

As the young officer turned around to see who it was, Colton lifted his hand curtly in greeting to the two men.

"Morning, Fred," Jim said. "Got a minute? There's somepin I want to take up with you."

"Can it wait, Billings? I've got to go out right away again. Got Granger outside in the car waiting."

"It won't take long. And it's on this case. I heard about the Baldwin girl, and there's something I think you should know."

"Oh. In that case, come in."

Jim pushed open the swinging gate and followed Colton through the door with a frosted glass pane lettered "Chief of Police."

Colton nodded to a chair. "Sit down." He took a cigar from the humidor on his desk and stood as he lighted it, still wearing his cap. "Well?"

Jim wished fleetingly that he hadn't come; but he turned his hat in his hands and stolidly said his piece: the likeness between the two murders, Ben Sterling's connection with each of the girls, the suspicions he had harbored before but had been unable to bring to any conclusion.

Colton had taken the chair behind his desk, and he watched Jim intently as the latter talked.

He leaned forward when Billings had finished. "What made you suspect Sterling then?"

Jim frowned. "Nothing you could put your finger on." He narrowed his eyes, recalling the past. "You know how it is sometimes; you get a feeling there's something wrong with a suspect's attitude. That's all it was. He was too calm, too innocent appearing when you questioned him. The others— they were all scared, upset, excited. Some of 'em blustered, some of 'em whined, some of 'em were too glib, showing you how they couldn't possibly of done it. But Ben, he was quiet, in perfect control, always polite— " He broke off. "Don't sound reasonable, does it," he grunted, "gettin' the wind up because a man don't act the way you expect 'em to when they're guilty? But that's the way it was. Somepin just seemed to tell me he done it. I never mentioned the way I felt except to the other men workin' on the case; and they just laughed at me. But when I heard about Dolores this morning, I decided, laugh at me or no, I was goin' to tell you how Sterling came right into my mind again."

He lifted his eyes sternly. "I'm countin' on you, Fred, to keep this conversation strictly under your hat. I don't want no trouble with Sterling; and if he ain't mixed up in it any way, I don't want him to ever find out what I been thinkin'."

"Of course not." Colton drew on his cigar, and with an abstracted gaze regarded the wall at the side of and behind Jim's chair. He held the cigar off, and let his eyes rest on Jim again. "I'll tell you frankly, Billings, if you'd come to me with this vague story about 'suspicions' an hour ago, I'd of thought you were a little cracked on the subject, just didn't like Sterling for some reason of your own, and so—wishful thinking like—had got it fixed in your mind he was a murderer."

He put the cigar down carefully. "But something came up this morning that puts a different face on things." He regarded Jim seriously and reached into his coat for the inside pocket. "I appreciate your motives in coming to me, and I guess you've proved you're a man that knows how to keep his mouth shut, keeping quiet all these years when you didn't have nothing to back up what you were thinking. So I'm going to let you in on something. For the present, it's not to get past these walls."

He pulled out a thick, red-covered book with a leather band locking the covers together by means of a tiny gold padlock. The word "Diary," written slantwise in Spenserian style, was stamped in gold across the leather binding.

"We searched the girl's room after we found her, and I found this in her desk. The key was on her key ring in the purse lying beside the body."

Jim was leaning forward tensely, and his eyes were bright and excited as they went from the book to Colton's face.

"She was careful," Colton said dryly. "Just used the initial 'B' when she spoke of the man she was having an affair with. I haven't had time to do more than glance over it, but you don't have to be much of a detective to figure out it was Sterling—references to things that happened at the store, for instance. Can't tell till I study it more carefully whether it'll even prove Sterling was the man, having only the initial to go on. But it shows there was trouble brewing. She was pretty broken up about losing her job, afraid he was going to break off with her. And just from what I had a chance to read, you could tell the girl was dead serious, meant to break up his home and get him for herself."

Jim let his weight back in the chair. "Of course that doesn't prove murder," he muttered.

Colton picked up the book and shoved it into his pocket resolutely. "No," he said grimly, "but it helps. It helps. I'm going out to his house now to talk to the womenfolks, checking on alibis."

Jim stood up abruptly. "Well, don't let me keep you. And good luck, Fred."

"Thanks, Jim. And I appreciate your coming around."

Billings paused briefly in the doorway, and his heavy face moved in a sardonic smile. "For once, I'm tellin' you, Fred, it won't make me mad to see another man succeed where I failed."

CHAPTER THIRTEEN

Beth and Shirley were working together in the living room when the police car pulled up in front of the house. The vacuum cleaner was running, with Shirley in jeans rolled to her knees pushing it over the rug. Beth, her hair covered by a silk scarf wound turban fashion over pin curls, was straightening up—emptying ash trays, gathering up newspapers, plumping cushions. They did not try to talk over the noise of the sweeper. Lucille Merritt had phoned them the news of the murder an hour before. Clarence at the city hall had heard it early.

Beth had gasped when Lucille told her, and felt the blood running out of her face. She placed both elbows on the telephone table, as if to brace herself while they discussed the news in horrified tones. When she laid the phone carefully in its cradle after Lucille hung up, she was trembling.

She sat still, her eyes open but looking at nothing. Choked to death, beside a flowering shrub—oleander this time. Disconnectedly it ran through her mind, Mrs. Malley sitting in the corner of the sofa and observing brightly, "*An American Tragedy* sort of thing."

Beth's fingers moved aimlessly on the smooth table top, and were still as she remembered that she and Ben had been safely at home together all evening.

She drew a long breath, and stood up.

Usually, when anything important or out of the way happened, she called Ben up at the shop to tell him about it or talk it over; but it did not occur to her to call him now.

Shirley was coming down the stairway. Beth stood in the archway and rested the palm of her hand against the casing as she told the girl what had happened.

While Shirley responded with low, shocked exclamations Beth moved across to a straight chair against the wall and sat down heavily.

"All I know," she said irritatedly as Shirley began to bombard her with questions, "is what Lucille told me."

Shirley paused in the midst of her excitement and looked at her mother closely. "Mother, you look so funny." She hesitated. "As if you'd had a terrible shock."

Beth's eyes rested on her daughter vaguely.

"Of course, it is awful," Shirley went on. "I can hardly believe it." She shuddered, then glanced at her mother again, and impulsively came forward and touched the woman's shoulder sympathetically. "But it isn't as if we really knew her so terribly well. And you look so pale and sort of dazed. Anyone would think something had happened to me or Pop, the way you look. What makes you take it so hard, Mom?"

"I don't know," Beth said dully. "I don't know. But, like you said, it was a shock—a terrible shock."

She shook her head slightly and stood up. "Well, we must get on with the work."

Later, when she saw Fred Colton and Barney Granger on her front stoop, Beth's eyes widened. As she led them into the living room Shirley turned off the cleaner and stood holding the wand, staring in astonishment.

"I'm afraid you've caught us in rather a mess," Beth apologized. "Cleaning, you know. I guess you can find a place to sit down though."

Barney perched uneasily on the davenport and jerked his head with a rather sheepish grin at Shirley. Colton took the straight-backed occasional chair facing the front end of the room, and Beth sat in the big armchair, pushing the footstool away with her knees so that her feet rested on the floor. Shirley came slowly and sat on the arm of her mother's chair, her elbow resting on the back.

Colton told them seriously that he was making routine checkups on the movements during the previous evening of everyone who had known Dolores Baldwin.

"You've heard, I suppose," he said, "what happened to her."

"Yes. And it's terrible." Beth twisted her hands together in her lap. "We—we couldn't believe it."

"Well, her having worked in your husband's shop, we thought you folks might be able to throw a little light on her activities and her associates."

"I just knew her casually," Beth said doubtfully, "from seeing her at the shop and so on. We hardly met socially at all." She glanced at her daughter. "And she went with an older crowd than Shirley did; so we knew very little about her private life."

"Well, the main thing"—he smiled at the two women ingratiatingly—"you needn't feel upset about it. It's just something we have to do—in order to be absolutely sure. But the main thing we want to find out is just where everybody that knew her was and what they were doing last night."

Beth smiled and leaned back in her chair, relaxing a little. "Alibis?" she said brightly. "Well, thank heaven, we're all accounted for. Shirley, you tell him what you did last night."

Somewhat disdainfully Shirley obeyed. She had gone from home sometime between seven and seven-thirty—she didn't know the exact minute—over to her girl friend Ginny White's, and they had gone to the movies and come straight home afterward. Ginny walked this way with her and left her at the front steps and went on alone. It was probably about eleven-thirty by then.

Colton nodded at her with an approving smile, and turned casually toward Beth. "And now," he said lightly, "you. Let's take it from the time your daughter left the house."

"There really isn't anything to tell, Mr. Colton. My husband and I just stayed home like a couple of old fogies and went to bed after the ten-o'-clock news."

Colton smiled genially. "Oh now, Mrs. Sterling, you two aren't such old fogies." His expression became apologetically serious. "I know I must seem pretty nosy, but that's the way we have to be in this work. We have to be awful fussy and exact. Now, you and Mr. Sterling were here all evening. Let's go over it step by step: what you heard outside in the way of traffic or unusual noises, if anybody came to the door or called on the phone, what rooms you were in."

Beth was regarding him with wary eyes. "I can't see how all that has anything to do with it."

Colton looked mysterious and professional. "That's the way our work is, Mrs. Sterling. All kinds of little details. We collect 'em from everybody, and when we get through and put 'em all together, some little old insignificant thing may mean something."

Shirley was eying him with open skepticism, and Beth looked unconvinced, but she sighed resignedly, then brightened. "I see. What we know or heard or something might throw light on what somebody else knows."

"That's it exactly." Colton beamed at her.

"Well, it seems sort of silly," she said with a reproachful chuckle, "but here goes." She frowned seriously. "Let's see. I was in the kitchen putting water in the ice trays when Shirley went out; she called good-by through the door. Then I went through the living room to our bedroom over there." She inclined her head toward the door beyond the staircase.

Colton had unobtrusively taken out a small loose-leaf notebook, and as she went on he jotted down a word or two from time to time.

"Ben was lying on the sofa there reading the paper. I went to the bathroom and combed my hair and put on fresh powder," she recited conscientiously, "before I came out. And then when I came back in here I picked up the San Francisco *News* off the coffee table, and looked at the radio log. I remember I said to Ben, 'I wonder if there's anything good on the air tonight.' And he said no, just crime stories, and there wasn't even a good television show. I'd been standing up, and I sat in that chair you're sitting in, Mr. Colton, and we talked a few minutes. Then I decided I'd work on the petit-point seat cover I've started, and I went back to the bedroom to get it. I settled down in the wing chair then, and Ben got up and went in the kitchen for a drink of water. He said something about straightening up the magazines in the garage, getting them ready for the Goodwill truck; but he came in and began to look through the record albums. I remember he asked if I'd like some music while I worked. And—and—" She paused and thought. "Yes, it was about then the phone rang. It was Mrs. Merritt—Mrs. Clarence Merritt, you know."

"And what time was that?"

"I really couldn't say." She pursed her lips, concentrating. "It must have been about eight-fifteen or eight-twenty though. Because I remember when I came back in the living room after we hung up I glanced at the clock, and it was eight-thirty. Ben was coming out of the bedroom, and I mentioned—just joking, of course—how you couldn't get away from Lucille on the phone, and we must have talked half an hour. And he said no, it was only ten or fifteen minutes. Well, then Ben laid a fire, and we sat down again, him on the sofa and me in the wing chair, and neither one of us budged until he turned on the news at ten and we went in the bedroom at ten-fifteen. We just undressed then, and were in bed by ten-thirty. And—I guess that's all."

"Thank you. Thank you very much, Mrs. Sterling. If everybody was as co-operative as you are, our job would be a lot easier."

He had noticed the telephone table in the hall as they came in, and as Beth talked his eyes had estimated its position in relation to the archway into the living room. From where he sat the telephone was out of sight; and he judged that only the far end of the room near the dining room could be seen by a person sitting at the table talking.

"Will you excuse me just a moment, Mrs. Sterling? I'd like to use the phone a moment."

As he rose he jerked his head toward Barney, who followed him into the front hall.

Out of sight of the women, he spoke in a low, quick voice to the other man: "Get over to Merritts' and keep talking to Lucille until I get there. I'll give you time to make it, and then I'll walk over. See that she doesn't answer the phone till I come. Flash your badge if necessary to keep her away from it."

"O.K." And Barney hurried out the door.

Colton picked up the telephone and called his office. He spoke in a low voice, holding his hand around his lips and the mouthpiece. "Send Charlie down to Sterling's shop, and bring Ben down to the office, and keep him there till I get there.... I don't care how the hell you get him to come. Just get him."

He came back into the living room with an affable smile, and began to thank Beth for her time and trouble, chatting along sociably, playing the part of the lingering guest as she ushered him down the hall. On the steps he let his attention be attracted to a camellia plant by the walk, and admitted ruefully that he and his wife just didn't have luck with camellias.

When he was sure Barney had had time to get inside at the Merritts', he took his leave briskly and hurried off up the street.

Beth watched him with a small uneasy wrinkling of her forehead. Shirley had come to stand behind her mother, looking over her shoulder.

With her hands on her hips, Shirley snorted scornfully: "Efficiency in the Los Alegres Police Department! Taking all this time to find out how you and Pop spent the evening. And here there's a murderer running loose, probably hundreds of miles away by now!"

Beth turned and snapped at the girl, "Shut up. It's not for you to criticize your elders."

Shirley took a step backward in amazement, her hands falling to her sides.

The girl's movement seemed to bring Beth back from somewhere; and she was startled at her own sudden eruption at the girl. But Beth only looked at her daughter flatly for an instant, then closed the door and walked back down the hall. "Come on, let's finish this living room," she said tonelessly.

She felt awfully queer. Troubled. It was natural, of course, with people being murdered all over the place. She did not pause to notice that she had lumped the Bailey murder in with this one, as if both had happened recently. It did not concern her or her family. All of them were accounted for at the time of the murder. Nevertheless, she was aware of a strange, heavy tension, as if her mind were pushing down hard against something.

Lucille was giving Barney a cup of coffee in the living room when Colton arrived there. The two of them were chatting like the old acquaintances they were, expressing horror over Dolores's fate.

"Barney said you were going to drop in, Fred," she told Colton as she admitted him, "so I brought out another cup." She indicated the glass pot set on a tile mat on the coffee table. "Will you have some coffee with us?"

"That'll go good, Lucille," he said with a smile.

As she handed him the cup Lucille said curiously, "Although what you're coming around here for I can't imagine. I know absolutely nothing about this horrible affair."

"I'm being thorough, that's all," Fred replied calmly. "Before we get through we'll know exactly where everybody in this town was last night."

"Well, that's an easy one in this case. Clarence and I were home all evening, alone, except that Linda White ran in about eight-thirty for a few minutes. I remember the time, because I had just finished talking to Beth Sterling on the phone." She nodded to the phone on the desk in the corner. "And that husband of mine, he was sitting there where you're sitting, Fred, and when I hung up he looked at his watch and said, 'Do you know how long you and Beth talked? I timed you, just for fun, and it was exactly forty-one and a half minutes.'" She grinned. "And then he made some crude remarks about women talking so much and never saying anything. So at least we're alibied from about ten to eight till nine, because Linda stayed about half an hour. After that all you've got is our word that one of us wasn't out playfully strangling young girls in the park."

Fred had made a notation in his notebook, and he glanced at Barney to see if the other had caught the implications of Lucille's remarks. Barney met his eyes intelligently, and Fred was satisfied.

"May I use your phone, Lucille?"

"Sure, help yourself."

Again Fred called his office. "Bill, run across the hall to Clarence Merritt's office and check on this—in front of a witness. One of the girls in Clarence's office will do." He repeated Lucille's story of the phone call and the time.

When he came back to his chair she was regarding him thoughtfully. "Have I done or said something wrong?"

"No. Something right. It all fits nicely."

She sighed. "Well, at least I guess I haven't talked out of turn and incriminated anybody. At least I've alibied me and Clarence and Beth and Ben. She said he was home too while we talked. Who are you trying to trip up with all this checking on phone calls?"

"Now, now," Colton chided genially, "mustn't try to pry secrets out of the Law."

"It's too bad, if this had to happen, it didn't happen while Roy was here. Not that I don't think you boys can handle it, but even if he is my own brother I will say Roy is a whiz at this sort of thing."

"I'm sure he'd be a big help," Colton said without enthusiasm, "but we'll bumble along the best we can."

As they were leaving the house Lucille said, "Well, I hope this time you catch the beast. Did it occur to you, Fred, how much like the Inez Bailey killing this is?"

"Yeah, it occurred to me."

CHAPTER FOURTEEN

Fred Colton's mind pulsed with elated excitement as they crossed town in the car. But he was silent, thinking carefully.

When he came into the outer office he raised his eyebrows at Bill, who said, "Sterling's across the hall with Charlie."

"You speak to Clarence Merritt like I told you?"

"Yep. He verified it just the way you told it. Said he's always teasing his wife about women gabbling over nothing on the phone; so just for fun last night he timed her. She always swears she never talks more'n ten or fifteen minutes to a time; so Clarence said he checked up on her, and she wouldn't hardly believe it. He said it was Mrs. Sterling she talked to. He listened off and on to the conversation while he read the paper."

Fred ran the tips of his fingers along his cheek, and picked up the telephone on the desk. Harvey, at the Sterling shop, answered the phone.

"Is Tim Bailey there?"

"Yes."

"May I speak to him? Fred Colton calling."

"Oh—of course. Of course, Mr. Colton."

When he heard Tim's voice Fred said, "Can you come down to my office right away? I'm going to have an interview that I'd like you to sit in on."

"Why—why, sure, Fred. Anything wrong?"

"No. Just have some things I'd like you to hear."

As he set the telephone down the police chief moved the tip of his tongue over his teeth, making a circuit of his mouth under the lips. Then with an air of decision he lifted the instrument again.

"Jim?" he said when a voice came over the wire. "Fred Colton. Got something kind of interesting coming up. Just thought—in view of everything—it'd be something you'd like to watch. Can you get over here to my office right away?"

Within ten minutes the little group was gathered around the golden-oak table in the mayor's conference room across the hall from the police offices.

Ben had expected to be questioned. He had, of course, been the girl's employer for over a year, would be expected to know something about her life. He was a little surprised at being brought to the city hall for the interview, but he had only the rigidly suppressed uneasiness that was to be expected in his situation. He was not specifically afraid of having to meet an accusation.

He kept up a desultory conversation with Charlie Jones, who seemed to be appointed to keep him company until Fred Colton showed up. When

Fred walked into the conference room with its cool north windows facing the street and Ben saw Tim accompanying him, even then he was not sharply alarmed. His defenses only braced themselves more rigidly.

The first stirrings of panic began when Jim Billings knocked and entered a few minutes later. Faintly Ben smelled a rat. His eyes swept quickly over the gathering. Tim wore an air of puzzled expectancy, and so, it seemed to him, did Charlie Jones, seated opposite Colton at the end of the table. Jim Billings looked watchful in a stolid way. Only Colton's manner was completely inexpressive, which, to Ben, indicated that the police chief knew perfectly what he was about.

Ben maintained a grave, concerned mien, as one who has come together on an equal footing with others to "get to the bottom" of a troublesome matter.

"I don't need to tell you why we're here," Colton began impassively. "It's in connection with Dolores Baldwin's murder. We've heard from the coroner's office that she died from strangulation sometime between eight and nine o'clock last night—could be ten or fifteen minutes either way from those times. Her family testify she ate dinner about six-thirty, and the contents of her stomach indicate closer to eight-thirty than otherwise as the time of her death. Now we've been doing a little checking up, and I find—"

He turned a level gaze upon Ben.

"—that your movements, Mr. Sterling, are unaccounted for from approximately seven-fifty to eight-thirty."

Ben stared back at him in unfeigned astonishment. "Why, I never left my own home last night," he exclaimed, "from the time I came in at six-thirty until I left this morning at eight forty-five."

"I have only your word for that."

"My wife can bear me out. We were together every minute."

"Didn't your wife have a phone call last evening?"

Ben's still astonished, uncomprehending manner did not betray the icy pricklings of wariness which traveled through his viscera. He frowned slightly, as one trying to recall a bit of trivia.

"Why—yes. Now that you mention it, I believe she did have a call—Mrs. Merritt." He seemed to be recollecting with difficulty. "A little after eight, I believe."

Colton pulled out his little black notebook and consulted it for effect. He knew to the letter what was written there. "The call was from Mrs. Clarence Merritt, and by the testimony of both her and her husband it lasted from exactly eleven minutes to eight until eight-thirty and a half."

Ben's face seemed frozen into the lines it had held when Colton produced the notebook. Who would have dreamed the Merritts would time a phone call?

"I can't see," he said with a stiff, rather reproachful laugh, "what that has to do with it. I was there in the living room all the time they talked."

He was thinking frantically, remembering the light in the garage. But the window which showed the light was on the Morrisons' side, and the privet hedges hid it from their house. Only from his own patio windows could it have been seen. He had decided to skip the magazine-Goodwill story; for Beth didn't know he had left the house while she talked to Lucille.

"To all intents and purposes you have no alibi for those forty minutes. Your wife at the phone table could see only a few feet of the living room area at the west end of the room."

Ben released an exasperated sigh. "Fred, do you seriously think that I would be crazy enough to try to run over to the Eastside Plaza, commit a murder and run back, and expect my wife not to know I'd left the house?"

Fred pursed his lips a little. "Well, you could have had an excuse ready in case it was needed. Mrs. Sterling mentioned you said earlier in the evening you might do some work in the garage later on. If she had come into the living room and you weren't there, she'd have assumed that's where you were and thought nothing of it."

Everything inside Ben's carefully normal exterior felt paralyzed. But he kept his outward aplomb.

"Ridiculous!" he sniffed. And glanced around at the other men as though to elicit their concurrence in his disdain of this farfetched reasoning.

Tim, his eyes going from the police chief to Ben, was listening with anxious concentration. Billings was scrutinizing Ben measuringly, drumming his fingers slowly on the table, and Charlie Jones was alternating glances of respectful amazement at his boss with ones of incredulous amazement at Ben.

"I don't know what you're trying to pull, Colton," Ben stated with dignity. "This sort of reasoning would get you nowhere in court. And"—he drew himself up a little straighter in his chair, concluding with an air of injured innocence—"if this sort of thing keeps up, I'll feel compelled to get in touch with Tracy Whitlock, my lawyer. I don't believe you have a right to cast aspersions on my character like this in the presence of my friends."

"Oh, I got reasons," Colton responded equably. He reached into his pocket and slowly drew out Dolores's diary. Every eye about the table fastened on it intently. "The first thing we look for in cases like this," he proceeded philosophically, "is motive. And this little book—the girl's diary," he explained to the others generously, "gives us a dandy—against you, Mr. Sterling."

Ben's face had gone a peculiar grayish white. He could not tear his eyes from the fancy script on the red cover. Who would have dreamed she kept a diary?

Inner resources of strength came surging up from somewhere inside him. He would not have thought he had such powers of adjustment, of self-control. As he realized swiftly that there was no hope now for his reputation, that his marriage itself was almost certainly threatened with destruction by the girl's written voice, he estimated the problem that faced him. His life. Regardless of all other losses a man will fight to the last for his life. And he felt a sudden inrush of unexpected strength at the knowledge that in spite of the book, in spite of the tenuousness of his alibi, they could never prove he had killed her.

In the deathly quiet which had fallen inside the room after the police chief's words, sounds from outside were loud and distinct: a man's laugh on the steps, the staccato blending of two women's voices on the sidewalk, the sudden muted explosion of an automobile engine coming to life at the curb, a shrill ascending trill of birdsong from one of the maples out front.

"We have it from this diary"—Colton tapped it gently with one finger—"and from the coroner's office as well that the girl was pregnant."

There was a faint gasp from Charlie Jones, and a hoarse, choked sound from Tim Bailey. He was staring at Colton with unnaturally brilliant eyes.

Colton turned the diary over and gently pinched the soft leather of the spine. He went on conversationally: "You all probably wondered why I asked Mr. Bailey and Jim here to sit in on this little—talk. But it struck me there were a lot of points of similarity between this case and the murder of Inez Bailey twenty years ago."

He glanced at Tim casually. The latter was staring at Colton as if he had turned to stone.

"For one thing, you remember, Tim, Mr. Sterling here was a neighbor of yours then, had known your sister for years, went out with her a good deal when they were in high school—"

Color was coming back into Ben's face splotchily. He leaned forward and snapped, "These insinuations are clear out of order. Of course I knew Inez. Everybody in town did. Billings here will tell you there wasn't a scrap of evidence to connect me with her death."

Billings regarded him levelly. "That's right," he said slowly, "no evidence."

"But this time we have evidence," Colton said silkily, and lightly tossed the book on his broad palm.

Tim seemed slowly to be coming to life after having allowed time for his mental processes to apprehend what he had heard. Both fists clenched on the smooth, grained wood of the table, and he turned his head and fixed his eyes on Ben's face.

With a lift of his chin implying bravado Ben stared back; but his eyes shifted under the growing balefulness in the other's.

With a growling oath Tim came to his feet, kicking his chair back with his legs.

"I said I'd kill the man if I ever found him, and by God—"

His snarl was interrupted by Fred's authoritative voice. Colton had already motioned to Charlie, who had moved with feline speed to stand beside Tim, his hand on the billy club at his waist.

"Take it easy, Bailey," he barked.

But Tim lunged across the table, his extended hands just missing Ben's shoulders as the latter jerked back in terror. Charlie caught Tim's arms, but Tim jerked loose savagely and started around the table. Colton was on his feet in his path, one large hand against Tim's chest, the other swinging his club at his side.

"That's enough, Bailey. Charlie and I both have our sticks, and we'll use 'em if we have to. We're keeping order here. Everything's going to be done legal, or it ain't going to be done."

As Tim glared into the officer's face reason reasserted itself in his eyes. "O.K.," he said sullenly. "But I'm warning you, that man's going to get his. If the law don't take care of him, I will."

Emboldened by the sight of the blue police uniforms barricading Tim's wrath, Ben scrambled to his feet.

"Fred Colton, I demand that you arrest that man. Threats of violence are a criminal offense."

Colton resumed his chair as Tim grudgingly sank back into his own, his eyes glowering murderously at Ben, who seated himself gingerly. Beads of sweat had gathered on Ben's forehead, and he was breathing jerkily. He noticed with a sort of detached interest that the flesh of his thighs was quivering uncontrollably.

Fred drew a folded sheet of paper from his inside pocket and spread it out, revealing several neatly typewritten paragraphs, and slid it across the table to Ben. He took the cap off his fountain pen, screwed it on the other end, and extended the pen; but Ben made no move to take it.

"This is a confession to the murder of Dolores Baldwin. Read it over and sign it."

Ben met his eyes defiantly. "This is intimidation," he declared in a high, shaky voice. "You can't get away with it. I demand a lawyer."

Colton shrugged. "If you won't sign it, I can't do anything about it. Matter of fact, I won't even detain you. You can walk out of here and go to your lawyer while we get out a warrant for your arrest. That we will do on the strength of the evidence we have. I'll ask Jim and Charlie here to stay for a few minutes to discuss some matters with me. You and Mr. Bailey will be free to leave."

Ben frowned at the chief, and glanced across the table at Tim's tightening lips, the eyes which had gleamed with comprehension at the chief and then turned malignantly on Ben.

"You can't get away with this," Ben shouted at Colton. "It's a form of third degree." He pointed a trembling finger at Tim. "You're threatening me with this man! This'll cost you your job."

"What have I done?" Colton looked from one to the other of those at the table with wide-eyed innocence. "Have I done anything illegal?"

Jim Billings hesitated, frowned, studied Ben for an instant, then reluctantly shook his head.

"Of course," Colton said virtuously, "if Tim happens to catch you outside and beats you up, if he should even go too far and you got killed in the—er—scuffle, naturally I'd have him arrested and brought to trial." He shook his head disapprovingly. "We don't let such things get by."

He shook his head again and gave a regretful sigh. "Of course, you know public sentiment, and juries in this county. Never can tell how they'll act. Practically impossible to pick out twelve people that aren't already prejudiced. If Tim here happened to—er—hurt you too much, they might even call it manslaughter—accidental, sort of. I ain't saying they would."

Ben listened with horror. His eyes fell upon Tim's large, hairy clenched fists. With terrified fascination his eyes rose slowly to the set, implacable face. Barbarians, those Baileys; lower class, primitive in their emotions. An eye for an eye.

He remembered the moment when he had sickly lowered his head on the cash register. *"I'd tear him apart with my bare hands."*

A quick, short-lasting rage rose in a last flare in Ben; and he ran his eyes rebelliously from one of the grimly watching men to another.

His voice was a low-pitched scream. "It's your responsibility to protect me. I'm not leaving this room alone."

Colton shrugged. "Then I guess Charlie and Jim and me will have to retire to my office for our little talk. I haven't taken you into custody, and it ain't my responsibility to baby-sit you till I do."

Ben's eyes rolled wildly over the encircling men. All in it together. Against him. They would lie—together. Even Charlie Jones. He could see them, bland and unperturbed, on the witness stand. They didn't know Tim felt so—strongly—about the thing. They wouldn't remember any threatening words or gestures. They had let Tim follow Ben Sterling from the room in perfect good faith.

And Tim. His hatred and his vengeance would be all his one-track mind would take into consideration until his murderous rage had vented itself. An animal—that's all he was.

If he refused to leave this room, Fred and Charlie and Jim would walk out, leaving him here with Tim; if necessary forcibly preventing him from accompanying them, lying their way out of it afterward. Or they would drive him out with that beast at his heels. There was no mercy, no compassion in these men he had thought were his friends.

His friends! The horrible irony of it. For what he had done, both times, had been done really with them in mind—or the men like them in Los Alegres. Actually he had killed in self-defense. But he would never be able to make them understand. Inez and Dolores—both of them had threatened his position among people like the Billingses, the Coltons—all the established, influential people in Los Alegres. He had killed so that he could go on being one of the respected, solid citizens of the community. Without Beth and her father's money and what they represented in town, he could never have been a prominent businessman, "in" with the very people that Billings and Colton represented—the Millers, Zangonis, Whitlocks, the people who were somebody. And now these very people—in the person of their agents, the police—were turning on him, hunting him down for the actions he had taken to ensure their friendship.

It was unjust, unfair. When he had done it, you might say, for love of them.

But he had always known, of course, that the world was like this, was like the fierce, malevolent faces now turned on him. That was why he had had to propitiate the society they ruled, stay in good with it, even to the extent of murder in order to maintain its approval.

The way they were acting now—merciless, ruthless, vindictive—proved that he had been right, that it had been self-defense when he killed those girls to keep them from dragging him down from a position among the cruel and self-righteous and implacable "best people," who, if you were not one of them, were against you.

And it had all been for nothing. Despite all his efforts they had turned on him brutally, rejected him, just as he had feared they would if they ever had a chance.

The ultimate horror was their sneakiness. Ben's eyes flickered frantically over Tim Bailey's hard, doubled fists. Using a man who was even yet "outside," who had never shaken off the traces of his origin on Railroad Avenue, to do their dirty work for them, to entrap and destroy him.

The hands opened, and closed again, slowly.

Ben's momentary rage had subsided, leaving only a whimpering terror inside him. He was afraid as he had never been afraid before. That fear barred his brain from consideration of anything beyond the immediate, inescapable, overpowering danger. Anything to be released from the threat of those murderous hands hovering over the polished wood of the table opposite him!

As a man who cannot swim will jump into the sea to escape the extended claws and exposed fangs of a wild animal on the bank, Ben took the pen and shakily signed his name to the paper before him.

THE END

The Three Widows
– – – – – – –
Bernice Carey

To My Father, Charles Carey

CHAPTER ONE

All day the cars had come shooting along the broad road which, like an assembly belt, passed them over the crest of the mountains to deposit them thickly in parking lots (50¢ All Day) or lodge them bumper to bumper along the narrow streets which crisscrossed to mark off squares covered by white-painted one-story apartment courts.

The cars were green or cream or red convertibles with the canvas tops down, or they were beetle-shaped black or blue sedans with sun visors cutting off half the view from the sloping windshields, or they were two-door coaches or coupes whose bodies still wore running boards and whose fenders were not in one piece with the rest of the machine's armored shell.

When the flow of traffic had swept them as close as possible to the shore and dropped them in a broadening mass like delta sands, the doors opened, and the people poured forth like brightly colored birds suddenly released from cages.

They came from the hot, flat inland valleys, from the San Joaquin, the Santa Clara, the Salinas. They came from the dry, uneventful small cities, seeking the moist air which flowed in from the sea. They came from fog-bound San Francisco seeking the sun on their faces.

They carried unwieldy cardboard cartons of lunch and army blankets and faded canvas cushions and beach balls and the Sunday papers and long, striped bath towels and bottles of sun-tan lotion, and they staggered toward the warm sand that curved inward in a long, semicircular border to the green-blue expanse of the Pacific.

Their walk was sprightly, and they talked happily, laughing a good deal, and the children, already barefooted, their stringy bodies electric with energy above faded trunks, were impatient with the pace; they darted and ran in and out among the grown-up legs and had to be yelled at at pedestrian crossings. The men wore crumpled slacks and shirts hanging loose, shirts printed with impossibly gaudy and frivolous designs—flying fish and hula girls and cowboys and horseshoes. Sometimes the women wore cotton slacks and tee shirts, and sometimes they wore shorts with halter tops, and always they wore sandals. The boys who were men in physique but not in experience were proudly and brownly bare in bathing trunks and striped towels slung carelessly over muscular shoulders; and the girls were glossy and loose of hair, with wide, reddened mouths and bright fingernails and toenails, their rounded young buttocks held firm by shiny lastex trunks as tight as girdles, their full breasts sticking out sleekly in matching material designed to cup and push forward the newly matured mounds of flesh. Not for an instant did they forget their figures, the smooth tan shoulders, the flat tan stomach showing between bra and panty, and the long, tapering legs ending in thick-soled sandals.

They were happy. All of them were happy—for the moment anyhow. Oh yes, there might be blots on the mood here and there. The mother who had to scream at the kid jumping off the curb toward the stream of traffic, who was a little tired already, having risen at seven and having put up lunch for six and collected bathing suits and towels and all the paraphernalia necessary for a day at the beach; and the father whose arms ached from lugging the big box of lunch for six blocks and whose eyes felt strained from watching traffic for seventy-five miles, and who knew it was going to cost more than they had allowed, what with all the rides the kids would go on and chocolate-covered bananas on sticks and pop for everybody and the rent of a beach umbrella.

And there was the boy with stormy red acne scars cut deep in his cheeks and the yellow pustules on his chin, the boy who came along with his folks because he couldn't get a date with a girl.

And the girl whose figure was adolescently thick and who wore a red-and-white crew hat with her name stitched on the brim and who was with three other girls because the boy she hoped would ask her to go with the gang had invited another girl.

Yes, there were little sore spots hidden by the holiday mood; but in general they were happy. They were going to the beach, and for all day there was nothing they *had* to do.

In the afternoon the Symphonic Beach Band played in the stand at the entrance to the pier from which speedboats departed for a run across Monterey Bay at—according to the voice over the loud-speaker at the end of the pier—"a speed of forty-five miles an hour."

People in street clothes stood in a dark line along the pier railing and were massed along the shallow steps extending for half a block above the sand in front of the plunge and the frozen-custard stand and the photography shop and the open-front cafés which dispensed hot dogs and hamburgers and had stools along the counter facing the walk. The long steps were filled with seated figures like the bleachers of a ball field—Sunday-afternoon strollers who sat on spread-out newspapers with their hands clasped around their knees, the men with light felt or straw hats shading their eyes, the women with the pink flowers on their hats and the pastel shades of their rayon blouses making dabs of color on the picture.

The band played Sousa marches and selections from Rudolf Friml and Victor Herbert. There were strings and a piano in the band, and the music carried out over the crowd, and heads on the steps and along the walk and on the pier moved gently in time to the music, faces inclined toward the men clustered around their instruments back in the orchestra shell.

A lyric soprano in a nautical blue jacket and white flannel skirt sang light-opera solos, and a tenor with unruly hair and a light brown suit sang "One Alone" and "Some Enchanted Evening," and a baritone sang "Cruising Down the River," and the soprano and the baritone sang "Indian Love Call" in duet; and the crowd along the walks and the people sprawled upon the sand which was dimpled from the pressure of many feet listened with attention and clapped their hands when the pieces were finished. American flags fluttered from the dome of the bandstand and from the roof of the pavilion at the other end of the beach. The fringe of the low waves was white, dazzling white in the bright sunshine; and the gulls were bright flashes of white above the sheen of olive-green sea water; and the pointed white speedboats trailed huge white feathers behind as they shot away for a tour of Monterey Bay, and far out the brisk northwest breeze raised gleaming white caps on the sea.

And on the buff-colored cushion of the sand the people sprawled, their flesh, where it was exposed outside the strips of colored cloth which bound their bodies at hip and breast, only slightly darker than the sand itself. The round parasols, tilted with their backs to the sun, facing the orchestra shell, were gay with rings of orange and red stripes on the green and blue and beige canvas.

While the music rode above the clatter of voices and feet on the board-walk and the muted roll of the surf at the damp, packed edge of the sand, life stirred languidly on the beach. A young father lay with his head on his arms while his wife leaned against his side, watching their baby as he wad-dled dragging his little brightly painted sand bucket among the supine forms on wrinkled blankets. A man in a soft felt hat and a pale blue dress shirt with gray suspenders over it leaned against the sea wall with his legs thrust out in front of him while his wife in a black silk dress lay on her side with her knees pulled up and her head on his thighs. The man smoked a pipe, his eyes upon the horizon far out between the two piers that shut in this section of the beach. They were no longer young, and their faces had the look of people who have worked for others in order to make a living.

A few feet in front of them two husky, long young women with dull, light brown hair lay flat on their backs with their eyes closed, determinedly deep-ening their tans. They might have been dead for all the motion their bod-ies made. A girl of about fourteen did back bends, the soles of her feet and the palms of her hands on the sand, her body arched in a one-piece black bathing suit; and her parents, sitting fully dressed on a blanket, looked at one another and smiled appreciatively and laughed when she collapsed on her spine, and told her how good she was.

No one paid any attention to the middle-aged couple, anonymous in mass-production Gantner suits, who drank soda pop and watched the scene without talking very much.

And on the broad concrete runway before the concessions the people marched up and down, eating dripping ice-cream sandwiches and popcorn and cotton candy on a stick, pausing to throw darts at balloons pinned on a wall and to take the ride in a little car through the Pirates' Cave or up and down over the Giant Dipper.

One wandered among the eating, laughing, aimless, moving crowd, or one sat on the steps before the bathhouse with eyes roving over the colorful sands strewn with people who let the sun beat down on their skins and who were glad to be doing nothing and were glad of the music coming to them free—the Stephen Foster medleys and the melodic light-opera tunes and the best of the popular ballads; and if one were of a mildly philosophic turn of mind, one thought about how innocent, how basically simple the human animal was; one could not help feeling that it was a nice animal, a likable one. When he was left alone to do as he pleased—to rest, to play, to eat and make love—not teased nor driven nor subjected to situations resembling the maze-like contraptions with which scientists produced neurosis in rats—man was a harmless creature, a live-and-let-live sort of being. He let people run past him and kick sand in his face and drip mustard on his legs and bump him on the sidewalk and crowd too close to his own spot with their blankets and their kids and their wet bathing suits, and he only frowned and stirred a little and let it pass. He knew they didn't mean anything. They were all just trying to have fun, everybody intent on enjoying themselves and willing to let him enjoy himself too. Nobody was trying to make him do anything today. He was doing what he pleased, and the others were doing what they pleased, and so you all got along together there on the beach. It was part of the fun, watching other people and how fat they were in their bathing suits and what kind of food they brought to eat and what kind of tones they used in speaking to their kids. Part of the fun was the show the other people provided.

CHAPTER TWO

The band concert was over. Fewer heads in white rubber caps bobbed up and down above the breakers. The tide inexorably ate its way back into the scimitar of dry sand. Only scattered figures sat hunched on the long stretch of steps before the roofed-in walk. The congestion was not so great on the sidewalk. There was more purposive movement on the sands. People folded umbrellas, gathered up sand-speckled cups and crumpled paper napkins and empty popcorn bags and crammed them into sticky hampers.

They drew on their shirts and wiped the sand off their feet with damp, discolored towels. They staggered in groups out of the clinging sand and trudged off up the alleyways between the amusement stands to pack themselves into cars that had become steel ovens from standing all day in the sun.

The shadows from the pavilion lay long on the crumpled, littered sand; the breeze had a chill in it that had not been there before. The waves crept farther and farther onto the warmth of the sun-baked sand.

A few parties listlessly ate the last sandwiches in their baskets and emptied the thermos jugs of coffee and then shook the sand from their blankets; and at last, when there was no more sunlight anywhere, even lying deeply gold and gentle beyond the shadows, when the beach lay lusterless and lonely in the twilight, they were all gone from the sands. There were only quiet strollers on the piers, scattered stragglers on the boardwalk, a few people having coffee and special-plate lunches in the open-front restaurants.

In the lull between the day and the evening trade the proprietors and the workers in the stands took time to sit on stools at the rear of their counters, eating supper from plates they had filled themselves, having cigarettes with coffee.

Mrs. White leaned on her crossed arms on the linoleum-covered counter and gazed out between the hollow square pillars above the bank of steps, her eyes casual upon the familiar horizon, the darkening sea, the frowsy sands. Her graying hair was fluffed lightly at the temples, drawn into a neat bun at the base of her head in back. Over a cotton print housedress she wore a figured apron that fastened with buttons behind her neck, fit neatly over her shapeless bosom, and was tied in a bow in the middle of her back.

Mr. White was eating his dinner, seated on the last stool of the counter that ran down the side of the rear wall of the building. The Whites specialized in barbecued sandwiches. Their nephew, Delbert, helped in the kitchen at the rear. A cousin acted as cashier; and both the White daughters worked as waitresses all summer before they went back to high school and college respectively. It worked out very well, and the Whites made a comfortable, year-round living from their concession.

Officer Doty approached with a leisurely gait, and Mrs. White greeted him with a, "Hello, Ed."

He drew to a halt, standing between two of the stools, his arm on the counter. "How's things, Delia? Have a big day?"

She sighed. "Did we? My feet're killing me." She glanced over her shoulder at a round clock on the rear wall. "And it'll go on till near midnight, I suppose. Sunday and all. Though it won't be as bad as last night. Boy, the place was really jumpin' last night. Biggest Saturday night we've had all season."

"Yeah, it's the nice weather, I expect. No fog."

"Like a cuppa coffee, Ed?"

"Don't care if I do."

He eased onto the stool and let his eyes rove casually over the beach. It was mostly just boring, his beat here along the boardwalk. Most of the people milling up and down in search of diversion never noticed that there were policemen on duty at all. As a matter of fact most of Ed's duties consisted of again bringing together parents and the squawling kids who had lost them. Santa Cruz was a quiet beach, criminologically speaking. The people who ran the concessions up and down the boardwalk were not the cheap, garish kind you read about in magazine stories dealing with carnival life. Santa Cruz had no freak shows, no glamorous-girlie shows, no loud-mouthed fortunetelling rackets. The people who ran the game concessions where you threw balls or darts or shot at moving clay pigeons, or who dispensed hot dogs and frozen custards, or operated the mechanical "thrill" rides were just local, small-town business people who belonged to lodges and the Chamber of Commerce and cast votes in city elections. They all knew Ed, and he knew all of them.

Mrs. White set his coffee down in front of him in its tall white mug without a saucer, pushing toward him the pitcher of cream with its sliding metal contrivance on the top that allowed a small, neat stream to flow when the handle was pressed back.

She leaned on her arms again and gazed past him toward the beach. The girls were attending to the few scattered customers.

The atmosphere was becoming grayly thicker with twilight, and those who passed now wore jackets or sweaters. Mrs. White frowned slightly.

"Ed, you notice that guy layin' out there? Another hour and the tide'll be up to him."

Ed turned with the cup in his hand and squinted toward the sand. "Damn fool'll have sense enough get up and leave before that. Half an hour and it'll be dark."

"I noticed him there ever since the crowd thinned out. Went to sleep, I figured."

Ed took a sip of coffee and gazed over the rim of the cup. He lowered the mug and sighed. "Probably been drinkin'. Get a bun on an' drop off an' seems like they can sleep through a four-alarm fire. Suppose I better go down an' get him movin'. Layin' there in a bathing suit, he'll catch his death of cold."

He pushed the cup back on the counter and grinned at her. "I'm supposed to be a policeman. But you know what I feel like sometimes? A God-damned nursemaid, and that's a fact."

Ed hitched up his belt. "Well, better get this guy roused up and on his way 'fore he gets washed out with the tide," he appended facetiously.

Mrs. White's appreciative answering chuckle followed him as he crossed the walk. She stood idly watching the officer descend the steps and plod through the sand. He bent over and grasped the shoulder of the man on the sand, obviously preparing to shake him awake. But Ed did not shake him. Instead, his hand drew back as if from a shock. He stood half pulled erect for a second, and then bent lower, his hand sliding under the prone figure's head as it lay on the folded arms, turning the face to peer into it.

Mrs. White's head was thrust forward intently, watching the policeman who slowly straightened and stood staring down at the sleeper. Ed lifted his right hand and scratched his cheek, then he turned and plodded back through the sand and up the steps. He came straight toward Mrs. White.

"What's the trouble?" she demanded.

Ed glanced about to see that no one was noticing them, and then said in a low voice, "Don't let on anything's wrong; but the guy's dead." He glanced at the fingers of his right hand, as if in recollection. "Colder'n a mackerel."

The woman gasped.

"Listen, tell George to just sort of casually wander down there an' keep an eye on him while I call in for the boys. Don't want anybody messin' around down there, or maybe somebody getting wise and causin' a lot of commotion, till we get the wagon here."

"Sure. Sure, Ed." Mrs. White took a deep breath. "Oh my, this is terrible. I'll tell George."

"It'll just be for a minute while I report, an' I'll be back. But I don't want to leave the body unguarded. You see?"

"Sure. Sure, Ed. Oh, dear." She hurried back to give her husband his instructions in a hushed voice.

CHAPTER THREE

It was a matter of minutes from the time Officer Doty relieved George at his vigil by the corpse before additional policemen emerged from the automobile which pulled up in the alley between the concessions and deployed toward the beach.

Darkness was settling down over the sands and the sea, and lights had begun to spangle the eaves of the pavilion and the outlines of the pier. The evening crowds were thickening along the broad cement foot thoroughfare, loitering in search of divertisement.

The police were quiet, unobtrusive about their mission. Two uniformed men took posts at some distance apart on the shallow steps to prevent the curious from following the medical examiner and the detectives down to the sands.

The news licked through the crowds, however, like the tiny flames of a prairie fire, and by the time the men moved up the steps carrying the basket with its betraying length and breadth it was necessary for Ed Doty and the other uniformed men to make a path for it through the gaping, murmuring people.

It was only minutes again after the wagon had pulled out for the county morgue before the suddenly concentrated crowd had lengthened out to become indistinguishable in the throngs wandering up and down the boardwalk.

At a little after ten the next morning the Whites pushed back the folding iron grilles which protected their counters from invasion at night and prepared to begin the day's business.

Mrs. White opened up the morning paper and leaned on the counter to look it over.

"Record-breaking Crowds Over Week End" was the main headline, but she found the article she was looking for near the bottom of the front page, headed in discreet type, "Unidentified Man Dead on Sands."

The article was chastely unsensational. Overdose of sleeping tablets. Traces of drug found in Cola bottle beside the body. Man about fifty years old, weighing one hundred and sixty pounds, five feet ten, scanty brown hair, gray eyes. Police suspect suicide. Anyone with information about the man, communicate with local police.

It was rather an unsatisfying news item—for a person, that is, who had, you might say, discovered the body.

Mrs. White understood perfectly, though, why the news was played down. Neither the newspaper, the city administration, nor the Chamber of Commerce—of which the Whites were members—wanted visiting tourists to get the impression that bodies littered the respectable sands of Santa Cruz.

She was anxious, though, for Ed to come on duty. He would be sure to have more details.

Since the vacation season was at its peak, the Whites were busy all day. There was more room between the umbrellas and the blankets on the beach on this Monday, however, and people could saunter along the boardwalk without jostling each other.

When Ed strolled up to the White Barbecue Nook about four o'clock to be offered his usual cup of coffee, Mrs. White was chatting with a patron who was consuming a glass of milk. Mr. Bladeswell had been a regular customer for two weeks now. He and Mrs. Bladeswell had been staying at the

Ocean View Motel and soaking up sunshine on the beach every day. They were retired people from Omaha, Nebraska who took a long automobile trip every summer. Mrs. Bladeswell was at the moment ensconced in her usual spot, knitting under a beach umbrella and watching the bathers in the surf. Mr. Bladeswell had a "nervous stomach," he had informed Mrs. White at the beginning of their acquaintance, which made it necessary to put something into it frequently, so every afternoon between three-thirty and four he came to the Whites' counter for his between-meals glass of milk.

Mrs. White had relatives in Council Bluffs, Iowa, just across the river from the Bladeswells' home town, and on the strength of this bond Mrs. White and Mr. Bladeswell had become close—if temporary—friends.

"You know," Mrs. White was saying, "it was practically the identical spot where your umbrella is that we found the body."

"Now don't you try to connect us up with it," he protested jokingly. "It was so crowded yesterday we had to set up our stuff down past the pavilion."

"Oh, of course not. I just thought you'd be interested. The coincidence of it."

It was at this point that Ed Doty arrived.

He, too, had become friends with the Bladeswells during their sojourn at the beach, and he greeted Mr. Bladeswell with casual familiarity.

Mr. Bladeswell pushed back his cloth hat with its little ventilating windows of copper netting and squinted at the officer. "Hear you had some excitement last night."

Ed glanced toward the sands and lowered himself to a stool. "Oh—that. Just routine," he said carelessly.

"Find out who he was yet?" Mr. White inquired, coming up to stand by his wife.

"No, not yet."

Dottie White, the younger daughter, moved up beside her father and peered curiously around his shoulder.

Her mother, noticing the girl's presence, commanded, "You get back and take care of your customers." Turning to the others, she observed virtuously, "It's no subject for a young girl to be listening to. Corpses. You think it was suicide, Ed?"

"Could be." He glanced about to see that no one else was listening. "Don't quote me now. I ain't really supposed to be discussing official business like this; but seein' as how we're all friends"—he took a sip of the hot coffee—"it's like this. Not a scrap of identification on him. He was layin' on an army blanket you coulda bought at any Surplus Store in the United States; an' he had on a pair of Gantner trunks. Well, you know how common *they* are. And the pop bottle. He coulda bought it here on the beach—even from you—or he coulda brought it with him from any place else. Now the thing is, if it's suicide, well, he didn't drop down there outa the sky; and an abandoned car'll turn up parked around somewhere close, or we'll hear from a rooming house or hotel or one of the courts pretty soon that some tenant never showed up since yesterday.

"But"—he raised his eyebrows at them meaningly—"if we don't hear from some of them sources, then it stands to reason somebody removed his clothes and stuff afterward from wherever they were."

"Then it would be murder," Mr. White said in a low voice.

"Looks like it to me," Ed declared.

"What are you guys doing," Mrs. White inquired curiously, "to find out who he is?"

"Oh, like I said, checking abandoned cars, checking with landladies and hotels, checking 'missing persons' reports, sending his description out to other offices. Sooner or later, I suppose, he'll turn up in 'missing persons.' Takes quite a while sometimes before the relatives or friends wake up to the fact a guy is missing."

"Sounds awfully complicated," Mrs. White reflected.

Ed nodded importantly. "People just don't realize how complicated our work *is*."

Mr. Bladeswell scratched his chin reflectively. "You know, this reminds me of something that happened two years ago when we were in Yellowstone. We spent a whole summer there. Had a cabin near the Lodge." He sighed reminiscently. "Beautiful place, Yellowstone Park. Well, early in the season the rangers found a guy at the bottom of a cliff. Been dead three or four days, just happened to run onto him." Mr. Bladeswell shook his head distastefully. "Wasn't in very good condition. All he had on was khaki shorts and a tee shirt and Keds. Same as this case. All stuff that coulda been bought anywhere. Naturally they figured it was accident. Guy hiking and loses his footing and goes off the edge of the bluff. Well, me an' Elsie got real friendly with one of the rangers—Jim Wade was his name. That's how we happened to hear about it. An', you know, they never did find out who the feller was. Leastwise they hadn't found out yet when we left the last part of August, and the thing happened around the Fourth of July."

Mr. Bladeswell nodded solemnly at Officer Doty. "And, come to think of it, this was a middle-aged man, too, around forty-five or so, and kind of medium, like the newspaper's description of this guy."

Mrs. White chuckled banteringly. "You better look out, Mr. Bladeswell. You were on the spot both times. The police might get to wondering."

Mr. Bladeswell's expression was alarmed as he turned distressed eyes on the policeman. "Oh, my goodness, nobody could think *we* had anything to do with it."

"I was just kidding." Mrs. White laughed.

Ed set his coffee mug down after a final swallow and said thoughtfully, "It's a funny thing. I just happened to remember something while you were talking. You know my brother, Ferd, the one I've told you about that's a private detective in San Diego. Well, he was at a convention of private operatives last fall, over in Fresno, and he came on over here and spent a day or two with me and the wife before he went on south. And, of course, we got to talking—about cases and stuff. You know how it is. And one case he told me about—it wasn't one he'd worked on, but another fellow told him about it. Happened in Yosemite just last summer. You speakin' of the rangers made me think of it. Forest ranger found this guy one morning laying on the shore by Mirror Lake, nothin' on but swimmin' trunks again; and of course nobody swims in Mirror Lake—too cold. He'd been killed by blows on the head. Well, by God, they never identified him neither. An' he was a guy between forty-five and fifty too. Ferd was interested in the case, and so was the guy that told him about it. Because Yosemite, you see, bein' smaller and not so many entrances, they should have found who he was by checkin' the camps an' hotels. Of course a lot of cars had left the park the evening before and early in the morning already before they got around to checking up; and they just never got nowhere on the deal."

"Sounds almost as if they might all be—connected," Mrs. White said thoughtfully.

Ed slapped his palm on the counter and stood up, hitching up his belt and settling the heavy gun holster against his thigh. "Coincidence, I s'pose. Pure coincidence."

"There's an awful lot of similarities, though, ain't there?" Mr. Bladeswell put in worriedly. "Always middle-aged men an' no identification, always summer, and in vacation spots, where there's thousands of tourists coming and going."

"Well," Ed declared, preparing to move along on his rounds, "if it is foul play an' one person's responsible for the whole thing, they'll probably never catch up with him."

Mr. White had taken a toothpick from the whisky-shot glass beside the cash register, and he said around it as he picked his teeth, "I dunno. 'The mills of the gods grind slowly, but they grind exceeding small.'"

"Now, George," Mrs. White chided jokingly, "don't go showing off your education."

Mr. White shook the toothpick at the officer solemnly. "Just the same, if I was you, Ed, I'd tell the chief about our talk, and have him check with Yellowstone and Yosemite. Won't cost nothin' but the taxpayers' money for phone calls."

"Won't do much good either," Ed retorted good-humoredly, "but I'll report it."

CHAPTER FOUR

The Bladeswells stayed on in Santa Cruz for the rest of the week. After that first day and the conversation which had revealed the coincidence of the middle-aged men in Yellowstone and Yosemite, Mr. Bladeswell had become rather anxiously interested in the Santa Cruz body; but every day Ed Doty reported no progress. A few "missing persons" descriptions had been compared with that of the man on the beach, but none had fitted him so far.

By the end of the week, when the Bladeswells packed up their sedan and moved on, the body had sunk to the status of an unsolved mystery.

Their itinerary had been carefully planned at the start of the trip, and the next stop on it provided for a week at a place which was half dude ranch, half motel—the latter a typically California corruption of the words "motor court" and "hotel." The place was called El Valle Escondido, and it lay indeed almost hidden in the hills between the San Simeon highway and the city of San Luis Obispo. The Bladeswells might never have heard of Escondido, as its patrons called it, except for a friend of Mr. Bladeswell in Omaha. Chet Hoffman's sister had spent a month there the previous summer and had raved about it, so Chet on his vacation this year was going to spend a week at Escondido; and he and Mr. Bladeswell had arranged that their trips should coincide at The Hidden Valley.

Chet ran a men's clothing store in Omaha, and he was a great one for traveling, a hangover, he always explained, from his days as a drummer. There was no Mrs. Hoffman now. Once there had been, but the alliance had ended in divorce many years before, so Chet took his summer tours alone in a snappy convertible, explaining with a meaning wink that "he travels fastest who travels alone."

The Bladeswells' reservations were made, and Chet would already be at the resort when they arrived that night. After this stop at Escondido the Bladeswells planned to drive south for a week around Los Angeles and then to swing east in a leisurely southern curve, reaching Omaha sometime in September.

For the first hundred miles along the San Simeon highway past Carmel and along the Big Sur country Mrs. Bladeswell was in a continual state of breathlessness over the sheer cliffs which dropped beneath them to a pounding surf, over the frightening distances rising ahead of them where masses of heavy brown mountain rose ominously as far as the eye could reach above equally appalling, vast expanses of sea that lay like a limitless sheet of hammered silver under the fog-gray sky.

There is a limit to how long a person can react adequately to the stunning grandeur of unfamiliar scenery, and Mr. Bladeswell was soon responding to his wife's monotonous exclamations of "Look! Isn't that *beautiful!*" with somewhat indifferent glances at the oncoming arrangements of land masses against sky and water. He didn't say so to Elsie, but he figured a person living in one of the weather-beaten, isolated structures that stared with glassy windowed eyes out across the rugged shoreline and the changeful sea would get just as used to the stark hills and the lonely grandeur of the Pacific as you would to the endless wheat fields of Kansas. After all, the plains were a sight that was not to be sneezed at either. Himself, he kept noticing it, how little *sky* there was in the west—except over the ocean, of course.

As his appreciation for scenery reached the point of satiety, Mr. Bladeswell's thoughts settled broodingly on Those Men again. Officer Doty had reported that the Santa Cruz police *had* checked with the rangers at Yosemite and Yellowstone—finding that no identification had ever been made of the two bodies in question.

Doty had been inclined to pass it off lightly, however. You'd be surprised, he said, how many unidentified corpses the police had to cope with, sometimes as a result of hit-and-run accidents, sometimes along railroad tracks, sometimes just heart cases on city streets.

Mr. Bladeswell argued to himself, however, that these cases were usually hoboes or other vagrants. They *could* appear in national parks or summer resorts, of course. But for all of These Men there should have been clothing, personal effects turning up somewhere nearby. After all, even a vagrant wouldn't be pursuing his way of life possessed of only a pair of bathing trunks—or, as in the Yellowstone case—khaki shorts, a tee shirt, and tennis shoes.

Mr. Bladeswell was convinced that all three cases had been cold-blooded murder, that someone had carefully removed all traces of his victim after each crime. But why had no "missing persons" inquiry ever connected up with either body? Perhaps the victims had been deliberately chosen for their solitary status in the world.

Mr. Bladeswell somehow could not get his mind away from these thoughts. The whole thing shocked him. Every one of these men younger than he was. All of them in some well-known pleasure spot, probably enjoying life there just as he did. And suddenly they were gone. With no one knowing or caring. That was the rub. It was unbearably pitiful somehow. Human beings like himself, to be left alone, unloved, unwept, unhonored even by decent burial with a minister and flowers and old friends filing past for a last sad look at the still, cold face.

There must have been a reason for the murders. The reasons could have been different each time, hatred, revenge—any sort of unholy passion. They couldn't have been for money. Men who had money usually had a standing in some community somewhere. Their disappearances would never pass unnoticed. And there were always people who were interested in a man with money—maybe not people who loved him, but people who were definitely aware of him, concerned with what would happen to the money when he died.

Yet money was the thing people would do practically anything for.

Earlier in the summer the papers had been full of the case of a dashing elderly man who went around garnering large sums of money from credulous women on the basis of planning to marry them, which he never did. And Mr. Bladeswell remembered a sensational case years back when some fellow—in England, he thought it was—actually married a whole slew of women, carefully killing off each one after he got control of her money.

Suppose this was a reverse of that case. Suppose it was a woman marrying men, getting their property in her name, and then pushing them over cliffs or dropping too many sleeping tablets in their pop bottles.

But how would she explain their sudden absences?

Mr. Bladeswell said, "Yeah, it's pretty," in response to another ejaculation of his wife, and thoughtfully negotiated a looping curve hanging over foam-bathed rocks three hundred feet below.

His eyes narrowed on the gray cement bisected by a white line.

All three deaths had occurred in summer in well-known vacation spots. Tourists. Far away from home and anyone who knew them.

Just suppose, for instance, something happened to *him* on this trip. Elsie, naturally, would have the body shipped home for burial. But no one would think it *very* strange if she didn't, if she had quiet services out here and stayed on somewhere in southern California to nurse her grief and try to forget in new scenes instead of in the heart-rending familiarity of their home back East which he would never share with her again.

Their checking and savings accounts were held jointly; the house was in both their names. There were laws, of course, that held everything up after the death of one party of a joint account. But suppose they had sold the house and banked the money. Before the bank ever knew he was dead, Elsie could have drawn all the funds out of both accounts. The people in the bank might think it was funny that so much money was withdrawn just before they heard Mel was dead, but Omaha was a big place—their own bank had thousands of accounts. Unless prompted by police inquiries no one would pay particular attention to the withdrawal of the Bladeswell funds.

That must be it, a wife murdering her husbands. The whole thing was pretty farfetched, and he had used his imagination pretty freely, but he'd be willing to bet he had figured it out right.

Mr. Bladeswell frowned behind his sunglasses and gnawed at his lower lip. They had been on the spot at Yellowstone and at Santa Cruz, and Officer Doty had just happened to know of the Yosemite affair.

Sickeningly it occurred to Mr. Bladeswell that there might be other cases. If he, having no connection with the police, had heard of *three*, how many more might there be that he hadn't heard of?

But surely if there had been an epidemic of unidentified male bodies over the course of years at famous resort areas the police, too, would have begun to add them up and get suspicious.

Death, however, was so common, and the police saw so much of it, and as Ed Doty had said, they were always having to deal with unidentified bodies. Still, they kept records; surely experts studied and co-ordinated them. A thing like this couldn't go on forever without the police beginning to discover a pattern.

But it was devilish clever—if he was right in his hunch. The bodies were so deeply buried in the mass of other accidental deaths and unsolved murders that even people who studied such things might pass them by in the crowd. It was only by accident that the pattern had been startlingly suggested to *his* mind, the accident of his being in Santa Cruz at this particular time and of hearing Doty's story of the body at Yosemite the year before.

Mr. Bladeswell was uneasy. As a citizen he felt he ought to do something about it. Who knew how many other innocent men were yet to become unidentified bodies in vacation spots?

The frustrating thing about it all was that there was nothing he *could* do.

CHAPTER FIVE

A little before five o'clock they turned inland off the highway clinging to the bluffs above the sea. Soon the countryside had radically changed. Instead of the overpowering grandeur of seascape they now found the more inviting contours of a landscape consisting of parched hillsides gliding into each other and softened by the olive-green balls of ancient live oaks resting on the slopes, their foliage nearly grazing the dried golden wild grass. Occasionally a driveway lined with cottonwoods led back to a ranch house spread out with its attendant buildings in a curve of the hills; and from the level meadows, which flattened out along the cement road here and there, red Hereford cattle gazed at them silently from white faces.

Mrs. Bladeswell said thoughtfully after a while, "You know, I think I like this better. If I was going to *live* in California I'd pick out somewhere like this. It's more human somehow. Back there on the coast—it was wonderful, of course, but kind of—stupefying, don't you think, Mel?"

"Yes, I guess so. It's all right to see, but this kind of country's better for a steady diet."

So they dismissed the stern coast and began to watch for the turnoff and the sign "El Valle Escondido, Reasonable Rates by Day, Week, or Month."

At last to their left they saw the sign and turned off on a well-kept blacktop road which after a quarter of a mile terminated in a graveled semicircle before the office, service ice station, and tiny grocery store at the entrance to Escondido.

When they had verified their reservations and asked about Mr. Hoffman, the attendant, who was a middle-aged man in faded jeans and a light-colored sports shirt, walked around the side of the office with them and pointed to one of the dirt roads leading off among the scattered cottages.

"You have Number 12, right up this road, and Mr. Hoffman is in 11 right next to it."

As they drove past the office Mrs. Bladeswell sighed happily, "Isn't this nice!"

It was a charming, a restful scene. In the center of a cool green lawn covering half an acre a tiled swimming pool surrounded by a broad cement runway winked a long, blue, sun-flecked eye at the occupants of striped canvas chairs and swings set on the grass around the runway.

Behind this spacious patio sat the ranch house. With its brood of white board-and-batten cottages scattered among the oaks and sycamores along the slopes which rose in a gentle amphitheater about the courtyard it reminded Mrs. Bladeswell of a mother hen surrounded by her chicks, for the ranch house was also white with a gray shingled roof rising to a peak over the two-story center and spreading like wings over the one-story ells which extended on either side. An old-fashioned veranda with a sloping roof and white pillars and a waist-high railing ran the length of the house with broad white steps breaking it in the center. A few people sat in rocking chairs there, idly looking out over the lawn and the swimming pool.

Back of the house and to its left, beyond a long grape-arbor, the sloping gray roof of a low barn was visible above the greasewood brush which covered the hillside, and to the right of the barn roof, between it and the roof of the house, one could see the gentle incline of a meadow where several cow ponies grazed in the slanting rays of the sun, ready to be ridden back into the hills on the morrow by those guests who craved adventure.

The Bladeswells drove up the dirt road, recognizing Chet Hoffman's car standing under a maple tree next to the cottage whose door was marked 11, and pulled up onto the driveway which ran between their own cottage and a sycamore tree which leaned with haughty, languid grace toward the little shingled house.

There was a tiny porch in front, only large enough to hold two wooden rocking chairs which reposed there in the shade. It was a little stuffy inside, but Mrs. Bladeswell immediately pulled up the sash windows on three sides of the living room to let in the breeze which stirred the cretonne draperies that would serve as shades at night. The room was plain but clean. The single-board walls were whitewashed and the pine floor painted brown with a homemade rag rug beside the double bed. A painted gate-leg table stood beneath the front windows with three straight chairs drawn up neatly around it. The only other pieces of furniture in the room were a bedside table and a golden-oak dresser with three drawers and a mirror held upright by knobbed posts. To their right as they entered were three doors, the first leading to a tiny kitchen with sink, electric plate, and cupboard shelves, the second to a clothes closet, the third to a bathroom with a lavatory, toilet, and stall shower.

Mrs. Bladeswell had not been inside the cottage three minutes before she had looked into all the doorways, shelves, and drawers, and after that she glanced about with a little nod of her head and passed approval on the whole setup.

"I think this is real nice, don't you, Mel?"

"Ain't very fancy, but it's comfortable," he agreed, "and clean, it looks like."

"Yes, sir, I think I'm going to like this place. I wouldn't wonder but I'd like to come here for all summer next year."

"You say that every place we go," Mr. Bladeswell observed equably, and went out to start unpacking the car.

He had just finished bringing in all the luggage when footsteps and a hearty voice sounded on the steps outside and Chet Hoffman appeared on the little porch.

"Well, I see you made it."

There was a merry outburst of greetings and handshakings, and in a few minutes Chet and Mrs. Bladeswell sat down in the rockers outside with Mr. Bladeswell bringing out a straight chair and sitting before the open door.

"I figured you'd want to eat at the ranch house tonight," Chet informed them, "so I put your names down. You have to let them know before ten in the morning if you want lunch or dinner or the next day's breakfast at the house. Lot of people do their own cooking here. But you get swell grub at the ranch house. Serve it family style." He glanced at his wrist watch.

"They eat at five-thirty, so I suppose we better get going in a few minutes."
Mrs. Bladeswell glanced at the white flannel trousers, white silk, open-collared shirt, and thick-soled tennis shoes which garbed Chet's robust figure, and murmured, "Maybe we ought to change clothes."

"Aw, you're all right," Chet assured her expansively. "People wear whatever they happen to have on—riding pants, sun suits, jeans. Nothing high-toned about this place."

"Well, I'll wash my hands and comb my hair anyhow."

As she rose and disappeared inside, two little boys in dirty jeans and black-and-white canvas-and-rubber shoes ran whooping by on the trail zigzagging down the slope behind the cabin.

"There's quite a lot of kids here," Chet remarked apologetically, "but that's one thing makes it nice. Family sort of place. Real nice class of people. No rough stuff, drinking parties, and all that. Just regular homey kind of people."

"You were lucky to hear about it," Mr. Bladeswell observed.

"What kind of a trip you been having?"

"Oh, fine, fine. How about you? Been in southern California most of the time, haven't you?"

"Yep, been on the road three weeks. Gotta head home next week though."

"Been having a good time, I suppose."

Chet grinned complacently. "Brother, you ain't kiddin'. Stopped in Las Vegas and done a little gambling. Came out ahead about a hundred bucks. Blackjack, that's my game. Took a run up to Arrowhead for a few days, but most of the time I stayed in Hollywood, had a room in a hotel on Sunset Boulevard."

"See many movie stars?"

"Well, not so many. Although I did see Humphrey Bogart on the street one day, and I saw Betty Grable in the Brown Derby once. Mostly, though, I took in radio programs. Guess I covered 'em all. Got on the air once myself. On 'Meet the Missus.' Can you beat that?" He laughed comfortably. "Got a real nice set of shaving stuff out of it. One thing you gotta hand it to 'em for in Hollywood, though. They got more damn good-looking women per square foot than I ever saw any place in the world."

"I suppose they all gravitate there, trying to get in the movies." Mr. Bladeswell smiled. "Make any time with any of 'em?"

Chet clicked his tongue against the roof of his mouth and raised his eyebrows suggestively. "Oh, I went out a few times. There's life in the old dog yet."

At the moment a young couple in slacks and tee shirts were passing along the road before the cottage, the man carrying a baby about eight months old, the woman pushing a trailer tot containing a toddler in coveralls.

"Wouldn't say this was such a good place for a ladies' man like you," Mr. Bladeswell observed.

"Oh, I don't know," Chet rejoined complacently. "There's two or three pretty good numbers in the bunch. Not as young as they used to be, but hell, I'm no spring chicken myself anymore." He chuckled ruefully. "Can't be too particular anymore."

Mr. Bladeswell smiled tolerantly, and his wife came out just then, closing the door and turning the key. They sauntered down the road and along the path leading past the lawns to the ranch house.

CHAPTER SIX

A woman came down the steps of one of the cottages overlooking the patio as they passed, and Chet paused to call out cheerfully, "On your way to dinner, Mrs. Meadows?"

She responded affirmatively in a light, gay voice, and floated toward them on a billow of pale blue organdy.

"These are the friends I was telling you about," Chet said genially, "Mr. and Mrs. Bladeswell, Mrs. Meadows."

"How ni-ice. Mr. Hoffman has been so looking forward to seeing you."

Mrs. Meadows widened her blue eyes between the thicket of mascaraed lashes which bordered them and smiled delightedly.

Mr. Bladeswell nodded, feeling bashful; and his wife smiled a little stiffly, taking in the froth of pinkish blond hair, the expanses of soft white skin escaping from the low round neck of the organdy, the high-heeled sandals with ankle straps, and the bright red toenails showing between the openwork of the frivolous slippers.

The pale blue organdy was not exactly an evening dress, but it could have passed for one; and although Mr. Bladeswell was not to think of it until later, Mrs. Bladeswell wondered at once what so fancy a lady was doing in this unsophisticated setting. She saw immediately that Mrs. Meadows was successfully concealing her age, which Mrs. Bladeswell estimated as past forty. There were little signs that another woman could read—the quality of the plumpness, for instance. It was not the sturdy flesh of youth. There was something flaccid, too yielding in it. And the little bit too much of make-up; and a certain droop to the flesh around the mouth and the jaw line.

Mrs. Meadows was not the sort of woman Mrs. Bladeswell warmed up to.

But she joined their party as if she belonged, putting a hand whose lit-

tle finger flashed a large sapphire dinner ring on Chet's shirt sleeve and trip-
ping along, chatting gaily.

"Don't you already *love* Escondido?" she chirruped. "It's just what its
name implies. Escondido means 'hidden' in Spanish, you know. And
that's just how I feel here, hidden from the world and all its troubles.

"I just *stumbled* onto it really. I made up my mind this summer I was just
going to get away by myself and be a gypsy, and I started out from Los Angeles—that's where I live—alone in my car without a single plan, just ready
to take whatever came. And I was skimming along on my way to the San
Simeon highway—really had Carmel in mind—but I investigated the sign
on the road, and"—her laughter trilled out—"well, here I am. I've been
here five days, and I'm having the most marvelous rest."

They had reached the foot of the steps, and Mrs. Meadows broke off to
deliver little cries of greeting to the guests distributed along the veranda
while they awaited the dinner bell.

Chet, too, nodded and smiled to right and left as they mounted the steps.

Mr. and Mrs. Bladeswell felt conspicuous as Chet introduced them to
people so fast that neither remembered a single name afterward: the
young couple with the children who had passed their cottage earlier; an
elderly couple who remained seated in their rocking chairs smiling ac-
knowledgments of the introduction; a bouncy family named Abernathy
whose five adolescent offspring seemed remarkably near the same age; a
Mrs. Smith whom Mrs. Bladeswell felt was more "her kind" than Mrs.
Meadows; two athletic-looking young men in jeans and high-heeled cowboy boots; and a pair of young women in sun-back dresses covered by
bolero jackets. Mrs. Bladeswell thought they were schoolteachers, and she
learned later that she was right.

Double screened doors led from the veranda to the dim room extending
through the length of the two-story part of the house. This was the
"lounge" which guests were free to use at all times, and Chet had guided
them into this room where some of the people they met were sprawled
about in easy chairs.

A rock fireplace rose at the far end of the room and an upright piano
stood against the east wall. There were sofas and chairs and end tables and
two writing desks disposed on the heavy linoleum floor. On three nights
a week the furniture was shoved to the walls, and a fiddler and an accordion player joined Mr. Fenn, the owner of Escondido, who played the piano while the guests indulged in square dancing down the length of the
shabby, home-like room.

While Chet was introducing the Bladeswells to a forthright lady in jodhpurs and a short-sleeved checked shirt, Mrs. Fenn came to the french doors
leading to the west ell of the house and rang an old iron cowbell as a sig-

nal, and the guests moved as one in a converging mass toward the low-ceilinged room completely surrounded by screened windows where three long tables were set for dinner.

Against the inner wall was a small and inconspicuous bar with a long, old-fashioned dining-room buffet serving as a backdrop and holding a few bottles of wine and vermouth. The hard liquor and mixes were stored under the wooden counter. When he wasn't too busy doing other things the Fenns' son-in-law acted as bartender. He rendered snappy service in cold beer or glasses of port, or highballs made either with soda or ginger ale, and he could even produce promptly a manhattan or a martini from already-prepared bottles of these concoctions; but he had been known to look blank over requests for whisky sours or pink ladies. In general, however, the Fenns' guests were indifferent to liquor, and the hosts' liquor license was a sort of defensive emergency measure in case of parties whose lives would be incomplete without frequent alcoholic interludes.

Meals were served family style, and the guests sat where they pleased. The lady in jodhpurs, Mrs. Fergusson, moved along with the Bladeswells and Chet to find seats at the table nearest the kitchen at the end of the room. Mrs. Meadows pushed through to Mrs. Bladeswell's side, squealing whimsically, "Almost lost you in the crush. Isn't it terrible? Regular stampede."

When they were seated Mr. Bladeswell glanced about and found Mrs. Fergusson sitting next to him, with Chet beyond her and Mrs. Meadows on Chet's other side. Across from him and directly opposite Chet the matronly lady that he *thought* was Mrs. Smith smiled at him in a friendly way. The schoolteachers and the athletic young men in cowboy boots had also found their way to this table. They were not exactly sitting together, however, because the table held only five on each side and Mrs. Smith's position marooned one of the young men away from the girls and his pal, beyond Mrs. Smith at the end of the table.

She was smiling and making some remark to Chet; and Mr. Bladeswell understood why Mrs. Smith had not volunteered to move so the youngsters could sit together. She wanted to face Mr. Hoffman.

Mr. Bladeswell's lips moved in a faint smile. Leave it to old Chet. Three unattached women, and all of them clustered around him.

The bouncing Abernathys had been unable to keep together in the "stampede," and at the last minute the two children who could be the eldest bounded to either end of the table, filling it out to an even dozen. They ate with gusto and speed, shouting down the length of the table to each other their uninhibited opinions on the provender supplied by the Fenns.

The Bladeswells were pleased with the food: generous platters of hot roast beef, plain boiled potatoes and smooth brown gravy, creamed string beans, and cool sliced tomatoes, served not as a salad, but on a plate passed from hand to hand up the table. There were homemade "raised" rolls, and crabapple jelly and little sweet cucumber pickles and either tea or coffee to drink, and for dessert fresh blackberries with cream and sugar and home-made nut cookies.

The Bladeswells could hardly believe their eyes or their taste buds. It might have been a real honest-to-goodness Middle Western dinner except that it was served at night instead of at noon.

Mr. Bladeswell leaned forward to speak to Chet past Mrs. Fergusson. "I see what you mean now about the meals here. I haven't had a supper like this since I hit California."

"That's one thing that brought me here," Chet returned. "Clarice said the food was real home cooking."

"I spent a week in San Francisco," Mrs. Fergusson declared, "and tried all the fancy restaurants—Omar Khayyam's, Solari's, French places, Span-ish, Chinese, and when I got through, 'By God,' I said to myself, 'I'll stick to good old American cooking.' They can have all their fancy sauces and flavorings, but me, when I eat a potato, I want to know it's a potato. And this beef tonight. It doesn't taste like garlic; it tastes like what nature meant it to taste like—beef."

Mrs. Smith leaned forward eagerly. "I'm glad to hear someone else say that. Back home I was always considered a good cook, but since I've been out here I was beginning to get an inferiority complex, because, like you said, Mrs. Fergusson, my food always tastes like what it is."

"Where is 'back home,' Mrs. Smith?" Mrs. Bladeswell put in sociably. "We're from Nebraska ourselves, and I always like to find out where other people come from."

"Well, Chicago was my home, but I've been traveling a lot lately. You see"—Mrs. Smith's face grew solemn—"I lost my husband recently; and—well, it's just hard to settle down without him."

Mr. Bladeswell set down his cup of tea and looked across at Mrs. Smith. He opened his mouth to ask a question, but the widow went on plaintively, after dabbing at her lips with a napkin, "You'll forgive me, Mrs. Bladeswell, but I don't like to speak of it. It's still too painful."

Mrs. Bladeswell clucked sympathetically, and of course after that it would have been impolite for Mr. Bladeswell to ask the question he had in his mind: "Where did your husband die, Mrs. Smith?"

He picked up his spoon and stirred the sugar which had settled in his cup of tea, his eyes on the clear amber liquid.

He felt pretty funny all of a sudden. These three women, all husband-less apparently, all hovering around Chet Hoffman. Chet, the eligible, the prosperous businessman. All three of them roaming around vacationing by themselves, each, he had gathered, driving her own car. Of course in this day and age thousands of women did that.

It couldn't be, of course, that one of them—

And anyhow it was only an idea of his—about the men—at Yellowstone, at Yosemite, at Santa Cruz.

But he raised his eyes speculatively and studied Mrs. Fergusson's firm profile. Her slightly waved brown hair swept back rather mannishly from a square forehead and well-shaped ears. She was evenly tanned, her jaw line cleanly cut, her sturdy neck firm and unwrinkled. At the moment her capable hands were engaged in lighting a cigarette. Mr. Bladeswell deduced that she was nearing fifty, a vigorous and surprisingly attractive fifty. She looked like a person of assurance, of competence.

Rather deferentially he inquired, "Are you a middle westerner, too, Mrs. Fergusson?"

She blew away a plume of smoke and turned her head to face him. "In California I suppose that's what they'd call me, but back home I'm a westerner. Denver, I come from."

"Oh. Well, we call that West in Nebraska."

"Wonderful state, Colorado. You've been there, I suppose?"

"Oh yes. Two years ago we spent a week in Denver. Climbed Pikes Peak too. Were you—er—were you in business there?"

She grinned and drew on her cigarette. "Everybody seems to get my number. Yes, I'm a businesswoman. Sell insurance." She laughed. "Can't sell you a policy, can I?"

"Well"—he chuckled—"not right now. You been traveling long this summer?"

"Been away from home six weeks now. First vacation I've had in two years, so I decided I might as well make it a good one. Last trip I took my husband was along; he's dead now, poor soul."

Having thus carelessly disposed of the "poor soul," Mrs. Fergusson led the way in the exodus from the dining room.

CHAPTER SEVEN

With his senses in a newly alert state Mr. Bladeswell noted how they moved in a body out to the veranda—he and Mrs. Bladeswell, Chet, and the three widows: Mrs. Smith, Mrs. Fergusson, and Mrs. Meadows—as if they were one party. Which, he saw, they were. The women were seeing to that.

There was an old-fashioned wooden swing hanging by chains from the roof at one end of the veranda, with sofa cushions in each corner, and Mr. Bladeswell and Chet took seats at either end of it. Mr. Bladeswell took out his cigar and pulled off the cellophane wrapper. Chet leaned back with his arms behind his head, one foot raised to rest with the ankle across his knee.

Mrs. Fergusson sat on the railing, her back against a pillar, one foot on the railing, her hands clasped about her knee, looking vigorous and athletic in the riding pants and checked shirt.

Mrs. Meadows, her legs slanted sidewise with the ankles crossed, snuggled into the chintz cushions of a wicker chair and tried to look like Billie Burke.

Mrs. Smith took a wooden rocker with a leather seat and, with her hands folded in the lap of her neat "shirtmaker" dress, rocked placidly, her curled, grizzled bobbed hair resting against the leather cushion of the chair back.

Mrs. Bladeswell sat in a reed "basket" chair and surveyed them all benignly.

The sunlight on the grass was mellow and amber beyond the shadow of the western hills. The swimming pool looked lonely and forlorn somehow, deserted as it now was.

The schoolteachers and the pair of young men in jeans were together in an awninged glider and canvas chairs down by the pool, and several children were playing some variety of "tag" on the lawn.

The Abernathys noisily occupied the end of the veranda opposite Chet's party. They seemed to enjoy one another's company immensely.

In the center of the porch several elderly people rocked and digested their dinners and watched the activities in the courtyard with philosophically indulgent expressions.

The group around the Bladeswells chatted desultorily. Mrs. Fergusson lighted another cigarette, and Mr. Bladeswell puffed on his cigar.

Mrs. Meadows said brightly after a while, "We must find another couple to make up two bridge tables, so the Bladeswells can play with us. You play, don't you?"

"Well, we play *at* it." Mrs. Bladeswell laughed.

"We got together last night," Mrs. Meadows went on with an arch glance at Chet, "with Mr. Hoffman, and had such an exciting game." Her gaze strayed down the porch. "Maybe Mr. and Mrs. Abernathy play."

"We'd love to play some night," Mrs. Bladeswell assured her, "but I think you'd better just go ahead without us tonight. We ought to turn in early. You see we drove clear from Santa Cruz today."

When his wife said "Santa Cruz" Mr. Bladeswell's eyes leaped swiftly from one face to another.

Mrs. Meadows' remained bland and Mrs. Smith's impassive, but Mrs. Fergusson brought her gaze in from the lawns to let it rest on Mrs. Bladeswell, who continued, "We spent about three weeks in Santa Cruz, were on the beach every day."

"I was there for a day or two," Mrs. Fergusson said flatly, "on my way down here. Took the Skyline Boulevard down from Frisco. Nice drive, and I liked Big Basin and the Trees; but as for the beach"—she shrugged dismissingly—"you can have it. Too crowded. It might be all right if you had a cottage and a private beach, but no public beaches for me, thank you."

"Well, we liked it," Mrs. Bladeswell murmured weakly. "I thought it was exciting—all those people and everything."

Mr. Bladeswell made a sudden decision, and observed casually, "It was exciting all right. Even had a murder while we were there."

Mrs. Meadows squealed and widened her eyes girlishly. "Oh, how horrid!"

Mrs. Smith lifted her head from the leather cushioning and repeated with a startled, questioning inflection, "A murder?"

And Mrs. Fergusson turned from the shoulders to look back and down at Mr. Bladeswell.

"When was that?" she demanded. "I never heard of it."

"Well, the police *thought* it was murder. Man died from an overdose of sleeping tablets right on the beach."

"Sleeping tablets?" Mrs. Smith said with a frown. "That sounds like suicide."

"Yes, it does; but they never found any of his clothes or anything, and that made it look funny, as if somebody had cleared up after him."

"Oh, the poor thing," Mrs. Meadows crooned.

Mrs. Fergusson drew in her breath and let it out, returned her gaze to the courtyard from which the slanting amber sunlight was now gone, and took a drag on her cigarette.

Mrs. Smith let her head fall back on the chair and observed musingly, "A person certainly runs into some strange things, traveling."

"I never seem to," Chet said with humorous plaintiveness. "Anything out of the ordinary happens I've always just left or haven't got there yet. For instance, they had a terrible smashup on the highway between Ventura and Santa Barbara on my way up here. Four people killed. Happened not five minutes after I passed the spot, and I never knew a thing about it until I read about it in the paper next day."

"I'd just as *soon* miss such things." Mrs. Meadows shuddered prettily.

Mr. Bladeswell's eyes probed the circle of bland faces, and again, on impulse, he threw out another hooked remark, "Seems as if the Mrs. and me're always running into one thing or another. Now you take two years ago this summer, we was in Yellowstone Park when they found another unidentified man. This one either fell or was shoved off a cliff."

"My goodness," his wife exclaimed, "I'd forgotten all about that. But they did, didn't they? Remember that nice ranger we used to visit with every evening? Wade was his name, wasn't it, Mel? He told us all about it. There was something *queer* about it. Foul play, they thought," she informed the others solemnly.

All three of the ladies had looked at Mr. Bladeswell while he was speaking, and it had been hard for him to analyze each of the three expressions in the brief period while their eyes were upon him. Elsie's voice, taking up as it had immediately after his, had brought their attention to her, and he had studied each face surreptitiously but with small success. Mrs. Fergusson's was somewhat grim before she turned her head to stare out over the courtyard; but, after all, it was a gruesome subject, violent death, enough to elicit a grim expression. Mrs. Smith had looked somewhat narrow-eyed—it could have been incredulity—as she glanced from him to his wife. And Mrs. Meadows had managed to look prettily shocked. But that could have been more of the acting in which she seemed to indulge freely.

"You folks sure get around," Mrs. Smith said. Did her voice have a rather inane ring, like that of one who feels compelled to say *something*—for appearance's sake? And had it sounded rather hollow?

Mrs. Fergusson laughed shortly, a somewhat harsh laugh, it seemed to Mr. Bladeswell. But then she tended to sound a little gruff at times. "Regular ghouls, you folks sound like, always on the scene."

"I've never been to Yellowstone," Mrs. Meadows said vaguely. But wasn't this a rather irrelevant bit of information—too quickly proffered?

The chains of the swing creaked a little as Mr. Bladeswell shifted his weight. He was suddenly glad he had not told Elsie the Yosemite story. She would surely have dragged in the body by Mirror Lake at this point; and then, if one of them were the husband slayer, she might jump to unwarranted conclusions, perhaps suspect him and Elsie of being detectives put on her trail. Certainly she would never believe their knowledge was the coincidence it was. The chain complained again as Mr. Bladeswell wondered uneasily if already they had talked too much. A woman who could bump off three husbands wouldn't cavil at rubbing out a fourth man who wasn't even a husband to her—if she thought he was on to her, and bent on exposing her nefarious career.

The conversation had bumped along without his assistance while Mr. Bladeswell was mulling over these considerations, and now his wife said briskly, "Well, Dad, shall we mosey along?" To the others she added, "We haven't even unpacked our bags."

"We'll be seeing you tomorrow, Mel," Chet said cheerfully, and the three ladies reiterated the pleasure they had found in meeting the Bladeswells.

As they walked down the path beside the lawns, however, Mr. Bladeswell chuckled dryly, "I'll *bet* they're glad we came. Afraid we'll be taking up too much of Chet's time so they won't be able to work on him."

"What do you mean, work on him?"

"Don't play dumb, Elsie. You could see as good as I could every damn one of those females's got her cap set for old Chet. How many men that own their own business and got money enough to run around half the summer in a new Oldsmobile do you suppose a single woman runs into? Can't fool me, every one of 'em'd like to marry him."

"Well, so supposing they would. That's no crime."

"Who said it was? All I said is they won't take to us cuttin' in on his time. With so much competition, they have to work fast."

"All right, then, we'll just keep to ourselves and not butt in more than we have to."

They were mounting the road to their cottage, and Mr. Bladeswell looked at his wife in some astonishment, "You want to see old Chet fall into some scheming hussy's clutches?"

"Mel Bladeswell, how you talk. He ought to be married. It's no way to live, a man in his late forties like that with no one to look after him. And I thought they were very nice."

They had reached the stairs to their house, and she hesitated before putting her foot on the first step. "Of course that Mrs. Meadows! There's a flighty one for you. I don't know as I'd trust her too much. But she is cute. And I can see how men would take to her."

"Not me. To tell you the truth, I didn't take to none of 'em."

Mrs. Bladeswell laughed teasingly. "You're just spoiled, having me all these years."

Mr. Bladeswell smiled and pinched her arm. As they began to unpack he pursued the subject as if he sought to gain something from his wife's impressions.

"What'd you think of the other two?"

"Well, of course I felt more at home with Mrs. Smith. She's more just plain folks like us." She paused with a coat hanger in her hand and frowned worriedly. "But I'm afraid she won't get anywhere against those other two. The homebodies just don't seem to appeal to men the way the other kind do. And it's too bad, because she'd make the best wife. You can tell just to look at her she bakes nice cakes and puts up fruit every year." She sighed and shook her head as she hooked the hanger with her husband's coat on it over the rod in the closet.

"No, I can't see Mrs. Fergusson putting up preserves," Mr. Bladeswell mused.

"If I was going to bet," his wife said judiciously, "I'm afraid I'd have to pick her. She looks like the kind of person who gets what she wants—by fair means or foul."

Mr. Bladeswell straightened abruptly from where he was bending to shove a suitcase under the bed.

"What made you say that— 'fair means or foul'?"

"Why, I don't know. It's just that she has such a determined way about her—and then she's been in business; and you know what *business* is."

Mr. Bladeswell went to the doorway and stood looking out into the dusk. A girl and a boy in their late teens, both wearing open-collared shirts and jeans, walked past on the road, hand in hand, oblivious to possible observers.

Behind him Mrs. Bladeswell turned on the lamp with a pleated paper shade which stood on the small table beside the bed.

"I can't say I've ever cared especially," she was going on desultorily, "for that *masculine* type. It's all right in the daytime; but, after all, pants for dinner. And she smokes too much, did you notice? Although I must say I thought Mrs. Meadows was overdressed. And she does something to her hair. Did you notice? Mrs. Smith was the only one who was suitably dressed." She sighed. "And you know, she's not bad-looking. Mrs. Smith, I mean. Of course she looks forty-five or so, but her features are nice, and she isn't really too fat, just plump enough not to be skinny."

"I can see Mrs. Smith's got one on her side anyway."

Mr. Bladeswell moved over to one of the rockers and sat down. There were occasional faint sleepy twitters of birds and an obbligato of frogs' croaking somewhere in the distance. A few stars were bright between the treetops above the road, and a little breeze was gentle on his cheeks. There was a radio playing dance music in one of the cabins whose lights flickered warmly among the trees, and from somewhere he heard a child's fretful cry and the cough of a starting motor.

He told himself it was foolish, this inquiring watchfulness which had sprung up in him—just because he met three women who had money to spend on vacations and who had no husbands and because a man had died a week before on a beach two hundred miles farther north.

Trying to build up some excitement in his life, he supposed.

Still, there was Chet, his old friend. He'd known Chet Hoffman since he was a kid in knee pants. He wouldn't want to see Chet taken in by some designing woman who might take him for all she could get and make him unhappy—the way his first wife Gladys had.

If one of these women was a murderess, he wouldn't feel right if he just sat by and watched her trap Chet.

But shucks! He shook his head and brushed at a mosquito which was investigating his ear. How often did ordinary, decent people run into murderers? And these women were all just plain, everyday people like him and Elsie.

He frowned, though, in the darkness. For somebody among those nice, ordinary people on the beach at Santa Cruz had committed a cold-blooded murder right there in the broad daylight.

It destroyed your faith in human nature, running up against something like that, that's what it did.

CHAPTER EIGHT

Breakfast was at eight the next morning; and when the Bladeswells and Chet arrived at the ranch house they were met by only Mrs. Smith and Mrs. Fergusson, the latter wearing her jodhpurs again but a plaid shirt this time. Mrs. Meadows apparently found the hour too early even for the sake of Mr. Hoffman's possible favors.

There was a smaller crowd for the chilled cantaloupe and hot cakes and bacon of the morning meal. Only the entire crowd of Abernathys, ready for the day in an assortment of sun suits, sandals, and eyeshades, the elderly couple whose name the Bladeswells were reminded was Finklestauffer, and a middle-aged couple who had not appeared at dinner the night before were there to answer the cheerful summons of the cowbell.

As Mrs. Fergusson shook out her napkin and spread it over her whipcord-covered thighs, she fixed her eyes on Chet and demanded, "Well, how about it? Going to take that ride with me this morning, Mr. Hoffman?"

"Didn't you notice my nice new Levis?" he retorted cheerfully. "Didn't put them on for nothing. But remember, now, we only stay out two hours. I haven't been on a horse in ten years. So even a couple of hours'll probably half kill me."

Mrs. Smith smiled at him comfortingly. "If it does, I'll try to dig up some liniment for you."

"Will you promise to rub it on too?" he challenged jokingly.

She returned his smile archly. "Well, now, I might just do that."

"Don't try to kid us," Mrs. Fergusson scoffed. "You're not that soft. I can tell just to look at you you keep yourself in condition. You look like a man who's used to exercise."

Sunning himself in this feminine attention, Chet ate his hot cakes with gusto; and Mr. Bladeswell calculated that the ladies had come out about even in the exchange, Mrs. Smith giving Chet a feeling that she was solicitous of his comfort and was also one who could take a joke, Mrs. Fergusson letting him bask in the admiration implied in her opinion that he looked fit.

By getting him off alone on horseback Mrs. Fergusson would be a few up on her rivals; and of course Mrs. Meadows was losing out by her absence. She probably intended to make up for it later in the day.

Inwardly Mr. Bladeswell laughed at himself a little for the way he was mentally keeping score on the ladies. After all, they only had a week to work, and you couldn't get far in seven days.

Before he went to sleep the night before he had deliberately made up his mind to be nosy. He was going to find out by direct questioning whether one of the three widows had a mysterious past.

He had decided to start on Mrs. Fergusson, since in some ways she seemed the most—well, dangerous—of the three; so he asked, as if trying to make polite social conversation, "Have you lived in Denver long, Mrs. Fergusson?"

"Off and on all my life."

"Was your husband in business there?"

"My first one was."

"Oh." Mr. Bladeswell cut a strip of bacon in two with his fork. You couldn't very well pursue the questioning by anything like, "And how many husbands have you had?" or "I meant your *last* one."

While he stumbled around in his mind looking for the most suitable next query Mrs. Bladeswell began a dissertation on the difficulty of getting mail regularly while on the road.

"I expected letters from our daughter and son to be waiting for us here, but there wasn't anything at the office last night." She beamed at the others expansively. "Our daughter, Margie, lives in Lincoln, has two lovely children. Her husband works in the capitol; and our son is in business for himself in Kansas City. Doing very well." She smiled expectantly at Mrs. Smith. "Do you have any children, Mrs. Smith?"

"No."

Mrs. Bladeswell looked taken aback, then rather pitying, and to change the subject, leaned forward to address Mrs. Fergusson, "How about you? Do you have a family, Mrs. Fergusson?"

"I have a daughter—in New York. She's in advertising," that lady returned shortly.

"Oh, so far away. I don't suppose you see her very often."

"Not very."

"By your first husband, I suppose," Mrs. Bladeswell prodded delicately.

Her husband knew that Elsie was merely trying to keep up conversation on the subject she assumed all women were most interested in: their offspring; but Mrs. Fergusson sent Mrs. Bladeswell a glance which indicated that the other was being nosy.

"Yes," she said, and moved so that her left shoulder met Mrs. Bladeswell's gaze. "I asked Mr. Fenn," she informed Chet briskly, "to save the pinto for you this morning. He's a nicely gaited little fellow, lively but not skittish.

I always ride a little mare—they call her Daisy—"

Rebuffed, Mrs. Bladeswell turned valiantly to Mrs. Smith. "Are you a native of Illinois?"

Mrs. Smith turned her head away and murmured, "Mr. Hoffman, would you be so kind—the cream, please?" She twinkled at Chet. "I shouldn't use so much cream in my coffee—plump the way I am—but I'm afraid I do spoil myself."

"Not at all," Chet responded gallantly. "I like to see a woman with a figure. Never could understand this fad of women starving themselves."

"I'm certainly glad to hear that. To tell the truth I've never felt I weighed too much, but with all the women trying to look like fenceposts, you begin to feel old-fashioned if you aren't skinny as a rail."

"Now I'd never call you old-fashioned."

Mrs. Fergusson broke in with a smooth laugh. "I should say not, Mrs. Smith. And what are fashions anyway? Just something for sheep to follow. I believe in everybody developing their own personality, having some individuality. Isn't that the way you feel, Mr. Hoffman?"

"Oh yes. Sure. Sure."

Since Mrs. Smith was conventional down to the last eyelet in her sturdy tie oxfords and the last pearl button in her mass-production cotton dress, there were somewhat dubious implications in Mrs. Fergusson's remark; and Mrs. Smith seemed to sense this, for the look she directed upon her fellow breakfaster across the table was not made up entirely of sweetness and light.

Mrs. Bladeswell had been left out of things for a while, and now she leaned across her husband and inquired of Mrs. Smith which cottage she occupied.

Mr. Bladeswell sipped his coffee, defeated. He supposed he could get each one of them alone and try to dig into her past, but he had a nasty feeling that Chet was the only man at Escondido any of them would want to be seen with be with at the moment, and that an old married man like himself might find it difficult to arrange tête-à-tête.

Already the attitudes of these two at least struck him as evasive about their personal lives. Which looked queer in itself. Usually you had to fight to keep from hearing complete biographies of the people you met on trips, down to the time they had measles when they were six and the time their oldest son swallowed a button when he was nine.

After breakfast Mr. and Mrs. Bladeswell strolled across the grass to sit under one of the big umbrellas shading a group of canvas chairs. Mrs. Bladeswell had brought her knitting along, and Mr. Bladeswell went down to the office where he bought a city paper which he read while his wife knitted and watched the pool which was already alive with young bodies leaping in and out of its cool depths.

They had been sitting there for perhaps an hour when Mr. Bladeswell, who had finished the paper, glanced toward the lawn at the end of the pool and blinked like one suddenly confronted by an apparition.

"My gosh," he said to his wife, "ain't that Mrs. Meadows?"

Mrs. Bladeswell lowered her knitting and straightened her glasses as she stared in the direction toward which Mr. Bladeswell had nodded.

"It certainly is. And oh, dear, she's spotted us. Here she comes." She waved her hand, smiling hypocritically at the dainty pink and white figure floating along under a ruffled pink parasol.

"A parasol, as I live and breathe," Mrs. Bladeswell muttered. "Haven't seen one like that since before we were married."

"Darlings, good morning!" Mrs. Meadows caroled.

She tipped her parasol and closed it as she slipped under the shade of the big umbrella, sinking gracefully into one of the canvas chairs and spreading her starched pink piqué skirt artistically over her limbs as she crossed her feet in their open-toed white wedgies.

"Isn't it a glorious morning?" she demanded happily, slipping out of the bolero jacket of her shoulder-strapped frock and carefully hanging it on the back post of her chair.

"Didn't see you at breakfast," Mr. Bladeswell observed.

"Oh, I never eat breakfast. Just orange juice and coffee in my room. But you should see me at lunch. I simply gorge."

She giggled; and with difficulty Mrs. Bladeswell smiled in response. Mrs. Bladeswell felt that someone should tell Mrs. Meadows that she was past the age for giggling. It was even more obvious in the daylight—her being past the age, that is.

"Where are the rest of our little bunch this morning?"

"I don't know where Mrs. Smith disappeared to," Mr. Bladeswell replied, "but Mrs. Fergusson took Chet horseback riding."

Mrs. Meadows' laugh rippled out. "Oh, she would, wouldn't she? Such an active woman. Poor dear, he'll be so sore and stiff after all that riding."

"They were only going to be gone two hours," Mrs. Bladeswell said flatly.

"Mrs. Fergusson's a lovely person, an awfully good scout, but"—Mrs. Meadows leaned forward confidentially and looked ingenuously from Mr. to Mrs. Bladeswell—"personally, I just can't bear athletic women. I suppose it's because I'm such a little hothouse flower myself."

"I wouldn't say Mrs. Fergusson was athletic exactly," Mrs. Bladeswell said primly, and then hated herself, because she did think just that.

"You look," Mr. Bladeswell said kindly and hastily, "as if you had always had an easy life, as if you'd never had to exert yourself very much."

Mrs. Meadows glowed at him. "Well, I have been fortunate," she said complacently. "You see, Daddy was a doctor, an awfully successful one,

and we just had everything, whole houseful of servants, and"—she sighed
prettily—"I guess I was spoiled. And then I married so young, and Rex,
that was my first husband—his folks had money, and we just *played* at life,
lived in hotels and traveled, and I just never did anything—in the line of
work, you know."

If he had been discomfited at breakfast because the other two women
shied away from personal disclosures, Mr. Bladeswell realized that now he
had run into the opposite pole in the way of chance acquaintances. Mrs.
Meadows was the autobiographical type. He listened, however, with a
sense of discouragement, because from the first he realized that her chrono-
logue was strung on a chain of exaggeration—not to say downright false-
hood.

Mrs. Bladeswell had stopped working her needles and was regarding the
other woman with her lips parted.

Mrs. Meadows had got to the second husband whom she had had to divorce—"drank, you know"—when Mrs. Smith sauntered up to them from
the runway by the pool. Mr. Bladeswell was still unclear about what had
happened to Rex, the first husband. His mind had wandered at that
point, and after Mrs. Smith's interruption of the monologue, he never did
find out.

He almost stared rudely as he recognized Mrs. Smith. For a moment he
*had*n't recognized her. She was, he realized, one of those rare people who
looked better without clothes than with them. A one-piece blue silk
bathing suit revealed full breasts held firmly in place above an honest-to-
God waistline and firm, rounded buttocks. The flesh on her thighs and legs
was smooth and tapered neatly to the knees and ankles. Without the
unimaginative belted dresses and the unyieldingly "sensible" shoes she wore
ordinarily Mrs. Smith was, in the terms of Mr. Bladeswell's youth, "a fine
figure of a woman."

Mr. Bladeswell glanced at his wife and saw a little self-satisfied smirk on
her face. She was chalking one up for her favorite. At least in the raw—
which in marriage was after all what counted—Mrs. Smith had both her
rivals beaten. Mr. Bladeswell was sure of it even though he had never seen
the other two in bathing suits.

"All ready for a swim?" he accosted the newcomer pleasantly.

"All ready," she agreed complacently, and sank into a chair facing them.
Mr. Bladeswell thought she looked rather smug.

"Isn't it rather hot, going in at this time of day?" Mrs. Meadows inquired
with patently artificial sweetness.

"I don't mind," Mrs. Smith said placidly. "The sun is good for a person."

"Some people's skin is tough enough to stand it," Mrs. Meadows said
with a smile which did not cover the tartness of her voice.

Mr. Bladeswell looked toward the pool, and pretended he was smiling at the children playing there. He had suspected that Mrs. Meadows wouldn't stack up so well against either of the other two in a bathing suit. He just had a hunch her legs were too fat above the knees, with a sort of squashed, doughy look to them.

If it hadn't been for the serious potentialities possibly present in one of these predatory females he would have found the prospects for the week ahead pretty amusing.

But he seemed to be haunted by the memory of that poor man on the beach and the elaborate theory he had built up around him. And the memory tinged his reactions to the comedy with somber suspicion.

CHAPTER NINE

Mrs. Smith was still sitting chatting with the others a little after eleven when Chet and Mrs. Fergusson strolled across the lawn toward the group.

Chet stretched out with a humorous groan in one of the longer chairs as Mrs. Fergusson dropped cross-legged to the grass. "I'll never be the same again," he moaned.

"Now, Chet," Mrs Fergusson reproved good-humoredly, "you're putting on. That horse didn't hurt you a bit. He rides like a veteran," she assured the others.

"Clara here is the one who rides like she was part of the horse," Chet said admiringly.

"How nice," Mrs. Meadows popped up eagerly. "You're using first names. Let's all call each other by our first names. I do hate formality." She beamed girlishly at Chet. "My name is Marice."

Mr. Bladeswell thought skeptically that it probably hadn't always been Marice. Probably Mary to start with. Mrs. Fergusson plucked at the cropped grass indifferently as Chet said agreeably, "That's a good idea. What's your name, Mrs. Smith?"

"Mabel," she returned without enthusiasm, as if she were not particularly thrilled with the name her parents had seen fit to bestow upon her.

"O.K., Mabel. And Mr. Bladeswell here is Mel—at least that's what we call him at the Elks Club back home. Melvin, isn't it, Mel? And the missus is Elsie." Chet chuckled. "Well, I guess that makes us all old friends."

"A person gets acquainted fast," Mr. Bladeswell observed, "out on the road like this."

In midafternoon, while Mrs. Bladeswell lay on her bed resting, Mr. Bladeswell and Chet sat in the rockers on the latter's little porch, visiting. After a while Mr. Bladeswell said slyly, "Pretty popular guy you are right now, eh, Chet?"

Chet had taken off his shirt, and he clasped his hands over his bare stomach and laughed. "You mean the girls? Well, I got to admit they do stick pretty close to me."

"Not scared one of 'em'll get her hooks in you, are you?"

"Don't worry about old Chet, Mel. I can take care of myself. And"—he sobered—"a man could do worse. They're all swell kids; you know that, Mel? Different types, of course, but all three of 'em good scouts."

"Not thinkin' of settling down, are you?"

"Well, I tell you, Mel, sometimes I don't know. I don't know but what if the right person came along I might not give some serious consideration to taking a whirl at it again. Some ways a bachelor's life is O.K., some ways it ain't. Wouldn't be bad to have a real home again, somebody to come back to at night."

Mr. Bladeswell hooked his thumbs in his suspenders and laced his fingers together over his shirt front. He realized now that the situation was more serious than he had thought. Chet had struck Escondido at a psychological moment, and the three husband-hunting widows had sensed his condition with deadly accuracy. When a man began to tell himself vaguely that it might not be such a bad idea to get married, it needed only the first single-purposed woman who recognized the symptoms to bring about the consummation of that vague intention.

And here there were three of them having correctly diagnosed Chet's mental and emotional state.

And suppose one of them were a professional husband killer. Mr. Bladeswell moved his bottom uneasily on the wooden seat of the chair. If only he could set his mind at rest that they were all what they seemed, just nice ladies of uncertain age who wanted a good husband and a comfortable home.

The chances were a thousand to one that's what they were. But Mr. Bladeswell would like to have been sure.

He had so little faith, however, in his detective abilities that he despaired of being able to find out.

Mr. Bladeswell didn't read detective novels except when they happened to run serially in his *Saturday Evening Post*, but from these magazine stories he remembered how the detective often set the stage and caught the suspect red-handed in a second crime—or third or fourth, as the case often was.

He, too, could probably pretend to each of the ladies that he "knew something." After all, he had been right on the scene a few hundred yards down the beach at Santa Cruz. He could pretend he had seen the woman that Sunday; and then, if she ran true to form à la fiction, she'd try to bump *him* off—to silence him, and he could expose her while she was doing it.

But Mr. Bladeswell had a nasty hunch he wasn't clever enough to pull it off. His trap would probably work only too well if one of them was guilty; and *he* would wind up under a bush with his head bashed in, and nobody ever would find out if one of the widows was leaving a trail of bodies through the West.

Regretfully he acknowledged that the fancy stuff was out of his line. He guessed Chet would just have to take his chances in the field of romance.

CHAPTER TEN

The Bladeswells had bought supplies at the store the day before so they could eat breakfasts at the cottage and have a few things on hand for Mr. Bladeswell's between-meal snacks.

The next morning, while his wife did the "housekeeping" this eating at home entailed, Mr. Bladeswell strolled down to the store again to replenish his supply of cigars and to pick up the daily paper. It was a bright, hot morning with the sun reflecting back from the leaves, the sky a uniform pale blue. Mr. Bladeswell mused on the sky, thinking that it seemed to be not the differences in the earth that he noticed most out here, but in the sky, which one would have thought would be the one thing the same the world over. He sort of missed the translucent white clouds which at home always drifted lazily somewhere above. There was something empty, almost harsh and unfeeling about the motionless, unvaried blue dome which curved high above the sunlit hills of California.

Several times Mr. Bladeswell tipped his ventilated cloth hat and smiled at passers-by as he proceeded toward the cluster of business buildings at the entrance, for already they were getting acquainted among the current population of Escondido.

The man who tended the store called him by name, and Mr. Bladeswell took a newspaper from the wire rack and selected three cigars and a box of crackers and a glass of cream cheese.

With his purchases under his arm he stood near the door and idly considered a wooden rack displaying paper-bound books in bright jackets set up so the sensational front covers assaulted one's attention.

Mr. Bladeswell read quite a few of these inexpensive books. For relaxation he usually bought Westerns; but he tried to keep up with things, and he often picked up informational stuff. He was surprised and rather complacent about what a lot of things he'd learned since they started to put out books at a price you could afford and where you'd run across them easily.

For instance, he'd always wanted to read that one everybody talked so much about a few years back, *How to Win Friends and Influence People*, and he never got around to it until it came out for a quarter. Lot of good common sense in it. And then there was deep stuff too. Like one called *What Happened in History*, and another, *Patterns of Culture*. Things he'd read in all of them he just never would have known if they hadn't been for sale at the newsstand.

He meditated, trying to decide whether he just wanted a good lively story like *Ghost Town on the Yellowstone* or whether he wanted to learn something as *The Birth and Death of the Sun* promised.

There were always lots of mysteries mixed in with the other books, and his eye lingered on one showing a frightened young woman in a filmy negligee staring up into the darkness of an open stairway. When he did read detective stories he liked them with mostly men characters and lots of action and guns; but he picked up the frightened young lady and thoughtfully turned the pages. The author was a woman, a name he was unfamiliar with. Ordinarily he would never have given the book a second glance, but there was something about the combination of women and mystery and murder that drew him right now.

He fished a quarter out of his pocket and turned back to lay it on the counter, holding up the book.

"O.K.," the clerk said, and rang up the sale.

Mr. Bladeswell started the book before noon, but it was soon time to go to lunch, and they spent an hour or so visiting with the Finklestauffers on the veranda afterward and then took a little swim. After that Mr. Bladeswell settled down to read in one of the rockers on the cottage porch, his feet up on the straight chair he had carried out for the purpose.

It was a reasonably engrossing story, longer than he thought was necessary. The action took place in an old-fashioned mansion where a group of exceedingly eccentric relatives had gathered for a rich elderly aunt's annual birthday party.

A little frown grew between Mr. Bladeswell's eyes as he penetrated deeper into the book. The characters seemed to spend an unconscionable amount of time and energy spying on each other and searching one another's rooms for some mysterious document of whose custody everybody suspected everybody else. A good deal of this behavior was practiced in the dead of night, embellished by ominous creaks of doors and ghostly footsteps on stairs and the flutter of draperies against people's bare arms.

The irritatingly knowing detective whose presence in the party was somewhat improbably explained outdid all the others in snooping, ransacking bedrooms and drawers and suitcases and even the ladies' handbags with perfect immunity, and—as it turned out—with perfect success. Not, of course, without several close shaves, and not without having been knocked unconscious three times from blows on the head any one of which would have produced concussion in an ordinary skull with a resultant period of hospitalization.

The detective sure did find out things about the characters, though, from reading the letters in their luggage and studying the condition of their clothing.

By the time he had finished the last page Mr. Bladeswell had forgotten all the clues laid out in the first fifty pages and couldn't even remember whom he had first suspected nor why he had done so. He just dumbly accepted the author's involved but glib explanation of motives and methods.

Mr. Bladeswell closed the slick covers of the book and gazed unseeing at his toes in their white cotton socks.

No one in the book had seemed to bother about it, but Mr. Bladeswell knew that you could be put in jail for messing around with other people's things. You weren't even supposed to enter their rooms without permission.

Still, an examination of somebody's personal belongings would sure tell you a lot about them. You would have to *deduce* a great many things; but Mr. Bladeswell was already somewhat astonished at himself for the deductions he had made concerning the three unidentified bodies.

He could hear his wife moving about inside the cottage, preparing to take a shower and dress for dinner. Elsie would be thoroughly shocked at the ideas that were forming in his head. He was somewhat shocked himself.

He lowered his feet and thrust them into his oxfords without tying the laces and shuffled into the cottage. In the kitchen he made himself a peanut-butter sandwich and poured out a glass of milk, both of which he carried out to the porch where he sat down and consumed them.

Mrs. Bladeswell was in the bathroom and consequently unaware of what he was doing, but when she came to the doorway a few minutes later and saw part of a sandwich in his hand and a third of a glass of milk standing on the chair, she exclaimed rather querulously, "You're not eating *now!* It's past five o'clock."

"My stomach felt kind of peckish," he replied mildly.

"But a sandwich! You'll ruin your appetite for dinner."

"I don't think I'll go down for dinner tonight. Later on I'll just eat some fig bars and a cup of tea."

"But what about me? I'm starved, and I certainly don't feel like making a meal out of a sandwich and fig bars."

"You go on down without me. I'll come down and meet you after dinner in the lounge. I hear they have a dance tonight, and we can watch. Might take a turn or two ourselves."

"Go down without you!" she said, aghast.

"Sure. Why not? You can walk down with Chet. Tell you the truth, my stomach ain't felt right all day. And I didn't lay down this afternoon the way you did, so I'll just take a little snooze while you're having dinner and then we can stay down at the ranch house and make a night of it this evening."

She scrutinized him with concerned eyes. "If you don't feel good maybe I ought to stay with you."

"I feel all right. Gettin' something in my stomach was all I needed. But I don't want a big dinner now." He yawned. "Feel kind of sleepy, and this is a good chance to catch forty winks while you're all down eating and it's quiet."

Wonderingly and unwillingly and a little suspiciously Mrs. Bladeswell surrendered to his wishes and finally went off down the road with Chet.

CHAPTER ELEVEN

Mr. Bladeswell pulled his watch out of his pocket and regarded it gravely. A quarter to six. The shadows were longer now and the sunlight had a mellow, slightly orange tinge to it, but the atmosphere was warm and unmistakably daytime-ish. He sighed and bent to tie his shoelaces. Even the gray and purple of early dusk would be better; but he had to take his chances.

He looked worriedly at the Yale lock on the door standing back against the wall inside, then rose and went into the cottage. As he looked toward the dresser top he thought back regretfully to the days when Elsie's hair was long and held up by sturdy wire pins. The light brown bobby pin lying on the ecru scarf beside her comb would have to do. He picked it up and dropped it into his shirt pocket.

After closing and locking his own door he went around to the trail behind the house. This path came out on a road lower down that branched off from his own to ascend the hill. Mrs. Fergusson's cottage, he had learned, faced that road, thus lying behind and diagonally across from Number 12, the Bladeswell cabin.

He left the trail before it reached the road and walked between two oak trees growing on the incline behind Mrs. Fergusson's lodging, the small dried leaves rustling a little under his feet. The slope of the hill hid him from view of Chet's or his own cottage and the road in front of them, but from the house across the street from Mrs. Fergusson's he could be seen plainly if anyone chose to look.

He had a good explanation, of course, if someone did see him. A man had a right to take a late-afternoon walk.

Soon, however, he was behind the cottage; and then he felt safe. It was the last house on the short road. Beyond was only a gully softened by willows. He walked around to the far side of the house where Mrs. Fergusson's car stood in nonchalant, rakish splendor. A deep maroon with brown leather cushions, its top was down, exposing a front and a back seat.

Mr. Bladeswell studied the machine thoughtfully. Some bus. It looked like money. And there was a Colorado license all right. She hadn't lied about that. He went around and peered at the ownership card under cellophane on the steering post. "Clara G. Fergusson." And a Denver address.

He pulled the clip of an automatic pencil loose from his shirt pocket and felt of his pants pockets with annoyance. Fine sleuth he was. Didn't even have a piece of paper for notes. There was a paper packet of matches in his shirt pocket, and he resorted to copying the address inside its cover.

Then he surveyed the house cautiously. So far, so good. They couldn't do anything to a man for looking at an automobile. Warily he walked to the corner of the little front porch and saw that the front door was closed. He nodded slightly and retraced his steps. Before the larger rear window he paused and studied the screen which hung from two brackets at the top and was caught at the bottom by a hook. He drew a deep breath and fished out the bobby pin, pulling it out straight and with some difficulty bending it into a curve at one end. He had to pry at one of the interstices in the screen to push the hooked pin end through it. One side of the tiny square broke from the pressure, and then he had more room to maneuver his improvised tool. In the process another strand of the aging mesh gave way, and then there was a small hole where before there had been neat little squares. It wasn't difficult after that to reach the hook and pull it away from the catch on the sill.

He returned the pin to his pocket and carefully lifted the screen off its brackets and set it on the ground so that it leaned against the house.

First glancing about uneasily, he hoisted himself up and wriggled over the sill. The room was sunny with light from the west window which overlooked the driveway. It was furnished almost exactly like the Bladeswells' place, yet it did not look the same. A copy of *Time*, an ash tray, and a tiny alarm clock with a luminous dial shared the top of the bedside table, and a pair of soft leather moccasins waited on the rug beneath the folds of a wine-colored flannel robe hanging half off the foot of the bed.

On the dresser scarf were a comb and a brush with silver backs, a closed box of face powder, a round metal container for rouge, a lipstick in a silver case, and a bottle of Tweed toilet water. That was all.

The gate-leg table by the front window had one leaf opened, and on it lay a closed brown leather correspondence kit and a camera in a henna-colored leather case with a shoulder strap.

One large brown suitcase stood against the wall, and a smaller but match-ing case lay closed on one of the straight chairs.

Mr. Bladeswell felt a discomfiture unrelated to his uneasiness over law-breaking. The room was uncongenial to him somehow, rather unfeelingly bare and efficiently neat. Mrs. Fergusson wasn't a homey person.

He glanced about uncertainly. It would be easier if you knew what you were looking for, like the people in the story. And what was he looking for? Well, one thing was for signs that a man had recently lived intimately with the woman.

He opened the closet door and peered hesitantly at the voluminous camel's-hair coat, the rust-colored herringbone-weave tweed suit, a brown-and-white-striped silk dress, and a light brown gabardine skirt slipped over the bar of a hanger with an eggshell satin blouse over it. The low riding shoes were on the floor and the jodhpurs and a plaid shirt hung on a hook. She must be wearing something else tonight.

Mr. Bladeswell went on to the bathroom and saw nothing personal ex-cept green soap in a white plastic container and a green toothbrush hang-ing in the metal claw provided for it.

He opened the little medicine cabinet and was treated to the sight of a can of toothpowder and a squat jar of cold cream.

In the doorway to the main room he took another deep breath and de-cided he must hurry a little more. He didn't have all night.

Without expecting much he crossed to the table and opened the corre-spondence kit. Envelopes were tucked neatly under the flap on one side, writing paper on the other. Loose on top of the paper were a few three-cent stamps, a blotter, two penny postcards, and a folded piece of paper.

He opened this sheet and suddenly his eyes widened. In one corner was a black-and-white print of a three-story building with waves lapping its base while underneath was the neat legend, "Sea Breeze Hotel, Santa Cruz, California, a view from every room."

Now at least he knew where she had stayed. Of course she might have told him if he had asked. But again she might not, and at any rate she sel-dom gave a person a chance to ask.

He folded the note paper and slipped it into his pocket, and with more spirit went to the dresser drawers. There was a safe at the ranch house where guests left their valuables, but he found a heavy hand-tooled Mex-ican leather handbag in the top drawer and began an inventory of its con-tents. In the wallet, besides a few bills and American Express checks, there were the usual driver's license and Three-A card; that was all.

Mr. Bladeswell thought of his own stuffed billfold, bulging with every-thing from lodge-dues receipts to snapshots of the grandchildren. Mrs. Fergusson traveled light, you could say that. Not even a checkbook, just the traveler's checks in her wallet.

Hastily he glanced through the rest of the drawers, finding nothing more exciting than knitted rayon shorts and ankle socks.

The big suitcase was empty, he found; and the smaller one, he decided, was a sort of supply case. There were camera films, a mending kit, a manicure set in a folding case, a wrapped bar of soap, a box of cleansing tissues, and a first-aid kit in it.

He sighed and felt a little futile as he decided to get out. Except for the name of her hotel in Santa Cruz, his snooping hadn't gained him very much in the way of information. At the window he noticed the drawer in the bedside table, and carelessly, just to be thorough, he pulled it open—and drew in his breath audibly. Beside a neatly folded, white, man's handkerchief lay a small but wicked-looking revolver. This Mr. Bladeswell did not pick up. He merely stared at it. A twenty-two, he thought. He was more familiar with hunting rifles and shotguns than he was with revolvers.

He pushed the drawer closed slowly. Of course it was not so strange. A woman traveling alone, she would want something for protection. And, remembering Mrs. Fergusson, Mr. Bladeswell's opinion was that she would protect herself with it, too, if she thought it necessary.

After landing on his feet on the dry ground outside the window he hung the screen in place carefully and managed finally to push the hook into the upright circlet of metal on the sill. She was a funny woman. He'd learned that much, anyway. Not at all the kind of woman he understood.

CHAPTER TWELVE

He drew out his watch. Six-sixteen. He stared at the Roman numerals on the dial. Was it possible? Had it been only half an hour since he left his own cabin? It seemed as if he had been in Mrs. Fergusson's room for hours.

He pushed his tongue against the back of his front teeth and considered. They would be in the dining room until seven—easy.

Mrs. Smith's cabin was farther down in the direction of the highway on a road that met Mrs. Fergusson's in a V at the intersection with his own road. He decided he had better take the closer cottage, Mrs. Meadows', which would leave him nearer the ranch house when he finished.

The road, when he came out on it beside Chet's house, was deserted, and he crossed it furtively. He pushed his way among the greasewood bushes and the horse-chestnut trees which hid the backs of the houses facing the courtyard from the view of the cabins on the upper road. He found the house easily, the dark blue club coupé with its California license parked beside it helping him to identify it. There was some risk in coming into sight beside the car, but the automobile registrations seemed important in his investigations.

The window was down only halfway, and he had to squint over it to read the white slip, "Gordon J. Meadows and Marice E. Meadows." Joint ownership. H'm. So there was a Mr. Meadows kicking around somewhere. Yet Mrs. Meadows was definitely acting like a woman who wanted to catch a man. Could the Gordon J. have died—say at Santa Cruz—or been divorced recently, and she was simply waiting to change the registration until she got a new license in January? Or was she a married woman pretending to be single and having her fling? Or was she planning to cut loose from Gordon J. and wanted to have another prospect staked out before she abandoned the present meal ticket?

The car was locked, so he couldn't investigate its interior. He edged along to the back of the house observing with relief that trees protected it from the view of its neighbors, and repeated the performance with the bobby pin.

The cretonne draperies were drawn across the windows and the room was warm and scented. The perfume declared itself the instant he had put his head inside. The whole room required a moment of readjustment after the Spartan severity of the one from which he had just come. This was as unmistakably Mrs. Meadows' setting as her own boudoir at home must be.

Blond leather luggage stood open everywhere with tumbled pastel contents spilling out. A magazine called *Glamour* lay face down on the bed where the white pillows were stacked against the headboard. A stiff-backed novel with a romantic title lay on the bedside table. The closet door was open revealing a row of summery frocks hanging above varicolored sandals scattered on the floor. The top of the dresser bewildered Mr. Bladeswell. Jars and bottles and shiny covered boxes jostled each other in no semblance of order. A crumpled lace-edged handkerchief had fallen to the floor beside a straight chair where a net brassiere hung by one strap from the back; a pair of chiffon panties lay wrinkled up on the seat. A peach-colored slip trimmed with eyelet embroidery hung by the straps over the corner of the closet door, and a pale blue robe trailed on the floor beneath the footboard of the bed across which it had been carelessly dropped. Two dainty blue satin mules lay one over the other on the floor beside the negligee.

Mr. Bladeswell pushed his hat farther back on his head and gazed about with dismay. In all that clutter you hardly knew where to begin.

A white patent-leather purse lay on the bedside table with the handle dangling. He reached out and opened it. A puff of scent rose from the satin-lined interior, but aside from a sheer linen handkerchief crisscrossed with cutout stitching and a silver compact monogrammed with intertwining *M's* the lingering perfume was all it contained.

Another larger purse in blond leather matching the luggage lay with the flap turned back among the scattered envelopes and picture postcards and part of a newspaper on the table under the front windows. The contents of this one looked more fruitful, although it was obvious that this purse, too, had been stripped, essential objects such as wallet and change purse having been transferred to whatever bag Mrs. Meadows had with her in the dining room. There were, however, a checkbook, an address book, and a little memorandum book with pencil attached still in it.

Mr. Bladeswell sank onto the chair by the table and prepared to do a thorough job. He opened the checkbook first and inspected the deposit book. His lips pressed together as he saw once more: Gordon J. and Marice E. Meadows. Turning to the check stubs, he found a balance of $525.06.

Uneasily Mr. Bladeswell now suspected Mrs. Meadows of trying deliberately to two-time a very-present Gordon J. Taking a trip by herself, for a "rest" perhaps, and bent upon having a good time with another man while she had the chance, deliberately posing as a divorcee or a widow to make her flirtations easier.

Impressed as he was by these deductions, Mr. Bladeswell almost abandoned further examination of Mrs. Meadows' belongings. But straight curiosity—now that he was in this deep—led him to finish his inventory of the handbag's contents.

The address book with its names and telephone numbers was too confusing to tell him very much. Most of the people she knew seemed to have suburban Los Angeles addresses, although the names of various states appeared here and there.

There were no letters, no postcards addressed to Mrs. Meadows. It seemed as if there should be some communication from Mr. Meadows, if she were still technically his wife, but there was nothing.

From the table top Mr. Bladeswell swiped a piece of pale gray notepaper with a design of violets in the upper corner, and copied the Meadows' home address from the checkbook.

He found no letters written on the notepaper which lay loose on the table; but one colored postcard depicting the Inn in Santa Maria was addressed to a Mrs. Mildred De Valle in Hollywood. The message on one side of the card, written in an up-and-down script that was rather attractive, read: "Dearest Mil—Having a grand time. Escondido is everything you said it was. Awfully nice people. One in particular paying little me a lot of attention. Will have a lot to tell you when I get back. Love, Marice."

Mr. Bladeswell laid the purse back as nearly as possible as he had found it and rather desultorily completed his search of the cottage. There were no male garments or sartorial appurtenances among her things that he could see, and no guns or other lethal weapons. He almost didn't go into the bathroom at all, but just as he was going to climb out of the window he remembered that room and decided to take a look.

Mrs. Fergusson's bathroom had had an almost unoccupied appearance. Not so Mrs. Meadows'. A box of bath powder stood on the tank of the toilet, and—although he couldn't figure out how she used them in the shower—a large bottle of bath salts stood beside it next to a low jar of cold cream with a box of facial tissues balanced on top of it. Pink soap shaped like a rose rested in the soap-dish, and a huge bottle of Honeysuckle cologne rode unstably on the other slippery corner of the washbowl.

He opened the medicine chest to a bewildering array of "things." He had no idea of the purpose served by most of them. One small cylinder-shaped bottle caught his attention by its typewritten label and the blue-lettered print which indicated that it had originated in an Owl Drugstore in Los Angeles, California. The typewriting stated that it contained capsules of sleeping powder, no more than one of which were to be used in any twelve-hour period, and listed the writer of the prescription as Dr. A. B. Levcowitz.

Mr. Bladeswell stood quite still, his hand on the edge of the mirror which constituted the door of the case. All his ideas underwent a painful readjustment. Perhaps Gordon J. had started the trip with his Marice. Perhaps it was his body which now lay unclaimed in the Santa Cruz county morgue.

Slowly Mr. Bladeswell opened the bottle. Four capsules lay in the bottom. He shook one out in his hand and replaced the bottle. Mrs. Meadows struck him as the sort of person who did not keep exact count of anything she owned, so she would probably not miss one capsule.

Out in the living room again he took one of the pale gray envelopes and folded it around the capsule, then thrust the packet down in a front pocket of his trousers where he wouldn't sit on it.

Now he looked once more to see if he had overlooked anything that would indicate a recent presence in Santa Cruz. But there was nothing.

When he was back on the tangled carpet of dry grass under the window Mr. Bladeswell consulted his watch again. It was ten minutes to seven, so he circled around past the car and came out on the path leading down to the lawns.

He walked with lowered eyes and hands in his pockets toward the house where a party of four teen-agers were sprawled on the steps exchanging badinage.

He had had no clear-cut plans when he started this snooping, but he figured now that the thing to do was to get in touch with Ed Doty by phone, telling him about the "clues"—that is, the hotel stationery of Mrs. Fergusson and Mrs. Meadows' sleeping potion, then leaving it up to the Santa Cruz police if they wanted to do anything. First, however, he must search Mrs. Smith's room, and make another try at abstracting information about their pasts from the three women.

CHAPTER THIRTEEN

There was no opportunity during the rest of the evening, however, to get away from his wife and the others to do further searching; and he had no chance for intimate talk with any of the three. All of them managed to dance fairly constantly, either with Chet or with the other men present. The clerk at the store and the attendant at the office had been pressed into service as partners for unattached female guests. From the youngest Abernathy to Mr. Finklestauffer, everyone participated during the evening in the square dancing, and it was past eleven when the Bladeswells broke away to return to their cabin.

On the way Mrs. Bladeswell suddenly broke the silence consideringly, "I think Mrs. Meadows is the best dancer."

But Mr. Bladeswell was not interested tonight in the relative progress the ladies were making with Chet Hoffman. The sleeping powder and the absent Gordon J. had him worried. Now that he thought of it, it struck him as odd that neither Mrs. Fergusson nor Mrs. Meadows had any photographs of a man in their possession, not even a snapshot.

He was almost ready to skip Mrs. Smith and to try to reach Doty by phone the first thing in the morning.

As soon as they had eaten breakfast the next day Mr. Bladeswell walked down to the store and the office to pick up the morning paper. Mrs. Fergusson, in navy blue slacks and brown oxfords, was striding down the graveled walk that divided the grass beyond the swimming pool, headed toward the office with a determined air.

Mr. Edwards, the attendant, was standing outside the little white-painted office, and Mr. Bladeswell saw the woman accost him in what seemed a belligerent manner.

Mr. Bladeswell approached the duo in time to hear Mrs. Fergusson's assertion, "I was certainly not mistaken. I tell you my cabin was entered sometime last evening."

Mr. Bladeswell's Adam's apple moved up and then settled into place. He felt pale, but he came up to the others with a mildly interrogative manner.

Mrs. Fergusson demanded, "What do you think, Mel? Somebody broke into my cabin last night."

"My, my!" He glanced at Mr. Edwards, who looked distressed. "Take anything?"

"No, that's the funny part of it. All that I can see is missing is a sheet of stationery from the hotel where I stayed in Santa Cruz."

There was no pretense in Mr. Bladeswell's surprised stare. But then Mrs. Fergusson was the methodical kind. She would know exactly how many sheets of paper she owned. Still, he hadn't expected her to miss it.

"If that's all that's gone," Mr. Edwards ventured placatingly, "maybe you just mislaid it."

She gave him a scornful glance. "I never mislay things. And several objects on the table were out of place. I might not have thought much about that, though, but it made me suspicious, so I examined the screen, and there was a hole in it right beside the hook, and the sill outside was wiped clean in the middle but still dusty at the sides. I tell you somebody climbed in through that window and went through my things. Since nothing valuable, like my camera or my gun, was taken, I assume it was just a prowler, some variety of peeping Tom. But I don't like it, and for the good of the place here you should take steps to stop it."

Both Mr. Edwards and Mr. Bladeswell had blinked when she said "gun." As far as Mr. Bladeswell was concerned he had a resigned feeling, his original opinion confirmed, that only in detective stories did people really get away with breaking and entering. Another thought was struggling through the froth of uneasiness at the surface of his mind. Would a woman who had a guilty conscience over a murder less than three weeks old be thus boldly risking the presence of police in her vicinity? For if the Fenns "took steps" to find the prowler it would mean calling the sheriff's office. On the other hand, why was she so incensed about the incident if no harm had been done other than the loss of a sheet of stationery?

"Well, I'll sure speak to Mr. Fenn about it," Mr. Edwards promised faintly.

"I would have told him myself," Mrs. Fergusson said, "but he doesn't seem to be around. For your sakes I won't say anything about this to anyone else. Mr. Bladeswell here will keep it to himself, too, won't you? But I warn you," she concluded ominously, "you'd better look into this or before you get through you'll have something worse than a stolen sheet of paper on your hands."

As she strode away in the direction of the ranch house Mr. Edwards and Mr. Bladeswell looked after her with worried frowns. At last Mr. Edwards broke out of his preoccupation and turned to Mr. Bladeswell. "Confidentially," he said, "I don't think anybody did break in. These women, they imagine things. Hysterical, you know."

Mr. Bladeswell grasped at the suggestion eagerly. "Sounded kind of screwy to me, too, to tell you the truth."

He went into the store and bought his paper, and when he came out he saw Mrs. Smith crossing the grass toward the pool, a bath towel over her shoulders, legs bare beneath her bathing suit. He tucked the paper under his arm and moved on more rapidly. Although his appetite for sleuthing had definitely abated in the last fifteen minutes, still, he was in it now, he might as well finish the job. It was risky, but he felt he was as good as in jail already. Mrs. Smith's back was to him, and he turned off the road leading to her cottage. He had to pass one house across the road from it, but he had learned that this was the one occupied by the schoolteachers, and he knew they spent their mornings on horseback.

To build the cottage Mrs. Smith occupied it had been necessary to bulldoze the side of the hill. Fortunately for Mr. Bladeswell's purpose a clump of box-elder bushes partially hid the house on the side toward the courtyard, and the cut-out bank loomed above the parking space where her neat black sedan stood.

Mr. Bladeswell walked past the cottage and ducked quickly in between the house and the car. Through the closed windows of the automobile he saw with surprise that the keys hung in the ignition. He opened the door and leaned across the seat to read the registration. Robert C. Smith and Mabel Smith. So she, too, had had a husband when the Illinois license was purchased that year.

The glove compartment was locked when he tried it, and he pulled the key from the switch and found the one on the ring that opened the glove compartment door. The contents were disappointingly impersonal: road maps, Kleenex, a package of gum, a chamois. Mr. Bladeswell's eyes roved over the interior of the car. It was a late-model Buick, but woven seat covers protected the cushions, and the tonneau was primly empty. Mr. Bladeswell tossed the keys in his hand and conceived a sudden notion to look inside the trunk at the rear. So he went behind the car and unlocked the storage space. One large piece of "airplane" luggage lay on the floor; it was nearly a small trunk. Absently he poked at the suitcase with his hand, and it moved under the pressure. Mr. Bladeswell's eyes steadied on the bag. Unconsciously he had expected it to be full of extra clothing that Mrs. Smith had not needed here at Escondido. He grasped the handle and the case lifted easily off the floor. It was obviously empty.

Thoughtfully he closed and locked the storage space. Empty. If she had taken necessary garments out of the case, would she not have left it in the house for repacking when she was ready to move on?

Now Mr. Bladeswell was no longer indifferent about inspecting Mrs. Smith's quarters. He peeked around the corner of the house toward the back window. But he was dubious about screens and windows since the recent encounter with Mrs. Fergusson. With a troubled expression he replaced the car keys where he had found them and walked around to the front of the cabin, studying it anxiously, wishing there were some easy means of entrance.

Without expecting anything he mounted the steps and took hold of the door handle. It turned, and he gave a little push, and the door stood open a crack. Startled, Mr. Bladeswell glanced over his shoulder. There was no one in sight on the road and only the front of the schoolteachers' cabin, blank and innocent in the morning sun, looked back at him from its position diagonally across the road.

He slipped in quickly and closed the door, speculating that Mrs. Smith had planned to run down for a quick dip and thought it unnecessary to lock up while she was gone.

A smaller suitcase, matching the one in the car, stood closed against the wall. Another lay on a straight chair with the top raised, still containing what seemed at a glance to be a few pieces of underwear. A fitted toilet case stood in the center of the dresser, and through the partially open closet door Mr. Bladeswell saw another medium-sized bag on the floor. He lifted the closed suitcase by the wall, judging by the weight that it was empty, and then moved over and pushed the bag on the closet floor with his toe. It slid weightlessly along the floor. Swiftly his eyes enumerated the chenille robe, the gabardine suit, the cotton and rayon frocks depending from hangers in the closet. He crossed the room and pulled open the dresser drawers. One of the two small top ones had a few handkerchiefs and a cellophane case of disposable powderpuffs in it. Only one of the longer drawers was in use, containing several flesh-colored knitted garments which seemed to be nightgowns and slips.

Mr. Bladeswell slowly pushed the drawer closed and stood immersed in thought, pinching his lower lip between thumb and forefinger. If he was any judge, Mrs. Smith's whole wardrobe would fit easily into the luggage now inside the house. Why, then, was the largest piece in the matching set locked up empty in the car? A car, incidentally, registered to Mr. and Mrs. Smith. Somehow this seemed the most suspicious indication he had picked up in any of the three cabins.

Suddenly Mr. Bladeswell froze in the attitude he had assumed. He had heard steps on the path outside. His eyes darted wildly around the small room, and unthinkingly he ducked into the kitchen. That is, it seemed an unthinking action, but in a flash he had known the kitchen was safest. She would be getting clothes out of the closet, entering the bathroom probably to take off her wet bathing suit.

With his back against the inside wall, he heard the door open and the plop of flat-soled sandals on the board floor beyond the partition. Sweat began to run down Mr. Bladeswell's temples and drip off his cheeks. His thoughts, however, were strangely and wryly philosophical. He had known all the time he couldn't get away with sleuthing, that *something* would happen.

It felt almost as if the nerves in his eardrums were rising to the surface and reaching out to catch the sounds of her movements out of the air. As he heard her steps in the bathroom just beyond him and heard the pipes suddenly singing hoarsely as water was released from them, he let his breath out softly and moved stealthily. Now was the time.

As he reached the doorway he swept the main room with one furtive, comprehensive look and took a long, breathless step toward the outside door. His hand was on the knob and he was almost ready to start breathing again when a choked scream reached out from behind him and stopped him cold in the middle of a movement.

Fearfully he let his head turn sideways on his neck, and sure enough there she was in the bathroom doorway, still in her bathing suit, her hair tousled, a towel in her hands, one end held a little higher than the other, as if she had been arrested while wiping her face.

Mr. Bladeswell dropped his hand and turned a little farther back into the room.

"Huh-hullo," he said with a weak smile.

Mrs. Smith was simply staring at him unbelievingly. Finally she demanded sharply, "What are you doing here?"

Mr. Bladeswell was not aware of consciously thinking it up, but he heard himself saying foolishly, "Well, I—I was just—out for a walk, and—and I thought I saw smoke coming out of your kitchen windows, so I stopped to investigate, and I found the door unlocked, so I thought I'd better go in and see, and—and then you came in. And, well, I thought you'd be—surprised, me being in here, especially as there didn't seem to be any—smoke, after all, so I thought I'd just slip out without startling you—"

He halted and met her eyes hopelessly, knowing that wasn't going over.

She had lowered her hands and they lay hidden in the towel at her waist, her elbows slightly akimbo. She said nothing, but her eyes were intent, measuring, as if she were trying to make up her mind. She took a step forward and rested one hand with the towel over it on the dresser top.

"Who are you?" she said quietly.

"Why—why, nobody. That is, I'm Mel Bladeswell, from Omaha, Nebraska."

She was eying him carefully, and after a moment she asked bluntly, "Have you been going through my things?"

"No. No, I swear, Mrs. Smith, it was like I said. I—I thought I saw smoke, and you know how dangerous fire can be this time of year."

She waited a few seconds, and then she nodded slightly. "All right."

"I hope—uh—well, no hard feelings, I hope," he said thickly.

"No. No, no hard feelings."

Mr. Bladeswell tipped his hat then, clutched his papers tighter under his arm, and escaped.

When he was out of sight of the cabin he stumbled toward a rock beside the road and sat down weakly. He laid the paper down, took off his hat, and wiped the bare front of his head and forehead with his handkerchief.

At the moment he didn't care if they never caught the murderer of those three poor men. He was through.

He sat there breathing deeply for a few minutes and then pulled out a cigar and lighted it. The stone was in the shade of the box elders which hid Mrs. Smith's cabin, and for the moment he had no inclination to move.

So defeated was he that now he hadn't even any desire to communicate with Ed Doty. The chilling impact of being discovered at his investigations had somehow jarred his "facts" into new focus, and he realized that the Santa Cruz police would probably only laugh if Doty conveyed to them that a middle-western tourist had "discovered" three suspicious females at a resort called El Valle Escondido. For what were his suspicions based on: three middle-aged women without visible spouses who had their caps set for an eligible man from Nebraska; a sheet of hotel notepaper; a bottle of sleeping medicine; and an empty suitcase.

What did his "clues" amount to, after all, even if his original theory about the Santa Cruz murder were correct? The very fact that suspicious circumstances existed in connection with all three of the women seemed to cancel out all of them. For certainly all three could not have had a hand in filling the Cola bottle with sleeping medicine.

Finally Mr. Bladeswell rose stiffly from the stone whose coolness had penetrated through the seat of his trousers; and he rose with the conviction that his detective career was over.

CHAPTER FOURTEEN

Mrs. Smith stood for several minutes with her hand on dresser, her eyes on the screen door through which Mr. Bladeswell had passed. His story of smoke had passed out of her mind as a puff of real smoke would drift away on a stiff breeze.

Anger, suspicion, fear: she could not have said which predominated in retrospective consideration of the mystifying little man.

Although he was not really so "little." It was just that he was so mild and unassuming that you thought of him as unimposing; and it was big people who were usually imposing. Like Mr. Hoffman—Chet. He was a big man. The kind of man she ought to have had. Years ago. Jolly. Almost happy-go-lucky. Someone who would make life fun.

As it had never been with Robert.

She was entitled to a little fun now. To laughter. Yes, even to romance. God knows she had had little enough of romance. A trip like this, for instance, it would be exciting with Mr. Hoffman—with Chet. She must get used to calling him that.

Even that, how hard it was to call him by his first name. It showed how stiff, how constricted she had become. How—there was no getting away from it—how dull she was. And it was living with Robert that had made her dull.

Everything came back to Robert. It was significant, when you stopped to think of it, that everyone called him Robert. You couldn't imagine anyone calling him Bob.

Mrs. Smith walked over to the rocking chair, the bath towel trailing from her hand, and sat down. She buried her face in her hands, the turkish toweling crushed against her cheek.

He had been a good man, Robert. No one could say he hadn't been; she had never said he wasn't. It made her feel bad every time she thought of it, his goodness. But he had been so dull. Surely no one could blame her for feeling—delivered, now that she had escaped that dullness.

Even this trip, which she had looked forward to with such hope, it hadn't changed a thing. The new sights, the scenery, and the strange faces, they hadn't been enough to counteract Robert. She would turn back from contemplation of a mountain peak or a waterfall or a stretch of shoreline, and there was Robert, and the horrifying realization that she was still bored—with him.

Instead of his usual inadequate two weeks this year he had been granted a whole month's vacation from his desk at the office. While they were planning the trip she had been excited. It had seemed as if this would change everything. It would be an adventure, a turning point.

But she had known after two days that it wasn't going to change anything, that in thirty days they would go back to exactly what they had left.

Mrs. Smith straightened up and let her hands fall to the chair arms, the towel trailing on the floor. Gradually the chair began to rock until it settled upon a slow rhythm while her eyes remained fixed on the casing of the kitchen door.

She could see what they had left as surely as if she were living through it again.

Breakfast in the nook of their upstairs flat, with perhaps a dozen words exchanged over the oatmeal or the bacon and eggs. It was partly that their kitchen was on the northwest corner of the four-family house on a conservative street that was neither "city" nor "suburban." Who could feel cheerful in the morning in a kitchen the sun did not reach until two in the afternoon?

The same housework every morning after Robert left at seven forty-five. The same midmorning telephone calls from one of the girls. The same marketing at the A&P; the same shopping trip downtown on the streetcar with Dora or Eleanor or Gladys; a matinee sometimes; the dinner for two, again in the breakfast nook. Bridge with the Ellisons once a week; twice a week the movies.

But most of all the same man. Just Robert, on and on and on. Until she had come to feel more insistently every day: Is this all? My God, is this all?

She read articles in the women's magazines. (After all, she tried to keep up on things.) And she tried to heed their authors' advice about "cultivating interests." She made an effort to be active in church affairs. She joined the League of Women Voters; but so many of the women were so much better educated than she was, she didn't feel at home among them, always afraid to open her mouth and say what she really thought for fear it would show her ignorance.

She had even tried ceramics. She and Gladys went to a class twice a week for a while.

But nothing had helped that terrible feeling, that, Is this all? Which had grown and grown—until she had known at last that what was really the matter was Robert, that her trouble was emotional.

And when the trip had done no good, when it hadn't changed Robert to see him in a different setting, when it hadn't changed the way she felt, she had become desperate. It had seemed as if he was to blame for everything. It was his fault that her life was so empty, so dull, his fault for being so unstimulating, so humdrum, so much a machine that walked away from a desk and took a streetcar and read the evening paper and said, "How about going to the show tonight?"

So why need she feel guilty now over wanting a man like—like Chet so soon? And she did want him. It wasn't just that he was well off, would be able to provide for her more than adequately. Life with him could be fun. And there was no time to lose. She wasn't getting any younger.

Those grasping, greedy other two women trying to get him for themselves.

And that snoopy, prying little man, Mr. Bladeswell. Why, *why* had he come in here? Was he trying to get something against her? Trying to ruin her chances for a new, fulfilling existence?

CHAPTER FIFTEEN

When Mrs. Fergusson came back to her cabin to prepare for lunch she let the screen door slam behind her, for entering the cabin reminded her that it had been broken into, and she was annoyed all over again.

She never had liked being interfered with, and this was interference of the first order, someone stealing into her private apartment and nosing about among her things. That had, in fact, been one of the most irksome factors about her marriages. It was the main trouble with men, the way they interfered with one's life, even in sharing one's bedroom. They pushed your coats out of the way in the closet, and tumbled the contents of drawers looking for things that couldn't possibly be in them. They strewed their belongings about clutteringly.

As she washed her hands in the little bathroom, her expression softened, and she made an exception, or almost an exception. Harry, her first husband, had not been so bad that way. He was naturally neat, methodical; and yet so easy-going, deferring to her judgment, letting her have the final say when it was something really important. She met her own eyes in the mirror as she dried her hands absent-mindedly. Poor Harry. Of course he had become a little boring. Too little spirit actually. Not like Edwin, her second. As a matter of fact she supposed she had been a little spoiled by Harry. After managing him so easily it had made it just that much more difficult for her to put up with Ed's insufferable bossiness. To *her*, a woman who could run rings around him in the race that was the business world.

She hung the hand towel neatly over the rack and brought her face closer to the mirror, her head slightly inclined, her finger pushing her nose a little to one side as she examined what had looked like a blemish. Satisfied that it was only a shadow, she dropped her hand and drew back.

Men, they were a problem. You got one like Harry that you could lead around by the nose and before you knew it you couldn't stand the sight of the poor thing; and then you got ahold of one like Edwin and he had you hating him before he knew what had happened, trying to reduce you to the status of the little helpmate when you knew all the time you had more guts and more brains in your little finger than he had in his whole insensitive body.

Perhaps that was her trouble. Too much rebellious spirit. It might have been better if she'd been the quiet type, like the Smith woman. Or the helpless kind, like that Meadows female, the one with no brains. Either way, you got along better where men were concerned.

But she had got off to the wrong start. She remembered Mamma. The psychologists nowadays said everything started in the home. And it had started there with her. The way Mamma deferred to Dad, the things she put up with, his evenings "out," while she stayed home with the kids and he came in drunk at 3 A.M. The way she never questioned at pulling up stakes and trekking on to a new town because Dad wanted to try a new job. The way she never had any money of her own, the incessant, "Bert, could you let me have ten dollars? Clara just has to have a new winter coat this year." The way she would make his favorite pie and wait breathlessly for his praise of the meringue.

Mrs. Fergusson shuddered now as she remembered Mamma's sycophantic dependence. And it wasn't just Mamma. She had seen them all, whether with more or less spirit than Mamma, playing second fiddle to the male who ruled the roost.

Before she was thirteen Mrs. Fergusson had known that *she* would never kowtow to a husband, be his handmaiden with palm outstretched for the necessities of life. No man would ever get the upper hand of her.

And none ever had.

Since Edwin she'd had better sense than to marry them; but it seemed to be a regular seesaw with her, from one type to the other. Andy who followed Ed had been the milksop type, and it hadn't taken long to get fed up with *him*. And the last one had been Maurice. He had fooled her for a while; but the first thing she knew *he* had started giving orders.

As she came out of the bathroom she dusted her hands together lightly. Well, she'd got rid of Maurice all right.

And now— She went to the window and looked out at the unimpressive hillside view of dried grass with the live-oak foliage hanging still and listless above it in the midday heat.

This man Chet was the problem. Her lips twisted in a faintly sardonic smile at her own expense. She knew herself, all right, even if some of what she knew was not exactly pretty. One reason she had gone after him was that those other two silly creatures had been so obviously bent on conquest. Her well-developed competitive spirit hadn't been able to resist the challenge.

But he did appeal to her. That hearty, uncomplicated, wholesome type always had attracted her. And he was so good-natured. You could manage him; and yet he was the sort—she was pretty sure—that wouldn't just lie down and let you walk on him. It might be that at last she had found the type she wanted—pliable but resistant enough to keep her interested. And he had enough money, apparently. She wouldn't be taking on a liability.

She turned from the window briskly, with a confident air.

CHAPTER SIXTEEN

Mrs. Meadows, alone of the three women, was blissfully unaware that anyone had been poking around among her scattered belongings. She had not been outside yet, for she always slept late, and afterward it took her all of two hours to make herself what she called "presentable."

Delicately she brushed the last dab of polish on the little toenail of her left foot whose heel was poised on the edge of the rocking chair where she sat in her slip with her left knee at the level of her chin. Sighing, she straightened her shoulders and carefully extended the left foot to join its mate on the seat of the straight chair two feet in front of the one on which she sat. As she screwed the brush back into the bottle of polish she surveyed her upturned toes with the satisfaction of an artist.

Then she leaned her head against the back of the chair and consciously relaxed while the polish dried. It was so important to relax all your muscles frequently, especially the facial ones, so they wouldn't get all set in ugly, tense lines.

With closed eyes she gave another little sigh. It was getting harder and harder lately not to worry about one's looks. And of course worry was fatal to them. You just had to keep a carefree mind.

Maybe she ought to have stuck to Gordon, not cast him off so lightly. He had, after all, been able to give her a nice respectable, *comfortable* life, even if it was so unstimulating. Maybe she was just a will-o'-the-wisp chaser. But that's the way she was, just a bundle of emotions, always being carried away by them. Romantic, that's what Earl had called her.

Forgetful of the necessity for relaxation, she frowned. That was Earl, always criticizing, always telling her she was this, that, or the other, none of it true, of course. Like it being time she grew up, and that there was more to life than romantic love.

Maybe, for men, that was true. But for a woman—if you were *really* a woman—what else was there but love? It was the most important thing in the world. All the books and all the stories in the magazines and all the movies said so. It was, in fact, one of the first things she had learned about life.

A little smile curved Mrs. Meadows' lips as she leaned back with eyes closed. She couldn't have been more than six years old when she first learned it—in a practical way. The little boy next door who got ten cents a week to spend and spent it all on her every Saturday morning at the candy counter of the corner grocery store.

It was always that way, all the time she was growing up. She had been such a pretty child, of course, with the curls Mummy put up on papers every night and the dresses with ruffles and lace. How dear Mummy used to sew and sew and sew for her. She used to say, "I have to keep my beautiful little Doll looking her best." Mummy used to call her that—Doll. Sweet it was, really. Mummy had been so high-minded too. She always said, "Doll, don't ever marry for anything but love. It's all that counts in this world. I'd rather see you marry a poor man you loved and live in two rooms than marry a rich man you didn't love and be just a bird in a gilded cage."

Sometimes even yet Mrs. Meadows wondered if Mummy hadn't been a wee bit impractical. Certainly as she got older she had grown away little by little from Mummy's philosophy. Love, of course, was the most important thing in the world; but there was no reason a person couldn't— well, guide it a little—toward men who had something to offer besides charm and sex appeal.

Mrs. Meadows opened her eyes and regarded her gay toenails. They were dry now. Next she must put on her dress and take her hair out of the pincurls and do her face. Her eyes remained fixed on the cerise-colored blobs at the ends of her toes, and suddenly she felt very tired, realizing that she didn't want to get up and work on herself for another hour. It seemed like a terrible chore.

She thought of Earl again. Fretfully she wished she wouldn't keep thinking of him. That had been one of the things she had resented most about Earl, the way he criticized her for spending so much time on her appearance. "What difference does it make," he would say, "what color your hair is?" and "Why the hell can't you leave your eyebrows alone? *I'm* satisfied with your looks."

But somehow it hadn't been enough for her that he was satisfied, even though she *had* loved him at first.

It was the strangest thing, the way it had always worked out. She slaved—yes, actually slaved, to make herself attractive to the man she was interested in, gave no thought to herself except to make herself desirable to him; and then, before very long, she always found herself resenting him. It was almost as if the resentment grew out of the fact that she had to give herself up so completely to the business of holding him.

It was certainly funny the way it happened every time, the way she gave herself up completely to pleasing the man, practicing every artifice of makeup and dress and personality to win and hold him. And then always— whether it was a matter of months or only of weeks—the revulsion, the bitter resentment that developed, and after that the inevitable, unreasoning, panicky desire to get away, to be free.

It was that way with Gordon, and it had been that way with Earl. Until she just couldn't *stand* him anymore. And even telling her she needn't think she'd get any alimony out of *him* if she tried to divorce him.

Naturally she'd got alimony those first times. A girl couldn't help it if she made a mistake in the man she married. And you had to have *something* to live on. It was different if you were clever like that horrid Mrs. Fergusson and could get out and earn your own money.

Her real trouble was, of course, that she fell in love so easily, sometimes while she was still married to another man. Even since she married Gordon there had been Joe. It didn't last *long*, of course, and Gordon would never know. And Joe had turned out to be such a washout. Thank heaven, after the way Joe turned out and especially being absolutely penniless, Gordon hadn't learned about him. Her mind shuddered away from the thought of Gordon learning about Joe. It would have put her in *such* a bad position.

Especially now when she had a *real* chance. She was just sure that this was it. Of course she had been sure every time. But this time, really, she thought it would be for keeps. She really liked Mr. Hoffman. She didn't know how she'd like living in Omaha, Nebraska. But Mr. Hoffman had more money than any of the other men she had married. And that would make a difference. It would be easier to stay in love with a man if you didn't have to be always scrimping and saving because he was too incompetent to supply plenty of money for his wife's comfort.

With this uplifting thought Mrs. Meadows terminated her period of relaxation and set her feet on the floor, ready to proceed with her dressing.

CHAPTER SEVENTEEN

The Bladeswells lunched at their cabin that noon, and it was the dinner hour before they saw any of "our little bunch," as Mrs. Meadows cozily designated them. Mr. Bladeswell had deliberately avoided the women all day, his uneasiness increasing with the hours. Suppose Mrs. Smith and Mrs. Fergusson compared notes. Mrs. Fergusson knew her cabin had been entered. Mrs. Smith had caught him red-handed. Mr. Bladeswell wiped drops of sweat off his brow. He didn't know the name of the county they were in, but he wondered if its jail were comfortable.

One thing, he should be able to tell when he saw them together again. If both women regarded him with fishy eyes, he could be prepared for the worst. Whether she had spoken to anyone else or not, Mr. Bladeswell expected Mrs. Smith to cut him dead.

But when they met on the veranda before six Mrs. Smith was only rather distant in manner, doing nothing which would reveal to the others that she had reason to feel harshly toward Mr. Bladeswell. Chet had walked down with them, and with quick insight Mr. Bladeswell deduced what had gone on in Mrs. Smith's mind that day. The Bladeswells were Chet's old friends. If she broke with them decisively or revealed Mr. Bladeswell's peculiar conduct, Chet would believe and side with his friends and she would be out as far as he was concerned. Mrs. Smith did not know that in Mrs. Fergusson she had a potential ally who would confirm her story; for that lady, out of consideration for her hosts, the Fenns, had agreed not to spread the report of a prowler in their midst. And neither of the women was on confidential terms with each other. As rivals their friendliness was a purely surface phenomenon.

So Mr. Bladeswell ate his dinner in the calmest state of mind he had experienced since morning.

They were sitting on the veranda later, in the same corner they had occupied on the first evening, when a taxicab turned into the graveled road which made a circle around the lawns and the swimming pool. Few automobiles drove up to the ranch house itself. Most of them turned off on the side roads to the cottages; but this cab continued straight ahead and pulled to a stop directly in front of the veranda.

Someone said as it approached, "Looks like somebody taxied out clear from Paso Robles," and added, squinting toward the machine, "That's the name on the side, Paso Robles."

"Bet that cost a pretty penny," Chet observed lightly. "Must be all of ten miles."

Everyone on the porch watched interestedly and in unaccustomed silence as the door opened and a man in a light suit and a Panama hat got out and scanned the veranda purposefully.

Mrs. Meadows had been watching the cab with the same idle curiosity that the others had, but as the man's head and shoulders emerged from the back seat, her breath came out in a little gasp, and she leaned forward incredulously, her hands clutching at the wicker chair arms.

The exclamation "Gordon!" broke from her lips involuntarily.

Mr. Bladeswell's first reaction as he glanced from the woman back to the man was one of relief—that "Gordon J." was not lying on a slab in the Santa Cruz county morgue.

The man's eyes picked Mrs. Meadows out from the crowd, and he waved with recognition, turning then to pull a small suitcase from the automobile.

Mrs. Meadows flashed a wild glance over her interestedly watching companions, and then in a flurry of pale blue draperies she was out of her chair and charging down the steps. The man had turned to the driver and taken out his wallet when she reached him. It was about twenty feet from the veranda to the driveway, and they all heard her shrill-toned but angrily subdued demand, "What are you doing here? What do you mean, following me?"

The motor of the taxicab was still running, and the sound blurred the man's low-pitched response given as he glanced uneasily at the driver's interested face and back toward the audience on the porch.

But they could hear Mrs. Meadows', "You can't stay here!"

Mr. Meadows, however, proceeded with his payment to the driver, who drove away and down the opposite side of the grounds, directing one last fascinated look toward the couple left standing at the foot of the path to the steps.

Out of politeness a buzz of conversation began to rise from the occupants of the veranda, but eyes returned repeatedly to the scene being enacted below.

Irritatedly aware of their prominence, Mrs. Meadows made a curt gesture to her companion and the two moved away several yards down the path toward the west.

Mrs. Meadows' own "little bunch," however, were on the end of the porch nearest the pair, and despite their having begun to exchange disjointed remarks to cover their amazement at and interest in the scene, all five of them caught a word and a phrase now and then.

"You certainly can't stay in my cabin—"

"How did you find—"

"Called up Mildred—"

"I meant every word—"

"—be hasty—I thought maybe—"

"I've never been so—no right—"

On the veranda Mrs. Smith and Mrs. Fergusson had exchanged looks almost of triumph, and indication that temporarily, at this evidence of a rival's downfall, they had forgotten their own opposing aims. Chet looked bewildered and somewhat distressed.

Mrs. Bladeswell had remarked rather inanely, "It must be her husband."

"She obviously didn't expect him," Mrs. Fergusson said dryly.

"Really," Mrs. Smith said, her voice lowered, her glance even including Mr. Bladeswell in the abrupt new intimacy engendered by this development, "I don't know what to make of it."

Chet's expression showed sympathy as he thrust his head forward a little and informed them confidentially, "She told me she was separated from her husband, getting a divorce. I guess he's made life pretty miserable for her. Kind of looks like it, him tracking her down like this." His eyes swept over them seriously. "This is strictly between us, of course. Just wanted you to know so we can be—uh—tactful about it."

Both Mrs. Fergusson and Mrs. Smith met his eyes with measuring, uncommunicative expressions; but Mrs. Bladeswell murmured regretfully, "My, it's too bad, isn't it? So embarrassing for her."

Mrs. Fergusson spoke coolly. "Let's not get sloppy about it. There's always two sides to these things."

Mrs. Smith was shrewder. She had obviously sized up Chet's soft-hearted reaction, and concluding that Mrs. Meadows had been pretty well eliminated anyhow, with a husband on the scene and a divorce not yet accomplished, she said magnanimously, "Well, it's too bad. Just ruins her vacation, you can see that." She smiled archly from Mr. Bladeswell to Chet. "The trouble you men make for us girls!"

"Sh-h, here she comes back," Mrs. Bladeswell warned.

Only Mr. and Mrs. Finklestauffer remained placidly rocking at the far end of the veranda. The schoolteachers and the young men had sauntered off across the lawn in pairs, and the young couple with the two babies had set out for their cabin while the Abernathys were pounding the piano inside, singing lustily in chorus.

The little party at the Bladeswells' end of the veranda watched the figure in the light suit and the Panama hat as it walked alone—looking forlorn and dejected—back toward the office at the front of the grounds. His suitcase still stood on the grass by the path to the steps, so they assumed he was going down to arrange for a cabin of his own, having been denied entrance to his wife's lodgings.

Like a wilted little bluebell Mrs. Meadows moved with bowed head back to her chair between the swing and Mrs. Smith, who was seated in the chair with the leather cushions.

Nobody said anything because no one could think of a really good opening gambit.

Mrs. Meadows fished a cobwebby handkerchief from her silver-mesh bag and pressed it pitifully to her eyes.

"I am so humiliated," she said in a muffled voice, "having you all witness this dreadful scene." She held the handkerchief down from her eyes and regarded them lugubriously. "You see, though, the sort of thing I have had to put up with. That man simply hounds me."

Mrs. Fergusson had been sitting on the railing as usual, and now she lifted one knee and clasped her hands about it. "Mr. Meadows, I presume," she said dryly.

Mrs. Meadows dabbed at her eyes again with the handkerchief. "Yes, my ex-husband."

"Some way," Mrs. Smith said affably, "I always assumed you were a widow, or divorced. But apparently you're still married to Mr. Meadows."

Despite the display of handkerchief Mrs. Meadows' eyes were quite dry, and now they shot a quick, venomous glance at Mrs. Smith. "I consider myself divorced," she said edgily, "even though it's not final."

"Do you have your first decree?" Mrs. Fergusson pursued relentlessly.

Mrs. Meadows brought the handkerchief back to her eyes and sobbed. "Please, I'd rather not talk about it. It's all so painful."

Chet moved in then to smooth things over. "Well, it's just one of those things. I wouldn't feel so bad if I was you, Marice. We all understand. I know what it is; I had a divorce once myself." He regarded them all solemnly. "Anybody that's never been through it just don't know what it is. It really takes it out of you, even if it's what you know you oughta do. So you just buck up. We're all friends here, and nobody's going to think a thing about it. We'll all just go on as if nothing'd happened. How about it if we see if we can pick up another couple of people and play some bridge?"

Mrs. Meadows brightened visibly at Chet's reassuring attitude.

"I suppose you're right," she said mistily. "But silly little me, I always take things so hard. I guess that's the penalty for being sensitive."

Mrs. Smith and Mrs. Fergusson looked a little sour, and Mrs. Bladeswell seemed withdrawn and uncomfortable. Mr. Bladeswell drew on his cigar and wondered. Perhaps the appearance of Gordon J. hadn't put Mrs. Meadows out of the running with Chet after all. It might even have served as the finishing touch, enlisting his sympathy, establishing a bond between him and "Marice" as the only two in the group who had undergone the devastating ordeal of divorce. Though even Chet should be able to tell that Mrs. Meadows hadn't even started proceedings. She had evidently just up and left the poor guy, in a fit of pique probably, although now, no doubt, she did intend to divorce him, Chet apparently seeming more desirable to her.

The thing, however, which most impressed Mr. Bladeswell was that now Mrs. Meadows—with a living spouse on the scene—was absolved from the Santa Cruz murder, leaving only Mrs. Smith and Mrs. Fergusson to worry about. At least, if Chet did finally marry her, she wasn't likely to kill him for his money someday. And now Mrs. Smith's excess empty luggage and Mrs. Fergusson's stay at Santa Cruz and the type of mind her carrying of a gun indicated rose to plague his thoughts again. Narrowing it down seemed to increase his suspicions.

And they centered more and more on Mrs. Smith. The car registered to Mr. and Mrs. The husband who by her own testimony had died recently, and her reticence on the subject. Add all that to the big empty suitcase.

She might, of course, be innocent as Mrs. Meadows was now proved to be. But he would like to know. If only he could get her to tell some kind of story about when and where the husband had died. Then he could check up on it, even though he had decided to cease playing detective.

He glanced meditatively at Mrs. Bladeswell's profile. Elsie and Mrs. Smith had hit it off pretty well. The woman had, of course, sensed that Elsie liked her best of the three. Maybe his wife could win her confidence, get her to talk.

The difficulty was that Mrs. Smith would be more cautious with both of them since catching Mr. Bladeswell in her cabin.

CHAPTER EIGHTEEN

With the exception of Mrs. Meadows, the "little bunch" all appeared at the ranch house for breakfast the next morning, and so they all got a good look at Mr. Meadows. Even Mr. and Mrs. Bladeswell had come down instead of eating alone in their cabin. They hadn't admitted to each other their real reason for this break in routine, but each of them knew it was because they couldn't wait for a closer look at Mrs. Meadows' husband.

He sat apart from the group which centered around Chet—at the table with the schoolteachers and the young men—and he looked like a man who has not slept well.

Mrs. Meadows' friends watched him surreptitiously all during the meal.

"Maybe," Mrs. Smith said, "we ought to introduce ourselves. He looks so lonely."

"I don't think Marice would like that," Chet demurred.

"No. There's no use in our getting mixed up in it," Mrs. Fergusson declared with finality. "Family fights are one thing I believe in keeping clear of."

"He's quite a bit older than she is," Mrs. Smith observed consideringly.

"You know something"—Mrs. Bladeswell chuckled—"he reminds me some of you, Mel. The same build, sort of."

Chet glanced down the table to the one beyond where Mr. Meadows was moodily sipping coffee, his elbows on the table, the cup held in both hands.

"'Bout the same amount of hair," Chet said jokingly.

"No remarks now," Mr. Bladeswell reproved tolerantly. He, too, looked toward the newcomer. "He does look about the same height and weight as me. But of course I'm better looking."

There was laughter and teasing repartee for a few minutes then, after which they politely quit stealing glimpses of the unfortunate candidate for the role of ex-husband.

Mr. Meadows preceded them from the dining room, and the little group lingered on the veranda for a few minutes, the men taking out cigars, Mrs.

Fergusson lighting a second after-breakfast cigarette. They took chairs near the center of the porch and observed Mr. Meadows standing by the swimming pool, his hands in his pockets as he stared into the water.

Mrs. Fergusson had seated herself on the top step, her back against the pillar, a brown leather envelope purse on her lap. A movement of her legs sent the purse sliding off and down the steps. The flap had been unfastened, and as the bag fell its contents spilled out: cigarettes, matches, a coin purse, and the neat little revolver Mr. Bladeswell had seen in her table drawer.

"Damn!" she exclaimed, as Chet obligingly moved down the steps to retrieve her belongings.

He picked up the gun and stared at it humorously. "Why the cannon?"

"Listen, I travel alone, and you never know what you're going to run into." Mrs. Fergusson was bent forward, stuffing things back into the purse.

"I don't think you'd run into much here at Escondido," Chet chided jokingly.

"I'm going for a hike this morning, and I always carry it when I'm on foot in the mountains. Rattlesnakes."

"Bet you couldn't hit a rattlesnake ten feet off."

"You think not? Come with me this morning and I'll give you a demonstration. I wasn't raised on a ranch for nothing. I've shot and killed more than one mountain lion."

She took the gun from Chet and tucked it into the bag, then pressed the gold catch into place.

Mrs. Smith chuckled comfortably. "My goodness, I'd be scared to death, carrying a gun in my purse, afraid it would go off by itself."

"I don't usually keep it on me," Mrs. Fergusson responded, and then looked around the group speculatively. "I've been keeping it quiet, but Mr. Bladeswell already knows, and I guess there's no harm in telling the rest of you." Her eyes swept over the empty veranda, and she lowered her voice. "Just keep it to yourselves, though. I don't want to start any trouble."

Mr. Bladeswell moved uneasily in his chair, but Mrs. Fergusson went on confidentially, "Night before last sometime while I was out of my cabin somebody broke in. I could tell by the screen and the window. The gun was there in the bedside table, and I just got to thinking, if there's somebody around breaking into things it's not a good idea to leave a loaded gun around."

"Did you tell the Fenns?" Chet asked with concern.

"I reported it to that man down at the office, but he pooh-poohed the idea. And nothing was taken; so I figured it could be just kids; but I'm not taking any chances. If there *is* some screwball breaking into the cabins, you can't tell what he may do next, so I figure I'll just tote little Roscoe around with me from now on. Then I'm *sure* nobody's going to try to get cute with me."

"Oh, I'm sure," Mrs. Bladeswell said reassuringly, "there's no criminal element around here."

"You can't tell what kind of prowlers might be lurking around these hills. And I damn well don't care about having somebody pawing through my things."

Out of the corner of his eye Mr. Bladeswell had watched Mrs. Smith. She had listened to the foregoing intently, obviously trying to come to a decision behind her expressionless countenance. He flinched as she suddenly put on an arch smile and glanced at him coyly.

"All kinds of mysterious things going on here. Shall I tell them about our little experience yesterday morning, Mel?"

Mr. Bladeswell managed a sickly grin. "Just as soon you didn't. Makes me look like an awful fool."

"Why, Mel, what have you been up to?" his wife exclaimed.

To Mr. Bladeswell Mrs. Smith's gayly joking manner was patently false. He could tell that she had been itching to get back at him for the start he had given her, and had decided to put him on the spot beneath the pretense of its all being a big joke.

"Mr. Bladeswell," she was informing them facetiously, "went into my cabin yesterday while I was out, and I came back and caught him there."

"Mel!" That was his wife, horrified.

"No-o?" Chet brayed on an amazed gust of laughter.

With his face a bright pink Mr. Bladeswell stammered through the story of seeing smoke coming out of the kitchen window. "Must have been an optical illusion," he concluded lamely.

Chet laughed heartily. "That's a good one. Wait'll I tell the boys at the Elks Club back home. Old Mel gettin' caught in a lady's boo-dwar."

"Melvin Bladeswell, I'm surprised at you! Surprised, that's what." His wife shook her head at him reproachfully.

"It certainly gave me a start," Mrs. Smith said complacently, looking at Mr. Bladeswell with a, "now I guess we're even" air.

Mrs. Fergusson had said nothing, but Mr. Bladeswell was keenly aware of her narrowed eyes and speculative stare.

"I was beginning to wonder, Elsie," Mrs. Smith was going on in a jolly tone, "whether your husband had been a private detective or a burglar or something before he retired."

"Mercy, no. Mel was in wholesale groceries."

"Say," Chet broke in, his eyes having wandered out over the grounds. "looks like Mr. Meadows is going calling."

All their heads turned to watch the shirt-sleeved, gray-haired man on the path up to his wife's door.

"I wonder if she's up yet," Mrs. Smith murmured.

"Well, it's his wife," Chet reminded them with a meaning chuckle.

Both Mrs. Smith and Mrs. Fergusson laughed then—with relief, it seemed to Mr. Bladeswell, as if they interpreted the man's facetious tone to mean that he was not particularly concerned about Mrs. Meadows' love life.

"She's letting him in anyway," Mrs. Bladeswell reported, leaning forward slightly.

"Bet that'll be a hot interview," Mrs. Fergusson contributed callously. "You've got to hand it to the old boy. He's persistent. Apparently doesn't fancy being an 'ex.'" She looked up at Chet. "Well, how about it? Want to go hiking with me?"

"O.K. Let's go shoot rattlesnakes."

As she rose to her feet Mrs. Fergusson quipped back, "The reptilian variety, I hope you mean."

CHAPTER NINETEEN

Mrs. Smith departed soon after Chet and Mrs. Fergusson did, but by tacit agreement Mr. and Mrs. Bladeswell remained on the porch, their eyes straying to Mrs. Meadows' door now and then. They had nothing else to do, and observing other people's activities was as good an occupation as any.

It was another half-hour before Mr. Meadows emerged. He came directly down from the cottage and crossed on the path in front of the ranch house, proceeding to one of the cottages facing the courtyard on the east where he stamped up the steps and disappeared inside.

Mr. and Mrs. Bladeswell studied him as he strode past without raising his eyes. He had the appearance of a man who is vexed but who has also become stubborn.

Mrs. Bladeswell looked at her husband. "Do you suppose he'll leave today?"

"I should think so. He doesn't seem to have got anywhere by following her up here."

"She must have flounced off mad, and he decided to go after her and try to make up," Mrs. Bladeswell said thoughtfully.

"That's about the size of it."

That afternoon, however, when the Bladeswells strolled down to the courtyard and found seats under one of the umbrellas, Mr. Meadows was doggedly swimming the length of the pool with overhand strokes. Mrs. Smith dived from the board as they watched, and they saw her come up beside Mr. Meadows where he clung with one arm to the draining ledge at the side. She spoke to him, and they exchanged a few words.

"Mrs. Smith is real good-hearted," Mrs. Bladeswell observed. "She feels sorry for the poor man and is trying to be nice to him."

Mr. Bladeswell had his own ideas—along the lines that Mrs. Smith's overtures were calculated more to embarrass Mrs. Meadows than to alleviate the man's loneliness, but he said nothing.

"Well! Here she comes," his wife announced sotto voce.

Mrs. Meadows was all in white—linen, it looked like—but she carried the pink parasol. She did not look as fresh as usual, however, as she joined the Bladeswells. Her face reminded Mr. Bladeswell of a pouty child's. After greeting them Mrs. Meadows let her eyes rove over the pool, coming to rest disapprovingly on her "ex-husband" who had climbed out and was sitting on the runway.

"I see," Mr. Bladeswell said mildly, "your husband is still here."

"He's the stubbornest man I ever saw," Mrs. Meadows burst forth petulantly. "Says as long as he's here and has leave from work he's going to stay till Sunday, whether I go back with him or not. He's just doing it to be disagreeable."

"Well, it's a free country."

"Unfortunately," Mrs. Meadows retorted snappishly.

Mrs. Smith approached them, pulling off her cap and shaking her hair loose.

"Hot today, isn't it?" she greeted them affably, and sat on the grass, her legs straight out in front of her.

"It is warmer here," Mrs. Bladeswell responded agreeably. "Not that I don't enjoy it for a change. It was really cool in Santa Cruz, evenings anyway. But that's one thing I like about the beach: it's always cool."

"I don't care much for the beach," Mrs. Smith said idly.

"I should think a swimmer like you would be crazy about the surf," Mr. Bladeswell put in. "Didn't you like Santa Cruz?"

Mrs. Smith turned her head and looked at him directly as she said flatly, "I was never in Santa Cruz."

Mr. Bladeswell had honestly abandoned his efforts to pry into the women's past movements, and he had spoken thoughtlessly, his mind now being more engaged with the Meadows' domestic crisis than with murder. But he had dwelt so long on the possibilities of each of the women having been in Santa Cruz two weeks before that he unconsciously felt that each one *had* been there.

Somewhat confused by his own lapse, he returned vaguely, "Oh—I had it in mind you had stopped off there on your way here. Must have misunderstood you."

Mrs. Meadows stood up restlessly and jerked her parasol open. "I haven't been down to see if any mail came in. Guess I'll run over now."

As she moved away with the parasol tilted behind her, Mrs. Bladeswell's eyes followed her and she murmured soft-heartedly, "Poor little thing; she's all upset over that man."

"He seems very nice," Mrs. Smith said curtly. "Personally, I always feel there's two sides to these things."

"Oh—of course. It takes two to make a quarrel. But I hope they make it up. It always seems too bad to me, people getting a divorce. It's so lonely being alone. But then"—Mrs. Bladeswell broke off apologetically—"I guess I don't need to tell you that, having lost your husband so recently."

Mr. Bladeswell saw Mrs. Smith pass the tip of her tongue across her lower lip and turn her head to look across the pool so that they could not see her face.

There was still enough of the virus from the bite of the detective bug left in him that Mr. Bladeswell could not resist following up this opening. "How long has it been since Mr. Smith passed away?" he inquired solicitously.

"About—about a month," she returned, still looking away, a rough note in her voice.

"Oh, then it was before you started on this trip. Somehow I got the impression it happened after you left the East."

Mrs. Smith turned her eyes on him for as long as a second and got to her feet. There was perceptible hesitation before she responded shortly and ambiguously, "Yes." She began to put on her cap. "I think I'll go in the water again before I go up and dress."

As she left them Mrs. Bladeswell, who had been screwing her face up warningly and reprovingly at her husband, said under her breath, "Mel, you shouldn't. You know it upsets her to talk about her husband's death. You can tell she took it pretty hard."

"If she did, you wouldn't guess it from the way she acts most of the time, makin' up to Chet, and chipper as a lark, eating and swimming and dancing."

"Well, what do you want the poor woman to do, be a hermit?"

"I s'pose," he charged with a note of raillery, "if I was to kick off you'd be makin' eyes at somebody else before I was hardly cold in my grave."

"Mel, how you talk! You know I'm *different*."

"Yeah?"

"You're just getting to be an old cynic," she retorted good-humoredly.

Later, when Mr. Bladeswell had been down to the store to pick up a quart of milk and a loaf of bread, he ran into Mr. Meadows and they walked back down the road together. The man seemed lonely and naturally not in cheerful spirits. Mr. Bladeswell felt sorry for him. Where the road branched toward his own cabin they stood chatting in the shade for a few minutes. Mr. Bladeswell learned that Mr. Meadows worked for a firm of stockbrokers on Spring Street in Los Angeles and hailed originally from New Jersey. They discussed the stock market and business conditions generally, and when they parted they had become friends in the sudden way people will at a vacation resort.

The Bladeswells walked down to the ranch house at five o'clock and found Mr. Meadows in one of the rocking chairs on the veranda listlessly scanning a newspaper. He nodded and said hello to Mr. Bladeswell, lowering his paper hopefully. Mrs. Bladeswell was deflected by greetings from the Finklestauffers, and she paused beside them, finally taking a chair near the old lady and pursuing an animated conversation about "Breakfast in Hollywood," which program the Finklestauffers had attended during a recent sojourn in southern California and to which Mrs. Bladeswell listened every morning when she was at home.

Mr. Bladeswell took the rocker next to Mr. Meadows and they resumed conversation like old cronies. In the course of comments about Escondido's qualifications as a resort, Mr. Bladeswell informed the other that they were moving on on Monday.

"I guess I'll go over and take the train Sunday." Mr. Meadows grinned wryly. "I was thinking of driving back with my wife. Guess you know Marice. But it didn't work out that way."

"Well, yes, we've got pretty well acquainted with Mrs. Meadows this week." He gave a low, embarrassed laugh. "Little place like this, we couldn't help knowing how things are—between her and you."

Mr. Meadows sighed. "Yes, it's just one of those things."

"How long," Mr. Bladeswell asked tentatively, "you folks been married?"

"Just since last October." Mr. Meadows uttered a dry sound. "One of those sudden things. I met her one week, we were married the next. Guess we should have taken more time, got to know each other better."

"Well, you know what they say, 'Marry in haste— '" He let the quotation die meaningly on his lips.

"I'm not saying anything against Mrs. Meadows, you understand"—the man hesitated briefly and cast a disgruntled glance toward that lady's cottage—"but *I* was not the one that wanted to break up. I'll tell you frankly, Mr. Bladeswell, Marice is—well, unstable emotionally."

He closed his lips in a straight line and regarded his new confidant sternly.

"Yeah. Well"—Mr. Bladeswell fumbled—"I'd say she did seem sort of high-strung."

"I should have suspected," Mr. Meadows proceeded bitterly, and moved his head closer, confidentially. "She's been married three times before. That's strictly between us, you understand, I don't want to say anything *against* Marice. But it goes to show, wouldn't you say? Of course I'd been married before, too, but only once. I was a widower."

"Were they all—divorces?" Mr. Bladeswell asked faintly.

"The first two were, but the last one—a Mr. Underhill—he died last summer."

"Oh." Mr. Bladeswell faltered, somewhat overwhelmed by this burst of confidences. But he could see how the poor guy felt, all alone among strangers, and mad, and nobody to tell it to. He had been bottled up fit to burst.

Mrs. Smith was coming up the steps, neat and matronly in her straight yellow dress and oxfords with sensible heels. She paused beside the Finklestauffers, not looking at Mr. Bladeswell.

The latter glanced out over the quiet lawns and saw Mrs. Fergusson walking beside Chet down the path before the cabins. Mrs. Meadows came out of her house to encounter them as they passed, and the three approached together. Chet glanced at Mr. Bladeswell and nodded uncomfortably, aware of Mr. Meadows.

The "little bunch" did not coalesce and move into the dining room together as usual. Chet was practically held captive by the three women who surrounded him and swept him into the dining room like watchdogs driving a blundering sheep.

Mrs. Bladeswell joined her husband and was introduced to Mr. Meadows, and when the dinner bell rang they entered the dining room together. Chet and his satellites had assumed their regular places at the table nearest the kitchen, and out of sheer mischievousness Mr. Bladeswell led Mr. Meadows along, and the three of them took seats at the end of the table. The other guests were well aware of how matters stood with the Meadows family, and there were covert glances from the other tables.

Mrs. Meadows glared at Mr. Bladeswell and turned so that one bare shoulder above a ruffled off-the-shoulder frock was displayed toward his end of the table.

Mrs. Smith smiled pleasantly at Mr. Meadows, and Mr. Bladeswell matter-of-factly introduced the man to Chet and Mrs. Fergusson. The latter grinned and said, "Hi," and Chet smiled foolishly and mumbled, evidently discomfited by Mrs. Meadows' frozen hauteur on his right.

Mrs. Fergusson, catching Mr. Bladeswell's eye, winked at him amusedly. But Mrs. Smith went through the meal as if there were a gap of empty atmosphere over the chair Mr. Bladeswell occupied. When Mrs. Meadows was forced to look at him her gaze pierced him balefully.

"Me and poison ivy," he thought to himself with rueful amusement.

Absorbing as the Meadows situation was, it subsided before the prominence Mrs. Smith was resuming in his mind. The stiffness had come into her manner and remained there after his questions in the afternoon. She didn't like being queried about the deceased Mr. Smith. Not a bit.

Mr. Bladeswell's uneasiness about the murders welled up again so insistently that he was no longer particularly interested in the Meadowses and their troubles.

He had learned his lesson. He was through. He wasn't going to try to do a thing about it. And yet— Suppose Mrs. Smith had disposed of Mr. Smith with sleeping pills. Was it right for him not to get her investigated?

CHAPTER TWENTY

To the relief of most of the party Mr. Meadows departed to his cabin after dinner. Things, however, were not the same. The "little bunch" had been frostbitten, the crisp vitality of their companionship turning brown at the edges.

It was dancing night again, and at eight-thirty the living room had been cleared of obstructions, the orchestra was taking its place. The rancher from the adjoining property, a man with a foghorn voice and a managing personality, always came over to call the square dances, and by nine o'clock the party was going good.

Mr. Meadows had come back, but he tactfully kept a little distance from the group centering around Chet. He danced once with Mrs. Bladeswell and with Mrs. Smith and Mrs. Fergusson, but he and Mrs. Meadows were not speaking.

About forty people, including guests and employees, enjoyed the festivities, between dances overflowing onto the porch which was lighted only by the glow from the house lights that shone through the front windows. In the dining room soft drinks were being dispensed at the bar along with occasional beers and highballs or sandwiches and coffee, and the screen doors leading from the dining room to the veranda were left unlatched for the evening so that people circulated through from porch and living room.

There was moonlight, and some of the guests, especially the younger ones, strolled outside between dances or sat one out in the chairs on the lawn.

The Bladeswells and Chet and his "harem," as Mr. Bladeswell had begun to think of them humorously, had a more or less permanent station in the corner of the room toward the veranda where an overstuffed davenport stood against the wall with occasional chairs angled close to it. After each dance they retreated there to fan themselves with handkerchiefs and to rest their feet, the women leaving their purses and jackets on the seats when they rose to dance. An old-fashioned overhead chandelier illuminated the area around the piano at the far end of the room and a bridge lamp against either wall served the rest of the space; so it was dim and therefore secluded in the corner.

Despite Mr. Meadows' embarrassing presence everyone seemed to be having a good time.

It was getting on in the evening, and couples were taking places on the floor for a quadrille. Mr. Bladeswell sat back in his chair, ready to sit one out. He had just danced a polka with Mrs. Smith, and he was not up to another caper just yet. She, too, sat in a corner of the sofa, apparently ready to sit still for a while. Mrs. Bladeswell and Chet were partners out on the floor, but he noticed idly that both Mrs. Fergusson and Mrs. Meadows were missing, and he saw the latter's pale blue organdy disappearing through the doorway that led to the bathroom at the end of the short hallway beyond the spot where the orchestra sat.

Mr. Meadows had been standing near the outside door, and as Mr. Bladeswell's eyes fell on him, the man turned and moved idly out onto the veranda.

Mr. McIntyre, the rancher who did the calling, was having some difficulty in lining up a couple to complete a fourth set, and Mr. Bladeswell decided to get out of sight before he got pulled in. They were always short of men.

"Guess I'll go out and stroll around a little," he volunteered politely to Mrs. Smith, who only stared at him indifferently.

He had thought of chatting with Mr. Meadows for a while, but the veranda was deserted except for Mr. Finklestauffer in one of the rockers to the right.

"The dancing too much for you?" Mr. Bladeswell inquired facetiously.

"Oh, I don't dance anymore. Just watch. Although we did the *Varsovienne* earlier in the evening. Still remember that one from when I was a kid, but we can't take these fast ones. My wife wanted to watch this set. Then we're going on home. Getting pretty late for us old folks."

In his white shirt sleeves and gray pants, his head bare, Mr. Bladeswell was suddenly aware of the coolness of the night. "Think I'll go in and have a cup of coffee. It's getting kind of chilly out here. Like to join me?"

"Well, maybe I will." The old man struggled up out of his chair. "Don't usually drink coffee this late at night, but I might as well dissipate for once."

Together they went through the doors into the dining room. Mrs. Fergusson was smoking a cigarette and holding a highball glass, talking to Mrs. Fenn and watching the other room through the doorway. While Mr. Bladeswell and Mr. Finklestauffer were being served the music began loudly with Mr. McIntyre's voice riding its crest in a jovial bellow. Mrs. Fergusson set her glass down on the bar and wandered to the porch doors.

Mr. Bladeswell and Mr. Finklestauffer stepped into the inside doorway and smilingly watched the vigorous pattern of the quadrille to the accompaniment of deafening strains from the accordion, the violin, and the piano, the commanding, rhythmical "calling" of Mr. McIntyre, and the hilarious cries and laughter of the dancers as they lost their places, were whirled into position again, and breathlessly continued to clap their hands and keep time with their feet on the linoleum floor.

"Make a lot of noise, don't they?" Mr. Bladeswell observed tolerantly, turning his head toward the older man.

Mr. Finklestauffer's face jutted forward over his cup. "Hey? What say?"

"Noise!" Mr. Bladeswell shouted. "Make a lot of noise."

"Oh—noise. Yep, sure do."

There were several figures in the quadrille which had been chosen, and it went on for almost fifteen minutes, counting the time lost when the caller had to stop and extricate couples from the tangles they had made with each other. About halfway through the dance Mr. Bladeswell saw Mrs. Meadows reappear in the doorway beyond the orchestra. She stood for a moment glancing about the room, then sidled along the wall to a straight chair. Just then Mr. Bladeswell felt someone brush against his arm and turned to find Mrs. Fergusson looking over his shoulder. She made some remark, but he could not distinguish its meaning, for the set directly in front of him was made up almost entirely of Abernathys whose bounciness was heightened by the music until it defied credulity.

As the dance neared its finale with the caller's instruction to "lead that girl to an easy chair," Mr. Bladeswell came in and took a chair beside the wall, Mr. Finklestauffer following him, and when the set was over he made his way among the sweating dancers back to the corner where the others in his party congregated. Mrs. Smith sat where he had left her. Afterward Mr. Bladeswell realized that he had no way of knowing whether she had remained there all during his absence or not, for his attention had been concentrated on the orchestra end of the room where Mrs. Bladeswell and Chet were "head couple" of the set nearest the piano.

That couple were now mopping their faces and sighing gustily and complaining about their feet. Mrs. Meadows tucked her legs under her girlishly in the corner of the sofa opposite Mrs. Smith, and Mrs. Fergusson began to rummage along the back of the sofa for her envelope bag. She pulled it out from where it had been lodged between the back and the seat cushions, then moved away to sink into the overstuffed chair next the davenport, drawing her package of cigarettes from her purse.

When Mr. Bladeswell happened to glance at her again Mrs. Fergusson was staring into the bag with a peculiar expression. Out of the corner of his eye he saw her fold the flap down slowly, her gaze directed vacantly at the floor. Then she looked off across the hall with an uncertain frown, drawing her eyebrows closer together.

His curiosity aroused, Mr. Bladeswell watched her surreptitiously.

Suddenly she stood up, tucked her purse under her arm, and without speaking to anyone marched down the room to where Mr. Fenn sat on the piano stool drinking a Coke and looking up at Mr. McIntyre, who talked to him with a beer bottle resting on top of the piano beside him.

Mr. Bladeswell saw Mrs. Fergusson speak to Mr. Fenn, who got to his feet with a surprised look and followed her toward the hallway door where she addressed him rapidly, motioning to the purse under her arm.

Even at that distance Mr. Bladeswell could see that the host was taken aback. He spoke earnestly, and became more distressed as Mrs. Fergusson replied sharply. He glanced worriedly over the crowd scattered along the walls and again addressed Mrs. Fergusson earnestly, shaking his head.

The colloquy lasted a few seconds more, Mr. Fenn apparently arguing unhappily, and then with a tightening of her lips, an annoyed shrug, and a hitching up of the bag under her arm, Mrs. Fergusson turned and stalked back toward the party in the corner.

After her return Mrs. Fergusson was taciturn and her eyes continually moved suspiciously from one to another of her companions.

In a few minutes the strains of the "Home, Sweet Home" waltz vibrated through the room. Mr. Bladeswell dutifully asked his wife to dance, but she moaned, "After that last one! I doubt if I can even walk home now, let alone dance."

Mrs. Meadows had grasped Chet's sleeve, pouting, "You haven't danced with me for *hours*, so I think I'm entitled to the last one."

Mrs. Fergusson was staring broodingly at the dancers. Her recent conduct had disturbed Mr. Bladeswell. Even his now self-discredited detective abilities had not been overtaxed in figuring out that something was probably missing from her purse, and that she had demanded Mr. Fenn to institute a search, a demand which he had refused, not wishing to alarm his guests, thinking perhaps that Mrs. Fergusson had left whatever it was in her cabin and forgotten about it. After her story the previous day of having been practically burglarized, he had probably put her down as a hysterical female who imagined things.

Mr. Bladeswell's curiosity prompted him to murmur, "How about you, Clara? Have the last dance with me?"

The slight, impatient movement of her head indicated an impulse to brush the invitation aside, but then her eyes focused on him, and she changed her mind. "Oh—well—O.K." She dropped her purse carelessly on the cushions and rose.

Neither said anything for several minutes as Mr. Bladeswell followed the music accurately. Then he said, "Is something wrong? You seem kind of upset."

She held her head back slightly and regarded him with open distrust. He deduced that she was remembering how he had entered Mrs. Smith's cabin, and was wondering if he were really the pleasant, friendly little man he seemed to be—or if he were a screwball who broke into ladies' bedrooms and took things out of other people's purses.

But her anger, her uneasiness, her enforced restraint were too much. She burst out bitterly, "You're damn right something's wrong. *Now* my gun has been stolen. And that damn fool Fenn won't do anything about it. I've a good mind to call up the sheriff and report it. The whole thing looks bad to me. First somebody breaks into my rooms, then they steal my gun. God knows what may happen next."

Mr. Bladeswell's expression was serious enough to satisfy her. He was, indeed, alarmed as much as she was, possibly more so. He was not even sure Mrs. Fergusson might not have hidden her weapon and made this fuss on purpose so that—if it *was* used—she could say she hadn't had it. Mrs. Meadows was out of it now, having produced a live husband; but knowing he had been on the beach in Santa Cruz on the fateful day, might not one of these two other women be planning to eliminate *him?* Or even—might not Mrs. Meadows have taken it to rid herself of the interfering Gordon J.? She had carried a capacious silver-mesh bag on a loop over her arm all evening.

Perhaps he, too, should go to Mr. Fenn and urge that an announcement and a search be made before the crowd dispersed. Except for Mr. Meadows, who had not reappeared, everyone was still there. And what did they know about Mr. Meadows actually? Maybe he had taken the gun from the bag as it lay tucked among the cushions, planning to murder his trying little wife. It was a cinch he didn't feel kindly at the moment toward his Marice.

"I'll tell you one thing," Mrs. Fergusson was saying pugnaciously, "I'm going to call the police in the morning—if I'm still alive to do it. I suppose there isn't much use in trying to do anything tonight. It's almost midnight, and I don't suppose you could even get any of these hick-town cops out of bed after ten o'clock. I'm not any crazier than Fenn is about having the law snooping around here, but guns were made for killing, and if somebody gets murdered, then we will be in for it."

Mr. Bladeswell shot a quick glance at her averted face. The woman was obviously keenly distressed. She was speaking with utter sincerity, prodded by her disturbance into talking without careful consideration. Suppose she had been the woman at Santa Cruz. She would indeed be frightened at being involved in a serious crime so soon afterward. She would rather risk having police around trying to prevent burglary or larceny than having them start really digging in a murder case.

Mr. Bladeswell felt frightened and confused.

"The first thing in the morning," he said abruptly, "if I were you I would call the sheriff's office. You're probably right about tonight. They'd just be mad at being called out so far from town."

As the crowd started home from the ranch house it seemed dark and cold out of doors. The moon had gone down, and only the lights from the ranch-house windows made a feeble pattern on the ground close to the house itself. They walked together down the road, Chet and the Bladeswells, Mrs. Fergusson and Mrs. Smith, Mrs. Meadows leaving them first while they waited until her light went on and she called a gay good night.

Flashlights bobbed ahead of and behind them as other guests walked along talking and laughing. Lights had come on in some of the cabins as Mr. and Mrs. Bladeswell and Chet walked up their own road. But Mr. Bladeswell was trembling as he closed the door safely behind him in their own cottage. He stood to the side of the windows as he pulled the shades, and it was not until he lay in the dark in bed beside Mrs. Bladeswell with the doors and the catches on the window screens securely fastened that he began to breathe easily.

CHAPTER TWENTY-ONE

Even without the disconcerting conjectures that the evening had stirred into activity in his mind, the coffee and the stimulation of the music and the unaccustomed exercise of dancing would have made it hard for Mr. Bladeswell to fall asleep. Elsie was soon breathing deeply, a soft snore escaping her once in a while; but Mr. Bladeswell lay wakeful and irritated at being so.

Outside there was the steady, liquid current of the night song of tree toads. There was no breeze, but the foliage of shrubs and tree branches seemed to rustle now and then.

Once he lifted his head and strained his ears, thinking he heard the slight crunch of leaves under a foot outside. But he lay back with an audible expulsion of breath and turned over, the springs sighing softly as he did so.

Nerves. He was hearing things. And it was no wonder. For he was utterly convinced that he was in danger. That gun had not been stolen—or reported stolen—for nothing. He had talked too much. One of the women suspected his suspicions about the Santa Cruz murder. And the one in Yellowstone. She must think he had "inside dope" on that one too. He remembered how he had rashly thrown out a feeler about Yellowstone that very first evening—in front of all of them, and how Elsie had elaborated on their intimacy with the ranger. Both he and Elsie had talked too much, she unwittingly, he carelessly. The murderer thought he knew more than he actually did.

He swallowed convulsively and pressed his head into the pillow. It was not just him now. It was Elsie too. The murderer would try to silence both of them.

If Mrs. Fergusson was on the level she would report the theft of her gun in the morning. Surely the arrival of the police to investigate would show up the thief. And somehow he was sure that thief was Mrs. Smith. But would she not wait until the excitement died down over the search for the gun before she used it?

He and Elsie must stay close to home in the morning. He would think up some excuse to cut short their stay, pulling out in the afternoon. Only away from Escondido would they be safe.

Chet and any other future victims would have to fend for themselves. He was not going to be quixotic enough to risk his life trying to pin her crimes on Mrs. Smith—or Mrs. Fergusson. He was still not convinced the latter wasn't a deep one, one who would hide her gun, accuse others of stealing it, and then use it herself under cover of the ensuing excitement.

Mr. Bladeswell lifted his head again. He *did* hear sounds—sounds that were not a legitimate part of the night, such as the brushing together of boughs in a stir of air, the rustling of night birds, the paws of little animals in the dry oak leaves. This was a steady crackling noise, and it seemed to come from beyond the open kitchen door, through the screened window in there.

And then he raised not only his head but his shoulders, and sniffed noisily.

Smoke! There was no mistaking it. He smelled smoke.

Elsie stirred slightly at his movement but slept on.

In one motion he had thrown back the covers and his bare feet were on the floor. He reached the kitchen doorway in two strides, and in the darkness of the room he saw the smoke gray and filament-like drifting through the screen.

"Elsie!" he shouted. "Elsie! Wake up! The house is on fire!"

He was grabbing the dishpan as he spoke, turning on the faucet over the sink. With the other hand he grabbed the filled teakettle on the stove and raced for the front door.

Mrs. Bladeswell was uttering confused little cries and disentangling herself from the bedclothes.

"Fill up everything in the kitchen with water and set it on the porch," he commanded, disappearing through the doorway.

With sudden comprehension she raced for the kitchen in her nightgown and followed him with the overflowing dishpan, running back to set a saucepan under the faucet.

Mr. Bladeswell had forgotten his other fears in the shock of recognizing smoke. The little wooden cabin would go up like cardboard once a blaze got a start, and if one house went others might follow. The trees, the grass, the fallen leaves were like dried kindling all around. And as a tourist in California he had been thoroughly impressed—by billboards, by Automobile Club publicity, by the rangers in state parks—about the disastrous possibilities of summer fires in California. This was not forest area, but the hills were overlaid with tinderlike dry grass, with mesquite brush, with clumps of small trees which would go up like torches. One house burning in a rural spot like Escondido might set off a conflagration that would sear thousands of acres before the state foresters could stop it.

Little flames were leaping merrily up the side of the house under the window from what looked like a miniature bonfire on the ground as Mr. Bladeswell dashed around the corner of the house, throwing off the lid of the teakettle and dashing its contents against the wall behind which stood the cooking stove filled with fuel oil. He ran back quickly and grabbed the dishpan off the porch floor, and when that two gallons of water struck the blaze it slowed to a few flickers. He ran back for two saucepans his wife had set out, and when he came back for more she was reappearing with the dishpan. The water slopped over its sides and down the front of his nightshirt, but with this inundation the fire sputtered and was out. They scattered a few more pans of water around on the ground and the wall, and then retired breathless to the house.

Mrs. Bladeswell had turned on the kitchen light, and when Mr. Bladeswell closed the front door behind him he snapped on the main room light which hung from a small chandelier in the ceiling. Mrs. Bladeswell put away the pans in the kitchen and turned out that light, and they stood in the living room and looked at each other.

Mrs. Bladeswell laughed shakily. Their nightclothes were wet down the front, Mr. Bladeswell's bare feet were dirty, and on both their heads the hair was tangled in disarray.

He let out his breath in an explosive, "Whew!"

"That was a narrow escape," she said weakly, and went over to sink down on the side of the bed, looking down at her skirt vaguely. "We'll have to change and wash our feet." She raised her head. "It's a good thing you noticed the smoke before it got a real start."

"Yes. Yes, it sure is." He rubbed the top of his head. "If I hadn't happened to be awake we'd never have caught it in time."

"We might *never* have waked up," Mrs. Bladeswell said in an awed tone. "You know—people get overcome with the smoke before they feel the heat."

Mr. Bladeswell rubbed his chin this time. "Yeah. That's right. And, by rights," he added thoughtfully, glancing at the clock, "we should have been sleeping like the dead, tired out from the dance. It's past two-thirty."

"Yes, and we'd better get cleaned up and back in bed," his wife said briskly. "I'll get you a dry nightshirt. Lucky your other one is clean or you'd have to sleep raw."

As he dried his feet and changed from his wet nightshirt Mr. Bladeswell's mind dwelt aghast on the implications of what had happened. Three, four minutes more, and the flames would have eaten through the paint into the wood, smoke would have poured in through the kitchen window with only a six-inch space of screened window in the front of the house from which to escape. He and Elsie, two elderly people unaccustomed to late hours and violent exercise, should have been sunk in the unconsciousness of exhaustion too deeply to be aroused before suffocated by the smoke and then buried under flaming timbers when the oil stove exploded, as it probably would have. It would have been a nice neat disposal of them with no clues left to the little bonfire set outside the window.

He was convinced now that this had been no "accidental" fire, started by a carelessly thrown match or cigarette butt. The sounds he had heard had not come from "nerves." Someone had been out there carefully piling twigs and leaves together on the ground and putting a match to them, then high-tailing it home before the fire was discovered.

Well, "Someone" must be surprised already that the cry of "Fire!" had not echoed through the trees as Number 12 went up like the funeral pyre for which it was intended to serve.

As he climbed into bed Mr. Bladeswell mused grimly that there would be more than a missing gun to report tomorrow. The location of the cinders outside was evidence that, along with the gun and his story, should start a real police investigation.

He was tempted to pour the whole tale out to Elsie, but he decided to hold his tongue until after he had talked to the sheriff. No use to upset her before it was necessary.

CHAPTER TWENTY-TWO

Mr. and Mrs. Bladeswell were eating cornflakes and drinking instant coffee at the little gate-leg table before the window the next morning when they saw Chet hustling up their path.

"Come in and have a cup of coffee," Mrs. Bladeswell called brightly as he started up the steps. She was looking forward, her husband could tell, to exclaiming brightly, "I guess you missed the excitement last night. I guess you don't know how lucky you are to even be seeing us this morning."

But the screened door was not closed behind him before Chet was demanding with grave excitement, "You haven't heard the news?"

Mr. Bladeswell swiveled around on the seat of his chair, a scared, empty apprehension of he-didn't-know-what mushrooming in his chest. His eyes were fastened on Chet as the latter pulled out the third chair and sank into it breathlessly.

"I just heard. I was standing on the porch, feeling the sun for a minute before I went in to shave." He felt of the faint brownish shadow on his jaw line. He was wearing only an undershirt above his jeans and leather mules on his feet. "That Mr. Sellers in the end cabin was coming back from the store, been out for a little walk, and he told me."

Chet drew in his breath.

"Told you *what?*"

"Mr. Meadows. He's dead. Shot through the head. The place is swarming with police already. I heard a lot of cars coming and going about half an hour ago when I first woke up. Must have been what woke me up, so much unusual traffic at this hour. But I never thought nothing of it." He paused, and said thoughtfully, running his hand through his uncombed hair, "God!"

"Shot?" Mrs. Bladeswell said weakly.

"Yep. Shot. This guy Sellers said one of the guys that works in the stables ran across him on the way to the corral this morning."

"Where was he?" Mr. Bladeswell asked raspingly.

"You know that grape arbor that runs from the east end of the back part of the house out kitty-cornered to the path leading to the cabins on the east slope? Well, he was about halfway along in there. Down toward the path. Sellers said he musta been layin' there all night." Chet lowered his voice, and his eyes stared away abstractedly, as if there were something particularly horrible about what he was about to say. "He was all damp, his clothes. There was dew last night."

"How did Sellers find all this out?"

"He's an early riser. Was down there before the police even got here, an' he heard it from Fenn and the hired man that found him. Sellers says he always goes out and walks around so he won't disturb his wife. Lets her sleep."

"But she wouldn't, she couldn't do *that!*" Mrs. Bladeswell muttered as if she were talking to herself and hadn't heard Chet's elaborations.

Chet took another deep breath and rubbed his head once more. "He— Sellers, that is, didn't know what kind of a gun did it; but"—Chet licked his lips and looked unhappily at the others—"I wouldn't say this to nobody else. But I keep remembering. Clara's gun. We—we was shootin' it off on our walk yesterday. She's a crack shot. And—and—it don't make a very loud report. It's so little—a twenty-two."

"But why would *she*— Oh no, we mustn't start getting ideas!" Mrs. Bladeswell cried softly.

Mr. Bladeswell sat in numb silence, his breakfast forgotten.

Chet stood up and moved toward the kitchen. "Can I have a cup of coffee, Elsie? God knows I need it."

"Oh, of course, of course. Just sit still." She rose bustlingly. "Only take a minute. The water's hot. I have the powdered coffee right here."

As Chet swallowed the hot drink greedily he went on talking as if it were a nervous necessity. "They're questioning everybody, Sellers said. Nobody supposed to leave the place."

Mr. Bladeswell had nothing to say. Except for monosyllabic replies to Chet's comments he was silent. In this death, with its plain label of murder, its weapon openly displayed, with its victim named and known, his murderer already supplied with possible motives, it seemed as if all three of those others were brought out from obscurity and shown in their rightful outlines. Gordon J. Meadows had proved his theories by bringing the number of slain men up to four.

Despite the shock and horror, he had a curious feeling of relief at knowing the sheriff's men were there. Now he could speak. Now he would tell them all he had thought and suspected and seen, no matter how foolish and irrelevant it sounded to the officers. At least now it would be their responsibility, not his. They had a good excuse now to investigate both Mrs. Smith's and Mrs. Fergusson's movements for the past month—if they didn't prove immediately that Mrs. Meadows had shot her husband.

When Chet had finished his coffee Mr. Bladeswell proposed, "Get your shoes on and let's walk down to the office, see what we can find out."

But at the Y where the roads led off to Mrs. Smith's and Mrs. Fergusson's cabins a state traffic officer was standing on the path in all the splendor of leather leggings, visored cap, and all-too-visible guns in leather holsters on his hips. He stepped forward as the two men approached.

"Going up to breakfast?" he inquired in a not-unfriendly tone.

"No, we was just taking a walk down to the store. Wanted to find out what was happening," Chet volunteered frankly. "Fellow in a cabin up the road told us what happened last night."

"Sorry, but I'll have to ask you to stay in your own cabins then. Sheriff Knight may want to talk to you later."

"You're a state policeman, ain't you?" Mr. Bladeswell asked curiously.

"That's right. The sheriff asked me to give 'em a hand. See that no cars or pedestrians leave the premises. His men got their hands full here, checking up on the guests. So if you'll just—" He looked meaningly back up the road.

"Oh. Well—sure," Chet said feebly, and they turned to retrace their steps, feeling like naughty schoolboys.

"Guess they don't want a big crowd milling around down at the store," Mr. Bladeswell said.

"Yeah, or people gettin' together on their stories."

"You better come in and have another cup of coffee or a piece of toast or something."

"O.K. Someway I didn't feel like going down for breakfast."

As they mounted the steps to the cabin they heard voices inside, and upon opening the screen door they found Mrs. Fergusson sitting at the table while Mrs. Bladeswell poured hot water from the teakettle over the brown powder in a cup.

The caller flicked out a match and looked up at the men. "I'm not supposed to be here, I suppose, but I sneaked across the back way from my cabin. Had to talk to somebody. God, I'm a wreck."

She did look less hearty than usual. Her facial muscles seemed to sag and there were shadows under her eyes. Mr. Bladeswell wondered if surprise at finding his cabin still standing had added to her discomfiture.

"They've been questioning Clara," Mrs. Bladeswell offered in shocked tones.

Mrs. Fergusson let out a breathful of smoke and said bitterly, "It was my gun, you know."

"I thought so," Mr. Bladeswell said heavily.

As she explained to Chet how the weapon had disappeared the night before Mr. Bladeswell tugged one of the rocking chairs in off the porch and sat in it near the door.

"Thank God," Mrs. Fergusson finished piously, "I didn't waste any time reporting it was missing to Mr. Fenn. He had told them about it, and also— after *this*—about somebody breaking into my cabin. If it weren't that I have no possible motive they'd probably suspect *me*."

"Poor Marice," Mrs. Bladeswell said anxiously. "I suppose they're raking her over the coals."

"Undoubtedly. I think they'd already had a session with her, from some remarks the sheriff let fall toward the end when he was talking to me."

"What's he like, the sheriff?" Mr. Bladeswell asked seriously.

Mrs. Fergusson shrugged. "Just what you'd expect. Typical small-town politician. Overweight. Taking it big. Probably not too efficient."

Nervously she extinguished her cigarette and took a sip of coffee. "Hell of a thing to happen on a person's vacation. I don't see why they had to use my gun for their dirty work."

Chet pursed his lips. "Let's see now, who knew you had a gun—besides us here, of course?"

"Well, Mrs. Smith—Mabel, that is. She was there yesterday morning when it fell out of my purse."

Mrs. Bladeswell's face puckered with concentration. "But Marice wasn't there. She probably didn't know you even had one."

"One of us could have mentioned it in front of her casually. About Chet and me shooting out in the hills yesterday. And don't forget, I tell you somebody did break into my rooms."

"I suppose they'll be along here pretty soon to question us," Mr. Bladeswell observed, to change the subject. "Probably talking to the people that spent the most time with Marice. And, of course, I talked to Mr. Meadows considerable yesterday."

"They went from my house to Mrs. Smith's—Mabel's," Mrs. Fergusson returned. "Two of 'em. The man with the sheriff took down everything in a shorthand notebook," she added sourly.

"Oh, dear," Mrs. Bladeswell murmured in dismay.

Mr. Bladeswell was sitting where he could look out onto the sunny roadway, and he saw the Mr. Sellers who had been Chet's informant wandering past with his hands in his pockets. Mr. Bladeswell rose and opened the door, stepping out on the porch.

"Hello there," he called affably.

"Morning, Mr. Bladeswell." The man paused willingly in his aimless saunter. "Terrible thing, ain't it? Suppose you've heard."

"Yes, Mr. Hoffman told me about seeing you. He's here now. We're just having a cup of coffee. Like to come in and have one with us?"

"Don't mind if I do." The alacrity with which Mr. Sellers moved up the path and the steps belied the casualness of his words. He was obviously far from "talked out" on the subject and was pleased at the prospect of a fresh audience.

"Mel," Mrs. Bladeswell reproved from within, "the bed isn't even made. What will he think of us?" But she went to the kitchen to heat more water, hoping the powdered coffee held out.

They had all met Mr. Sellers at the dances in the ranch house, and he took his place among them like an old friend. Mr. Bladeswell dragged the other rocker inside, and the little room was cozily crowded and sociable with the coffee cups and cigarette smoke.

"Yes, guess I was the first one of the guests to hear about it," Mr. Sellers said complacently, and graciously accepted a steaming cup from Mrs. Bladeswell. She had had to rinse out her own and give it to him, for the furnishings supplied only four cups, none of which matched.

"Always been an early riser," he proceeded informatively. "Guess it must have been about six o'clock. I seen Mr. Fenn and this ranch hand—Vic, they called him, I think—and that guy George that works in the store. They was all over by the grape arbor, and I could tell from the way they acted somepin was wrong. When I got up to 'em I see Mr. Fenn hadn't even combed his hair. Had on slippers."

"You—you saw—the body, then?" Mrs. Fergusson said.

"Sure. Layin' right in plain sight from the path that runs from the porch along the road to the cabins on the east slope. You know how they got them grapes trained to run along the logs on top, and the sides are all clear. Just them log uprights holdin' up the arbor, and seats along here and there."

He paused to chuckle—a little ghoulishly—it seemed to the others, and glanced banteringly at Mr. Bladeswell. "You know at first glance when I came up I thought it was you—"

Mrs. Bladeswell uttered a horrified, rejecting sound.

"Yes, sir, I did. I seen you at the dance last night, and you had on gray pants and a white shirt just like him, and all I could see at first was the back of his head, an' you both got gray hair, you know." He sighed. "One good thing, it didn't blow his head all to pieces. Nice, clean shot, went in the temple and clean through. At least"—he paused to consider, and stirred his coffee—"I *think* the bullet went on out the other side. Couldn't swear to it. Mr. Fenn wouldn't let 'em touch the body again. Of course Vic had touched him to begin with and found out he was dead."

"Did you see the gun?" Mrs. Fergusson demanded.

"Did I see it? Why, it was me discovered it! Yes, sir. You see, I cut straight across the lawn and the road and over the grass by the house toward where they was standing by the arbor, and I seen it layin' right there on the grass between the path and the arbor, not more'n fifteen feet from the body. I just about bent over an' picked it up, and then I thought, 'Nope. No you don't, Rupert my boy. Fingerprints!' An' I just left it lay there and pointed it out to Mr. Fenn."

It seemed as if everyone sighed at once, and there was a momentary silence while all mused uncomfortably.

Chet said tentatively, "You said the gun was about fifteen feet from him.

Did you gather they thought it was fired from there? What I mean to say"—he cleared his throat awkwardly—"his being hit square in the temple like that don't necessarily mean it was a good shot did it. Anybody could have hit his head from there, whether they were any kind of marksman or not."

His eyes fastened hopefully on Mr. Sellers, and all but the latter were uncomfortably aware that Chet hoped the suspects weren't going to narrow down to people like him and Mrs. Fergusson who had practiced with the little gun.

"They didn't say, of course," Sellers replied importantly, "but it ain't more'n fifteen feet from the path to the arbor, and come to think of it the gun was in three or four feet from the path as it was, so it must've been closer to ten feet from the body than fifteen. So I'd say it didn't *have* to be a crack shot. Anybody can hit a target a dozen feet away. Of course"—he paused pontifically—"it was night—nothin' but the moon to see by, and shadows from the grapevines."

There was a thoughtful silence. The eyes of each member of the little party looked vacant as each seemed to be mentally visualizing the moonlit scene around the grape arbor.

"They sure got on the ball fast," Mr. Sellers resumed after a sip from his cup. "Only about an hour from when Mr. Fenn went in and phoned before they was all over the place—the sheriff in person and a ambulance and photographers, and some guy with a little black bag, guess it was the coroner. I hung around and watched. Quite a bunch collected, people from the houses facing the center there, got woke up by all the traffic. I saw the sheriff and one of his gang go up and knock on Mrs. Meadows' door after they'd looked the ground over an' talked to Vic and Fenn. They went inside, an' then I went on down toward the store and the office. They'd took the body off in the ambulance by then."

He regarded the others brightly. "Fellow in plain clothes took my statement down there. 'Spect they'll get around to you folks sooner or later. Sure a lot of excitement. Even a motorcycle cop stopped off. He's helpin' to keep people from escapin'."

Mrs. Bladeswell glanced at the little traveling clock on the dresser. "It's after ten," she said nervously. "I suppose they'll get to us pretty soon."

Mrs. Fergusson rose. "I'd better go back. It may not look so good if they find us all here. They'll think we're getting together on our stories. Thanks for the coffee, Elsie."

"Guess I might as well go home and shave," Chet observed, following her out the door.

Since his audience was dispersing like this, Mr. Sellers also took his leave to go in search of fresh listeners.

CHAPTER TWENTY-THREE

Mrs. Bladeswell chattered in shocked, incredulous tones as she cleared the table, and to escape her voice Mr. Bladeswell went out to the porch. He stood with his hands in his pockets and stared unseeingly at the thicket of maple trees across the road.

He had not spoken since Sellers' words: "I thought it was you."

That was it, of course. In the light of the quarter moon, under the shadow of the grape arbor, Meadows had been mistaken for Bladeswell by someone standing on the path or on the lawn between it and the arbor.

When Chet first told them he had been so shocked by the grisly fact of Meadows' death that he hadn't thought of mistaken identity. But it was clear enough.

And then the murderer had seen Mr. Bladeswell walking around big as life after the man in a white shirt and gray pants fell face forward under the grapevines. So she had set fire to his house, determined to shut him up before the sheriff appeared in the morning.

What a night the creature must have spent.

Poor Meadows. Dead by mistake. But wait. There was no proof that it was Bladeswell for whom the shot was intended. He only suspected that to be the case. Meadows was being a nuisance to his wife. Was it, after all, no mistake, his death?

Mr. Bladeswell had eliminated Mrs. Meadows as the past murderer, but was he sure? Meadows had told him she had a husband who died last summer. He hadn't said how or where.

And there was the body in Yosemite last summer.

True, she had had a husband to show—in the person of Gordon J. But suppose she had been on an illicit escapade with some *other* man at Santa Cruz, and had found it expedient to get rid of him?

Had he eliminated her too easily?

Mr. Bladeswell's brain felt mushy from the rapidity with which events had bombarded it in the last twelve hours. But the death of Gordon J. Meadows reared up out of the mush of his speculations most conspicuously.

When had it happened? During the dancing last night, of course. Only then was there a chance of the shot going unnoticed. The east wing of the house, which consisted of bedrooms, all empty at the time, had intervened between the shooting and the big center room. The music and the clapping and the stamping had blotted up the crack of the revolver.

He tried to remember the evening and its sequence of events, to establish times when the accident—for he was almost sure that it was an acci-

dent that Meadows was dead—could have taken place. It was more difficult than he would have imagined to disentangle people's movements.
Who was dancing with whom. When they were all together, when scattered. There was that last quadrille. He frowned painfully. It was not at all
clear, but he seemed to remember seeing Mr. Meadows by the door before
it started, then not seeing him again. But he couldn't actually *swear* the man
had gone out. And he had left Mrs. Smith sitting alone. And coffee with
Mr. Finklestauffer. And Mrs. Fergusson in and out of the dining room. And
Mrs. Meadows slipping in through the rear doorway to a chair on the side
lines.

He moistened his lips uneasily. Neither Mrs. Meadows nor Mrs. Smith
had seen him across the room in the dining room. One of them might have
done it then, while he was inside. But Mrs. Fergusson had seen him. She
could have already shot the wrong man, though, before she saw him enter with Finklestauffer.

It was impossible, trying to figure people's movements and make anything
out of it. Only one thing seemed sure now. He had been right all the time.
One of them had committed murder at Santa Cruz. And he had tipped off
his hand to the murderer. She thought he really knew something. She did-
n't realize it was all mere conjecture on his part. And she was so scared she
had tried to silence him for good.

Whoever the murderer was she had discovered her mistake after the last
square dance. But no one of his three suspects had displayed any surprise
when the bunch reconvened by the sofa before the last dance. Both Mrs.
Meadows and Mrs. Smith would have had time to compose themselves after catching a glimpse of him across the room. Mrs. Fergusson, though, had
been confronted with him and Mr. Finklestauffer rather suddenly in the
dining room and hadn't turned a hair. Did that let her out?

The palms of Mr. Bladeswell's hands felt damp and he rubbed them up
and down on his pants' legs. Almost twelve hours had elapsed now since
the murderer had discovered her mistake. Upon discovering her error, she
must have felt more desperately than ever the need to silence Mr.
Bladeswell, since police would soon be interviewing him, as they did
everyone else, over Meadows' death. Why had she not simply gone back
after the gun she had thrown down and aimed it at the right man this time?

Looking back, Mr. Bladeswell could see the impossible situation the killer
had been in.

For the sake of an alibi for the first murder she had to stay with the others as they left the ranch house and went along home. By throwing the gun
on the grass, she had disarmed herself, and by the time it could be retrieved
Mr. Bladeswell would be safe in his own cabin. Once there, the criminal
had two people to deal with. If she inveigled Mr. Bladeswell outside, Mrs.

Bladeswell might see who she was and raise an outcry which would bring witnesses before the murderer could escape, even if she shot Mrs. Bladeswell too. The fire had been safer, and it had the additional advantage of stilling Elsie's tongue, too, in case she knew anything damaging.

Now, however, in the broad daylight of morning, after the discovery of the body, undetected action was almost impossible. The presence of the police was an insurance for him and Elsie.

Mr. Bladeswell could hear his wife still talking to him through the open kitchen window. He backed up into the doorway and poked his head forward and peered down the road. He wished feverishly that the officers would hurry up. Once he had talked to the sheriff the murderer would know it was too late. The beans would have been spilled.

CHAPTER TWENTY-FOUR

There was not long to wait. A medium-sized, businesslike black sedan glided slowly up the road and stopped before Chet's cottage, and a man emerged from either side of the front. Mr. Bladeswell deduced that the shorter, stockier one in a light brown gabardine suit and a Stetson hat was Sheriff Knight. He was accompanied by a younger, taller man in slacks and a plaid jacket. They disappeared inside Chet's cabin, and Mr. Bladeswell restlessly peeled the cellophane off his second cigar of the morning, turning back into the house.

Mrs. Bladeswell frowned at the cigar as she stood by the dresser powdering her face. "Aren't you afraid you'll upset your stomach, two cigars before noon?"

"Can't help it. I need a smoke." But he went out and poured a glass of milk and ate a graham cracker, prowling around the small rooms as he consumed them. He went out to the porch again as he lighted the cigar.

Fortunately for Mr. Bladeswell's nerves the officers' stay with Chet Hoffman was fairly brief, and they descended the steps and came on foot across the space between Number 11 and Number 12. Standing on the path, the sheriff looked up to the porch.

"Mr. Bladeswell?"

"That's right."

"I'm Sheriff Knight of San Luis Obispo County. Investigating the death that took place here last night."

The two men were already on the steps, and Mr. Bladeswell held the door open. "Come in. This is my wife."

Mrs. Bladeswell fluttered a little and came to a perch on the side of the bed as the strangers took chairs and Mr. Bladeswell settled into the rocker which had been brought in. Sheriff Knight placed his hat with its slightly exaggerated brim squarely on his knees, his hands on its edges.

Dispassionately and without preliminaries he began to ask questions: about their own and other people's movements on the previous evening, about Mrs. Fergusson's gun, about their impressions of the Meadows' behavior toward one another.

Mr. Bladeswell answered as accurately and as fully as he could, but he was impatient to have done with this routine stuff. What he really had to tell this man he didn't want to say in front of Elsie. If she knew of his snooping, he'd never hear the last of it.

So when the officers filed out onto the porch he was right behind and following them down the path.

Sheriff Knight regarded him unenthusiastically as Mr. Bladeswell fell into step beside him.

"I didn't want to talk in front of my wife," Mr. Bladeswell confided in a low voice. "No use upsetting her, but there may be more to this shooting than meets the eye."

"You have further information?"

"I think so."

"Well—" The sheriff's voice was a little weary. He was used to these busybodies who had theories. But you couldn't afford to ignore anything in a murder case. Clues turned up in funny places sometimes. "Come on over to the car, and let's have it."

He opened the door by the steering wheel and sat on the seat, facing Mr. Bladeswell, his feet on the ground. The younger man leaned against the front fender and listened listlessly.

Being as concise as he could Mr. Bladeswell started with the body on the beach at Santa Cruz and the conversation with Ed Doty which had brought to light the men at Yellowstone and Yosemite, going on to outline his own speculations about a possible link between the three and coming down to his "investigations" here at El Valle Escondido.

At first the sheriff listened with a lackluster eye which wandered around Mr. Bladeswell's figure, apparently studying the sunny front walls of the cabins and following the antics of a squirrel which scampered up and down the trunk of the sycamore tree between Number 11 and Number 12. The younger man had stuck his shorthand notebook in the side pocket of his jacket and lighted a cigarette which he smoked lazily, his eyes on the bushes down the road.

Drops of sweat appeared on Mr. Bladeswell's forehead as he became increasingly aware that they were not impressed. But when he got to Mrs. Smith's vagueness about time in regard to her husband's death, the Mr. and Mrs. registration of her car, the large empty suitcase, and Mrs. Fergusson's

Santa Cruz notepaper, and the sleeping-powder capsules in Mrs. Meadows' medicine chest, both of which Mr. Bladeswell triumphantly drew from his pocket, the sheriff's eyes focused on the narrator steadily.

He lifted his hand to deter Mr. Bladeswell, and without taking his eyes from the latter's face said briefly, "Better get this, Paul."

Rather surprised, Paul drew out his tablet and pencil, went around Mr. Bladeswell to the rear door of the car, opened it, and sat on the seat in the same position Knight had assumed in front.

"Go over those times again about the deaths in Yellowstone and Yosemite," the sheriff instructed, "so we can make a note of it. And Paul, get that about his search of the cabins."

Mr. Bladeswell had a blessed sense of relief. They were taking him seriously. He was getting tired, so he sank to his heels, one foot a little before the other, his elbow on the forward knee, and carefully repeated the points the sheriff had mentioned.

"It looked to me," he said finally, "as if Mrs. Meadows was cleared when he turned up, but now I don't know. She had another husband die last summer. I didn't find out the circumstances, but it might bear looking into."

The sheriff was eying him strangely, and Mr. Bladeswell remembered one of the main things he had wanted to suggest. He shifted his weight on the balls of his feet.

"Another thing. I got a nasty feeling it was me they meant to kill last night."

Paul glanced at Mr. Bladeswell curiously, his pencil continuing to move on the slick paper.

"So? How's that?" Knight prompted impassively.

"Well, at dinner last night somebody said they thought Meadows and me looked alike, same build and all, and I judge we're about the same age. Then this morning this Mr. Sellers up the road that saw the body before you came, he said at first glance he thought it was me. It was done during the night, probably during the dance, and outdoors, a few feet away, it would have been easy to mistake Meadows for me. We were dressed something alike. I had on a white shirt and gray pants too. So, if it was like that, it makes me think I was on to something, and one of those women got scared of me and wanted me out of the way."

The sheriff pushed his hat back on his head and crossed his legs. His eyes shifted, and he stared thoughtfully at a blotch of white on the sycamore trunk. "Could be," he muttered. "Could be."

Mr. Bladeswell lifted himself stiffly out of the crouch and put his hands in his pockets. "Something else happened last night that made me think it was like that." He went on then to describe the fire, and when he had finished Sheriff Knight heaved himself to his feet.

"Let's take a look."

The three men walked around to the side of the cabin and thoughtfully regarded the irregular circle of cinders under the window and the scorched paint of the siding above it.

"H'm." He thrust his hands deep in his pants' pockets and stared glumly at the ashes. Then his eyes slowly ranged over the adjoining ground.

"I'll have one of the state fire wardens come out and take a look," he grunted gloomily. "Looks like a set fire, all right, but we'll get an expert's opinion."

As they turned to walk back toward the car Mr. Bladeswell observed sententiously, "It ain't any of my business, I suppose, but if it was me I'd check back on all three of them women, when and how and where their men died, and if they was off on any trips with husbands last summer and the one before. If you turn up anything suspicious it'd help to narrow it down on this case. Personally," he volunteered expansively, "I sort of favor Mrs. Smith. As I said, Mrs. Meadows is sort of out. For one thing, she wasn't there when Mrs. Smith told about me being in her cabin or when Mrs. Fergusson's gun fell out of the purse. Although that don't mean she hadn't heard about both things some other time. Mrs. Fergusson, she might have figured it was me broke into her place after she heard I was in Mrs. Smith's, and might have made a to-do about the gun being gone, just to throw suspicion off her."

"We'll look into it," Sheriff Knight said abruptly. "Meantime, you better keep your mouth shut about what you've told us, and sit tight. If somebody did try to shoot you and got Meadows instead and then tried to burn you up, they may try again. Anyway, thanks for the help. We'll check up on the ladies' husbands and see what comes up. I've got their home addresses."

The men were taking their places in the car, and Mr. Bladeswell leaned forward, his expression almost wistful. "You'll let me know—whether they're on the level or not. It's been a burden on my mind."

For the first time the sheriff smiled. "We'll let you know."

As they drove away Paul looked at his boss curiously. "What do you think of it?"

"Well—sounds farfetched. But you never know. That's just how you catc' up with people sometimes. They get away with it once and then they
†   cute again and it leads back to the first crime. I'd of checked on
            ws and the Fergusson dames anyway with the authorities
            me from. Won't do no harm to include the Smith woman,
            at it we'll just find out if any of 'em were in the national
            and the one before, and if they might've been in Santa
            Shouldn't be hard to find out how their husbands

died. Matter of fact," he said thoughtfully, "we'll see a few more people so the trail won't lead straight from this old geezer, Bladeswell, and then we'll drop in on the girls again before we pull out and get their stories as to how their husbands died—so we can check with the reports we get. Find anything fishy about one of their stories and we'll put the heat on."

"Sounds awful coincidental," Paul said dubiously, "this bird gettin' a line on three murders, one of 'em two years old."

"That's what makes life tough for criminals. Sheer Goddam Chance is always steppin' in and trippin' 'em up. Somebody hears somepin and somebody else sees somepin and somebody else just happens to be someplace he has no business to be, and boom! the whole thing goes up higher'n a kite."

Sheriff Knight lifted his hand from the steering wheel and shook his finger at his deputy as they pulled up beside the office. "If you want to get ahead in this racket, that's one thing you gotta remember, son. Never overlook nothin'. So you gotta listen to a lot of crackpot theories from innocent bystanders; but once in a thousand times you hear something that throws the whole thing wide open; and you can't afford to risk missing that one little piece of information. Criminals can take chances, but we can't afford to."

"All I got to say is, it makes a lot of extra work, checkin' up on everybody's ideas of what might have happened."

"Part of the game, my boy, part of the game."

CHAPTER TWENTY-FIVE

It was after noon before the sheriff's car pulled out of the main driveway and away down the black-top road leading to the highway. A deputy in plain clothes remained stationed in the office out front for the purpose, Mr. Fenn spread the word, of seeing that no guests left the ranch without permission until after the inquest which would be held, Sheriff Knight believed, on Monday.

It was now Saturday, and general opinion at Escondido was to the effect that the delay in conducting an inquest was meant to give the authorities more time for investigation previous to it. A few people were being permitted to depart on Sunday per their plans, but none of the group who had been friendliest to Mrs. Meadows was granted that liberty.

Thinking of how telegrams and telephone messages would soon be winging across country to Colorado, to Chicago, to Santa Cruz, of detectives setting out to ask questions in response to Knight's requests for information, Mr. Bladeswell relaxed as he had not since he met the three widows and grew suspicious of them. Naturally the guilty person would sit tight now. For she would see that the fat was in the fire. If Mr. Bladeswell were going to talk, he should already have done so; and it would be dangerous to stir up further police activity by another attack upon him. All she could do now was wait and trust to luck and Sheriff Knight's possible inefficiency.

Chet went to the ranch house for lunch, but the Bladeswells remained in their cabin eating canned soup and a salad of canned asparagus and mayonnaise. Chet came by at one-thirty and reported, "None of our little bunch showed up for lunch but me. Mrs. Fenn told me Marice asked to have a tray sent over. They don't usually give room service, but Mrs. Fenn said, considering the circumstances, she sent the oldest girl over with a tray of lunch. Boy, the whole place is buzzing. You oughta heard 'em."

He had taken the rocker opposite Mr. Bladeswell on the porch, and he sighed dejectedly. "Everybody thinks she done it."

"What do you think?"

"Why would she? That's what gets me. Right here where nobody else really knows him and they're bound to suspect her."

"Of course they have to prove it."

"Yeah, but I just can't see her doing a thing like that."

Mrs. Bladeswell had brought out a straight chair and sat between them. "You didn't see Mabel or Clara?"

"No, they didn't come down."

"Sulking," Mr. Bladeswell suggested dryly. "Probably mad at being questioned and not allowed to leave."

"I was wondering," Mrs. Bladeswell said meditatively, "if maybe we oughtn't to call on Marice. After all, it is a death in the family, even if it is a sort of queer one. And the poor little thing alone there, nobody going near her except cops and the Fenn girl with the tray."

"Wouldn't do no harm," Mr. Bladeswell agreed.

Chet considered for a second or two. "Yeah, I think we ought to. After all, a person's innocent till they're proved guilty."

So, after conferring a little more, they set off down the steps for the call of condolence. On the road Mr. Bladeswell suggested, "Let's cut through here. No use going clear around by the road."

"Isn't it kind of rough?" his wife protested doubtfully.

"Naw. It's a little steep, but the ground is clear after you get past these bushes."

"Never thought of taking a short cut like this," Chet observed. "How come you know about it, Mel?"

"Oh— Well, I—I was just walkin' around one day, lookin' over the lay of the land."

So they came out at the rear of Mrs. Meadows' cottage, walked around her car, and went up the steps. The wooden door was open behind the screened one, but the shades were down inside, making it so dim in the cottage that they could not see in as they stood on the little porch. It seemed as if Mrs. Meadows appeared very suddenly beyond the screen.

"Oh. Oh, hello. Come in," she said, pulling open the door.

"We just thought we'd run over," Mrs. Bladeswell said, "and see how you were, see if there was anything we could do."

They filed in awkwardly, the men mumbling embarrassed greetings. Mrs. Meadows indicated the straight chairs and one of the rockers which she had moved into the house. She herself sat on the bed, leaning against the rumpled pillows at its head. The room was as untidy as it had been on the day of Mr. Bladeswell's search, and Mrs. Meadows murmured helplessly, "You'll have to excuse the way things look. I've been lying down." She sighed pathetically.

She did not offer to raise any of the shades which gave the room a twilight air, and Mrs. Bladeswell could see why. Today Mrs. Meadows' appearance could not tolerate strong lighting. In her fluffy blue negligee, her loosened hair, she looked merely pale and fragile in the dusky room, but out in the cruel sunlight she would have looked haggard and faded.

She picked up a chiffon handkerchief with a wide, fine lace border from the bedside table, and pressed it gracefully to her eyes.

"That awful man, the sheriff," she quavered, "he thinks I d-did it!"

"Now, now," Chet chided reassuringly, touched by her misery, "nobody thinks anything of the kind," he declared rashly. "It—it was probably an accident."

Mrs. Meadows raised herself on an elbow. "You know what I think?" she demanded. "I've been lying here just thinking and thinking, and I think it was suicide. Despondent—over me. You know, you hear about those things all the time. People get turned down and they shoot themselves."

"No, it was murder all right," Mr. Bladeswell denied matter-of-factly.

Mrs. Meadows glared at him, and Mrs. Bladeswell reproved in a vexed tone, "Melvin!"

"Well, it was. That don't mean she did it, but somebody did."

"But who would?" Mrs. Meadows cried despairingly. "I didn't even know there was a gun on the place. That awful man showed it to me, and I never saw it before."

"You don't know whose it was?" Mr. Bladeswell asked quickly.

Mrs. Meadows looked at him sharply. "No. Do you?"

The visitors glanced at each other uneasily. So the sheriff hadn't told her. And now they were afraid to, although they knew she would find out as soon as she saw Mrs. Fergusson again.

"You mustn't just stay in here and brood," Mrs. Bladeswell put in hurriedly. "Now you get up after a while and have a nice bath and change clothes and come out to dinner tonight with the rest of us. You'll feel better if you get out and see people." She glanced at her wrist watch. "It's two-thirty now, and we'll stop out in front at five and yoo-hoo for you, and you just come out and we'll all go to dinner as if nothing had happened. I'm sure that's what it all was, like you said, an accident. You'll see, they'll find out; it's all a big mistake."

"Oh, Elsie, I do hope you're right. I just can't bear people thinking such awful things about me." She gave a little gasping sound, half-sigh, half-sob.

"Now, nobody thinks a thing about you," Chet assured her heartily, and Mr. Bladeswell gave him a sidelong look and let his eyes slide along over the room and the pitiful little figure on the bed. Scent was as pervasive in the air as before, and there was an overwhelming femininity about the room. Pastel-shaded things showing through the partially open closet door, lacy odds and ends strewn about the room, all those fancy boxes and bottles on the dresser, and bare white ankles and the curve of her insteps showing above the frivolous mules which hung from Mrs. Meadows' toes as her feet dangled over the edge of the rumpled bed.

He was damned if the murder wasn't turning out to her advantage as far as Chet was concerned. Her hunted, disadvantageous condition aroused his sympathies, made him feel masculine and protective toward the weak and persecuted little woman. For all Mr. Bladeswell knew Chet might think she would have been justified in shooting the man who had "hounded" her. You could never tell about people where their feelings were involved. They did the damnedest things. Again Mr. Bladeswell's eyes ranged over the perfumed, frivolous room with its crinkled sheets, its dented pillows. There was no getting away from it. There was something downright sexy about the atmosphere the woman created around herself.

When they left the cottage after receiving Mrs. Meadows' misty-eyed promises to "buck up" and "be brave," by common consent they wandered across the grass to a glider which happened to be unoccupied and sat together looking down toward the pool.

CHAPTER TWENTY-SIX

No one, surveying the scene, would have suspected that a man had been shot dead on the premises the night before. The water was noisy with splashing children, sun bathers lay on mats nearby, people in play clothes sat under the umbrellas laughing and playing cards.

As they sat looking on in silence, Mrs. Fergusson came striding toward them from the road, wearing a skirt and blouse and flat oxfords and an-kle socks. She grabbed the canvas back of a small chair standing in the ad-joining group of furniture and dragged it with her as she came forward, swinging the chair around and flopping into it with a glum, "Hullo," as she reached them.

"Didn't see you at lunch," Chet said affably.

Mrs. Fergusson directed a furious glance at him. "You know why? I had company—again. That stupid sheriff was back, asking me more questions about things that have nothing to do with all this. And I suppose you know the latest. We can't leave until he says so. And I was planning to pull out Monday morning. If people have to shoot other people I wish to God they'd pick on somebody else's gun to do it with."

Mr. Bladeswell was looking beyond her, and he nodded and smiled. Mrs. Fergusson turned her head and jerked it in greeting at Mrs. Smith, who was approaching barefooted in her bathing suit, her folded cap clenched in her hand.

"Don't get up," she said to Chet, who had started to rise, "I'm wet, and I'll sit here in the sun."

She had smiled as she spoke, but as she lowered herself to the grass, her face settled again into grim lines of which she seemed unaware.

"I'm burned up," Mrs. Fergusson went on, bringing out her cigarettes. "Here it is, an open-and-shut case, and we all have to be dragged into it."

Mrs. Smith looked up at the other woman and came into the conversa-tion as if she had been there from its beginning. "That's what I say. Just because that woman attached herself to us like a leech—I certainly didn't associate with her from choice—they act as if we had something to do with her filthy murder."

Chet leaned forward sternly. "Now look here, I don't think that's any at-titude to take. How do we know Marice had anything to do with it either? She could be—uh—the innocent victim of circumstances."

Both women had turned startled eyes upon him, never having expected this championship of their erstwhile rival.

"Innocent!" Mrs. Fergusson snorted.

"It was her husband, wasn't it?" Mrs. Smith snapped.

"Yes," Mrs. Bladeswell interpolated worriedly, "but it seems so strange—killing him so—publicly, when she's bound to be suspected."

"If it wasn't her," Mrs. Smith addressed Chet acidly, "who's the next best suspect? I don't suppose you've stopped to think. Everybody saw the way she was running after you. The police might figure you were sweet on her and bumped her husband off to clear the way."

"Yeah. Think that one over," Mrs. Fergusson added waspishly.

Chet looked blankly from one to the other of the women. "Why, I—I—

Why, I never heard of anything so—" he sputtered incredulously.

Mr. Bladeswell studied the two women alternately through narrowed eyes, realizing that an unforeseen development had taken place. Their determined pursuit of Chet had taken second place—if it had not been abandoned completely—to their zeal for pinning the murder on Mrs. Meadows and thus disposing of it so that the "stupid" sheriff's attention would be diverted from themselves.

Both of them had the wind up. There was no question about that. And with one of them, at least, it was because of panic over having her past dug up. Mrs. Fergusson, of course, was in a bad spot because of owning the weapon. That could be the only source of her desire to see Mrs. Meadows safely convicted of murder.

"Don't forget"—Chet was getting his speech under control in self-defense against this unexpected attack—"it was your gun, Clara, the shot was fired from."

"Are you implying I might have killed him!"

"I'm not implying anything. But I, for one, am not going to turn against a friend just because circumstantial evidence looks bad for her."

Mrs. Smith's eyes had been moving from one to the other of the speakers during this interchange, and now her contribution to the conversation indicated a deliberate shifting from the accidental position of ally to Mrs. Fergusson into which she had slipped.

"Well," she said, as if having thought the matter over judiciously, "the circumstantial evidence does seem to point your way, Clara."

"It does nothing of the kind! Mr. Bladeswell here can tell you I missed my gun at the dance last night."

"It was lucky, wasn't it," Mrs. Smith said sweetly, "that you thought to mention the loss to him before the murder was discovered?"

Mrs. Fergusson's eyes were hot with anger as she retorted, "If I remember correctly, you were sitting on that sofa where I left my purse while I went in for a drink."

"That was a smart move, leaving your purse around so it seemed to give others a chance to get into it."

Mrs. Fergusson came to her feet in a violent movement and stalked away in speechless rage.

Mrs. Smith looked after her, and then turned with a rather smug expression to Chet. But he looked away with a worried frown.

"Maybe I shouldn't of said what I did. We've got no right to go around casting aspersions at people. But"—he eyed Mrs. Smith severely—"you girls made me mad, being so quick to turn on poor little Marice."

Mrs. Smith's expression showed that she was grappling with a number of conflicting impulses, but after a speechless second she burst out, sitting rigid on the grass, her rubber cap clenched in both hands, "Poor little Marice! Really, Mr. Hoffman, how can you be so—so blind! You say you don't really think it's Clara, even though it was her gun. And you won't hear of it being Marice, even though it was her husband. What do you think it was—spontaneous combustion?"

Annoyed at this fresh attack, Chet lashed out, "Why are you so anxious to have us pin it on somebody? That's the police's job. I'm damned if I'm going to go around suspecting all my friends. *I* don't have to worry about convicting somebody else to clear myself."

Mrs. Smith scrambled to her feet, made awkward by fury. "Are you insinuating *I* need to clear myself?" she demanded shrilly. "Maybe you feel perfectly comfortable living in the same neighborhood with a murderer, but *I* don't—especially"—she glared down at Mr. Bladeswell malevolently—"after already having my house broken into."

Snapping her lips shut after this telling rejoinder, she threw up her head defiantly and marched off.

The Bladeswells and Chet stared after her in stunned silence for a moment before Chet announced bewilderedly, "I can't understand it, everybody turning on everybody else like this."

"There," said Mr. Bladeswell quietly, his eyes following the direction both Mrs. Fergusson and Mrs. Smith had taken, "are two mad and frightened women."

"You know," Chet observed sententiously, sinking back on the cushions, "it's true what they say: in a crisis people show their real nature."

Mrs. Meadows came out when they halted in front of her house a little after five-thirty. Mrs. Bladeswell had been curious to see what the new widow would wear for her first public appearance, and her first reaction was: Well, I should have known; whatever the part was, she'd play it in the right costume.

For Mrs. Meadows had on a heavy gray linen dress made on simple lines, the only fripperies being a pink turnback collar and cuffs and small pink buttons fastening the waist. Conservative gray-and-white spectator pumps and smoke-colored stockings completed the costume, which Mrs. Bladeswell guessed was the one she wore on the road.

Mrs. Meadows managed to remind one of a dove, yet her face showed the ravages of an anxiety-ridden day. The flesh hung wearily on her small-boned features.

Mrs. Smith and Mrs. Fergusson arrived separately at the ranch house, and for the first time neither joined the group Chet Hoffman was in, only nodding with cool smiles and finding it necessary to speak to some of the other guests.

About Mrs. Fergusson she didn't care, but Mrs. Bladeswell was still par-

tial to Mrs. Smith as a mate for Chet, and she was annoyed with her candidate. Mrs. Smith wasn't playing her cards right. Not at all. When she saw
that the man's sympathies were aroused by Mrs. Meadows' plight, Mabel should have chimed in, pretending to see things his way, and, if she really didn't, using later opportunities to arouse in more subtle ways his suspicions of and to undermine his confidence in Mrs. Meadows. Then, if the
officers decided Mrs. Meadows *had* done it, she would be out of the running anyway, and Mrs. Smith would have nosed out the blunt and more
forthright Mrs. Fergusson. Honestly, it seemed as if some women never did
learn how to handle men.

Everyone was painfully careful to speak politely to Mrs. Meadows, but
everybody stared at her surreptitiously all through the meal which the little woman in gray only picked at; and no one missed the fact that the "little bunch" had broken up, Mrs. Fergusson and Mrs. Smith sitting at different tables. Their removal both from Mrs. Meadows' company and from
one another's bore its own connotations; and opinions were almost visibly taking shape among the guests. If the woman's own friends felt like that
about her, it must be true: she probably had shot her husband.

There was something ominous about the officers' continued absence from
the ranch (with the exception of the one man who hung around the office
seeing that no one who was forbidden to do so left the place).

The next day was Sunday, and nothing happened, simply nothing.

Mrs. Meadows was perking up under Chet's solicitude. Mr. Bladeswell
was somewhat aghast over his friend's reactions. He wouldn't have believed
Chet could be so soft-headed, that he could be blinded by the appeal of
the woman's helpless pathos. Couldn't he see how she had treated the late
Gordon J., whether she had actually shot him or not? Couldn't he see how
spoiled and petty and mean she was? But apparently Chet couldn't. All his
bemused eyes took in was her perfumed femininity, her need of a stalwart
protector.

The other two women also showed the strain, whether from fear or from
rage at Mrs. Meadows' unexpected advantage in the contest for Chet's af-
fections.

One seldom saw Mrs. Fergusson without a cigarette between her fingers,
and her face had set in harsh lines.

Mrs. Smith looked as if she hadn't slept for weeks, and there was a prim,
prudish restraint in her expression and manner which covered who knew
what emotions seething beneath the surface.

Mr. Bladeswell waited impatiently for the sheriff's return with his find-
ings. He spent hours calculating and recalculating how long it would take.
Say Knight sent off his phone calls or his telegrams or whatever he did by
three o'clock Saturday afternoon, give the various local authorities twenty-

four hours to check up on the past private lives of the ladies. Surely Knight would have his answers by Sunday evening. On the other hand, maybe the police didn't work on routine stuff like that on Sundays; maybe they would wait till Monday to ask their questions and do their investigating. Still, when murder was involved, surely they didn't bother about observing the Sabbath.

CHAPTER TWENTY-SEVEN

It was past ten o'clock on Monday morning when the deputy, Paul, came striding up the road and turned in at the Bladeswells' path. Mr. Bladeswell was sitting at the edge of the porch in the rocking chair, taking advantage of the warm morning sun which still reached a little way under the porch roof.

Paul looked chipper and rather pleased with things in general. His eyes resting on Mr. Bladeswell were speculatively admiring.

"Mr. Knight would like to have you come with me down to the ranch house," he stated cheerfully.

"You got some—news?" Mr. Bladeswell asked eagerly, rising from his chair.

"Yep, we got news," the young man rejoined noncommittally.

Mr. Bladeswell turned to his wife who had come to the door. "I'm going down to see the sheriff," he informed her. "I'll be back after while."

As he stepped briskly along beside the young man, he questioned anxiously, "Well, what did you find out?"

"You'll see, you'll see," that person assured him smugly.

They went into the living room of the ranch house where Mrs. Meadows in a soft white dress huddled shrinkingly in one of the overstuffed chairs. Mrs. Smith woodenly occupied a straight-backed occasional chair, looking at no one, neither the sheriff who sat beside one of the writing tables with his legs crossed, nor Mrs. Meadows, nor the man in a brown suit who sat near the kitchen doors, nor the man in a gray suit and close-cropped hair who sat by the dining-room doors, nor the tough-looking individual with a rather mashed-looking face who stood looking out of the front doors, wearing herringbone-weave tweed and picking his teeth meditatively with a succession of tooth-picks produced from his vest pocket. Mrs. Smith's eyes flicked coldly over Mr. Bladeswell and Paul, and resumed their contemplation of nothing.

Mr. Bladeswell had hardly settled himself in the corner of the sofa when steps sounded on the veranda, and Mrs. Fergusson, wearing jeans and a tan blouse, came in followed by still another man in plain clothes who stood beside the tooth-picking person and exchanged seemingly casual remarks with him in a low tone. Mrs. Fergusson looked indignant, and glared at Mr. Bladeswell and the other women and sat down on a straight chair. Paul had seated himself at the second desk and arranged his notebook on the blotter. Mr. Bladeswell glanced around the room interestedly, impressed as he counted the representatives of the law: six of them. It made a person feel kind of important, so many of them taking an interest.

Sheriff Knight uncrossed his legs and recrossed them the other way and began dispassionately, "I called you all together for a little talk in view of information I have in my possession. I invited Mr. Bladeswell to join us because it is due to his powers of observation and his ability to put two and two together that we got a line on where to look for these facts—"

All of the women looked at Mr. Bladeswell as if he were a fat, slimy yellow snail that had crawled across a garden path without its shell. He cast his eyes down modestly.

"Our main interest, of course, is in the death of Gordon J. Meadows. For various reasons we think one of you women killed him—"

"That's outrageous," Mrs. Smith broke in. "I hardly knew the man. And it wasn't *my* gun."

"Well, you see," the sheriff said kindly, "we don't think the murderer *meant* to kill Mr. Meadows. We think he was really after Mr. Bladeswell."

A deathly stillness sank into the atmosphere. It was cool, and the light was subdued in the long room whose front windows were shaded by the porch roof, the rear ones facing north. A few shrill cries from the direction of the swimming pool penetrated the screen doors in front, and from the kitchens to the rear a sputtering, unintelligible radio voice was audible.

"I'll be honest with you. We don't know for sure which one of you it was who shot Mr. Meadows. It seems as if any one of you had opportunity and a motive for stopping Mr. Bladeswell's tongue."

The sibilant drawing and release of breath were audible in the silence, and one of the officers cleared his throat.

"I'm afraid, however," the sheriff went on regretfully, "I'm going to have to hold all three of you at our county jail." He sighed resignedly. "Although we may never solve the riddle of Mr. Meadows' death—unless, of course, the guilty party decides to confess."

Mr. Bladeswell shot a quick glance from one woman to another. He was puzzled. Each of the ladies was regarding Knight warily.

"I don't get it," Mrs. Fergusson whipped out, her lips pale.

From his inside coat pocket Sheriff Knight drew out a sheaf of folded papers and sorted through them, as if uncertain as to which were the pertinent ones. With maddening deliberation he pulled a spectacle case from his jacket pocket and carefully settled the glasses in place. He then proceeded to unfold the sheets of paper, inspecting each one with his head slightly back, peering through the lower half of the glasses.

Mr. Bladeswell saw Mrs. Fergusson's knuckles whiten as she grasped the wooden arm of her chair. Mrs. Smith was sitting closest to him, and he saw a bead of sweat in the hollow between her upper lip and her nose. Mrs. Meadows was pulling at a chiffon handkerchief with clenched fingers.

"It's sure kept us busy this week end," the sheriff volunteered with a chuckle, as he got his papers in order. "Not just us, but members of other law-enforcement bodies here and there around the country." He paused and regarded the ladies severely through his spectacles. "That's one thing people forget sometimes, the Long Arm of the Law." He moved one paper up and down. "Now, you take this report. It took detectives in Denver, and the rangers' office in Yellowstone Park, and the county recorder in Portland, Oregon—and, oh yes, an airplane flyin' in to Denver with a photograph originally taken at Yellowstone, to get together all the information I've got here."

Mr. Bladeswell felt hollow in his chest, and he looked at the frozen, staring-eyed Mrs. Fergusson with sick eyes. So it was her, after all.

"Now you told me, Mrs. Fergusson," the Sheriff was speaking inexorably, "that your husband Edwin D. Fergusson died of acute indigestion in Portland, Oregon, while you were on a vacation trip a year ago last summer. Well, it's a funny thing, but the authorities in Portland had no record of any such death, and you know it's a law that death certificates are always put on file. Now there was an unidentified man found dead in Yellowstone Park early in the same month of July when you said your husband died later in the month in Portland. Well, naturally the officers there took pictures of the body. The face wasn't in A-one shape when they found it, but still it wasn't past recognition, and when that picture was flown in to the Denver police they took it around and sure enough several people identified the man as Edwin D. Fergusson. 'Nother interesting coincidence, you and Mr. Fergusson was registered at Old Faithful Lodge and had checked out three days before they found the body."

Mr. Knight directed a benign glance at Mr. Bladeswell. "Way we got onto all this, Mr. Bladeswell happened to be in Yellowstone that summer when Mr. Fergusson's body was discovered."

Without moving her torso Mrs. Fergusson turned her head toward Mr. Bladeswell.

Mr. Bladeswell looked away uncomfortably. Both Mrs. Smith and Mrs. Meadows were gazing at him fearfully, as if he were something horrid and unclean. He met their eyes defiantly. Well, so he *had* spied and informed on one of their little bunch. They shouldn't look at him as if he was a traitor. For now the miasma of suspicion would lift a little from around their heads.

CHAPTER TWENTY-EIGHT

The sheriff was still fiddling with his papers.

"We come next to last summer, a year ago, that is. And Yosemite National Park—"

Mrs. Fergusson jerked forward in her chair. "I've never been in Yosemite in my life!" she cried in a choked scream.

"No," Knight said equably, "but you have, Mrs. Meadows."

Mr. Bladeswell turned uncomprehending eyes on the little woman in white who cowered in her chair but whose face was twisted into an ugly shape of anger and fear.

"I guess I pretty well outlined our procedure in telling about Mrs. Fergusson's case. Of course you haven't been living in the same neighborhood as Mrs. Meadows that you did as Mrs. Underhill, but Mr. Bladeswell here remembered a 'Mildred' to whom you had written a postcard, and we found her address in your address book which we—er—appropriated when we searched your cabin Saturday morning, and the Los Angeles police found out something about your activities for the past few years from her—"

Mrs. Fergusson's face had been working, and now she burst out, "Bladeswell! Postcard—" Her voice sputtered out furiously.

"Yes, it was Mr. Bladeswell who entered your cabin—and yours, too, Mrs. Meadows. He was doing some—er—investigating on his own."

Mr. Bladeswell, dazed as he was, cringed before the malignant eyes of the women. The thought uppermost in his confused mind was one of thankfulness for the stolid men stationed about the room—armed, he hoped.

"Well, Mildred—Mrs. DeValle, that is—was very helpful. She told us you had taken a trip north—she thought up the Redwood Highway last summer in company with Mr. Underhill, and that Mr. Underhill was killed in an auto accident near the Oregon border. At least that was your story, Mrs. Meadows, when you returned from the trip. And she identified the photograph of the man found near Mirror Lake in Yosemite last August. You stayed in a cabin at Camp Curry, I believe; at least the camp's records show a Mr. and Mrs. Earl Underhill registered there for three days prior to the discovery of Mr. Underhill's body."

"You'll have to prove it," Mrs. Meadows cried, but her voice shook uncontrollably.

"That shouldn't be too hard," the sheriff replied easily.

He turned his face toward Mrs. Smith. "And now, Mrs. Smith, we come to you. I guess you've been expecting it, especially since you know Mr.

Bladeswell suspected—or, you were afraid, knew—that you'd been in Santa Cruz recently. Matter of fact, *you're* my choice for this last murder. You thought Mr. Bladeswell might have actually seen you in Santa Cruz while you were there. And you wanted to be sure his mouth was shut for good. I figure you slipped Mrs. Fergusson's gun out of the bag where she had obligingly shown you she carried it, followed Mr. Bladeswell out on the porch only to find he had vanished, and then prowled down the path looking for him, saw a man strolling up and down in the arbor, a man in a white shirt and light pants, and bang! let him have it, tossed the gun over on the grass, having handled it with a handkerchief around your hand, and came back inside. Must have been disconcerting to see him come back into the room."

Mrs. Smith sat up straight in her chair, her hands folded in her lap. "You're going to have a lot to prove," she said in a voice that strove to be calm.

"Well, me and Paul can prove you told us Mr. Smith died of a heart attack in San Francisco two months ago. And if he did, the San Francisco authorities never heard of it. No death certificate's been signed on him there. And your neighbors in Chicago all identified the picture of the man they found dead on the beach as Mr. Smith."

She brushed her clenched hand over her upper lip where Mr. Bladeswell had seen the bead of sweat. "All that doesn't prove I killed him."

"Well, it's up to the district attorney of Santa Cruz County to prove what happened. Seems they want you for trial up there, although the Wyoming police and the Merced County authorities over Yosemite way are willing to leave the other ladies up to us since we took 'em in custody. It can be done either way."

"It's like she says," Mrs. Meadows cried in cracked tones. "Nobody can prove anything. So our husbands died. So what? That doesn't mean we had anything to do with it."

"Maybe not. But I know if I was on a jury the whole thing would look awful funny to me, every single one of you lying about the circumstances of her husband's death." He leaned forward confidentially. "And you know something? It's quite a coincidence. In every single case the couple had their money in joint accounts. And every single time, right away after the husband died, before the banks knew about it, most of the money was drawn out by one party, the wife." He shook his head. "Sure is going to look suspicious."

Suddenly he straightened and drew a deep breath, folding the papers together and removing his glasses as he ordered with an abrupt, curt change of tone, "Take 'em away, boys."

An officer approached each woman. Mrs. Fergusson raised her chin defiantly, glared at the man, and stalked from the room ahead of him. Mrs. Smith shrank in her chair, her eyes raised to the policeman. As he put out his hand to take her arm, she cried out, and her eyes darted frantically from one occupant of the room to the other. "No. No!" Her voice became a sob, and she looked straight at Mr. Bladeswell.

"It was him. He's responsible. He got under my skin. Watching, prying, poking his nose into my life. I lost my head. He—he frightened me. He's—he's like Robert, some ways. It was as if Robert were—after me—" She broke down, crying in deep, gasping breaths. "I'm not a killer. I'm not! It's his fault—that Mr. Bladeswell. He was driving me crazy. I didn't know what I was doing. I just felt I had to get rid of him—"

Inexorably the officer pulled her to her feet and escorted her, sobbing, from the room.

Mrs. Meadows had stared wide-eyed at the collapsing woman opposite her. As if in a trance, she lifted her eyes to the man beside her; and she, too, drew back with a little moan.

"Oh no, oh no."

The officer touched her shoulder phlegmatically. "Come along."

Mechanically she rose to her feet, her eyes fearfully on the man's face. Then she put her hands over her face and began to cry softly. The officer put his hand under her elbow and almost gently guided her out of the room.

Mr. Bladeswell remained hunched in his corner of the sofa, not looking up. When they had gone he lifted his eyes to the sheriff who had risen and come around the desk.

"Well, you sure put us on to something," Knight was saying genially. "Of course (in the course of our investigations) we'd prob'ly have stumbled onto what they'd been up to, but your theories speeded things up, gave us the clues about where to look."

"I can't believe it," Mr. Bladeswell said dully. "All three of them. I never thought. I wasn't even sure it was *any* of 'em. But—all three."

"Does kind of take your breath away, don't it?"

Mr. Bladeswell raised horrified eyes. "And they all had their cap set for Chet. My God, he might have been next."

"If he had any money and if she got bored with his company, he might have been at that."

Mr. Bladeswell got to his feet groggily. "We live in a terrible world, don't we?" he said solemnly.

"Oh, now I wouldn't say that. These dames just all happened to come together in one spot."

They had approached the double doors with Paul following, and the sheriff gestured toward the expanse of green surrounding the bright swimming pool where two little boys chased each other along the runway. Mr. and

Mrs. Finklestauffer were placidly watching from canvas chairs, and one of the schoolteachers and one of the young men crossed the lawn arm in arm, their eyes upon each other.

"There's nothing wrong with the rest of 'em. Most people behave themselves. It's just that once in a while some of 'em get greedy."

Mr. Bladeswell shook his head, uncomforted, as he descended the steps.

CHAPTER TWENTY-NINE

The white line pushed the gray pavement ahead toward the south, through little hollows where sycamores drooped over streams, over the rise of sunburned foothills, turning and dipping outward to parallel the bleak sand dunes extending along the endless beaches. Mr. Bladeswell kept his eyes upon the line, staring ahead grimly under the brim of his cloth hat. Even Mrs. Bladeswell had less than usual to say about the scenery as they headed steadily south on the next lap of their trip.

"One," he broke out suddenly, "yes, I expected it; but all three of them. I tell you, it's more than a man can take in. None of 'em seemed like that kind of people. I can't figure out why they'd do such a thing."

"Well," Mrs. Bladeswell said thoughtfully, "you take Mrs. Meadows. I don't think it's so hard to see why she would. You saw how she just up and got tired of Mr. Meadows, decided she needed a change, and might do better."

"Then why didn't she just divorce the other one—Underhill, wasn't it?"

"Well, you see, she wanted to get as much out of it as possible; and you can't be sure how much you'll be able to get in a divorce settlement. Having had a couple before, the courts might not have been so generous this time, especially if he was a nice, respectable man, as he probably was. And working his death the way she did, she got everything and could be comfortable financially while she looked around for somebody more interesting." Mrs. Bladeswell sighed. "Yes, I can see how she figured. She's pretty spoiled and headstrong; you saw that; selfish and no sense of responsibility."

"I suppose so," Mr. Bladeswell said reluctantly. He negotiated the passing of a 1938 model sedan traveling at thirty miles an hour ahead of him. When he had the car straightened back on the road he continued, "But Mrs. Fergusson, there wasn't anything childish or impulsive about her."

"No; but she was such a managing person, determined to have her own way. It would be hard to live with a person like her. They probably didn't get along very good, and being in business together, he probably kept trying to interfere, have some say too. I could just tell about her; she had to be boss—or else. And they'd only been married a few years, and she never succeeded in breaking him in the way she probably thought she could when she married him. So she just got tired of it, and the first good chance she had she just up and got rid of him."

"She was a kind of hard-boiled type," Mr. Bladeswell agreed.

"Now Mrs. Smith was the one that really surprised me," Mrs. Bladeswell went on with a little disapproving cluck. "But the more I think of it the more I can see what happened. You see she'd been married to this Mr. Smith for over twenty-five years."

As she paused after this conclusive statement and sat looking out at the field they were passing as if she had no more to say, Mr. Bladeswell shot her a puzzled glance.

"What's that got to do with it?"

"Well, she was only forty-six, you know; and around in there a person feels it's kind of a crucial time of life. You sort of look back and check up and look ahead and think about—life and things. From what came out after the police looked into her past, you can see she'd led a rather—well, quiet kind of existence with Mr. Smith. Nothing much ever happened— not even children. And the way I figure, Mr. Smith must have been that kind of person, the kind that didn't mind just jogging along in a rut. I can see how Mabel got to feeling. Here she was forty-five years old, ready to start growing old, and nothing had ever *happened* to her. She figured if she was ever going to *live*, she'd better start doing it. So she probably talked him into this trip, thinking a change of scene might be the answer; and then, my goodness, she finds out it's almost as dull traveling with him as it was just living along the way they'd always done. He bored her, that's all; and she had a kind of desperate feeling, 'My goodness, am I never going to have anything different in my life, just Mr. Smith forever?'"

Mrs. Bladeswell sighed again, sadly. "And, well, one thing led to another."

"She didn't have to murder the poor guy," Mr. Bladeswell snapped.

"No-o. But there must have been times when she *felt* like murdering him, and one of those times, in a moment of weakness, she did it."

Mr. Bladeswell withdrew his eyes from the back of the car fifty feet ahead and glanced briefly at his wife's placidly regretful face.

Now that the excitement and amazement and shock that had shaken everyone at Escondido had died down, Elsie seemed to be very calm about the whole thing. She had figured out the reasons—you might almost say the excuses—with an astonishing lucidity.

The idea of a woman "feeling like murdering her husband" was not at all inconceivable to her.

"Maybe," he blurted out with sudden bitterness, "*I* better look out. You might have a weak moment and bump me off so you could start fresh."

She chuckled amusedly and patted his thigh. "My goodness, no. I'm *fond* of you, Mel. You see, they had all got so they weren't."

He gazed ahead rather sulkily, but she didn't seem to notice.

"Besides," she said inconsequentially, "I'm sixty-one."

He grunted. With a sudden burst of speed their car shot around the one ahead.

After a few minutes Mrs. Bladeswell said thoughtfully, as if mostly to herself, "I think maybe it's partly the men's fault. Not Mr. Smith's or Mr. Fergusson's or What's-his-name's indi*vid*ually, but just men in general. You see, us women get everything *from* them, our homes and clothes and even food. If we're going to have any money us married ones have to get it through a man. And maybe it builds up a kind of—unhealthy—attitude. For one thing, men become means to an end. It makes it harder to love them for themselves. And then when they get kind of irksome for one reason or another, like interfering with your pleasure—like it was with Mrs. Meadows—or trying to run you like it probably was with Mrs. Fergusson—or just plain boring you like I think happened with Mrs. Smith—why, there isn't enough disinterested love to act as a brake on the mean impulses that some people seem to be subject to. Their feelings get in a tight spot where it seems as if a lot of things are pressing on them too hard, and they just seem to turn on the man they're dependent on. Sort of relieves their feelings temporarily."

Mrs. Bladeswell drew still another gusty sigh, and declared ruefully, "I guess it boils down to men just being too important, every way, to most of us, not just as people to love, but as sources of support and protection and all. And some women get kind of restless and don't have enough self-control at the critical moment when they're hating them the hardest."

As he grimly manipulated the wheel Mr. Bladeswell wanted to ask sarcastically if she had ever hated him—temporarily. But somehow he didn't dare. And anyway, she would probably laughingly deny it.

At any rate, he tried to comfort himself, Elsie was capable of more love than those other women had been. And besides, as she had pointed out, she was sixty-one. If there had been a crisis, she had passed it successfully.

Nevertheless he didn't feel happy about the ideas she had musingly expressed.

THE END